THE ROSE OF SHARON

A NOVEL

BOOK 1 OF *THE BRIAR HOLLOW SERIES*

THE ROSE OF SHARON

A NOVEL

LORI WAGNER

The Rose of Sharon
Book 1 of *The Briar Hollow Series*
Copyright © 2011 by Lori Wagner

Design and layout by Laura Jurek
Cover model, Audrey Cayten

ISBN: 978-0-9798627-8-6

Library of Congress Control Number: 2011900928

Scripture quotations are from the King James Version.

Requests for information should be addressed to:
Affirming Faith
1181 Whispering Knoll Lane
Rochester Hills, MI 48306
loriwagner@affirmingfaith.com
www.affirmingfaith.com

Printed in the United States of America.

*D*EDICATION

To Bill Wagner,
my husband, my love–

Individually, we faced some of life's thorns
before God brought us together as one–
united in a special kind of love
that remains fragrant and sweet
like a rose abloom in the summer sun–

ACKNOWLEDGMENTS

Thank you, my dear family,
  –for putting up with the back of my head as I worked many long hours on this book
  –for listening as I read you re-write after re-write
  –for loving the story and characters with me
  –for your unending support in all my Affirming Faith ventures.

Thank you, Les Stobbe, my literary agent,
  –for believing in me, encouraging me, and taking a chance on me.

Thank you, Barbara Westburg,
  –for all your helpful suggestions to improve the manuscript and my writing skills.

Thank you, my Facebook friends,
  –for critiquing little passages here and there. It's a small world after all, and I'm glad to be your friend.

And, of course, I have to thank my God–as Balim would say, the "sweet Lawd Jesus!" He is my life, my strength, my song, and my inspiration!

I am the rose of Sharon,
and the lily of the valleys.
As the lily among thorns,
so is my love among the daughters.

– Song of Solomon 2:1-2

To appoint unto them that mourn in Zion,
to give unto them beauty for ashes,
the oil of joy for mourning,
the garment of praise for the spirit of heaviness;
that they might be called trees of righteousness,
the planting of the LORD,
that he might be glorified.

– Isaiah 61:3

*C*HAPTER 1

"**A**re these the ones?" Rosalie held the arching stem of a salmon-colored cabbage rose between her long fingers. Pansy Joy nodded and beamed her approval as her sister bent for a drink of the flower's heady scent.

An unexpected shriek of delight from Pansy Joy startled Rosalie. She jerked upright and let out a soft cry as a thorn punctured her finger.

"Ouch!"

"Oh, I'm so sorry," Pansy Joy exclaimed. "I didn't mean to make you prick yourself." She rushed to her sister's side and reached for her hand. "Let me look at that."

Rosalie flinched and extended her throbbing finger. Usually the first person to tend to another's physical ailment, the sight of her own blood befuddled her senses.

Pansy Joy examined the wounded digit. "No thorn. That's good." She pulled a handkerchief from her sleeve and pressed it against Rosalie's bleeding finger. The older girl watched. Her green eyes, watery from the pain, held a look of amusement as her sister continued to apologize and apply pressure to her finger.

"Oh, Rosalie. I'm dreadful sorry. Truly I am." She lifted the handkerchief to check the bleeding then clamped it back down. "It's just that I'm so excited for the wedding I can hardly keep still . . . or quiet, for sure." Pansy Joy lifted beseeching brown eyes to search her sister's face. "Do you forgive me?"

"You know I do." Rosalie smiled at her animated sibling. "It's not your fault. I should have worn gloves. I've been working with Mama's flowers long enough to know roses don't grow without thorns."

Since he mother's death over three years ago, Rosalie had faithfully tended her mother's children, home and gardens. The eldest of the Johnson children, she had a special knack with plants—with people too, except where young men were concerned. While plants thrived in the rich Kentucky soil at the Johnson place, Rosalie's love life seemed a desolate wasteland.

She knew she didn't share Pansy Joy's vibrant beauty. She was terribly tall and thin and freckled, after all. Rosalie had been overlooked by suitors for so long that when Clayton had started finding excuses to visit the Johnson place, helping out during her mother's difficult pregnancy, she had been both pleased and surprised. Certain she had been destined for spinsterhood, dormant hope had sprung to life in Rosalie's tender heart.

But that was then. In one horrible moment her dreams had swooped off like a gaggle of geese in the fall. Life had dealt troublesome blows to Rosalie. The year that should have been most joyful, the year her mother finally delivered a son, the year she at long last had a beau of her own, had become a year of double losses.

Seasons had come and gone. She was 19 years old, and she was truly thankful for her life full of activity and the genuine love of her family. Most girls her age were married and had a babe riding a hip by now, but Rosalie made the best of things and, for the most part, accepted her situation. Her days held purpose and fulfillment, if not romance.

Rosalie lifted the edge of the handkerchief. "It stopped bleeding," she said. "I'm fine." She withdrew her hand from Pansy Joy's and pulled a pair of scissors from her apron pocket. With practiced ease, she clipped the flower just below the sepal and placed the blossom in Pansy Joy's cupped hand. As her sister sampled the rose's fragrance, Rosalie tugged on her straw hat. She adjusted its brim to shade her porcelain skin and hopefully ward off the formation of any new freckles. In her estimation she already had too many dotting her cheeks and the bridge of her upturned nose.

Pansy Joy worried her bottom lip, concerned for Rosalie's finger, while behind Rosalie's smile and clear celadon eyes, her thoughts drifted.

Rosalie was genuinely happy for her sister. The love flowing between Pansy Joy and Garth Eldridge was something to behold. One look at the cow eyes they made at each other erased any concern. Those two were smitten, for sure. Pansy Joy practically sparkled from the inside out. Without a doubt, Rosalie was pleased for her sister, while at the same time she could not deny the bittersweet mix of gladness for Pansy Joy and longing in her own heart.

Rosalie schooled her thoughts to count her blessings. With the upcoming wedding and the babies sure to follow, she reminded herself she had much to be thankful for. Being an auntie was a delightful thought indeed.

"These peach ones will dry into a deeper color," said Rosalie. "I think they will be perfect for your bouquet and decorations. A nice complement to the calico you ordered for your dress, too."

Rosalie turned to survey the bushes loaded with buds and blooms. "Summer will be over before we know it. We'll keep our eyes on these and cut the roses as they peak. I've got racks and twine set up in the drying shed, so it will be easy to hang them as we cut each one at full bloom."

Pansy Joy cupped the showy bloom in both hands and drew it to her chest. "I've always liked cabbage roses best. They open up so big and full, and that's just how I feel right now. My heart is near to bursting."

Rosalie shook her head at her sister's dramatics. "It better not burst. We don't have time to clean up any such messes," she said, wagging a finger at her twitterpated sister.

"Well, fine. That's just fine, sister." With a flip of her blond curls, Pansy Joy harrumphed, set her hands on her hips and marched out of the rose garden. She headed toward the barn with a playful smile on her face that belied her spirited retort. "I'll sure be careful not to add to your workload with my poor exploding heart," she pronounced over her shoulder as she stalked away. "I'll just take my heart and hands over to the barn and milk Clover. She never teases, and she's always happy to see me."

At 15, Pansy Joy was halfway betwixt hay and grass—part girl and part woman. Matthias, her father, concerned she was too young to marry, had insisted she and her beau, Garth Eldridge, wait until her sixteenth birthday before they wed. Four years older than the vibrant beauty, Garth had eyes for none other than Pansy Joy since she was wearing short skirts and braids. He was most willing to wait the eight months her Pa required for this girl so full of life to be his own.

Unlike most brides, Pansy Joy scheduled her wedding in the dead of winter. It would take place directly after midnight following the ringing in of the new year and Pansy Joy's January 1 birthday. The couple planned to exchange vows by candlelight and start the new decade as man and wife. Folks in this part of Kentucky had never heard of the like; but Pansy Joy said if she had to wait eight months, she wasn't going to wait one day more than she had to. Besides, she imagined it would be the most memorable wedding Washington, Kentucky, had ever seen.

Rosalie watched her sister tromp across the grass with swinging arms and lumberjack steps. Before she arrived at the barn door, Matthias opened it and walked out. He took in the scene and shook his head. Nothing new here. Two girls. Two completely different dispositions. He cleared the way, and Pansy Joy slipped inside with a wink and a kiss to his bristly cheek.

A bucket in one hand and leaning on his hickory cane with the other, Matthias Johnson took the same path his second daughter had crossed only a moment before, but at a much slower pace. His oldest waited for him enclosed in the beauty of his late wife's rose garden.

Matthias and his bride had moved to Kentucky 19 years previous. The land had been vacant, but the bubbling creek and seclusion of the green hollow had thrilled the young couple. They both thought it was just the place to establish their homestead and family.

Matthias had brought tools and supplies to build the house and barn and establish the orchard. Along with the barest of newlywed household necessities, Sharon had brought cuttings. For months before the move she collected slips from family and friends of the many varieties of roses that now grew on trellises and in clusters in the cordoned area. Not only did she know the names of the plants, but when she pruned and fussed over each one, she prayed for the person who had given it to her. She said it helped her feel connected to the loved ones she left in Texas, and there was no better place to feel close to God than in a garden.

"God used to meet up with Adam and Eve every evenin' in the Garden," she often said in her lilting Texas drawl. "The good Lord wrote in the good Book that Jesus is the same yesterday, today and forever. So I reckon God still likes to meet up with folks in gardens."

Sharon had not stopped with the rose garden. She expanded her planting to include herbs in containers and rows beyond the house. To the left of the path leading up from the road, a perennial garden of wildflowers every height and hue waved in the wind. A grapevine, started from one small slip, now completely covered the arbor on the path from the rose garden down to the orchard. It made a pretty sight, as did Rosalie standing tall in the morning sunshine watching her pa trek up the slight incline.

She fits in there, Matthias thought. *She does. Looks like a stem of Queen Anne's lace.* With the big straw hat perched on top of her tall, slender frame, the willowy girl did resemble the flower that grew prolifically along the roadside–especially when she tipped her head like she was doing just now.

"Morning, Pa."

"Morning, Rosalie."

"Breakfast will be ready in a few minutes. Pansy Joy wanted to show me something first."

"That girl's a conniption." Matthias set down the pail that held a tincture he planned to apply to his trees directly after breakfast. Resting his cane against his leg, Matthias slipped his dusty slouch hat off and combed his fingers through his thick brown hair with his free hand.

"You're right about that," Rosalie said. She restrained herself from showing her pa her wrapped finger. She figured there was no point in adding to what he already considered lovesick foolishness.

"Is Marigold up?"

"Yes. She was helping Lucas get dressed, and then they were going to fill the wood box." Rosalie started for the house. Smoke curled out the fieldstone chimney of the three-room log cabin. A steep-pitched roof topped the half loft, and a narrow covered porch spanned the cabin's face.

"I've got the coffee on and the bacon finished. The griddle is hot. The flapjacks will be ready by the time you get washed up."

Matthias followed his daughter to the cabin and stopped at the lean-to to scrub the nicotine sulfate residue from his hands with lye soap. Methodically, he cleaned off his work boots, washed his face and prepared for his favorite time of day. Every morning his family gathered for breakfast and to share a Scripture reading and devotion before heading out in different directions around the homestead, orchard and town.

Matthias opened the door and looked inside at his busy family. Rosalie worked at the cast iron stove putting the last of the flapjacks on a stoneware plate. Marigold, his 12-year-old tomboy, stood next to the table, all set and ready, pouring his coffee. It smelled like a bit of heaven. In front of the large stone fireplace, little Lucas knelt stacking wooden blocks into a teetering tower.

His mind flashed back, and Matthias recalled his beloved Sharon kneeling in front of the same fireplace. A great stone, three feet by six feet, formed the hearth. Before Matthias had earned enough money to buy his wife a cook stove, Sharon used to prepare their meals on the large stone. Many times he walked in the door to find her pulling the big coals out of the fireplace and placing them under the skillets and placing embers on the lids. The tripod she used to hold pots and kettles was still secure on the side of the fireplace and used on special occasions.

A bustling Pansy Joy skidded to a stop behind her father who had stalled in the doorway. "Can you take this, Pa, while I wash up?"

"Sure." Matthias took the pail of frothy milk and walked inside. Three-year-old Lucas leapt up from his spot in front of the fireplace. He watched his Pa put the milk pail on the counter, and waited for him to sit in his ladder-back chair. When Matthias was settled, Lucas climbed onto the big man's lap and wrapped his chubby arms around his neck. Matthias tucked the boy's head under his chin and hugged him back, silent and content.

With the meal preparations complete, the three girls took their places at the trestle table. "Go on, now." Matthias gave Lucas a gentle nudge. The boy jumped down and hurried to his seat ready to eat.

When every head was bowed Matthias offered the blessing. "Lord, we thank You for this day, this food, and all Your bountiful provisions. We ask Your blessing on this meal and the work we set out to do this day in Jesus' name. Amen."

Rosalie offered the flapjacks to Matthias. He stabbed five of them with his fork and plopped the thick stack on his plate. "We must have finished off the last of the maple syrup." Matthias reached for a smoky jar of thick sorghum molasses and poured a generous fall on his tower of flapjacks. "Looks good, Daughter."

"Thanks, Pa." Rosalie started the platter of bacon around the table. She enjoyed watching her pa eat, the whole family really, but especially Pa. He was a big man who appreciated a well prepared meal, even a simple one like this.

"Pa." Marigold broke the silence around the table. She waited until her father met her eyes in acknowledgement. "You think we could go fishing today?"

"Hmm. I'm afraid not." Matthias slowly shook his head. "I've got to get the trees taken care of, golden girl. The webworms are nesting in the pecans."

Marigold tried to mask her feelings, but between the honey braids, Matthias read the disappointment on her freckled face.

"How about you take Lucas out and see what the two of you can snag?" Matthias offered. "There are some mighty fat wiggly worms out by the scrap pile."

Marigold brightened at the prospect of fishing–and her Pa trusting her to care for Lucas, with fish hooks and all. "That'd be fine as cream gravy, Pa."

"Fetch the good Book now, Marigold," Matthias said. "We'll have us a word before you go."

Marigold scooted back from the table, disappeared into her father's bedroom and returned with his worn leather Bible. Before going to sleep each night, Matthias read a chapter or two. Morning devotions usually turned out to be a verse from the previous evening's reading.

Matthias cradled the book in his left hand and thumbed the gilded pages with his right until he reached the passage he was looking for.

"Here." Matthias transferred the book to Rosalie and indicated the verses. "Read this."

"'For a good tree bringeth not forth corrupt fruit; neither doth a corrupt tree bring forth good fruit. For every tree is known by his own fruit. For of thorns men do not gather figs, nor of a bramble bush gather they grapes. A good man out of the good treasure of his heart bringeth forth that which is good; and an evil man out of the evil treasure of his heart bringeth forth that which is evil: for of the abundance of the heart his mouth speaketh.' Luke 6:43-45."

"I think you know every verse in the Bible about trees and fruit." Pansy Joy grinned at her father.

"The Lord uses things in nature to give simple folks understanding." Matthias bowed his head, and the children followed his lead. Quiet meditation and silent prayers concluded the morning devotion. Matthias pushed back his chair, grabbed his slouch hat and headed out the door.

CHAPTER 2

"Let's go, Lukey." Marigold grabbed a worn tin can from the kitchen shelf. "We'll stop by the barn for a shovel to dig up some worms. Then we'll grab some hooks and line."

"Jussa minute."

"Aren't you in a hurry to get fishing?" Marigold threw a puzzled look at the boy scurrying in front of the fireplace.

"I am, but I gotsta put my blocks away."

"You have to do everything according to Hoyle, don't you, little brother?" Marigold swung her braids and rolled her big brown eyes.

"Who's Hoyle?" Lucas implored his sister with an inquisitive look on his cherubic face.

"Oh, that's just a saying." She knelt and began putting blocks in the basket beside the fireplace. "Come on. I'll help you, and we'll get a wiggle on."

The twosome made quick work of picking up the blocks while Rosalie and Pansy Joy took care of the breakfast clean-up. Rosalie washed and Pansy Joy rinsed, dried and put the dishes away on the open wooden shelves that lined the cabin wall.

"Marigold, come back after you get your worms and gear ready," Rosalie said. She dipped a speckled platter in a tub of sudsy water and scrubbed it with a crocheted dish cloth. "I'll pack you a picnic so you can take your time at the creek. You know

Lucas will tire of fishing way before you're ready to call it a day if he gets hungry. Come home by one o'clock so you can get your chores done and Lucas can get his nap."

"That'll be grand." Marigold grinned from ear to ear. She picked up her tin cup a second time and headed to the door.

"Don't forget your hats." Rosalie passed the clean platter to Pansy Joy, wiped her hands and pulled Marigold's bonnet and Lucas's straw hat from pegs on the wall.

"Hats are for dudes. That's what Mar'gold says."

"Hobble your lip, Lucas," Marigold retorted.

"You, two!" scolded Rosalie. "Hats are not just for *dudes*. Easterners wear hats, and Westerners, too. And not just for fancy dress, either." She plopped Marigold's poke bonnet on her head. "You, young lady, need to get it in your head that wearing a bonnet is good for you. You can stay out in the sun without getting burned, and wearing a bonnet actually keeps you cooler."

"Not to mention, wearing a bonnet will keep you from freckling," Pansy Joy chimed in. "Not that freckles are unattractive," she quickly added looking from Marigold's profusely freckled face to Rosalie's sprinkled one.

Rosalie pursed her lips to capture the exacerbated smile attempting to make an appearance under her sparkling eyes. With a brisk movement she firmly placed Lucas's straw hat on his head and tied the strings beneath his pudgy chin. The fishers departed in the morning sunshine. As the door closed behind them, Rosalie and Pansy Joy exchanged glances and then filled the cabin with the giggles.

"I declare," said Pansy Joy. "I don't know where that girl comes up with all those peculiar sayings."

"Me neither. But she surely has an endless supply."

"I best get down to the lodge," said Pansy Joy. "If I hurry, I can meet Garth at his place and he'll walk me the rest of the way."

"I finished the lotions for Mrs. Erlanger. Will you be able to take them with you today?"

"Oh, sure. Garth will help me carry them."

Rosalie packed several jars of lotion in a sturdy, handled basket. She loved making her own concoctions with flowers, herbs, oats, goat milk, beeswax, and other ingredients at her disposal from their orchard and gardens. This batch was scented with lavender and decorated with Rosalie's loving touches. She embroidered flowers on circles of pure white cloth that she tied over the tops of the jars with purple ribbon. The lotions not only smelled wonderful, they looked lovely, as well.

Florence and James Erlanger were the proprietors of Comfort Lodge, and Florence Erlanger never lacked for customers for Rosalie's lotions. She sold them to travelers who stayed over, tempting them with complimentary samples beside their washstands. So many women traveling from the Old States found themselves ill-prepared for the harsh climates of the western territories. Their dry faces and hands drank in Rosalie's lotions that not only smelled pretty, but healed their chapped skin. Even townsfolk made special trips out to buy them; and since the lodge was an official business, Florence was able to sell them at a higher price than Rosalie could from her home.

To make the batch of lavender lotions, Rosalie had first created a base of grapeseed oil and beeswax. Prepared in the top of a water bath, she combined the two ingredients and kept them over low heat until the beeswax melted. While that was warming, she heated water, borax and crushed lavender in a different pot until just before it came to a boil. She strained the flowers, and when both mixtures were ready, she transferred them to a porcelain mortar in which she mixed the recipe thoroughly with a wooden pestle. A thick, fragrant lotion formed, which she poured into small canning jars to be decorated after they cooled.

Martha Matheny, who owned the general store with her husband Donald, tried more than once to convince Rosalie to sell her lotions to her at wholesale prices. Florence Erlanger wouldn't hear of it. One of Rosalie's mother's best friends, Florence insisted all the profits on Rosalie's sales go directly to the girl. She asked only that Rosalie provide enough for use at the lodge for herself and for their boarders' use. It was an offer Rosalie could not refuse. And since she had been running the Johnson household after her mother's passing, she did not have extra time to make enough to supply both the lodge and the general store.

"What are you working on today?" Pansy Joy asked.

"By the time you meet up with Garth, I'll have bread dough ready to rise and the beans soaking for supper. After that, I'm planning to harvest some St. John's wort before I weed the vegetable garden."

"I hope your finger is feeling better. Wear your gloves today and keep it clean."

"I will. You have a good day. See you at supper."

Pansy Joy took the basket from Rosalie, gave her a quick hug and headed out the cabin door.

Before Rosalie assembled the ingredients for her bread dough, she remembered her promise. She pulled out a pail, lined it with a napkin and filled it with a picnic lunch of smoked ham and biscuit sandwiches, apples, oatmeal cookies and a jar of Clover's fresh milk. The door opened just as she folded the napkin over the top of the lunch pail.

Marigold never missed a step. She walked into the cabin, grabbed the pail, and headed back out. "You're ace-high, Rosalie," she said as she swung the door to a close behind her.

Rosalie peeked out the window. She watched Lucas take the pail from Marigold and Marigold grab the fishing gear. She tapped on the glass. Both children turned, and Rosalie waved. Lucas and

Marigold waved back, and then clasped their free hands together and headed off to the creek. Daisy, the Johnson's brownish-colored mutt of unknown heritage, gave a big stretch, jumped off the porch and followed after them. The dog's skinny tail stuck straight up and swayed like a cattail in the wind with each step.

Blissful silence filled the cabin. Rosalie usually enjoyed the quiet, a trait she inherited from her Pa, but this morning she was anxious to be outside. She mixed and kneaded the bread dough and put it in containers she covered with cloth and set close by the stove to rise. Pulling a heavy pot from the shelf to the stove top, Rosalie transferred dried beans from a canister and then filled the pot with water from a pail. She would add the ham hocks once she started the pot cooking, but first the beans would soak until after dinner.

Rosalie checked the stove and added a couple of sticks to keep the fire going. She didn't want to waste time restarting the fire to prepare meals later in the day. After gathering her basket, gloves and scissors, she retrieved her straw hat from its peg and tucked her thick auburn hair beneath its wide brim. "Thank You, Lord," she whispered as she left the cabin and stepped down the wooden porch steps, gratitude for the glorious June day filling her heart.

Not one given to superstition, Rosalie did appreciate tradition. She was a day late. Her mother always gathered St. John's wort on June 24 in honor of St. John the Baptist's birth, but the 24th fell on Sunday this year, and Rosalie did not feel right about harvesting flowers on the Lord's Day.

Rosalie's birthday was coming up soon. She had been born July 1 when the roses were in full bloom. Her mother, a sentimental woman and great lover of flowers, named her Rosalie in honor of her beloved roses, but also so she could call her firstborn daughter her "Rose of Sharon."

Sharon's second daughter came in January, when the pansies pushed through the snow, bringing joy in the middle of the cold winter. Marigold was born in the fall, and last came Lucas. Sharon survived the birthing, but the bleeding would not subside. The new mother passed on to her eternal reward several hours after the long-awaited baby boy entered the world with a lusty cry. Matthias named the child Lucas after Luke in the Bible. Luke had been a physician, and Matthias believed if the doctor had been in Washington for his Sharon maybe she could have been saved.

Rosalie and Pansy Joy both played vital roles in caring for Lucas. Having a baby to raise helped ease the terrible unexpected loss of their mother. In addition to the new load of household chores, diapers, and baby duties, Rosalie resolved to tend her mother's flowers as best she could. Under her mother's tutelage, she had learned to care and nurture the plants her mother loved.

She also resolved to learn as much about medicinal herbs and plants as possible. If she could help ease someone's pain through her plants and prayers, she was determined to do it. She read every bit of information she could get her hands on and experimented with different preparations of tinctures, poultices, teas and such.

Never in a hurry to weed the vegetables, Rosalie meandered from the cabin to the wildflower garden ablaze with color. She ambled through, enjoying the sights and scents. At the patch of St. John's wort, a perennial plant with yellow five-petaled flowers, Rosalie began harvesting both flowers and translucent green leaves. These would not be used for lotions, but dried in paper in the shed until they were crumbly. Some would be steeped for several weeks in olive oil to make a pain-relieving antiseptic used on wounds and bruises. The remainder would be saved for poultice treatments for rheumatism and arthritis and teas that eased emotional ups and downs.

"Lord, You are just amazing." Rosalie fell into her habit of talking to God out loud among the flowers, snipping and praying. "When I think how You make these little flowers come up each summer, year after year, each one holding a gift of healing and encouraging, it just makes me love You all the more."

Her finger, a bit tender from the morning's prick, reminded her to pray for Pansy Joy. "It doesn't seem like my sister will be needing any Wort to ease her spirits this year. She's flying as high as the eagles. And Lord, I'm happy for her. Truly I am. Pansy Joy's so young–a child in so many ways, but a young woman in love and set on marrying and keeping her own house. Please help her, and help Garth too as they prepare for their wedding day. And Lord, help me prepare for it, too."

CHAPTER 3

Pansy Joy passed the wildflower garden on her right and entered the tree-canopied lane that led to the main road. She knew Rosalie loved the flower gardens best, but this was her favorite place. It was a quarter mile of fairyland–a place of dreams and romance where treetops bowed to one another, where limbs intertwined in a magical embrace and swayed in gentle breezes crossing the hollow.

The earthy smell of pine and ferns saturated the air. Fairy dust surely sparkled in the tiny beams of light intermittently peeking through the leaves and providing a bit of light for her way. This was the perfect place for some time alone, hidden from the world, or a secret meeting between lovers or friends.

Admittedly, Pansy Joy had been scared here a time or two. Daytime fairylands can transform into habitats for hobgoblins when the sun goes down. What looked warm and welcoming in the daylight seemed cold and threatening with no stars or moon for a light beneath the dense foliage.

Thoughts of Garth filled her mind and senses as Pansy Joy exited the tree-covered passage and stepped into the sunshine with a full smile. Comfort Lodge lay a mile south of Briar Hollow. The Washington city line was a mile further. The Eldridge farm was between the Lodge and the Johnson place, and Pansy Joy hoped Garth would be on the look-out for her as she walked by.

Yesterday, after Sunday morning worship, Pansy Joy had whispered to Garth, "I'll be coming by around 7:30 tomorrow. It's my day to help at the lodge."

Garth had lowered his lips near her ear and quietly voiced his reply. "It seems I recall having some fence mending to do on the corral. I might find myself out by the road directly after breakfast." That was what Pansy Joy was hoping for as she covered the half mile between her home and Garth's place.

The corral sat on the western part of the Eldridge farm, the structure closest to the road. As she neared the entrance, Pansy Joy saw Garth straddled across the fence rail before he caught sight of her. He cut a swell with his broad upper body wrapped in a blue cotton shirt with a crisp standup collar tucked into fawn-colored pants at his trim waist. Beneath his hat, sandy brown hair was neatly trimmed and his face clean shaven. He played with a piece of straw, twirling it in his fingers and then popping it between his teeth like a cigarillo.

When Garth spied his girl, he nearly jumped off the fence. Instead, he forced himself to move slowly. He reminded himself he was a man in control; but what he really wanted to do was run like a colt in an open field jumping and kicking with delight. That's the way Pansy Joy made him feel.

The way Garth figured, God never made anyone prettier than his Pansy Joy. She was a trim but curvy 5 feet 2 inches of delicious womanhood with wonderfully expressive eyes and ashy blond hair that curled up all on its own. When Garth first fell in love with her, Pansy Joy wore braids that hung down her back like ropes, but now the heavy mass was pinned up in a loose style. Runaway ringlets taunted him to twirl wayward curls around his fingertips.

Garth shoved his hands in his pockets and walked out on the rutted dirt road to meet his betrothed. "How's the prettiest girl in Kentucky?"

Alone with Garth, Pansy Joy turned bashful. A downward tip of her chin and a shy look in her big brown eyes melted Garth's already warm heart. Those eyes got him every time. Doe eyes, he called them, framed in long thick lashes under beautifully shaped brows. It was best to focus on those eyes, too, because he knew if he took a long look at those cherry lips, he would be a goner for sure. *God help me make it through December,* Garth prayed silently.

Pansy Joy was a fetching sight in her beige and green calico work dress. Flattering her fine features, the fitted bodice was darted on both sides of the front button line ending at a straight natural waist. The sleeves, fitted also, tapered down her arms, and the floor-length skirt covered petticoats that swooshed with every step intoxicating Garth in their wake.

"I'm just fine, Garth," Pansy Joy answered sweetly. With her feet planted in the middle of the road, she held her basket with both hands and rotated her shoulders back and forth—tick, tock, tick, tock—like the pendulum on the mantle clock marking time. "How nice it is to see you out this lovely morning." A coquettish smile played across her pretty face.

"I think I might have mentioned I had some fence mending to do today," Garth said. "You know how men folk always have work to do."

"I see." Pansy Joy looked Garth over, head to toe. "I didn't notice any tools out or any loose boards on the corral. You must be a mighty fine worker to finish up a big project like that before eight o'clock in the morning."

"Right you are, missy. I'll be a right fine catch for some lucky young lady." Garth puffed out his chest and threw back his head, looking for all the world like a rooster in suspenders.

"I see you have a basket there, ma'am. Do you need some assistance toting your load? I might be able to help out a young lady in need."

"That would be such a gentlemanly thing to do. Are you sure you can spare the time, sir?"

"Oh, I'm sure. I'm thinking it's the Christian thing to do, exhibiting one of them fruits of the Spirit Reverend Dryfus preaches about, don't you think?" Garth gave her a wink and reached for the basket. "Let's see. Walking with you . . . would I be exercising longsuffering or temperance?"

Pansy Joy gave a playful shove between Garth's shoulder blades. "If that's how you feel, I can carry my own basket. A real gentleman would use other words to court a lady, like love, joy and goodness."

"Like, 'goodness me' or 'it will be a joy to finish this unselfish act of mercy'?" Garth arched his eyebrows and made a face at Pansy Joy before his voice took on a more serious tone. "I notice you left off peace. I reckon we could both use a little of that about now."

Pansy Joy tucked her arm through Garth's elbow. The couple started down the road in step, Garth closing his wide gait to match Pansy Joy's shorter stride. "I really do have peace," she said, the teasing in her voice now markedly absent. "With everything in me, I'm ready to be your wife. I've been so excited I injured Rosalie this morning. She got stabbed by a thorn to the point of bleeding, bless her heart."

"What did you do to that sister of yours?"

"Nothing, really. She jerked her finger on a thorny stem when I let out a little joy in Mama's rose garden."

"Let out a little joy? A little Pansy Joy? I'd like to see some of that myself."

"You sure you won't get hurt like Rosalie?"

"Sure as shooting," Garth said, but he wasn't as sure as he made himself out to be. Having his darling so close, holding on to his arm, occasionally brushing against him as they walked, it was getting to his manhood. "Do you think Rosalie's all right with everything?

"I think so," said Pansy Joy. "I know she's genuinely happy for us. There's not a kinder soul than Rosalie. She doesn't have a selfish bone in her body."

"No question about that. The way she's taken over since your ma passed–it's been something to watch and admire."

"You're right." Pansy Joy stroked the firm bicep beneath the woven cotton. An innocent touch that proved downright distracting to both of them. She shook the cottonwood from her brain and thought again about her sister.

"Nobody knows Rosalie better than me. She's all smiles and helping hands, and it's genuine, for sure and for certain. Still, I sense she has a longing in her heart. After Mama died and Clayton moved to Nevada . . ."

"I thought Clayton was in love with her."

"We all did. Rosalie, too, I'm thinking. He was a couple of years older, but he was definitely interested. He kept finding reasons to be out to the orchard, usually some little something in his pocket for Rosalie, helping out around the place when Mama was so sick while she carried Lucas."

"Then why'd he up and leave?"

Pansy Joy had explored this subject before, but had never shared her thoughts. "After Mama died, Rosalie took over most of the womanly duties at the house, including the raising of Lucas and Marigold. I've often thought Clayton figured if he married Rosalie, he'd be marrying the orchard and the rest of our family, too. Seems he wasn't willing to do either, or wait for the situation to change."

"So he went west to seek his fortune."

"You know his ma and pa always wanted to move out to Death Valley. They finally did it a few months after Mama died. Clayton was old enough to make his own decision to stay or go, but he went with them. We haven't heard from any of them since."

The half mile walk ended before either was ready to say goodbye. "Here's your basket, ma'am."

Pansy Joy released her hold on Garth's solid arm, already missing the feel of it between her hands. She took the basket, and Garth gave a formal bow before he clicked his heels together, made a sharp 180 degree turn and started his walk back to the farm. Pansy Joy watched him, waiting and then receiving a last loving look and a wave before she turned on the path that led to Comfort Lodge.

CHAPTER 4

The perennial early riser, Balim was up before his young master and had the coffee ready by the time Zion Coldwell stretched his way out of his bedroll. Dawn split the sky in glorious pinks and lavenders as Zion sauntered across the sparse grassland to meet Balim by the open fire.

Balim handed Zion a cup of steaming coffee. "It looks like your plan's working just fine, Massa Zion."

Zion had to agree. "Who would have thought a few newspaper advertisements would change our lives?"

"Funny how things work out that away." More than the postings had changed the lives of the Coldwells in the last few months, and not much escaped Balim's watchful eyes. He was very aware that Zion, a cheerful lad from infancy, now carried an underlying heaviness even when he gave a rare smile. "How was Miss Penny's night? She sleep clean through?"

"No nightmares, thankfully."

"Thank Ya, Jesus."

"Yeah."

"Poor little darlin' hasn't been the same since the accident."

Zion poked the fire with a stick. Sparks flew. "We'll make Washington before nightfall."

"Mm hm." Balim studied the tall young man beside him like a mother watching her child on the first day of school. He seemed to be holding up well, but Balim wondered how he was handling the challenges of their rigorous travels and recent losses.

"I can't help but wonder if any of the others beat us to the rendezvous point. We've made good time, but the river crossings took longer than I expected." A spark of humor lit Zion's eyes and a dimple appeared on his right cheek. "It's a good thing we learned how to cross rivers before we pick up the other folks."

"Yes, suh. That's of a truth," Balim agreed. "You got game, Massa Zion. Why'd you pick Washington fo a meeting place? 'Tain't Maysville right close by Washington?"

"You're right. Maysville and Washington are just a few miles apart. The steamboat carrying the Coventrys is chugging down the Ohio right now. Maysville would have been convenient for them, but folks coming by land don't need to go all the way to the river." Zion shot down the rest of his coffee, picked up the pot with a towel and refilled his cup. He offered some to Balim.

"The L&N pulls in at Louisville station. The ladies and Mr. Ballard will take the stagecoach from there to Maysville. With the newlyweds coming across North Carolina, I thought it would be easier to find each other in a smaller settlement."

"Good thinking, Massa Zion. The Lord done blessed you with a fine mind. Yes, suh."

"And who knows who will be waiting for us when we arrive? The advertisement said we would take on additional travelers if they were well-outfitted and had the money for the transport fee."

"Zion!" A raspy cry came from the wagon.

"Be right there." Zion rose from the stump he'd been sitting on and hurried to the wagon. One small hand held the wagon's white canvas covering open, while the other rubbed the sleepies from cornflower blue eyes. Peeping from beneath a silky blond mane that contrasted with Zion's coarse chestnut hair, eleven-year-old Penny Coldwell's eyes perfectly matched the color of her big brother's.

"Morning, Buttercup." Zion reached in and hoisted the girl with ease. He gave her a quick squeeze and dropped a kiss on her head before settling her tenderly on the ground.

Still in her nightdress, Penny looked sweet and vulnerable. She wore the fine features of their mother, an aristocratic nose, high forehead, and thin pink lips set in a lovely oval face. Zion recalled a daguerreotype he had seen of his mother around Penny's age, and she was the spitting image of her.

"Good morning, Zion." Penny gave a stretch and surveyed the landscape. "I'll be right back."

"You want your wrapper? It's a might nippy this morning."

"Thanks." Penny took her shawl from her brother and disappeared behind some bushes.

"You ready for a cup of Arbuckle's, Missy Penny?" Balim asked when she returned.

"Balim. You know I don't drink coffee. I'm too young for that." The serious look on her face broke into a slight grin and she shook her head at the big black man. "One of these days I'm going to surprise you and say yes."

"Maybe when you get a few more inches on you," said Zion. "Until then, it looks like we'll have to rustle up something else for a young lady of your discriminating tastes." Zion ladled some water from a barrel into a speckled tin cup and handed it to Penny. "Drink this, and we'll get you some milk when we reach Maysville later today."

"That sounds so good. I'm surprised how much I've missed having fresh milk. Being on the trail and everything . . . well, I guess I never appreciated all we had before." Penny took a sip from the cup. "It's hard to believe we're almost there, and we'll be meeting up with all those strangers."

"They won't be strangers for long. It's over 2,000 miles to Nevada, and I'm sure we'll all be as friendly as a basket full of kittens by the time we get there."

The mention of kittens sent Penny's mind back to Virginia and her lost pet. "I miss Prissy."

"She was a sweet cat," Zion said. "Had the prettiest long hair I ever saw. I'm sorry we couldn't save her."

"I know." Penny turned her eyes to the puffs of clouds skittering across the azure sky. "Do you think cats go to heaven?"

Zion did not know what to say. He felt a familiar tightening in his chest, and he knew he needed to pull himself together before he spoke. His voice would surely crack, and he did not want Penny to hear it.

Balim came to Zion's rescue. "The good Book says lots about critters. Did you know that, Missy Penny?"

"Really?" Penny turned her attention on Balim. "I just remember poor things being killed for sacrifices–oxen, lambs, doves, and such. Does it say they go to heaven when they die?"

"Cain't say for certain those very animals do, 'cause that's not told us in the Holy Scriptures, but I do know they's animals in heaven, chile."

"It says that? In the Bible?"

"Sure 'nough does. John the Revelator done told us all about how the Lawd Jesus is gonna come back riding a white horse. Where you think He's gonna get that mount, little Missy? Must be up in heaven with Him already. Ain't so?"

Penny perked up a bit. "It does say that. Right in the Bible. I remember now."

"And what about them lions and lambs lying down with each other in peace? That's in paradise, too."

A real smile lit Penny's face and she turned flashing blue eyes on her brother. "If there are lions, lambs and horses, then there might be cats, too."

"There may be, at that," Zion answered.

Reluctant to change the subject that offered his sister a bit of hope, Zion forced himself to face the realities of the day. They needed to break camp and hit the trail. "Why don't you get dressed now, Penny? We'll have our breakfast and get on the trail."

Zion tousled Penny's hair and offered the girl a hand. "Come on. I'll help you into the wagon."

Balim watched brother and sister cross the campsite. Zion lifted Penny into the wagon. A sturdy transport built in the Conestoga Valley in Pennsylvania, this commercial wagon had a unique design. Huge and heavily built, the 18-foot wagon could hold up to 8 tons of cargo in its bed that curved upwards on both ends to prevent contents from shifting during travel. A wooden framework and suspensions secured a white canvas covering that offered protection from the elements. Wide, iron-plated wheels supported loads so heavy that six mules were required to pull a fully loaded wagon—which is just what Zion hoped for.

Zion had calculated the fees he would earn transporting a hodgepodge group from the Old States to the new frontier out west. Almost everything he owned was invested in this wagon, team and supplies. He anticipated a good profit from the venture and the chance to make a new beginning anywhere he decided to make his abode. After he saw the settlers safely to their destinations, he could transport goods back East for a fee and pick up new folks. Or, as he and Penny traveled, they might just take a fancy to Denver or Virginia City themselves. He could sell the rig and make a good start on a friendly piece of land.

Zion took a quick mental inventory of his passengers. The Coventry family from Boston had forked over a hefty deposit that would fund the food and supplies needed for the trip. Mrs. Coventry, willing to adventure into the unknown, was not willing to do so without her heirloom furnishings. Her husband could not deny her, especially with the extensive library he packed for himself. Uncertain what educational materials would be available for his children, Rachel and Henry, he planned to bring every resource necessary to accomplish the task. Zion didn't mind. He got paid by the pound and the mile. Mr. Coventry was welcome to bring as many books as he wanted, at least as many as the steam ship could haul without sinking into the Ohio River.

The newlyweds would not net a large profit for Zion. They were bringing their own team and wagon, so they had no need to pay cargo fees. For a reasonable charge Zion would serve as their escort and protection. Clarence and Louella Sweeney were concerned about the Mormons. They had been known to attack wagons in the Utah Territory and strip their owners of all their belongings.

Travis Ballard, the minstrel photographer, wanted to document the gold rush and migration to the West, to show the new frontier to the world. The optimistic fellow dreamed of publishing photographs and articles in periodicals and then turning them all into a book.

As for the three single ladies, Liza, Penelope and Beth Ann, Zion was hesitant at first to transport them. He was uneasy with women traveling unchaperoned and unprotected. Miss Liza Waterson worked at a saloon in Nashville, one Travis Ballard frequented when he was in town. While bellied up to the bar one evening, Travis showed Liza the solicitation Zion had placed in the *Nashville Daily Union*. In the next column over, Liza read a notice for a mail-order bride. Ned Hall, a miner in the Nevada Territory, had a viable gold claim and was looking for a wife. Travis contacted Zion and Liza wrote Ned.

Although Liza had a colorful background, Ned was understanding. He had gone west for his own fresh start and he would not deny one to Miss Liza. Besides, she was a looker. Travis helped Ned and Liza get their plans in place by volunteering to escort Liza. By the time the final arrangements were made, he had agreed to escort two other women from Nashville to the rendezvous point, as well.

Penelope Ford had also answered an ad for a bride, and Forrest Evans contracted with Zion to transport the young lady to him. A seamstress from St. Joseph, Missouri, Penelope owned little to haul to the new frontier. Besides a trunk of clothes and a bag of personal items, she asked only to bring her heirloom spinning wheel. It belonged to her granny, and she had promised her she would keep it in the family.

Bunking up in the middle of the two brides-to-be, Beth Ann Sparks was cut of a different cloth altogether. She traveled on a mission from God to the Paiute Indians of Nevada. The missionary society in Little Rock had gathered barrels of clothing and supplies to send with Beth Ann. A contact in Virginia City would see her to her final destination.

Once all his travelers were safely transported west, Zion had one more obligation. He had promised Balim his freedom, and he meant to see to it. Of course, Zion had heard about the Underground Railroad and thought of it as a means of escape for Balim. Although his family legally owned Balim, Zion did not believe in one man possessing another. It just didn't seem the natural order of things. Providence had placed him an owner; but he knew if the situation was reversed, he would not want to be one of the owned–unable to make decisions for his future or create his own destiny.

Zion wanted better for Balim than an empty-handed escape on the Underground Railroad. He owed him–his family owed him much more for his years of faithful service. Zion had big dreams for Balim. It was only last spring he had discovered Balim had a wife. Minnie, a beautiful mulatto owned by their neighbors, had asked Balim to keep their marriage a secret. She said things would be hard for her if her master knew. The arrangement worked for several years, their secret kept until the Browns planned to move to South Carolina last spring and Minnie chose to run. She thought if she could be free in Canada, Balim might somehow find her. If it was up to Zion, Balim would.

CHAPTER 5

Raised on a horse farm in Virginia, Zion had been confident he could handle the mules and wagon; but as the party crossed the state headed for Kentucky, Balim found himself driving the team more often than not. Zion preferred the saddle. It seemed a shame to bounce on the buckboard when he could be riding West, his thoroughbred stallion. And, in the horse's best interest, of course, Zion reasoned that his mount fared better in the fresh air than being tied to the back of the wagon eating trail dust with Star and Absolom.

The mild temperatures of early morning quickly dissipated in the summer sun, replaced by stifling humidity. Sitting tall in the saddle, Zion removed his hat and wiped the perspiration with a bandana. "I'm going to let West have a bit of a run," he called out to the two wagoneers. He mashed his hat down firmly on his head and gave a simultaneous click of the tongue and flick of the reins. West let out a snort and then broke into a full run.

On a good day the wagon covered 15 miles, and the monotony of the slow pace fatigued both horse and rider. Exhilarated by the wind on his face and the rush of the ride, Zion relished the feel of the powerful animal beneath him as they flew over the open road. Thoughts of Penny and Balim reined him in. He eased West into a walk and turned back.

"Hello, the wagon!"

"Hello, the stallion!" Balim greeted Zion as the horse met the wagon, turned, and flanked the buckboard. "You an' that hoss take the rag off the way you two skedaddle all over the countryside."

"I would be scared to death to ride that fast," Penny said. "I'd fall off for sure. But you and West look beautiful, the way you lean into him and move together."

"I would be scared to watch you ride that fast, little girl," Zion said. "You want to walk for a bit or ride Absolom?"

"How much farther do you think we have to go?"

"Not much. Homesteads are getting closer together. I think we'll make town mid-afternoon. We'll stop in about an hour for dinner and have a home-cooked supper at the lodge."

"And a bath?" Penny was unable to disguise the longing in her voice. Washing in streams or in basins of water along the trail lacked the delight of submersing in a tub of warm water with a bar of fresh smelling soap. And having two men around afforded little privacy for proper hygienic care. The Coldwells, while not pretentious or of the elite society of Virginia, adhered to a strict policy of personal cleanliness impossible to maintain in the wild.

"I'm sure Mrs. Erlanger will have proper facilities for a bath, Buttercup."

"I hope so. I feel more like a stinkweed than a buttercup."

"Ah, Missy Penny, you's sweeter than any ole stinkweed."

"Thank you, Balim. Would you mind stopping so I could walk for a bit?"

"Sure 'nough, Missy Penny. Sure 'nough will." Balim pulled the reins and the mules slowed to a stop.

"How many rooms will they be needing?" Pansy Joy asked Mrs. Erlanger.

"Every one we've got."

"That's unusual, to have a group so large all at the same time."

"Arrival times vary from one group to the next, but they all plan to meet here before they set out for Nevada Territory in a wagon train."

"They are either brave or crazy or both," Pansy Joy said. "But boarders are boarders, and that's money in the bank."

"I'm glad your sister sent more lotions. I sold the last jar to Lark Matheny last week." Mrs. Erlanger smoothed the sheet and fluffed the feather pillow. "You know she sneaks it in the house. Martha would take on to beat the Dutch if she knew her daughter was buying Rosalie's lotions on the sly."

"I can just see Lark in her lace-trimmed nightgown and rag rollers pulling the jar out from under her canopy bed–slathering Rosalie's lotions on in the dark." Pansy Joy let out a hearty laugh that sent her curls bouncing. "Wait until I tell Rosalie."

Mrs. Erlanger folded her arms across her chest and shook her head at the capricious girl. "You are a caution, Pansy Joy."

"Florence?" James Erlanger called up the stairs. "You got chickens up there? I hear cackling."

"Your ears must be playing tricks on you, Mr. Erlanger. Me and Pansy Joy just made up the big room for our guests."

"I hope they enjoy the room as much as you two seem to be," James said as he climbed the steps. He entered the suite, thumbs hooked in his suspender straps, and looked from one woman to the other. Pansy Joy shot a sideways glance at Florence and burst out laughing again.

"Well, if it isn't the rooster come to check on the biddies," Pansy Joy said.

"Rooster?" "Biddy?" The Erlangers answered in unison. The comical indignation hit Pansy Joy's funny bone. She let out a giggle that started a fresh round of laughter.

"I declare, Pansy Joy," James said. "You're a bit of sunshine in calico and pinafore. Mrs. Erlanger looks forward to the days you help out around here. She says you're a tonic to her soul."

"A merry heart doeth good like a medicine," Florence said.

"I'm thankful for the job, Mr. Erlanger," Pansy Joy said. "I enjoy my time working here with you both."

Penny, once so excited to think of finally arriving in Washington, drew her knees to her chest on the buckboard and hid her face from the horrific sight ahead. Right in front of the county courthouse inhumanity slapped her tender cheek with a bitter sting. Of course, she knew Balim was a slave. He was part of her earliest childhood memories. But to her, and all the Coldwells, Balim seemed more like family than tangible property that could be sold away at a man's discretion.

The barbarity of one human being owned and sold to another, in chains, on the courthouse steps—the injustice shook Zion to the bone. Of all places to have a slave auction, who chose the courthouse? Wasn't the courthouse the symbol of due process and equity? The place of righteous judgments by honorable men who upheld laws of decency and civility?

A granger ascended the steps for a closer look at the man newly offered for bids. He pulled at the black man's lips to check his teeth and pinched his limbs to determine muscle tone. "Take a walk, Simon." The auctioneer ordered the slave to walk back and forth, and then touch his toes. "He's the picture of health, gentlemen. Who will start the bidding on this young buck?"

"I'll never forget his face as long as I live," Penny cried into her skirt. The anguish and defeat written on the man's face as he was separated from his wife and child was more than Penny's young heart could bear.

"Chattel." Balim mumbled. Not men, but property.

"Let's move out, Balim," Zion called.

Balim slapped the reins. "Giddyup," he called out to the mules, and with a start the big wheels moved the rig forward with two saddle horses tied behind.

The team traveled up the macadamized road, heading north past the city line. The mules responded well to the pavement. Maysville Road, the first macadamized road in Kentucky, originated as a buffalo trace. Herds of the massive animals carved a path through the wilderness that became the main conduit for travel in the region. Plans were in place to make a modern road that ran from the Ohio River to New Orleans.

Less than a mile out from town, Zion saw the sign for Comfort Lodge. "We turn left 100 yards up."

"Haw, mules," Balim called to the team as they drew near the entrance.

Comfort Lodge lived up to its name. The grounds themselves welcomed the travelers. A weeping willow opposite the pond waved them in, bidding them down the lane for respite. In the center of the pond edged with fuzzy cattails, a goose house perched on a little island. Mama goose led a curving line of seven goslings from the backside of the island, and Penny forgot her misery.

"Oh, baby gooses."

Zion didn't bother to correct her grammar. Under the willow tree, two benches invited folks to sit a spell and enjoy the quiet surroundings. Down a ways from the pond, stood the corral and a large barn painted a cheery red with white trim and a big white X on the door. The black roof of the barn arched over a haymow with a crane. A henhouse and springhouse completed the outbuildings, and across the lane, Comfort Lodge nestled in the shade of tall timbers.

Painted a deep green, the vastness of the lodge blended into the lovely scene. A large wrap-around porch swung across the front and both sides of the first floor. Four ladder-backed rocking chairs wore the same floral cushions as the bench swing suspended from the porch ceiling. The black-shingled roof donned eight gables, four facing front and four looking into the woods. Clusters of black-eyed Susans lined the flagstone path to the door decorated with a grapevine wreath and dried wildflowers.

"What a beautiful place," Penny said. "I think I could stay here forever."

"Looks a bit like paradise, don't it?" Balim said. "Shady and sunny, wet and green, fresh smelling, too—all at the same time."

"And I bet it's got feather beds." Penny clapped her hands. "Oh, hurry, Balim. I mean, please stop. I want to get down."

"Hold on there, Missy Penny. Don't go up the spout." Balim pulled the reins and lowed a deep whooooa. The team slowed, and a flop-eared hound dog rounded the corner of the house. Before Zion dismounted to help Penny down from the wagon, the door swung open. A petite blond bounded out, and then stopped abruptly.

"Welcome!" Pansy Joy said. "You must be the Coldwells. I'm Pansy Joy from down the road. I was just helping Mrs. Erlanger get your rooms readied up. Everything's in apple pie order."

Zion and Penny's eyes fastened on the attractive young woman, bonnet and basket in hand. "I was just headed home, but let me get Mrs. Erlanger for you." Pansy Joy disappeared in the doorway.

"She's dreadful pretty," Penny said.

"That's so," her brother agreed. Quick seconds later, Pansy Joy returned with a smiling Mrs. Erlanger wiping her hands on her apron.

"Welcome. Welcome." The ladies descended the steps to greet their guests.

"Thank you, ma'am," Zion said. "We're right pleased to be here."

"You've beat the others, so you'll have time to rest and recover before you have to set off again."

"We're thankful for your hospitality, Mrs. Erlanger. This here's my sister Penny, and Balim." Zion assisted Penny down from the wagon.

"Penny. Balim." Mrs. Erlanger nodded to each. "Why don't you drive the wagon down to the barn? Mr. Erlanger will help you stow it inside and take care of your mules."

"Yes'm." Balim clucked the team to motion and they plodded down to the barn.

CHAPTER 6

"You should have seen the little girl Penny," Pansy Joy said. The Johnson family sat around the table for the evening meal. "She was the cutest little thing with the bluest eyes and sunny blond hair–about your age, Marigold."

"She was traveling with her brother?" Rosalie asked.

"Yes, she was." Pansy Joy buttered a piece of johnny cake and handed it to Lucas. "I think we should invite them over. Penny seemed sweet as strawberry jam, but there was something sad behind her eyes."

Rosalie passed the platter of fried fish compliments of Lucas and Marigold's fishing excursion that morning.

"Her brother's name is Zion Coldwell, and he organized this group heading out to Nevada Territory. A black man named Balim drove the wagon in."

"You say it was one of those big ones made in Dutch country?" Matthias asked.

"Yes, sir, Pa. It looked like a ship sitting high up on its big wheels. The white cover rounded over the top and made an opening in the front and back to protect their belongings."

"Did they have any animals with them?"

"Leave it to you to ask about critters, Marigold."

"Well, did they?"

"I saw three horses, and a team of six mules pulled the wagon, but that was all."

"Six mules, you say?" Matthias rubbed his chin in thought.

"Yes, sir. That's how big that wagon was. It took all six of them to pull it down the lane."

"Would you like some more beans, Pa? Or catfish?" Rosalie offered.

"No thank you, but I'd take another piece of johnnycake if we've got some of Marigold's honey left."

"Sure do, Pa. I'll get it for you." Marigold jumped up from the table to get her prized honey, still in the honeycomb, pleased to have a special request from her father. Marigold tended the beehives in the apiary on the perimeter of the orchard. Bees never lacked for some flower or another at the Johnson place. Spring through fall, they found plenty of nectar that produced the most delightful honey blend in the region. "It's the last of it, but more'll be coming soon."

"You entering your honey in the fair this year?" Pansy Joy asked.

"You know it. It'll make a mash for sure." Marigold handed the crockery jar to her father. "I can't really take the credit for what the bees make, but the good Lord led them here for me to tend. The honey will be coming in in a couple of weeks now, in plenty of time before the Germantown Fair. I aim to win me a blue ribbon."

"I like your honey, Mar'gold." Lucas cheered his sister on. "It's the bestest."

"Thanks, Lukey." Marigold beamed at her protégé, her faithful shadow and biggest supporter for every adventure.

"I like your johnnycake, too, Rosalie."

"Thank you, Lucas. I like to watch you eat it."

"The fair's celebrating its fifth anniversary this year," Pansy Joy said. "I think we should all enter something."

"How about your blackberry cobbler with Clover's sweet cream?" Rosalie suggested. "The blackberries will be coming in strong over the next few weeks."

"I thought the same thing. Folks do make over my blackberry cobbler. I just need to beat the birds to the bushes."

"What about you, Rosalie?" Matthias asked.

"I haven't decided for sure. Maybe honeysuckle syrup. It's simple to make, but not everyone knows how. It's a nice change from maple syrup or sorghum."

"Goodness knows we've got plenty of honeysuckle," Matthias said. "I clip it back every year, and every summer it tries to take more ground."

"Oh, but the hummingbirds do love it so," Pansy Joy said. "And I love to watch them flying around the hollow."

"Between me and Lukey, the hummingbirds and the bees, you'll have a time getting enough nectar for syrup," Marigold teased.

"Yeah," Lucas said. "Don't need no cooking or nothing. Just pluck 'em and suck 'em." Marigold grinned at her brother and ruffled his saddle-brown hair.

"What about your lotions?" Pansy Joy asked.

"I don't think there is a category to compete for such things. I've only seen handicrafts and baked goods, jams and jellies, that sort of thing, besides the livestock, plants and such."

"That's because Mr. Matheny is on the fair committee, and you know his wife would have a conniption if your lotions won. She already has a bur in her saddle since you won't sell them to her for the mercantile."

"Mr. Matheny's not the only man on the committee," Rosalie interjected. "Representatives from all over Mason County have a say. I just don't think enough people make that sort of thing—not enough to warrant a judged exhibition at the fair."

"Fairs are about showing and sharing, educating and celebrating," Matthias said. "Just because there's not a judging, doesn't mean you can't exhibit your goods. Folks bring newfangled inventions and farm implements every year. It's a way to help each other out."

"I might just do it, Pa." Rosalie warmed at the idea of sharing her special creations with others. And if people liked the exhibit at the fair, she might pick up production and make a few more sales. "Speaking of newfangled inventions, Katie told me Evan and Ethan Matheny said a hot-air balloonist will be selling tickets for rides at the fair this year. Can you imagine being up in the sky with the birds?"

"Don't seem natural like, folks floating above the ground," Matthias said.

"The way Evan and Ethan compete for Katie's attention is something to behold itself. Garth said they act like two tumbleweeds on the prairie falling all over each other to see who can get the closest to his sister."

"Katie is awful pretty . . . a sweet girl, too," Matthias said. "Best she not go up in that balloon with both of them Matheny boys, though. If they get in a tussle in that basket, it could come to naught."

"I'd like to try that balloon myself," Marigold announced, always up for adventure regardless of the risk. "You know, Rosalie, you could enter your rose petal custard with the caramel syrup. It's top-notch."

"It is good, but I don't want to compete with Pansy Joy's blackberry cobbler."

"Pansy Joy's cobbler's a heap better than that pasty ole angel food cake Mrs. Matheny's sure to enter." Marigold said. "That woman thinks her recipe is a local legend."

"That's enough, Marigold," Matthias said. He threw a stern look at his saucy daughter.

"Yes, Pa." Marigold gave a repentant look and held her tongue. Matthias changed the subject.

"You're a fine sewer, just like your Ma."

"Your needlework is pretty as a picture," Pansy Joy said.

"I haven't made anything new to enter. It's not right to enter something from previous years." Rosalie's handiwork embellished many of the items in the Johnson cabin. She edged the simple muslin curtains with redwork embroidery. Meticulously she fringed basket liners and cross-stitched floral patterns in the corners. On Sundays and special occasions, all the girls wore collars crocheted by Rosalie of thin cotton thread, many dyed to match special outfits.

"What about the quilt?" Matthias asked.

Rosalie swallowed and then turned slowly to face her pa, cheeks tinged with a blush of humiliation. "I . . . I've tried to work on it, but I . . . I've been so busy with other things." Matthias didn't press for more. The quilt belonged to Rosalie. Her mother had cut the pieces and bundled them into separate squares ready to be stitched up. Matthias was convinced she chose the calicos for the girls' dresses so she would have just the right color scraps to squirrel away for the quilt. Beautiful pinks, reds and yellows were cut into petals, and a host of green prints and solids formed leaves, stems and sepals. Pregnant with Lucas when she finally collected the last bits of fabric, Sharon's fingers swelled up so much she was unable to begin the needlework. She passed on before she stitched a single flower in place.

Rosalie enjoyed appliqué, but could not bring herself to work on the quilt. Everyone knew the Rose of Sharon quilt pattern was traditionally made for newlyweds. And Rosalie knew her mother spent years collecting and cutting the fabric she intended to use in the making of a wedding quilt for her firstborn. Many times Rosalie retrieved the pieces from her mother's cedar chest with every intention of putting needle to cloth. On top of the canvas bag holding the pieces laid the Scripture Sharon had intended to embroider into the binding of the quilt.

I am the rose of Sharon, and the lily of the valleys. As the lily among thorns, so is my love among the daughters. The Song of Solomon 2

As much as she loved the feeling of the fabric in her hands and the tangible connection to her deceased mother, Rosalie's heart forbade her contrary fingers from doing the practical thing. Her normal sound reasoning and pragmatism fled like a moth before a monsoon. And when Clayton left Washington shortly after Sharon died, Rosalie gave up altogether. Certain she would never need a wedding quilt, she thought about making it up for Pansy Joy. She even prayed about it, but something stopped her every time she thought she might be ready.

Pansy Joy felt the heaviness in the room. "How about the greased pig contest, Rosalie?" she interjected. "You could enter that." Lucas guffawed and Marigold laughed out loud at the thought of Rosalie dashing around a filthy pigpen in long skirts and petticoats after a greased pig.

"Oh, I don't know if I'm up for that," Rosalie answered with a grin. "How about you, Pa? You want a turn with a squealing porker?"

"Don't reckon I'd have much of a chance with this bum leg." Matthias rubbed his knee with a familiar stroke. "I'll try my hand at the shooting contest, though. How about you, boy? You want to catch the greased pig at the fair?"

"Sure, Pa!" Lucas lit up like a sparkler. "You mean I'd get to play in the mud and Rosalie wouldn't even get mad?"

"That's the way of it." A slow grin crossed Matthias's face.

"Do you think the Coldwells will be in town for the fair?" Marigold asked.

"Can't say for sure," Pansy Joy answered. "They're waiting for the rest of their traveling party to meet up with them before they head west."

"I hope I'll get to meet Penny," said Marigold. "Maybe she'd show me the mules."

"I'm sure Mrs. Erlanger will invite them to Sunday service. They seem like churchgoing folks. Maybe they'll come to prayer meeting tomorrow night," Pansy Joy said.

"Which reminds me, tomorrow is wash day," Rosalie said. "I need everyone to gather everything that needs cleaning. I'm going to turn in early so I can finish up before prayer."

"I can't remember the last time I felt so good," Penny smiled up at her brother as he tucked her in clean smelling sheets on a real feather tick. Mrs. Erlanger had accommodated Penny's desire for a hot bath. The lodge had a special room set aside for private ablutions, complete with lavender-scented soaps and lotions. Penny soaked so long Zion actually worried she drowned in the tub and banged on the door to check on her. By the time she finally came out, her fingers looked like raisins, but her drowsy eyes and contented smile were a sight for sore eyes.

Mrs. Erlanger had taken the girl to her knee and worked the tangles out of her silky golden hair and then braided it and sent her off to bed with a full belly, clean body and happy heart.

"Will you pray with me, Zion?" Penny asked.

"I'll listen to your prayers like I do every night."

Penny nodded. The accident that changed their lives had wounded Penny's heart, but not her faith. Zion, on the other hand, struggled with concepts that tripped up many good men and women. How could a loving God allow horrific tragedies into peoples' lives? And not just any people? Fine, God-fearing ones? And in the struggle to make sense of it all, Zion lost more than his parents and home. He lost his trust in God.

Prayers complete, Zion stood by Penny's bed. Just as he anticipated, she drifted off to sleep in a matter of moments. He opened the door, stepped into the narrow hallway lit by a hurricane lamp mounted to the wall, and then descended the steps to the parlor. The big room covered the entire base beneath the rental rooms above and provided a comfortable meeting place for the lodge's guests. The Erlangers often used the room for community events when weather necessitated an indoor meeting place.

Zion walked through the spacious room to the front door and stepped out into the cool, dark night. A bullfrog sang in the pond and crickets played an accompanying tune. A crescent moon hung overhead lighting Balim's silhouette on the porch steps.

"Is Missy Penny sleeping, Massa Zion?"

"Like an angel." Zion stretched his six-foot-three-inch frame and eased into the rocking chair closest to the steps.

"Reckon she was played out."

"Guess so." Brilliant stars lit the clear night sky while lightning bugs sparked golden enticements to one another under the willow tree. "Whoo," a barn owl called in the distance.

"Thank you, Balim."

"Why, whatever for, Massa Zion?"

"For sticking with me and Penny when you could have left long ago–right now, for that matter."

"Ole Balim's not going to desert you in yo time of need. No, suh, Massa Zion. No, suh." Zion watched the big black man shake his head in the moonlight.

"We both know Maysville is a major station on the Underground Railroad. Freedom's right across the Ohio."

"Freedom's being in the will of King Jesus, Massa Zion. And I's been a free man a good long time."

Zion remembered the freedom Balim talked about. He grew up knowing what it felt like living with the peace of God in his life. His mother and father, holiness people, were sanctified at a camp meeting where Methodists, Baptists and Presbyterians alike met together and experienced a baptism by fire, what Charles Finney called waves of God's "liquid love" flowing into their hearts. Zion's mother and father had genuine relationships with Jesus, but their son felt betrayed.

"Just the same, I thank you for staying on, and I'll do my best to see you and Minnie reunited after this trip."

CHAPTER 7

Before the sun crowned the horizon birthing the new day, Rosalie stepped outdoors and lit the fire under the kettle, thankful Pa and Lucas filled the big pot the night before. The water would be boiling by the time she finished the scrubbing.

Rosalie had soaked the clothes in warm water overnight. She pulled out Pa's broadcloth work shirt and began the process, scrubbing it with lye soap on a washboard. Next the shirt would be boiled and stirred in a big pot of water, and then removed from the vat and rinsed twice, once with clear water and once with bluing, wrung out, and hung on the line to dry. When everything was pulled off the line, Rosalie used a flatiron and starch as needed.

Wash day took much time and effort, but with one washboard and tub, only one woman at a time was able to work at the scrubbing. Rosalie sometimes took shifts with Pansy Joy, but she knew her sister detested the task and often spared her from it. Most folks did their wash on Mondays, but Rosalie cherished every bit of her Sundays of worship and rest. Toting water and firewood and soaking clothes could wait until Monday night as far as Rosalie was concerned.

The laborious work of wash days, though taxing to the body, gave Rosalie time for meditations. As she scrubbed Matthias's shirt, she thought about the conversation around the dinner table the evening before. Life generally settled into a peaceful routine in Briar Hollow, the site of the Johnson's home and orchard two miles north of Washington.

One of the first Kentucky settlements, and the first city named after George Washington, the town's origins lay with the North American bison. The great buffalos crossed the Ohio River at Maysville and, in their search for salt, cut a broad path that led four miles south into Washington–a path that became the main road from Maysville to Lexington. A thriving community with flourishing mercantile houses, taverns, mechanics shops and churches, the bustle of the city quieted outside its boundary lines.

Rosalie liked it that way. Routine, the familiar, was comfortable. Living outside the city, sheltered from conflict, she had learned to be content and thankful. It had taken time. The wound from her mother's death had not yet healed when Clayton's departure rent it anew. There was no denying the pain, although Rosalie reminded herself he had never officially declared matrimonial intentions.

Over the past three years, the Lord had brought healing to Rosalie. As she tended her mother's flower gardens, she grew. She grew in her spirit. She grew in her knowledge of plants, their care and their practical uses. She grew in her desire to bring healing and beauty into the lives of others, and she grew into a delightful young lady.

Rosalie learned to count her blessings, and they were many. Not everyone lived in such a lovely place, a cozy home surrounded by wildflower and rose gardens, fruit trees and pumpkin patches. Family, friends and community gave Rosalie a sense of well being. She felt secure, loved and appreciated. She counted these as gifts from God.

Rosalie worked the fabric up and down the scrub board, her mind returning often to the little girl traveling alone with her brother and driver. She wondered about her family and home, filled with a sense of sorrow she didn't understand but that led her to pray. "Lord, bless Penny today. It hurts my heart to think of a little one without a ma or pa around and so far from home. I don't know the details of her situation, but it can't be easy traveling the countryside in a wagon with no women folk.

"Help her brother tend to her needs as best a man can. And if there's some way I can show Your love to her and be a blessing, I pray you will give me the opportunity and show me the way."

The cabin door opened and Pansy Joy erupted through it, blond hair flying out beneath her nightcap and her nightdress flapping as she hurried to greet her sister. "I overslept, Rosalie. I think it's one of those unconscious, built-in things. It seems if I ever oversleep it happens on wash days."

"I don't mind. I like being out in the quiet of the morning." Rosalie squeezed soapy water from her father's shirt, put it aside and retrieved a dish towel. With a practiced rhythm that played a graceful song on the washboard, she moved the fabric methodically up and down over the ridged metal.

"I'll get dressed and start breakfast then. The fire went out in the cook stove, so it will be a little while." Pansy Joy hugged Rosalie from behind, pressed her cheek into her shoulder blade and gave her upper arms a squeeze. "I love you, Rosalie."

"Love you, too, Pansy."

Rosalie stoked the fire under the kettle and completed the scrubbing by the time Pansy Joy called her in for a breakfast of soft-battered eggs, fluffy biscuits and coffee. Matthias chose a Scripture in Psalms and handed the book to Pansy Joy for the reading.

"'God setteth the solitary in families: he bringeth out those which are bound with chains: but the rebellious dwell in a dry land.' Psalms 68:6."

After the reading, the family dispersed, each to their own tasks. Rosalie returned to the yard and transferred the scrubbed laundry into the boiling kettle. As she stirred, she thought on the verse and little Penny Coldwell came to mind again.

Zion studied the handwritten notes in his journal and compared them with the map stretched out before him. Daylight streamed through the curtained window. He heard Penny stir and turned to watch her eyes slowly open. She blinked and took a moment to place where she was and then smiled when she saw her brother watching her.

"Morning, sleepyhead."

"Morning.

"Did you sleep well?"

"I haven't slept that well in a long time."

"You slept through breakfast, but Mrs. Erlanger saved you a plate." Florence insisted Zion let the child rest, and he had willingly obliged.

"If breakfast this morning is as good as dinner was last night, I'll really think I've died and gone to heaven." Penny swung her feet off the side of the bed and stepped on a braided rag rug. Pulling her shawl from the foot of the bed, she wrapped it around her shoulders and headed to the door. "Will you come with me?"

Zion set his journal and maps aside. "I think I could do with another cup of coffee."

"I can be ready in ten minutes." Zion stepped out in the hallway while Penny readied herself. After seeing to her toilet, she put on a simple day dress made of a pink calico and white floral print with a crocheted collar. She brushed and re-braided her blond hair, all within the promised ten minutes, and brother and sister descended the stairway together. To the left of the massive parlor, a large dining room abutted the kitchen, washroom, two bedrooms and a private parlor used by the Erlangers.

In the dining room, still smelling of bacon and molasses, four matching tables with walnut balloon-backed chairs sat atop a gleaming wood floor. Cream-colored basket-weave cloths covered each table, all with red and cream cross-stitched embroidery sewn around their fringed perimeters. Paned windows capped with ecru lace valances marched along the front wall that overlooked the porch. In the corner, the flat lid of a dormant wood stove held a crockery pitcher of burnt-red coneflowers and Queen Ann's lace, a colorful complement to the cheery tablecloths. Beside the wood stove stood a functional sideboard crafted in a simple rectangular style with a rich walnut finish.

Zion pulled back a chair and Penny sat down. "I'll let Mrs. Erlanger know you're up." Before he reached the kitchen door, Florence entered the room with a plate in one hand and a frothy glass of milk in the other.

"I heard you coming." She smiled at the little girl and sat the plate and cup on the table. "Would you like some coffee, Mr. Coldwell?"

"Please, call me Zion." He tipped his head. "And thank you. Some coffee would be right nice." Florence went to the kitchen for the pot, and Zion seated himself next to his sister.

"Here you go." Florence returned from the kitchen, filled a mug with coffee and set it before Zion.

"Thank you, ma'am."

"Oh, you're welcome." Florence grasped the handle in one hand and rested the hot pot on a thick towel in the other. "I saw to your man, Balim. He's back out in the barn with Mr. Erlanger. That's some team of mules you have there."

"I'm sure Balim extended his appreciation for the fine breakfast."

"Yes, he did. He's a well-mannered negro."

Penny's eyebrows shot up and Zion was immediately on alert. Although he detected no malice in Florence, living in a slave state often colored a person's perception of black people, slave or freed. Zion would have intervened if the situation was different, but he and Balim had agreed they best lay low as long as their travels kept them in territories where slavery was the law of the land.

Balim slept in the haymow in the barn and took his meals in the kitchen. He kept to his station and would until he crossed the Ohio to freedom, and hopefully, ultimately, to Minnie. It didn't sit right with Zion, but for Balim's safety, it was best. Many black men had been kidnapped and drug into the Deep South to face new taskmasters and hopeless situations. He refused to take the risk.

"He's a good man," Zion said, watching for Mrs. Erlanger's reaction.

"Seems so. I'll be in the kitchen if you need anything else. Enjoy your breakfast, Penny."

"Thank you, Mrs. Erlanger. I will."

Florence left the room. Penny's appetite, so voracious moments before, suddenly dulled. She picked up the fork and pushed the fried potatoes around on her plate.

"Eat up now, Penny. That's a fine meal set before you."

"I'm not so hungry."

"Don't get downhearted for Balim, Buttercup." Zion reached across the table and lifted Penny's chin with his fingertips, their blue eyes met and fastened. Zion probed the distraught face before him and tried to comfort the girl with a tender smile. "Balim's at peace."

"Balim's sleeping in the barn while we're on feathered ticks. It just doesn't seem fair."

"Well, you're right, Penny. It's not fair, but it's the way things are right now." Zion and Balim had kept the details of their arrangement between themselves. He considered sharing their plans with Penny, but he was concerned she might spill the beans on the long trip west, and who knew what kind of folks they would run into along the way. They didn't really know the people they had contracted to transport. Zion had decided to tell Penny that Balim would be freed after they escorted the last travelers safely to their destinations and began the trip back to Maysville.

"Balim would be more pleased to see you eating that fine breakfast than fussing about him. You've gotten too thin, and we both want to see you get a little meat on your bones and flush in those pale cheeks before we leave."

Zion sipped at his coffee while Penny managed to eat a portion of the food before her. She forced down a few bites under Zion's watchful gaze before the sound of Balim singing floated through the open dining room window.

King Jesus is a listnin' when I pray
King Jesus is a listnin' when I pray
Said if I'd just hold my peace
Then de Lawd will fight my battles
King Jesus is a listnin' when I pray

"May I be excused, Zion?" Penny perked up, and Zion could see she had finished her meal. The sound of Balim's rich baritone beckoned her like a sailor to a siren's song.

"Sure, Penny."

Penny scooted the chair back from the table. Wiped her mouth and neatly folded her napkin before placing it on the table. She walked to the door, the picture of a dignified young lady, but once she descended the steps, she ran, straight into Balim's arms.

"Whoa, what's all this, Little Missy?"

"I'm just happy to see you this morning." Penny burrowed her head in the big man's chest. He smelled the familiar mix of horses and leather and Balim—a scent more comforting than the sweet lavender soap and lotion she had enjoyed so much the evening before. "I heard you singing."

"Well, Missy Penny, the Scripture says it's a good thing to give thanks unto the Lord and sing praises unto His name."

"Balim, you know more about the Bible than anybody. I thought colored folks were uneducated."

"Ain't never been to no schoolhouse, but I've had me some learning. Sure 'nough."

CHAPTER 8

S he couldn't take it any longer. The promptings had persisted throughout the day. Rosalie, tired from the exertion required to complete the washing for a family of five, resisted the urge to rest and walked out into the orchards to talk to her father. Matthias stood amidst the plum trees, loaded with developing purple fruit.

Dinner complete and supper hours away, Rosalie's appearance in the orchard surprised her father. "Everything all right, Rosalie?"

"All's well, Pa." Rosalie looked over the rows of laden fruit trees, their sweet scent filling the air. "How are you?"

"I'm fine. Just checking these trees for brown rot. We've had a lot of rain."

"Have you found any patches?" Rosalie remembered the year so much of the plum harvest was lost to the dark fungus. Matthias babied his trees, making sure they got a good mulch of rotted farmyard manure and garden compost in the spring, and then pricking it into the surface in the fall. His established plum trees, on a good year, yielded about 20 pounds of fruit each. Delicious eaten fresh, the plums were also canned or made into leathers. His daughters made jams, jellies and dried prunes that could be stewed and used in delicious fillings for pastries or mixed with other fruits to make stuffing. And, of course, they sold bushels and bushels at the farmers market every harvest season.

"The trees look good this year. I found patches in a couple of areas, but I trimmed them off. It shouldn't be a problem." Matthias looked at his daughter standing in the full sun. The wide brim of her straw hat shaded her fair complexion, and her large green eyes held an expression Matthias recognized. "What's on your mind, Daughter?"

"I woke up thinking about that little girl, Penny. All day I've felt a pressing in my spirit to pray for her. I've got the wash on the line, and since Pansy Joy's home, I thought I might walk down to the lodge–see if there's anything they need."

"Why don't you take a few plums? There are some early ones ready." Matthias ruffled his hair with a brawny hand and wiped a bead of sweat from his brow. "Send my best to the Erlangers."

"Thanks, Pa." Matthias jammed his hat on his head and turned back to his tree. Rosalie plucked a half-a-dozen ripe plums and carried them in her apron to the house where she fetched a basket and told Pansy Joy her plans.

As she walked past the wildflower garden, the cheery yellow buttercups beckoned to Rosalie. She pulled a few stems, tucked them inside her basket, and then entered the tree-lined lane that led to the main road. She covered the mile walk from Briar Hollow to Comfort Lodge in good time, wondering with every step what she might say to the girl who captured her thoughts. A verse came to mind as she turned in the lane leading to the Erlanger's–something about the Lord filling a mouth with just the right words at the right time. Remembering the Scripture put her mind at ease and she left the matter in God's hands.

The Erlangers kept the place up well. Nestled in the natural setting surrounded by trees, the pond, the tidy buildings and grounds all created a welcoming haven. On the front porch, a tall broad-shouldered man sat on the bench swing with a petite little girl. Her blond head rested on his shoulder and her feet hung free as the man tipped the swing back and forth in a gentle motion.

Rosalie climbed the porch steps and her resolve melted in a puddle beneath her balmoral boots. The girl slept, creating an awkward moment for the young man who would have stood in a lady's presence, but who was reluctant to wake the girl beside him. Rosalie put her index finger to her lip. "Sh. I'll just go inside and see Mrs. Erlanger," she whispered.

Rosalie opened the door as quietly as possible and disappeared inside. She walked into the dining room and passed into the kitchen where Mrs. Erlanger worked. Florence Erlanger, her back to the interior door, placed a loaf of bread dough in a pan and covered it with a cloth. She pushed the pan next to two others and turned to wipe her hands on a towel.

"Oh," she exclaimed when she saw Rosalie in the kitchen doorway. Her hand flew to her chest in surprise. "You startled me!"

"I can see that," Rosalie said with a smile. "I really didn't mean to sneak in your kitchen. I just didn't want to wake the little girl asleep on the swing."

"Well, let's sit a minute whilst my heartbeat slows back to normal. You want a cup of coffee? I've got tea and lemonade, too."

"If the coffee's ready, that sounds good."

"I pretty near always have coffee on, especially when we have boarders." Florence pulled the coffeepot forward on the stove to the heat and grabbed two mugs from the lined kitchen shelf. She placed them and a plate of molasses cookies on the table and filled the mugs with hot coffee.

"I see the first of your guests arrived."

"Yes. The Coldwells pulled in last night. You should see the wagon and mules they drove in. Good thing my James built a cavernous big barn. They drove the wagon right in and shut the door behind."

"Pansy Joy said there were only the three of them, two men and a little girl."

"That's right. The others will be along any day. It's not an easy feat to time a meeting of folks from all over the country in one little backwoods lodge."

"No, I imagine it wouldn't be, now that you mention it."

"So you say little Penny was sleeping on the swing?"

"She looked like an angel with all that golden hair for a halo. Of course, I didn't get to see much of her face. Is she well?"

Mrs. Erlanger considered the question before answering. "As far as I know. She's a slight little thing, but she wasn't coughing and didn't look feverish or anything."

"I have to tell you, she's been on my heart all day–ever since Pansy Joy told us about her at the supper table last night, really."

"She seems to be a good girl, and hasn't been a bit of trouble. She ate real well last night, but not so much today. She loved your soaps and lotions, by the bye."

The front door opened and footsteps crossed the dining room floor. Zion Coldwell's tall frame filled the entryway to the kitchen. "Pardon me, Mrs. Erlanger." He tipped his hat at Florence, and then at Rosalie. "You, too, ma'am."

"Yes, Mr. Coldwell. Let me introduce you. This is Rosalie Johnson. She's our neighbor down the way. Pansy Joy's sister, the girl you met yesterday."

"Pleased to meet you, Miss Johnson."

"Pleased to meet you, Mr. Coldwell."

"Is there something I can do for you, Mr. Coldwell? Did you need anything?"

Zion shuffled his hat from one hand to the other. He felt awkward asking for food when Mrs. Erlanger had prepared a more than adequate mid-day dinner. "I don't mean to inconvenience you, ma'am."

"No inconvenience."

"Do you have a little something that might hold Penny over till supper? She was a might upset earlier and didn't eat enough to fill a sparrow's belly. She woke up from her nap hungry. The girl doesn't have a lot of meat on her bones to keep her going."

"I noticed that." Mrs. Erlanger stood. "I'm glad her appetite has picked up. Do you think she would like some bread and apple butter?"

"I brought some plums fresh from the trees in our orchard. Does she like plums?" Rosalie offered.

"I think she'd like both, and I might be able to assist should she need some help finishing things off." Zion flashed a bright smile and his right cheek dimpled. Rosalie looked into his tanned face. Her clear celadon eyes connected with his smoky cornflower blues. Something in her stomach did a little flip, and she felt a rush of heat on her face, but Zion did not seem to notice.

"I'll have Penny come in here if you don't mind. She's likely to drip plum juice all over your pretty tablecloths if she eats one in the dining room." Zion left the room and returned with Penny. He gave her a nudge through the kitchen door and guided her to the small worktable where Rosalie sat.

"This is Miss Rosalie Johnson, Penny."

"How 'do?"

"I'm very well, Penny. How are you?"

"A little tired, but I had a nap. I think a snack might help."

"Sit right down, Penny." Mrs. Erlanger placed a cutting board on the table with thick slices of bread and a jar of apple butter. "Would you like some milk?"

"Yes. And thank you." Penny took the knife and dipped it in the apple butter. The spicy smell whet her appetite.

"I just picked these plums. Pansy Joy told us you'd come, and I thought you might like some fresh fruit. It's probably hard to come by fresh things when you're traveling."

"You're right about that," Zion said. "Balim does his best, but beans and hard tack every day could cause a fellow to throw up the sponge."

Rosalie laughed. "My sister Marigold would like that—'throw up the sponge.' She's always coming out with some new phrase or another. Maybe I'll use that one on her at supper tonight."

Rosalie looked like a different girl when she laughed. Her fine features, not stark, but not ample by any means, seemed to brighten and fill out when she smiled; and her eyes sparkled with good humor.

"Oh, look, Zion!" Penny pointed to the basket Rosalie lifted to the table. "Buttercups!"

"Well look at that."

A real smile filled Penny's face. She turned to Rosalie with awe in her voice. "I think that means we're supposed to be friends."

"I don't doubt it at all," Rosalie answered. "I walked past the flower garden on the way here, and the Lord impressed me to pick these just for you. But tell me, why are buttercups special?"

"Because she's Buttercup," Zion answered.

"I thought your name was Penny?" Mrs. Erlanger said.

"It is." Zion and Penny answered in unison. They looked at one another and grinned from ear to ear. "And it's Buttercup, too," Penny added.

"When Penny was born, I wasn't allowed anywhere near the house. I kept pestering Pa to go in. I wanted to check on Ma and the baby. Pa had a tough time keeping me occupied. He said we should pick some flowers for the new baby, so he took me on a long walk. There were all kinds of flowers along the lane, but the only ones I wanted to pick were buttercups. They just seemed so cheerful."

"And when he brought them into the house, I was tucked in Ma's arm while she rested on the bed. Zion handed Ma the flowers and said, 'Here, buttercups.'"

"Ma was so done in from the birthing she must have thought I called Penny Buttercup, and with that yellow hair of hers, well, it just stuck. Buttercup's been her pet name ever since."

"You'd fit right in over at Briar Hollow," Mrs. Johnson said. She looked at Rosalie and the two burst out in a new round of laughter.

"Oh, that's rich," said Rosalie. She pulled a handkerchief from her sleeve and dabbed at the tears in the corners of her eyes.

"What's rich?" asked Penny.

"My Ma, bless her soul, she loved flowers to distraction. She planted them everywhere. Spring, summer or fall something is always in bloom. She had Pa make a special shed to dry them in so she could have them in the house in the cold winter months, too." Rosalie wiped the tip of her nose with the handkerchief.

"Guess that wasn't enough, now, was it, Rosalie?"

Zion watched Rosalie as she shared a knowing glance with Mrs. Erlanger. Not the vivacious beauty of her sister, Rosalie's features were attractive in their own right. Where Pansy Joy was petite and curvy, Rosalie was long-limbed and graceful. Her thick auburn hair topped a pretty heart-shaped face that reminded him of a china doll Penny used to have, except for the freckles. But Zion didn't mind freckles. They looked quite nice on Rosalie, and her pale jade-green eyes sparkled with a secret ready to burst forth.

Penny, filled with curiosity, bit her lower lip to keep her manners in check.

"You were there for each one, weren't you?" Rosalie looked from Mrs. Erlanger to Penny. "Mrs. Erlanger was Ma's best friend. They spent lots of time together, but every now and again over the years she came for a special visit, about the time a new baby girl was being born."

"You?"

"Yes. I was the first. Mama had a particular affection for roses. You'll have to come to Briar Hollow and see the rose garden. It's a sight to behold and in full bloom right now."

Penny gave Zion a silent entreaty, and Zion nodded in return. "I'd love to see your rose garden," she said. "Thank you."

"Her ma's name was Sharon." Mrs. Erlanger picked up the tale. "When her first little girl came along, she named her Rosalie– her little 'Rose of Sharon.'"

"Some folks thought it peculiar, but Mama was sincere as she could be." Rosalie's eyes softened with sweet memories of her mother. "You see, she loved flowers so much because she considered them beautiful gifts from the Lord. She said there were lessons in every one, and healing in many."

Hanging on every word, Penny felt a familiar ache for her own mother, at the same time, she relished every moment of Rosalie's story. Zion watched the emotions playing across both girls' faces and witnessed a silent knitting together of two tender hearts.

"My pa husbands an orchard in the hollow, and he thinks the same about his trees."

"That's so." Florence said. "Matthias is always relating pruning, fertilizing, and tending his trees to Scripture."

Rosalie nodded. "There is a lot to learn from God's gift of nature."

"Balim says the same," Penny said.

"Balim must be a wise man."

"He is, Miss Johnson. I can introduce you to him."

"That would be nice," said Rosalie. "Where was I? Oh, yes. Ma did like roses best of all. She said there were special lessons in the roses, and folks call Jesus Himself the Rose of Sharon."

Mrs. Erlanger picked up the story. "A couple of years later, I made another trip out to Briar Hollow. We'd had an early warm spell that year. I remember it clear as day. The day your sister was born a light snow blew in. The pansies were already up. They looked like they were shivering, but they poked their purple and yellow heads out of the snow. 'Twas a cheerful sight."

"I know Ma saw those pansies, too, though I'm not sure she knew it snowed that day. And you met Pansy Joy, so you already know her name."

"And you said something about Goldenrod?" Zion asked.

"Marigold. She was our fall baby–hardy, resilient and yellow-haired. She's 12 and quite the tomboy."

"That girl does have a heart of gold," Mrs. Erlanger said.

"Three girls and three flowers," observed Zion.

"I wonder what she would have named a boy," Penny mused aloud.

"I wonder that myself sometimes." A melancholy settled over Rosalie as she remembered the day of her mother's passing. "Pa named him Lucas, after Luke the Physician."

Rosalie stood to go. Zion stood with her. "I best get home. Pansy Joy will be wondering what became of me, and I need to get supper started. It was a pleasure to meet you both; and you, Penny, have an open invitation any time you want to see the gardens."

CHAPTER 9

*Z*ion and Penny walked Rosalie to the front door and out of the lodge. They stood together on the porch and watched her leave. Carriage erect, basket in hand, her calico skirts swished past the pond, down the lane and out of sight.

"She's nice." Penny brought the bouquet of buttercups to her nose and drank in their light fragrance.

Zion withheld comment. The impact Rosalie had made on both Penny and himself took him by surprise. Penny had not smiled like that for months. There was a clear connection between the two. As for Zion, Rosalie possessed some quality that left him wanting to know more about her.

"Massa Zion."

Startled, Zion realized Balim had done it again. For such a big man, he traveled noiselessly at times, seeming to appearing out of thin air like Hiawatha's ghost. "Yes, Balim."

"The shoes on the mules is holding up fine, but your West needs some blacksmithing or you'll be riding shank's mare to Virginia City."

"Well, since I'm not planning to walk to Nevada, I better take West into town and have the smithy take a look. Would you like to come?"

"I done seen enough of Washington to satisfy me, Massa Zion. If it's aright with you, I'll keep Missy Penny company here at the lodge. She might get to chasing after those goslings and fall in the pond."

"You know I wouldn't do that." Penny crinkled her nose at Balim.

"I'll head right out then." Zion turned to Penny. "You tell Mrs. Erlanger where I've gone and let Balim know if you need anything."

In a matter of minutes, Zion had West saddled and was on his way into town. He asked at the livery and was directed to Jim Cooper's smithy the next block over. The sound of metal on metal rang out as Zion approached the building and watched a muscular man hammering a red hot shoe on the flaming forge. The blacksmith took a well used bandana from his back pocket and wiped a stream of sweat running down his tanned face. When he looked up he saw Zion across the yard.

"Afternoon. That's a fine animal," Cooper admired the black stallion as Zion dismounted and walked the horse closer.

"Thank you. I'm Zion Coldwell. This is West."

"My name's Jim Cooper, but everyone calls me just plain Cooper." The blacksmith took off a worn glove and extended a large, sinewy hand to Zion.

"My man tells me West needs some shoeing. Do you have time to see to him today?"

"I can work him in. No emergencies here."

"I would appreciate that." Zion wrapped the horse's reins around a post. "About how long do you figure?"

"A couple of hours if you want all four shoes done. I need to finish this filly first."

"All right. I'll be back in two hours then. Thanks, Cooper."

Zion left the smithy and walked to the log post office. A middle-aged, bespectacled man greeted him. "What can I do for you, sir?"

"I'm meeting some folks in these parts. I told everyone to send any messages to me in care of the Washington Post Office. Have you gotten any mail for Zion Coldwell?"

The man rubbed his chin. "Zion Coldwell, you say? The name's not ringing any bells, but I'll check the general delivery."

Zion watched the man pull a bin down from a shelf and riffle through the letters inside. "Nope. Nothing for Zion Coldwell."

"That's good, I think."

"No news is good news, so they say."

"So they say. I'm staying at the Comfort Lodge. Just came in town to get my horse shoed. Would you let me know if anything comes in?"

"I'll see the Erlangers get your mail if something comes for you."

"Thanks. Good day to you."

"You, too."

Zion wandered through town. Washington, the seat of Mason County, Kentucky, until 11 years previous in 1848, was a well established settlement with rope walks leading from building to building. Zion walked past the limestone courthouse, a venerable structure with a modest steeple that looked like a pencil writing in the sky. Its pristine appearance belied the activities that had taken place there only a few hours ago.

Zion's strong feelings about slavery stirred as he recalled the auction. He knew he was only one voice, and a voice quieted by his circumstances–just a young man with no home and a delicate sister to care for. Aware of the little affect he might have on the blight marring his great nation, he resolved anew to see Balim freed and reunited with his wife.

The issue of slavery sweltered on the nation's back burner, threatening to boil over and scar the countryside. Abolitionists met in the north, and slave owners gathered in the south, each camp believing God was on their side. The thought added to Zion's confusion about his faith.

Zion poked along the rope walk and stopped at the Paxton Inn, a two-story white clapboard building with black shutters on its many windows. Compelled to go in, he stepped to the door with the arched window set in above it, opened it and walked inside. It took a moment for his eyes to adjust, but when they did, he noted the fine appointments in the room. Shock registered when he recognized the man seated in one of the fine parlor chairs, the auctioneer. He spun on his boot and left the building before anyone spoke a word.

His jaw set, Zion strode quickly away from the building. He felt his heart beating hard in his chest, the blood quickening in his veins as memories of the auction replayed in his mind. His boots clacked on the limestone walkway. A woman tucked her children behind her skirts as he approached, and he realized the severity of his countenance. Slowing to a normal pace, Zion inhaled a long breath and forced his thoughts from the courthouse of yesterday to the Washington of today.

No use taking the ugliness of some folks out on the whole town, he thought. Zion passed a mechanic shop and came to the entrance of a large mercantile. He still had some time to kill, so looking for a distraction, he stepped inside Matheny's General Store. Perhaps he would find a small gift for Penny.

The scents and vast selection of goods in the store came as a surprise, everything from ladies unmentionables to garden hoes all scattered about in different displays. Barrels of flour and sugar stood right across from the ammunition counter. Wagon tongues and beef tongues, ribbons and rifles, bonnets and bric-a-brac all laid out in the same building testified to the unique positioning of the town. Maysville, only four miles away, was considered the pioneer gateway to the west, and businesses catered to those traveling out and those staying on.

"Can I help you?" A middle-aged woman greeted Zion from behind the counter. Slightly plump, her ample figure filled out a pagoda-sleeved gown with multiple rows of blue plaid cotton skirts trimmed in deep navy. Her smile didn't reach to her eyes, and although he could not put his finger on it, something about her made Zion a bit uncomfortable.

"Thank you, ma'am. I'll just look around if you don't mind."

"Let me know if you need any help."

"I will." Zion moseyed the aisles looking from display to display. He approached an array of toys and stared at a porcelain doll with auburn hair and pale jade eyes. It reminded him of someone, a younger version of Rosalie, perhaps. The way the she and Penny had connected, Zion was certain Penny would enjoy this doll, especially once they hit the trail. Lacking the funds for such an extravagant purchase, he picked up a bilbo catcher from the table. The simple cap-and-ball game made of wood and string could entertain a girl for many miles.

A pretty young lady with golden ringlets descended the steps from the residence on the upper floor. She seemed a bit young for long skirts and an up hairdo, to Zion's estimation, but she was nice to look at, nonetheless.

"How do you do?" A velvety voice greeted Zion.

"Fine, thank you, ma'am." Zion tipped his hat and offered a polite nod.

The girl sent her hips into motion and her floor-length skirts rustled in the sway. Long lashes batted, sending signals no man would miss.

"My name's Lark." The swaying and batting continued as she extended her hand to Zion. "If I can help you with anything at all, you be sure and let me know."

Zion took the hand offered, discreetly flipped it from horizontal kissing position to a vertical orientation and gave it a quick shake. "I'm Zion Coldwell. I was just looking for a little something for my sister."

"How nice. What a thoughtful man you are. How old is your sister? Is it a special occasion?"

"She's 11, and no ... no special occasion. Just a little something to put a smile on her face."

"I'm sure you know how to put a smile on a girl's face." The winsome words hung in the air between the two. Zion, unaccustomed to such directness in a girl, was at a loss for words. He stared at Lark with a blank look before he regained his senses. "I'll just take this game. Good day, Miss Lark." Zion tipped his hat again and made quick time to the counter.

"Did you find everything you were looking for?" Mrs. Matheny asked.

"Probably more," Zion muttered under his breath.

"What was that?"

"Sorry, ma'am. I'll just take this." Zion placed the appropriate coins on the counter.

Mrs. Matheny wrapped the bilbo catcher in brown paper and tied it with a string. "Will you be in town long, Mr. Coldwell?"

"I'm not sure exactly how long. I'm meeting some folks here and then we are traveling west. They're coming from points north, south and east. As soon as we're all ready, we'll be heading out."

"How interesting." Lark sidled up against the counter. "Mother, don't you think that would be a romantic adventure?"

"Not likely. You've no idea what life is like on the trail. There's no room for canopy beds and claw-footed bathing tubs."

"I would miss both, but with the right company, it might be worth it."

"If you will excuse me, ladies." Zion left the mercantile, package in hand, and headed to the blacksmith. He was ready to bid farewell to Maysville and settle in for the night at Comfort Lodge.

"I hope to see you again soon, Mr. Coldwell." Lark waved her hanky at Zion as he made a hasty exit from the mercantile and returned to the smithy.

"The horse is ready, Coldwell." Cooper stroked West's flank in admiration. "Bring this one back any time."

"Thanks, Cooper." Zion examined his horse with satisfaction and paid the blacksmith for his services.

"Oh, I plum near forgot. You had a visitor while you were gone."

"A visitor?" Zion stroked his chin and wondered who would have stopped by the blacksmith to see him.

"Ole Jenkins from the Post Office. He said to give you this."

Cooper pulled an envelope from beneath his heavy apron and handed it to Zion. "Thanks, Cooper."

"Sure thing. See you around."

Zion grabbed West's leads and left the yard, saddling up in the street. He rode a quarter mile out of town and opened the envelope from the Sweeneys.

Dear Mr. Coldwell,

We made good time through North Carolina, but have been held over for wagon repairs in Knoxville. We expect to arrive three to four days behind schedule, arriving by the 29th or 30th.

Sorry for any inconvenience.
Sincerely,
Clarence Sweeney

Zion folded the letter and stuck it in his saddlebag next to Penny's gift before he headed back to the lodge. The Sweeney's delay, he figured, wouldn't set them back too much. The others had not yet arrived, although they were expected any time.

When Zion neared the lane to Comfort Lodge, he went with his impulse and decided to continue down the road another mile. West clipped along at a comfortable pace until Zion pulled the horse's reins. A hand-painted sign marked the entrance of a tree-lined lane. In scrolled letters, not too fancy, but not too plain, the words "Briar Hollow Orchard" were painted in red on a plank made of several wooden boards joined together. Scrollwork and little pictures of fruits and flowers bordered the sign.

Zion peered down the lane, but the trees blocked his view of the hollow. With a tinge of disappointment, Zion turned West around and flicked the reins. "Let's go see Penny, boy."

CHAPTER 10

"It smells so good in here." Pansy Joy inhaled the distinct fragrance filling the air in the Johnson cabin.

"I love the smell of lavender," said Rosalie. She held the edges of the tiny pillow she was working on and closed them with a whipstitch. Embroidered purple flowers on mossy green stems donned the front of the sweet smelling sachet. She placed the finished piece with several just like it in a basket on the kitchen table and yawned. "It makes me sleepy, though."

"Me, too," said Marigold, and echoed her sister's yawn with an exaggerated stretch.

"I don't really mind waiting to get married," said Pansy Joy, "but it would have been nice to have fresh flowers. Sally's wedding was so pretty and sweet smelling."

"I know," said Rosalie. "But I have an idea, and I already have some things collected–like rose hips and pine cone, juniper shavings and rose petals."

Marigold looked up from the numbers she was calculating on her slate. "What are you going to do with all that?"

"Around Thanksgiving, about a month before the wedding, we take all these things, and we can get more, too. I was thinking about cinnamon bark."

"Cinnamon? Are you making tea?" Marigold asked.

"No, but a cup of tea sounds good. Would you like some?"

"I'll put the kettle on. You keep talking." Pansy Joy pulled the kettle from a shelf and filled it with water. She poked up the fire in the stove and set the kettle on top.

"Nice to see I have your undivided attention," Rosalie teased.

"Oh, you do, Sister. If you're talking about my wedding, I'm all ears."

"Let me explain. It's kind of like these sachets. There is more than just lavender in there. There is filler, too, and fabric holding it all together. I plan to take all the things I have saved, and some others I want to get before Thanksgiving, and then we will mix them all up with some rose oil. If we put some orris root in, that holds the scent especially well. The mix will be sweet for a long time."

"I see." Pansy Joy said. "What a great idea. But what will we put it in? You aren't planning to fill Comfort Lodge with sachets, are you?"

"You could sew some on your wedding gown," Marigold chimed in. "Might look real pretty."

"I don't think so." Pansy Joy held her chin in her hand and shook her head at Marigold before turning to Rosalie. "Why don't you tell me what you had in mind?"

"Until right before for the wedding, we keep the mix in air-tight jars. It takes several weeks before they're ready. The day before the ceremony, we fill pretty dishes and bowls and set them around the big parlor. I thought we could put some of the dried cabbage roses you liked on top of the bowls."

Pansy Joy clapped her hands in delight. "I love it! We can put a candle next to each bowl. It will look so pretty and smell so good."

"That does sound grand." Marigold smiled at her love-struck sister, shook her braids and rolled her eyes and then turned her attention back to the figures on her slate.

"Would you like to take a walk?" Zion asked Penny after supper.

"Sure." Penny bit her bottom lip and flicked her wrist. "I almost got it that time." Zion enjoyed watching Penny play with the bilbo catcher. Although she had not yet mastered the simple toy, she had made progress, getting the ball in the cup about one in four tries.

"Why don't you let me put that in my pocket while we walk? You're liable to trip." Penny handed the toy to her brother. Zion tucked it safely in his pocket and reached for Penny's hand.

"Let's tell Balim. Maybe he'll want to come."

"I already did. He said he wanted to reorganize our things in the wagon–make it ready for when the others get here with boxes and trunks. The Coventrys have some furniture that will take up quite a bit of room."

Brother and sister left out on the main road and turned north away from town. They walked in silence for a half a mile. "Look at that," Penny said as they approached a farm, neat as a pin on the east side of the road.

"Nice spread."

"Do you think that's where Miss Johnson lives?"

"No. They live at an orchard, and that's a farm. See those fields of corn? It looks like a good crop, too. Remember what Balim always says, 'Knee high by the Fourth of July'?"

"Oh." Penny tried to hide her disappointment, but Zion read it easily.

"Were you hoping to see Miss Johnson?"

"She did invite us."

The thought caused Zion to perk up a bit. He'd been heading the direction of the Johnson place, but had not fully committed to showing up on their doorstep.

"You're right, Buttercup. She sure did." Zion picked up the pace. "We're about halfway there. Are you up to it?" Penny's energy level, which had lagged the last couple of days on the trail, had not revived since they arrived at the lodge. Zion was concerned for her health, but thought some fresh air and exercise might be just what the girl needed.

Penny's blue eyes sparkled with surprise. "Sure, Zion. I'm up to it," she said, and she did her best to keep stride with her brother's long legs. They quickly covered the last half mile and stopped in front of the sign. "That's it!" Penny pointed to the canopied lane.

"I think you're right, Buttercup. Let's turn in."

The juniper-lined lane delighted Penny to no end. She studied the leaves overhead, and then the ferns on the ground. "Look, Zion–a fairy ring." Penny let go of Zion's hand and dashed between two trees. She jumped in the middle of a three-foot mushroom circle surrounded by a ring of flowers. A glass jar sat right in the center. "Listen."

Penny stood completely still in the ring. They both heard a tinkling sound. "Do you think it is fairies?" Zion asked. He saw the chimes hanging in the trees behind Penny, but did not want to dash the child's fancy.

Penny closed her eyes, a peaceful expression on her face. "No." Her shoulders set, she turned to her brother with a resolute countenance. "I don't really believe in fairies. But if they were real, I think they would like it here."

His sister's maturity often amazed Zion. Part of him wanted to clap for her while another wanted to grab her hands and dance a jig in the fair ring sweeping her back into childhood innocence.

"It reminds me of the story Pa told us about how he got saved." Zion chuckled. "I haven't thought about that in a long time."

"Tell me again, Zion." Penny turned bright eyes on her brother. "I don't want to forget, and I know you remember more than I do."

Zion dredged the recesses of his memory for the details. "All right," he began. "Let's see. Before Ma and Pa married, Pa worked a side job delivering cotton. One day he was traveling through the woods, just his horses and a wagon full of bales, and he heard angels singing. It scared him. He knew he was a hard case and the fear of the Lord gripped his soul."

"I can't imagine Pa a reprobate," Penny said. "He loved the Lord so."

"Maybe that was the reason. He loved all the more because of it."

"Maybe so. What happened next?"

"He was so drawn by the sound he left the wagon and walked to it. He saw three figures all in white singing in a language he never heard. He said he felt the glory of God and he lit a shuck back to the wagon and hurried on home.

"He told Mamaw and Papaw Johnson, Uncle Charles and Aunt Mary, and Ma. Only Ma would go back with him. She said she'd like to hear angels singing."

"Ma always did love singing."

"Yes, she did." Zion ran a hand down one of Penny's golden braids and tapped the end of her nose with his forefinger.

"When they got back, they found the white-clad singers–a traveling minister and two ladies. They had been worshipping God and praying in preparation for a camp meeting. Pa was so impacted by what he had heard, he decided to help them make the brush arbor for the meeting. He worked beside them, cutting saplings and brush from the edge of the forest and driving long poles, uprights, into the ground. They laid rafters across the uprights for the roof and tied them into a lattice they covered with brush and hay."

"I've always wanted to attend a brush arbor meeting," said Penny.

"You never know," said Zion. "Maybe we'll run across one during our travels."

"And they stayed for the meeting, right?"

"That's right. Pa said he never saw the likes before or since. Folks from all over, black and white, sinners and saints–men and women from all denominations and all walks of life gathered for the meeting. It lasted three days."

"But Pa didn't," Penny interjected.

"No." Zion smiled at his sister. "Pa didn't. At the end of the first evening, he knew he had to get right with God. He walked down to the anxious bench in front of everyone. The whole crowd witnessed his conversion. Ma was so excited she started a laughing and jerking under the power of God."

"I remember she said the presence of God was so thick some people were laid out on the ground."

Zion agreed. "Yes, they were. Ma herself was full as a tick with the joy of the Lord."

"And Pa was baptized in Jesus' name the next day, and he and Ma got married right after harvest."

"That's the way of it." Zion wrapped his arm around Penny's slight shoulders. "You ready to move on?"

Penny looked up at her brother. "I'm ready." Her thoughts left the past and hurried before her to the Johnson cabin. "I hope they are home."

As they neared the end of the lane, the thinning foliage opened to a clearer view of the hollow. Penny took in the sweetness of the orchard, gardens and home. Her lips parted in wonder and a quiet "Ooh" slipped out unbidden.

The hollow, a circular clearing between the woods on the west and the creek on the east, was abloom with colors every spectrum of the rainbow–its air filled with intoxicating perfume. To the north, left of the lane, a wildflower garden greeted their approach to the cabin. The orchards lay in neat rows beyond. Between the cabin and creek, an enclosed rose garden and a grape arbor loaded with dangling clusters flanked the worn path to the orchard. Across from the cabin, a kitchen garden neighbored a hen house. A serviceable stable and corral, small shed and an apple barn lined the southern perimeter.

A brown dog loped from the porch of the log cabin to the lane where Zion and Penny stood. "Hey, fellow." Zion scratched the mongrel between the ears and the trio approached the cabin together. Zion rapped on the front door.

Inside the cabin, Marigold looked up from figuring numbers on her slate. "Who could that be?"

"Why don't you open the door and find out." Pansy Joy lifted the lid to the kettle and dropped some leaves and cinnamon bark inside to steep.

Marigold happily left her slate at the table and opened the door. "Hello," she greeted the strangers.

Zion took his hat in hand. "Hello, Miss."

Rosalie recognized the voice, stood quickly to her feet and smoothed her skirt. Her long fingers moved from her skirt to her hair, tucking strands of auburn in place before finally settling at her sides. Normally serene, Rosalie's reaction to their visitors did not escape Pansy Joy's keen eye.

Rosalie moved to the door. "Marigold, this is Mr. Coldwell and his sister, Penny." She placed her hand on her sister's shoulder and turned to their guests. "Won't you come in?"

"Thank you." One by one, Penny, Zion and the dog entered the door of the lavender-scented cabin.

"Not you, Daisy," Marigold ordered the interloping animal back out the door. "You know Pa don't abide critters in his house."

"Nice to see you again," Pansy Joy said.

"You, too, Miss Johnson," said Zion. "Penny and I were out for a walk. We saw the sign by the road, and thought we'd take your sister up on her invitation to see the flower gardens." Zion looked at Rosalie, and one glance at her sister's face confirmed to Pansy Joy what she already suspected. For the first time in years, Rosalie flushed in the presence of a man.

CHAPTER 11

"I'm so glad you came," Rosalie said.

"Me, too." Penny sniffed the air in the cabin. "It smells like the lotions Mrs. Erlanger uses at the lodge."

"That's because Rosalie makes them from the same lavender bushes," said Pansy Joy.

"You make them?" Penny asked.

Rosalie's flush deepened. "Yes." She trained her focus on Penny, purposely avoiding Zion's cornflower blue eyes framed in long, dark lashes that reminded her of the bachelor buttons in the wildflower garden.

"Rosalie makes lots of things with Mama's flowers," Marigold said.

"And Pansy Joy makes delicious sugar cookies." Rosalie motioned to the plate on the kitchen work surface. "We were just having tea. Would you like some?"

Looking for Zion's nod of approval, Penny gratefully accepted. "Oh, yes, thank you."

The front door swung open. Matthias and Lucas entered the cozy cabin.

"Hi, Pa," Pansy Joy said. "This is Mr. Zion Coldwell and his sister Penny."

"I'm pleased to meet you, sir." Zion extended his hand to Matthias.

"You, too." The big men clasped hands in a firm shake. "I'm Matthias Johnson. This here's Lucas." Lucas smiled up at Zion and then flashed a heart-melting grin at Penny.

"It's hotter in here than outside," said Lucas. "Can I have mine out on the porch?"

"I have cider for you, little one," said Rosalie. "Marigold, Penny, would you like to sit out on the porch with your cookies?"

Penny looked again to Zion for approval, and then started for the door with his nod of consent.

"You go on out and I'll bring it to you." Pansy Joy held the door open and the three children walked onto the covered porch. Marigold scooted the two outside rocking chairs and a wood stump used for a stool around a wooden crate. By the time she had everything in place, Pansy Joy came out with cups of cider and a plate of her thumbprint sugar cookies topped with dollops of strawberry jam.

"These are wonderful," Penny said as she reached for a second cookie.

"Fine as frogs' hair," Marigold said.

"What's that?"

"Have you ever seen a frog's hair?" Marigold asked.

"No."

"That's 'cause they're fine." Marigold bobbed her head and crossed her arms in front of her chest. "Real fine."

Penny burst out in a laugh followed by Lucas.

"You got me."

Zion heard Penny's laughter from inside the house and it warmed his heart. Seated around the kitchen table having tea and cookies with the Johnsons gave him a fine feeling indeed.

"I hear you're heading up an expedition to Virginia City," said Matthias.

"Yes, sir. I'm expecting folks in any day."

"No one's arrived yet?" Pansy Joy asked.

"I got a letter today from the Sweeneys. They're a newlywed couple hailing from North Carolina. They got held up in Tennessee with some wagon trouble, but they expect to be here by the end of the week."

"That shouldn't delay you too much," said Matthias.

"I haven't heard from the Coventrys yet. They're traveling from Pittsburgh on *The Messenger*, a steamboat coming down the Ohio to Maysville. I thought they would be in today.

"Four more took the L&N line from Nashville to Louisville and are coming the rest of the way by coach." Zion took a bite of cookie. "This melts in your mouth, Miss Johnson. Can't remember when I had such a good cookie."

"Pansy Joy's known for her baking around these parts." Matthias reached for a second cookie and dipped it in his tea. "She'll be entering her famous blackberry cobbler at the fair coming up. You think you'll be around mid-July?"

"I hope to be well on the way to Virginia City by then."

A sinker dropped in Rosalie's middle, befuddling her usually calm spirit. *What's gotten into me?* she wondered. She knew the Coldwells would not be staying on in Washington. Why then did she feel this disappointment?

The sound of a horse approaching at a fast clip halted the talk around the table. Matthias and Zion went out to investigate, followed by the girls who remained on the porch with the children as the men stepped into the yard.

"Whoa, there. Whoa." Pulling the reins on the roan mare, the peculiar rider brought the panting animal to a stop in front of the cabin.

"Evenin'." Matthias greeted the man in the saddle, a slight man with a narrow face and tawny straw-like hair that shot out beneath a faded slouch hat. "Can I help you?"

"I'm looking for Zion Coldwell. His man Balim said he'd gone for a walk this way."

"You've come to the right place. This is Mr. Coldwell."

The rider dismounted and threw the reins at Matthias who grasped them firmly and stroked the mare's heaving neck with his free hand. "Name's Bug Perkins." Zion shook the skeletal, outstretched hand. "I'm here on business."

"What can I do for you?"

"Is your pa here?"

A warm glow started at Zion's neck and crept up over his face, but Zion schooled his expression and gave a firm reply. "I'm the only Mr. Coldwell here and the only one coming. What can I do for you?"

"I . . . I was expecting an older man."

"What's your business, Mr. Perkins?"

"Me and my traveling companion, Mr. J.T. Nester, met the Coventrys on the steamboat coming down from Pittsburgh. They arrived in Maysville this afternoon, but we've been unable to arrange transportation for their things. J.T. sent me to fetch you with the wagon."

"It's too late to come this evening. It will be dark soon," Zion said. "Have them room in town for the night and I'll be there first thing in the morning with the wagon."

Zion turned to Matthias. "Where's a good meeting place in Maysville, Mr. Johnson?"

"You can't miss the courthouse or the post office."

"Did you notice either of those buildings on your way out of town?" Matthias asked.

"I saw the courthouse. But you better make it quick. The captain wants everything off the riverboat. His hands threatened to dump the Coventry's things off on the dock, but J.T. talked them into leaving it on 'til we could see to it."

"I'll leave at sunrise," Zion said. "Meet me at the courthouse at 7:00 a.m. with Mr. Coventry. We'll go to the riverfront, collect their belongings and then pick up the family on the way out of town."

"Would you care for some refreshments, Mr. Perkins?" Rosalie offered.

"Thanks, but I've got my canteen here. I need to get back to J.T. with the plans." He mounted his horse, tipped his hat and sped off the property.

"Poor animal," Matthias shook his head.

"The horse doesn't have a canteen," said Marigold. "I hope she'll be ok."

"Must not be his mount, or he'd surely treat her better," said Zion.

"The bridle had the name of the Maysville livery burnt into it. I'm sure they'll take care of the mare when Perkins returns it." Matthias rubbed his scruffy chin in thought. "I hope so, anyways."

Still seated in the rocking chair, a pale Penny forced out a weak call. "Zion."

Alarm shot through Zion as he looked at Penny clutching her abdomen.

"Zion," she repeated in a whisper.

Zion rushed to her side. "What is it, Penny?"

"I need to go to the privy, but I don't think I can make it on my own."

Rosalie noted the distressed look on Penny's face and the exhaustion in her tone. "This way," she said.

Zion swept the girl into his arms and Rosalie wasted no time leading him to the outhouse behind the cabin. He rushed the girl to the door and Rosalie helped her inside. "I'll see to her."

Panic flooded Zion as he waited. What was happening? How could something set on so quickly?

After several long minutes, Rosalie opened the door. With one arm holding Penny's elbow and another wrapped around her slight shoulders, the older girl supported the younger, and the two stepped out of the little building. Zion lunged forward and folded Penny once more in his arms.

"Let's go inside and lay her down," said Rosalie. Zion carried Penny inside the cabin and followed Rosalie to a first-floor bedroom. Penny moaned and grabbed her stomach again. Rosalie turned to Zion and gave an authoritative command. "Get Pansy."

Zion hurried out into the big room where the remaining Johnson family had gathered in shocked silence. He locked eyes with Pansy Joy. "Your sister is asking for you." Pansy Joy wasted no time and hurried to Rosalie's side.

"I need something to use for a chamber pot. Something old we won't miss if we have to throw it out from the sickness. She's not got the strength to make it back to the outhouse."

"I'll be right back." Pansy Joy strode to the lean to, grabbed a dented tin bowl and returned to the bedroom she shared with Rosalie. "Excuse me." She shut the door leaving Zion to wait with the others.

Sensing Zion's distress, Matthias turned to his source of comfort and extended it to the young man. "Sit down, Mr. Coldwell." Matthias placed a firm hand on his shoulder and guided him to the table. "Marigold, Lucas, let's take Penny to Jesus."

"What are you saying?" Zion spun and Matthias's hand fell away. "I don't want Penny to go to Jesus. He already has our ma and pa."

"You misunderstand." Matthias remained calm, unflustered by Zion's outburst. "I meant we should pray for the girl–ask the Lord to touch her with healing mercies."

Humbled by his ignorant eruption, Zion sat meekly in the chair next to Matthias. A large hand extended to his, and Zion was pulled into a circle of prayer.

"Lord, we know You are aware of every situation. What comes as a shock to us and to the Coldwells is no surprise to You. I pray that You would help us rest in that reassurance, and that You would touch this precious little girl. Whatever's ailing her, we pray You would mend her up good and whole in Jesus' name."

"Amen." Lucas and Marigold said in unison. Zion nodded and stared at the plate of cookies still sitting in the middle of the table.

"Why don't you take Lucas out for a game of checkers."

"Sure, Pa." Marigold retrieved the game from the chest and the two headed to the porch.

"She's gonna be all right, Son." Something in Matthias's tone raised Zion's hopes. He locked eyes with the big man sitting beside him. He had watched Matthias use a cane to maneuver around the cabin and yard, but the strength in this man belied his crippled physical state. Zion felt the power of Matthias's faith, a faith his own pa had shared, and he nearly wept.

The door to the bedroom opened. Pansy Joy walked out, shut the door and sat next to Matthias across from Zion. Zion studied her big brown eyes looking for clues, but found only compassion and the same calmness emanating from her father. Pansy Joy reached across the table and patted Zion's hand.

"Penny's in good hands, Mr. Coldwell."

"Of a truth," Matthias said. "Rosalie's a fine caregiver and knows how to use the herbs and remedies the good Lord provided for us."

"How is she? Do you know what's wrong?"

"Rosalie's concerned it might be cholera."

"Cholera!" Zion rose to his feet. "That could kill her!"

"Truly, Mr. Coldwell. Cholera is a serious ailment. I can't explain it, but Rosalie and I both feel confident she's going to pull through. It may not be cholera at all, but we can't take a chance."

"What do we do?"

"We let her rest and keep her well hydrated. Rosalie knows the best ways to help her with that."

"What can I do?"

"Besides praying, you can dispose of the stool, rags and water. If it's cholera, we can't take a chance on passing it on to others."

"We can bury everything out back of the barn," Matthias offered.

"And make sure nothing comes into contact with anyone. Bury everything."

"Can I see her?"

"Rosalie said to send you in with some fresh water." Zion followed Pansy Joy to the pail and filled a basin which Zion carried to the bedroom. Rosalie looked up from her position over his sister where she bathed her heated brow with a damp cloth. Zion knelt beside her.

"How is she?"

"She's resting now, but I knew you'd want to see her."

"I do."

"I'm going to make a special tea of passion flower and blackberry root. It will help stop the flow and ease the pain from the swelling inside. That and keeping fluids in her are the best things we can do–that, and pray."

CHAPTER 12

The hours passed slowly. Pansy Joy followed Lucas and Marigold up to the loft for the night. Matthias sat with Zion several hours before retiring himself. With the house settled, Rosalie left the bedroom door open allowing Zion to see his sister from the front room.

Zion rose from the rocker and crossed the floor to the bedroom. Seated in a chair at the bedside, Rosalie hummed a soothing song. As she breathed out the melody, the words sang out from Zion's memory.

May God bestow on us His grace,
With blessings rich provide us,
And may the brightness of His face
To life eternal guide us
That we His saving health may know,
His gracious will and pleasure . . .

Rosalie looked up to see Zion watching her. A wave of awkward shyness washed over her, but she set aside her feelings to encourage the troubled young man.

"She's resting peacefully." Rosalie looked into Zion's tired face. "I think she'll be fine."

"How can you say that? If it's cholera . . ."

"Some of her symptoms are the same as cholera, but some are not. I wasn't certain at first, so we had to take precautions." Rosalie placed two fingers on Penny's wrist and counted the beats of her pulse. "Her pulse is normal and her skin hasn't dried out. She hasn't thrown up, either. Once she got past the initial impact on her system, she hasn't had any more nausea or cramping. I think it's more a case of flux."

"Flux? How would she get that?"

"Flux is a body's response to a bug in its digestion. It can come from something a person eats or drinks, contaminated with unclean water or animal waste; but who knows where Penny might have gotten it? There are a lot of animals around."

Relief flooded through Zion. Bloody flux could be serious, but did not pose anywhere near the threat of cholera. People contracting the dreaded disease had been known to die in as little as three hours or only last a few days.

"Why don't you let me get you a blanket? You can stretch out on the floor and get some rest. You have to leave soon for Maysville."

"Maysville. I forgot all about that." Zion studied Rosalie's face looking for assurance beyond her words. "You really don't think Penny's in danger?"

"She swallowed all the fluids I've given her. She's still passing more than I'd like, but that's normal. This should run its course in a few days, but I don't think you should move her yet. I can see to her."

"You're sure?" Zion liked the confidence he saw in Rosalie. The sweetness, too. Rosalie nodded. "I better get word to Balim, then. I . . ."

"Pa already took care of that, Mr. Coldwell. He sent Pansy Joy with word a few hours ago. Her beau lives at the farm between here and the lodge, and she's glad enough for any chance to walk by."

Zion studied Rosalie before he spoke again. "Thank you. Thank you for everything." Rosalie warmed under his gaze and attention. "I'll take that blanket, if you don't mind."

"Not at all." Rosalie, thankful for a chance to break the spell binding her to the chair, rose and walked to the foot of the bed. "I've got a crocheted blanket right here in my hope chest." Her own words hit her hard. How could she have been so foolish to say such a thing–offering a single man a blanket from her hope chest? She'd only thought to keep from disturbing her family by offering what she had available in her room, but the impropriety weighed heavy as she reached in the wooden chest and drew out the blanket.

Zion caught it all. He thought of Lark and her blatant invitations in such contrast to Rosalie's innocence and sense of shame. Zion smiled at the girl with the hang-dog look. She peeped up at him as she extended the blanket. "Thank you kindly," he said.

"Welcome," Rosalie whispered.

Zion was tempted to lift Rosalie's chin the same way he did Penny's when she needed a talking to, but he took the blanket and walked out of the room. His blue eyes met Rosalie's green almond ones when he turned to say goodnight. "I was wondering if you'd do me a favor, Miss Johnson."

"Why, if I can, Mr. Coldwell, I'd be happy to."

"Would you call me Zion?"

The flutter in Rosalie's middle returned. She successfully restrained herself from worrying her lower lip, but her untamed fingers found their way to a loose auburn curl and gave it a nervous twirl. She nodded her head slowly, the corners of her lips curving up ever so slightly. "If that would please you . . . Zion."

"That it would."

"Then, please, call me Rosalie."

Matthias woke early, before the rooster crowed. Rosalie, still seated in her chair, was leaned over at the torso, her head on the bed, and fast asleep next to Penny. Zion lay stretched out on the floor in front of the fireplace. Although Matthias normally left kitchen duties to the women, he decided to make some coffee. After all, he reasoned, he had a good night's sleep compared with the others in his cabin.

Rosalie stirred at the sound of her father filling the pot with water from the bucket. She realized she had fallen asleep, the ache in her back and neck proof to her poor position when she dozed off. She rose from the chair and walked into the kitchen, rubbing her back with balled fists. "Morning, Pa."

"Morning. How's the little one?"

"I think she's doing fine. I watched her for hours. Her symptoms lean more to flux than cholera. She should be on her feet soon."

The smell of coffee woke Zion. Rising from the floor, he pulled the blanket up with him and attempted to fold it.

"Rosalie, why don't you help Mr. Coldwell wrestle that blanket down?" The early morning conversation about the afghan replayed for both Rosalie and Zion as they grabbed the corners, met in the middle, grabbed the new corners, and then met in the middle again in a dance that ended with the blanket folded into a neat package. Rosalie took the bundle from Zion and placed it on the foot of her bed. She checked on Penny, who slept soundly.

In the kitchen Zion drank from the mug Matthias handed him. Strong coffee scalded his tongue, just the way he liked it. "I sure thank you for your hospitality, Mr. Johnson."

"'Tweren't nothing. Rosalie done the most." Zion watched Rosalie exit the bedroom.

"She's still sleeping," she said. Matthias handed her a mug of coffee which she accepted with gratitude. "Pa, I hope you don't mind, but I offered to keep Penny here until she gets her strength back."

"That would be fine, Daughter." Matthias turned to Zion. "Your sister's welcome as long as you need."

"Thank you, sir. Rosalie thinks it's safe for me to ride into Maysville this morning, so with your permission, I'll take my leave. I hope to be back by noon."

Matthias noted the familiar use of his daughter's first name, but kept his thoughts to himself. "Godspeed, Son."

"Thank you."

Matthias's salutation stirred a sense of well being in Zion. He turned to Rosalie. "And thank you, Rosalie. Is there anything I can bring you from town? Anything you might need?"

"God's provided everything we need right here in Briar Hollow."

"It seems that way." Zion tipped his hat and walked out the front door. In the predawn light, the trip back to the lodge passed quickly without stopping at fairy rings or having to pace himself to Penny's short stride. As he walked, Zion contemplated Rosalie's words, "God's provided everything we need right here in Briar Hollow." The sentence resonated in his spirit, and for the first time in several months, Zion wondered if perhaps God hadn't forgotten him. Maybe he had found everything he needed–right here in Briar Hollow.

The mules hitched and the wagon pulled out of the barn, Balim readied the team for Zion's return. When Pansy Joy arrived the evening before with the news of Penny's illness, Balim took the matter to King Jesus. He prayed and listened until his heart received an answer. Penny would be just fine. God was working things out for good, for sure and for certain.

Zion advanced on the lodge with purposeful strides, and then stopped in the lane when he saw Balim at the ready with the big wagon. "Mornin', Massa Zion."

"It is a good morning, Balim." Zion smiled at his friend and servant. "I wasn't sure what it would bring, but when I walked down the road I remembered that verse you're always spouting about the steadfast love of the Lord never ceasing. His mercies never come to an end but they are new every morning."

Balim's wide black face split into a huge smile. "That's right, Massa Zion. That's right."

"It looks like we're ready to go. Thank you, Balim. You're a good man." Balim extended a hand to Zion who used it to pull him into the wagon.

"Yes, suh. We're ready." Zion gave Balim a hearty slap on the back, and with a giddy-up, the team pulled out on the road. Balim handed Zion a cloth filled with ham and biscuit sandwiches. Between bites, Zion filled Balim in on Penny's condition and how the Johnsons opened their home to her.

"The blessing of the Lawd, Massa Zion. Sounds like the blessing of the Lawd to me."

"You could be right," Zion said. "I've been walking around like a bleeding man not even noticing the good things right in front of my nose."

Penny opened her eyes, still foggy and unfamiliar with her surroundings. "Are you a fairy?" she asked the figure beside her. Rosalie turned in surprise. Auburn hair cascaded over creamy shoulders, as she stood in a white chemise performing her morning toilet.

"It's me, Penny, Rosalie." Understanding dawned in Penny's tired eyes.

"I remember now. Zion and I were walking here and we stopped at a fairy ring. You look just like a fairy, if they were real."

"I was just washing up. We had a long night, remember?" Rosalie took a clean dress from a peg on the wall and slipped it over her head.

"It all seems a bit foggy, and my insides are aching, but I don't think I'll ever forget last night." Penny watched Rosalie brush through her thick auburn hair and then pin it up in a loose knot.

"I don't think I'll forget last night either. Are you up for some breakfast?"

"I'll try, but I'm mostly thirsty." Rosalie brought a cup of water laced with goldenseal tincture to Penny. She knew the herb relieved diarrhea, and if Penny was bleeding intestinally, it should help that too. Rosalie slipped her arm beneath Penny's back and held her while she drank. Exhausted, Penny melted back into the feather bed.

"I'll bring you something to eat in here. You just rest for now."

"Can I see Zion?"

"Your brother was here all night. Once we realized you were out of danger, he decided he better go to Maysville for the Coventrys. Do you remember Mr. Perkins coming last night?"

"I do, but not very well. That's when I started feeling so poorly. Odd how quickly it came on."

Part of Penny felt deserted by Zion, left in a cabin with people she hardly knew; while on the other hand, she felt reassured that her condition was not critical. Zion would not have gone to Maysville if something were seriously wrong. Besides, Penny liked being with Rosalie–all the Johnsons, really–such a warm family in such a beautiful place.

"You rest, and I'll see to your breakfast." Rosalie smiled at the weary girl and then left for the kitchen. She returned a few minutes later with a garlic-seasoned vegetable broth, but Penny had fallen fast asleep.

CHAPTER 13

Katie walked the familiar path from the Eldridge farm to Briar Hollow. She had been concerned when none of the Johnson family showed up for prayer Tuesday night. When Pansy Joy came by on her way back from the lodge later in the evening, she knew she had to see Rosalie as soon as possible.

Swinging a basket of doughnuts in one hand, Katie walked the short distance to her friend's house. In the morning sunshine, orange tiger lilies stood at attention as she passed, and a giggle escaped when she thought how they reminded her of the gangly, red-haired Matheny twins.

Entering the lane to the Johnson place, Katie reached in her basket and pulled out a note on a tiny piece of paper. She held it in her hand contemplating its contents until she reached the fairy ring. With thoughtful determination, she lifted the jar from the center, unscrewed the lid and tucked her wish inside with two others. She bowed her head in prayer.

"Lord, you know I don't really believe in fairies, but this just seemed like a fitting place to write down my prayer. You said to have faith, to believe as if the things we haven't seen yet have already come to pass, and to give thanks as if they already have. So I put my prayer of thanksgiving in this little jar, believing in Jesus' name that You've already got things working to bring it to pass. Amen."

Katie replaced the lid and set the jar back on the circle. Peace washed over her spirit as she stood in the delightful spot, flowers about her feet and a lush arbor of teeming branches bristling overhead. Shafts of light, like royal swords, pierced the canopy in bright sheaths reaching from heaven to earth, reminding Katie of Jacob's ladder and the angels traveling back and forth between the natural and the supernatural. Cheered, the girl picked up her basket and continued to the cabin.

"Good morning, Katie." Pansy Joy stopped sweeping the porch and waved at her soon to be sister-in-law. She tucked her chin on the handle of the straw broom and watched Katie cross the yard.

Katie always looked fresh as a daisy, and pretty as a picture, even in a simple work dress. She wore a periwinkle floral calico with a slightly fitted bodice that met at a front closure. Gathered on a waistband, the matching skirt swung over several rustling petticoats. Glistening raven hair was tucked neatly beneath a straw poke bonnet trimmed with a sprig of flowers and organdy ruching at the base of the crown. Jauntily tied to one side of her chin, the wide blue ribbon bow complemented the deep blue of her eyes.

"Good morning, Pansy Joy." Katie lifted her skirts and walked up on the front porch. "How's the little girl today?"

"Not strong, but better. Rosalie tended her during the night. She said her symptoms leaned more to flux than cholera."

"Neither one's a day at the fair."

"You're right about that. The poor little thing's plumb wore out. Rosalie, too."

Katie reached into her basket and flipped the napkin open. She lifted it so Pansy Joy could get a whiff of the sugary, fresh fried doughnuts. "I brought you something. I thought these might perk folks up around here."

"That'll perk me up right quick." Pansy Joy leaned the broom against the side of the house and opened the front door. "I bet we've got some coffee to go with those. Come on in."

Inside the cabin, Marigold sat at the table sewing netting on a wide-brimmed straw hat. "Look at you, Marigold," said Katie. "I never thought I'd see the day you were sewing pretties on your bonnets."

"That will be the day." Pansy Joy giggled.

Marigold rolled her eyes and shook her head. "Now don't be starting any such scuttlebutt, Katie Eldridge." She lifted the hat she was working on so Katie could see it better. "This here's my beekeeping hat. It needed mending."

"I see," Katie said with a laugh. "Don't worry. I won't start any rumors about town."

"Good." Marigold winked and turned her attention back to her sewing.

"You collecting honey this morning?" Pansy Joy asked.

"No. I found a swarm in one of the trees yesterday. If I can catch the queen in a frame, the rest will follow her scent into a hive."

"You amaze me," said Katie. "You sure know lots about beekeeping. I just know I like the honey."

"Me, too," Pansy Joy chimed in. "Marigold's got a knack with all sorts of critters–even the little flying ones."

The bedroom door opened and Rosalie stepped out. Exhaustion marked her delicate features, but she wore a peaceful countenance. "Hello, Katie. So nice to see you this morning."

Katie crossed the floor and gave her friend a quick hug. "I came to check on you and the little girl. Pansy Joy stopped by last night and filled us in. How's she doing?"

"Penny's improving, thanks be to God." Rosalie brushed a wayward strand of hair behind her ear and suppressed a yawn.

"Pansy Joy said you thought it was the flux?"

"I do. I'm more certain even now. Without going into detail, I'll just say that the stuff she's passing and the way her body is responding line right up with flux, which is much better than cholera. She could be gone by now if it had been cholera."

"And your family could have been in danger, too."

"We have a lot to be thankful for this morning," said Pansy Joy.

"Yes, we do." Rosalie turned to the stove. "A cup of hot coffee sounds good. Will you join me?"

"We will," Pansy Joy said with enthusiasm. She grabbed the basket of doughnuts off the table and showed them to Rosalie. "Look what Katie brought."

Rosalie peeked under the napkin. "Mmm. Smells heavenly."

"Too bad Pa and Lucas are out in the orchard," said Marigold, an impudent smile on her freckled face.

"Now, now, young lady." Rosalie waggled a finger at her sister. "We'll save some for them to have with their dinner. They'll be back in a couple of hours."

"Oh, all right." Marigold bit the thread to break it free from her hat. "All done," she said, triumphant at her domestic achievement. "Let's eat."

Pansy Joy pulled mugs down from the kitchen shelves while Marigold cleared her sewing away. Rosalie brought the coffee and napkins, and Katie uncovered the bounty in the basket.

"Is your pa picking plums already? I didn't think they would be ready this early," said Katie.

"A few early ones have come in." Rosalie poured coffee in Katie's mug. "Pa and Lucas are out thinning the crop. Too many plums growing on one branch, and the whole harvest will be puny."

"That's what we do with our seedlings," said Katie. "If too many come up in one spot, we have to thin them, or they'll choke each other out."

"I feel like that when we get too many people in the house."
Marigold laughed at her own humor. "I'd rather be outside any day."

"It's a good day to be out." Katie wiped a crumb from the corner of her mouth. "It will be dripping hot soon, but it's been a beautiful morning."

"I hope Zion finishes loading his wagon before the heat of the day sets in," said Rosalie.

"Zion?"

"Mr. Coldwell." Rosalie blushed and stumbled a bit on her words. "He . . . he's Penny's brother."

"I see." The edges of Katie's lips turned upwards as she watched her friend squirm. She held her tongue to see what else Rosalie would offer on her own, but Marigold interjected first.

"Mr. Coldwell looks like he could load up a wagon pretty quick. He's thick-shouldered."

Rosalie's blush deepened. Pansy Joy and Katie cut quick glances at each other and smiled in cahoots. Both young women had witnessed Rosalie's quiet suffering when Clayton left with his family; and they both watched her tireless, sacrificial care for her family and others.

"I was thinking to make some peppermint and chamomile tea for Penny." Rosalie stood and began pulling together the ingredients. "She kept down the slippery elm bark I gave her this morning in a bit of applesauce."

"Ma says slippery elm is good for healing innards," said Katie.

"It is. I'll give her some more after lunch and before bed tonight."

"So you're planning to keep her here then?"

"Z . . . Mr. Coldwell and I discussed it before he left." Rosalie twirled a strand of auburn hair between two fingers. "At first we thought she might be contagious, so we couldn't take her back to the lodge for sure. Before morning broke, we knew she was better, but Mr. Coldwell had to drive over to Maysville to pick up cargo he was hauling for a family he's transporting west. I told him it would be best not to move Penny while she was so weak, and I could tend to her here."

"When do you expect him back?"

"After noon." Rosalie looked at the mantle clock. "A couple of hours yet."

"He'll need to drop the Coventrys at the lodge first," said Pansy Joy.

"Too bad," said Marigold. "He'll pass right by but won't be able to stop. Maybe I'll keep a look out for him so I can fill him in on how Penny's doing."

"That would be nice, Mari." Pansy Joy stood and collected the empty mugs. "Guess I'll wash these up before I head out. I mean to get me some of the blackberries, ahead of the birds this year."

"What are you planning to make?" Katie asked.

"Her famous blackberry cobbler," Marigold answered for her sister.

"I like just about anything you make with blackberries, Pansy Joy, but your cobbler is a work of cooking art."

"She's practicing up her recipe for the fair," Marigold bragged. "What competitions are you planning to enter this year?"

"I thought about entering a pecan pie, and maybe some peach preserves." Katie picked her basket up from the table. "The double wedding ring quilt is near finished. It just lacks the binding, and I can easily finish it before the judging. But I wanted to talk to you about it first, Pansy Joy. Would you mind it being on display?"

Pansy Joy lit up. "Why not at all, Katie. I would love to see it at the fair. I'd be right proud."

"I just thought that since it was for your wedding, you might feel strange about it. I wasn't sure how I felt myself. It might seem like giving you a used wedding gift."

"I don't feel that way. Since Garth and I have to wait, it will make the wedding seem like it's really going to happen, you know?"

"You never know," said Marigold. "It might win a ribbon. Wouldn't that be nice to have an award-winning quilt for your wedding day?"

"Award or no, it's a beautiful quilt," said Rosalie.

"Have you done any quilting yourself, Rosalie?" Katie asked.

"Not recently. I've been busy stitching up sachets and covers for my lotions . . . after mending and keeping Lucas and Marigold in clothes. They're growing like weeds."

"It's true," said Marigold. She stood up and smoothed her skirt. "My dress is getting shamefully short and there's no more hem to let out. If I don't get a new one soon, my knobby knees will be airing."

"We can't have that, for sure," Katie said. "I have some muslin left from the quilt backing. Since your dress still fits everywhere else, we could add a solid border on the bottom, even make a matching collar and cuffs."

"That would be wonderful," said Rosalie. "I hate to admit I've gotten behind on my sewing. I'm thinking after the fair I will have time to catch up."

"I'm sure you will, but in the meantime, we can make this dress serviceable awhile longer with just a little work."

"Thank you, Katie. You're a good friend."

"And so are you, Rosalie." Katie headed to the door. "I best get home now. I'll be praying for Penny."

"Thank you."

"Tell Garth I said hey," Pansy Joy called after Katie as she descended the porch stairs.

"I will. Bye now." Katie waved over her shoulder. She passed the wildflower garden and entered the woods. When she came to the place where the fairy ring hid between the trees, she thought about her prayer resting in the jar and her friend Rosalie. "Seems like You might already be working on that prayer request, Lord. Thanks, again."

CHAPTER 14

Balim and Zion arrived at the Maysville courthouse ahead of the rest of their party. The brief wait ended when promptly at 7:00 a.m., Perkins arrived on foot accompanied by Thaddeus Coventry and J.T. Nester.

Mr. Coventry appeared every bit the affluent Easterner in a double-breasted dark frock coat with notched collar over medium blue pin-striped pants. He wore a wool felt topper with a matching ribbon around the base of the six-inch crown. Beneath the tailored jacket, over a crisp white shirt, he wore a blue and taupe paisley vest and a taupe silk cravat tacked in place with a diamond pin.

"Good morning." Thaddeus looked up at Zion and Balim in the massive wagon. "I'm Thaddeus Coventry. You've met Mr. Perkins, and this is Mr. J.T. Nester."

"How do you do?" Zion tipped his hat and jumped out of the wagon to shake hands with the peculiar looking trio.

"We're fine, but we need to get the freight unloaded from *The Messenger*," Nester said. "Captain Perry about had a conniption last night. He's headed to New Orleans and needs everything cleared off the ship."

"Balim and I will see right to it then," said Zion. "Where's she's docked?"

"Mr. Coventry, why don't you slide up on the buckboard?" suggested Nester. "Me and Bug will ride in the back."

"That will work just fine," Thaddeus responded.

Zion wondered how J.T. Nester had become part of the Coventry party and just why he was making the arrangements. Something niggled in the back of Zion's mind, but he couldn't quite place his finger on it. The men climbed on board and Mr. Coventry directed Balim to the riverfront.

Arriving at Limestone Landing, the group descended onto the dock. "Wait here." J.T. boarded *The Messenger* on one of its large front planks and located a deck hand. Zion stood too far away to hear the conversation, but he saw J.T. pass something to the hand, and then turn and walk back to the wagon.

"We're all set to board, Mr. Coventry. Why don't you wait here with the wagon while we load up?"

"I'd like to make sure nothing is left behind."

"I'll let you know when we reach the end of it. You can come on board then and check."

Thaddeus nodded, acquiescing to J.T.'s plans, and watched the four men plod down the dock to the double-decked steamboat. *The Messenger*, a sternwheel, wooden hull packet, laid out 230 feet long by 30 feet across with a 26 foot paddlewheel. Five boilers with 16 inch flues powered the great wheel. From the dock to the front of the boat, two planks provided access to a deck encased with a metal railing. Between the first and second decks, a large crane was mounted.

Nester knew the way, and navigated the boat easily, leading the men to the cargo hold. Working in two-man teams, they carried large crates and carefully wrapped furniture one-by-one out of the belly of the boat to the deck where a man operating the crane assisted in removing them from the ship. Once all the items were safely dropped on the dock, the men made their first trip to the wagon, muscles bulging under the weight of their burdens. Zion was thankful he partnered with Balim instead of the spindly Bug Perkins.

"We cleared out the hold," J.T. said. "You can check if you want, but the room's empty."

"I think I will, at that," Mr. Coventry said, and then ambled down the dock to the boat. He disappeared inside, and the men continued to march the cargo from the dock to the wagon.

Zion wiped the sweat from his brow after carrying the last piece of furniture from the ship. "Balim will organize the load inside the wagon."

"That's not a job for a darkie," said Perkins. "Takes some brains to order all this up so it will fit in just so."

Zion, jaw set, considered his options. He nodded to Balim and then addressed Bug in a deferential manner. "I believe you're right, Mr. Perkins." Zion looked at Balim. "Why don't you got sit under that tree over there while Mr. Perkins handles the organizing. A man of his intelligence surely doesn't need help from a simple black man."

"Yes, suh, Massa Zion. I'll do just as you say. Yes, suh." Balim turned his back on the men, a grin splitting his wide face as he ambled to the tree Zion indicated. He broke out in song on the way and sat down beneath a juniper tree.

Standing on the banks of the Jordan River,
waiting for the water to rise . . .

A black man crossed the grass and stopped beside Balim. "That be the Jordan to some," he said, indicating the Ohio River stretched out before them.

"That so?"

"Yes, suh. And Ohio's the Promised Land." The man leaned against the tree. "Name's Arnold—Arnold Gragston."

"I'm Balim Johnson."

"You ain't from 'round here, are ya?

"No. Me and Massa Zion hail from Virginny."

"That yo massa over yon?"

"The one in the brown shirt."

"How'd you end up over here while them white folks are toting the crates?"

"The blessing of the good Lawd, I'd say." Balim smiled at Arnold.

"Blessings come in all sorts of packages, I suppose."

"Sure 'nough."

"If you got a hankering to be free, I have ways to help folks out."

Arnold had Balim's full attention. "You part of the Underground Railroad, man?"

"I know the stations."

"I heard Maysville was one of 'em." Balim examined the nondescript man with the hooded eyes. He was calm. He looked like he was just shooting the breeze–while he offered Balim information that could cost his life.

"You were right on that. They's sev'ral here." Arnold looked over the water's edge and tipped his head in the direction of a big white house. "You see that three-story house over yon?"

Balim spied the building perched on a high point nestled in the trees a few hundred yards from the riverbank. "Yes. I see it."

"That's the Bierbower place. Mr. Jonathan Bierbower, him and his missus, they conductors, fo sure. Underneath the floorboards of the sleeping rooms on the bottom floor they's a room for hiding folks on the rail."

"You don't say." Balim stroked his bristly chin and tried to imagine the white folks that would take such risks to free black men and women, and the lengths some men went to enslave them.

"I belong to Mr. Jack Tabb down the way. He's a pretty good man, not a Demmecrat, like the rest of them in the county."

"Why don't you leave, if you can?"

"Well, Balim, it's like this. I never thought I could really do it until last year. Mr. Tabb, he let ole Arnold go a courtin' at a neighboring plantation. While I was there, I met a girl, and she was such a perty little thing–brown skinned and kinda rosy, looking all scared. An old woman asked me to row her to the other side.

"I didn't want to do it, mind ya. Didn't think I could. I went home, and darned if I didn't find myself fetching that girl in the night and rowing her over."

"How did you know where to go?"

"Mr. Rankins, he has a lighthouse on the other side in Ripley. I rowed hard against the current, keeping as quiet as a mouse and aiming for the light shining across the river. When we reached the landing, two men reached down and grabbed the girl. I started trembling all over and praying. Then one of the men took my arm and I just felt down inside of me that the Lawd had got ready for me. 'You hungry, Boy?' is what he asked me, and if he hadn't been a-holding me I think I woulda fell backwards in the river."

"I would have been a praying, too, brother." Balim smiled at Arnold. "What made you come back?"

"I've thought about that. Not quite sure, but over the past year I've rowed a good many others to freedom. Guess I figure I can help others that don't have it as good as I do."

Balim nodded in appreciation. "What about you, Balim?"

"Got me a wife in Canada. Some day soon I'll be seein' her again."

"Are you plannin' to ride on the rail?"

"No, suh. The good Lawd's got other plans for ole Balim. Yes He does. I have a job to do first, and then I'll be seein' my Minnie."

"What kind of job you talking about?"

"I've got to see to Massa Zion first–and Missy Penny."

"Who's Missy Penny?"

"She's Massa Zion's sister. We done left her sick outside Washington."

"When she gets on her feet, and you're ready to go, check out the Paxton Inn. The folks there will get you to the next station on the line."

"That's not the way of it, Brother Arnold. Massa and Missy, they lost their ma and pa. They's on their own, and I'm traveling west with them on a job. I know King Jesus has got me on this special mission, and I aim to see it through."

"Guess I can understand that."

"I guess you can, Brother Arnold."

"What happens after that? You plannin' to escape then?"

"Massa Zion–he's a good man. He wants to write me papers and send me on to Canada a free man with something jingling in my pocket to help me get settled."

"Pleased I am to hear it, Balim. Yes, pleased indeed." Arnold stuffed his hands in the pocket of his worn pants. "I best get moving on. Massa Tabb, he gives me freedom to run, but I cain't be gone too long."

"Right proud to know you."

"You, too."

Balim wanted to shake the man's hand, but didn't want to risk drawing anyone's attention. "Godspeed," he called softly as Arnold Gragston strode down the street.

"Balim!" Zion called from the wagon.

"Comin', Massa Zion." Balim pulled himself to his feet and walked over to the wagon.

"I think Mr. Perkins got everything worked out here." Zion winked at Balim. From beneath the canvas cover, Bug poked out his sweaty head.

"Fine work, Massa Zion. Fine indeed."

"Mr. Coventry went to rent a carriage for his family," said Zion. "Then he was going to the inn to pick up his wife and children. They'll meet us here any minute."

J.T. circled around the wagon. Something about the man puzzled Zion. His dress was that of a gentleman, but his face and demeanor did not seem to match. The moustached man had smallish eyes with bushy black eyebrows and a full head of black hair over which he wore a straw top hat with a black band. Tan and white checkerboard pants contrasted the jacket J.T. pulled over his shoulders as he approached, a plaid made of navy and medium blue worn over a white shirt and vest and black neck tie.

"Bug, let's head over to the livery for a couple of mounts," J.T. said. "The livery driver can return them when he brings the carriage back." Bug and J.T. started on the road to town. "We'll be back in a jiffy."

CHAPTER 15

Twenty minutes later, the group was ready to leave.

"We'll take the lead." J.T. motioned to Bug, and the two spurred their rented horses onto the road. The Coventrys followed in their rented carriage, and Balim and Zion pulled out behind them. The noonday sun shone directly overhead as the caravan headed out of Maysville.

"We're making good time. I can't wait to check on Penny," said Zion. The wagon rolled out of town and entered a covered bridge, one of many that dotted the rough Kentucky terrain. Consisting of an 81-foot span of a double post and brace design, the bridge provided passage over one of the state's numerous streams. It had been covered to protect its complex system of rigid trusses.

"Yes, suh," Balim said. "I know it's only been a few hours, but it sho seems longer."

Zion's head was full of thoughts. He turned to his faithful friend and asked, "What do you make of these folks, Balim?"

"Well, Massa Zion, you want ole Balim to speak plain?"

"I've never known you to do otherwise." Zion looked in Balim's laughing eyes and enjoyed the light moment.

"You got me there, Massa Zion." Balim thought for a minute. "Well, suh, the Coventrys seem like nice enough folks. I don't think they's much suited to life on the trail, but hopefully once we get to a settlement, they'll find their way."

"They are right proper folks, aren't they?"

"Yes, suh. Right proper." Balim held the reins securely yet comfortably in his big hands as the wheels of the great wagon rolled south down the road to Washington.

"I think we need to make sure Henry stays towards the front," said Zion. "The dust won't help his asthma any."

"His sister Rachel seems spry 'nough."

"She does, her ma, too–just accustomed to finery and comforts. I hope they know what they've signed up for," Zion added. "What about Perkins and Nester?"

"Well, Massa Zion, them two's another story altogether."

"What do you mean?"

"I mean that Mr. Nester, he looks to be playing to the gallery, puttin' on some kind of show. And that Bug fellow, he's on the shoot, for sure."

"I don't know what they're up to, Balim, but I think you nailed it. They just don't seem to be on the up-and-up."

Balim clicked the reins. The hodge-podge group traveled quietly beneath clear blue skies accompanied by the rhythmic sounds of clicking horse hooves and rolling wheels.

"Nester!" Zion called out to the lead horseman. J.T. turned his horse and trotted back to the wagon.

"Yeah, Coldwell?" The finesse in J.T.'s tone when he addressed the Coventrys was notably absent when he spoke to Zion.

"You seem to have things well under control here," said Zion.

J.T. sat high in the saddle and adjusted his hat, waiting for Zion to continue.

"I left my sister sick at a cabin just before the lodge. When we get there, I'm going to stop off and check on her. Your man Perkins knows the way in, and the Erlangers are expecting you."

"I can handle that. And I forgot to mention, me and Bug are planning to ride west with you to Virginia City," J.T. nodded and jabbed his horse with his boots spurring him back to the front of the line.

Zion looked after J.T. in shock, speechless.

"That there's a curly wolf if ever I seen one," Balim said.

As they reached the turn in to Briar Hollow, Balim slowed the wagon and Zion jumped down.

"Hey, Mr. Coldwell," Marigold greeted Zion as he turned in the lane.

"Hey, Marigold."

"Wait 'til you see Penny. She's doing so much better." Marigold and Zion walked side by side through the wooded lane. "And Rosalie and Pansy are just putting dinner on the table. You'll stay, won't you?"

"If you're inviting me, I could use a good meal. I carried enough furniture to outfit a small town in the west."

"Who would bring a bunch of furniture on a wagon when they could make new ones once they got there?"

"Some folks don't know how to make furniture, and then some pieces of furniture are special . . . family heirlooms."

"I see." Marigold and Zion exited the lane and walked out into the open hollow next to the wildflower garden. Coming from the lean-to, washed up and ready to eat, Matthias and Lucas met them in front of the cabin. Matthias held out his hand.

"Good to see you, Son. How did your trip to Maysville fare?"

Zion pondered the events that had played out over the morning but decided not to trouble Matthias with his concerns about Nester and Perkins. "We collected the Coventrys and their belongings off the steamboat and Balim's taking them on in to Comfort Lodge." Zion looked at the cabin door. "I just couldn't drive by without checking on Penny."

"Well, let's go on inside then. I'm sure the girls have a fine meal laid out." Matthias opened the door. "After you." He nodded to Zion, and then to Marigold and Lucas.

"Rosalie, we need to set another plate," Marigold called as she entered the cozy room. The girls inside watched the line of people slip in the cabin door.

"I'll see to it," Pansy Joy said. "I'm sure Mr. Coldwell is anxious to see Penny. Why don't you take him in, Rosalie?"

"Thank you so much." Zion joined Rosalie in the middle of the room and they walked together to the bedroom door. Rosalie rapped softly on the door and then peeked inside.

"Penny," she called softly, "your brother is here."

Zion watched Rosalie go to his sister's side, brush her golden hair back from her forehead and hold her delicate wrist for a pulse.

"Zion." Penny greeted her brother with a weak but sincere smile. "It's so good to see you."

"You, too, Buttercup. Looks like you were in good hands here with Miss Rosalie." Zion offered Rosalie a gratitudinal grin, his cornflower blue eyes crinkling in a way that made Rosalie a bit weak herself.

"Oh, yes. It's awful to be sick, but awfully nice to be here." Penny gave Rosalie's hand a squeeze.

Rosalie took a small cup from the bedside table. "I want you to eat this, Penny. It might taste a bit funny, but it's good for you— slippery elm bark in a bit of applesauce."

"Can I sit up?" Penny asked.

"Do you think you can?"

"If Zion will help me. I'd rather eat sitting up than lying in the bed."

Rosalie looked to Zion who immediately went to the bedside. He seated himself on the bed and slipped a sturdy arm behind Penny's pillow, supporting her upper body on his. Dipping a spoon in the applesauce, Rosalie brought it carefully to Penny's lips. Zion watched her expressive eyes as she fed his sister. Although he was still concerned about Penny's health, he couldn't help but notice how adorable Rosalie looked when her lips formed an "o" and then closed and chewed, mirroring Penny's motions.

Rosalie, keenly aware of Zion's gaze, resisted the urge to look past Penny's sweet face into his. Instead, she concentrated on the task at hand.

"That's enough," Penny said after a few bites.

"Enough sitting, or enough eating?" Rosalie asked.

"Both, I think."

Zion laid Penny back down on the feather mattress and tucked the blanket around her. He reached for her small hand, and on the other side of the bed, Penny reached for Rosalie's. The feelings flooding Rosalie were so sweet they caused an ache deep in her chest. She dared not lift her eyes to Zion's face, lest he read the emotions playing across hers.

Zion leaned over Penny and kissed her forehead. He released her hand and caressed her cheek with the back of his. "You rest now. I'll check on you in a bit."

Penny used her free hand to cover a yawn, and her heavy eyelids closed without a word. Reluctant to let go of the little girl's hand, Rosalie watched Zion leave the room, and then knelt beside the bed. "Thank you, dear Jesus, for bringing Penny here, and for keeping her through this illness. I pray You continue to heal her everywhere she hurts, inside and out." She wanted to pray for Zion, but the words didn't know how to come together.

"And Lord," she said after a slight pause, "I ask you to bless Zion as he bears the weight of her care and all the folks You are bringing together for this trip west. In Jesus' name. Amen."

Rosalie's hand slipped easily from Penny's relaxed hold. The sound of her even breathing reassured her that the worst was over and Penny was now resting peacefully. She left the room and joined her family and Zion at the table where they waited to say grace together. Taking the only empty seat next to Zion, she closed her eyes and lowered her head. According to the Johnson custom, everyone at the table joined hands for prayer, and Rosalie placed her hand in Zion's open palm.

Zion wondered if Rosalie felt the same current he felt pulsing from their joined hands. Excitement, tension and anticipation coursed through him, and he marveled at the difference he felt when only two minutes before he had held Penny's hand. Holding Rosalie's was completely different.

Confusion, delight and dismay mixed together in Rosalie's response to Zion. How could she feel this way at one simple touch from a man she barely knew? Why did it feel so amazing, and where could it possibly lead? Zion and Penny would be leaving soon, traveling west just like Clayton, while she stayed on at Briar Hollow tending her family and her mother's flowers.

Matthias offered thanks. Platters and bowls began their first trip around the table losing their loads of glazed pork chops, mashed potatoes and gravy, green beans slow cooked with strips of bacon, chunky applesauce and thick slices of crusty bread served with creamy butter. Zion's attention turned to the food, but the sweetness of Rosalie's hand in his lingered.

"I was wondering, Mr. Johnson, who you might recommend to see regarding the purchase of a wagon and horses."

Matthias scooped a forkful of applesauce before he answered. "I'd see Cooper for the horses."

"I met him in town. Seemed a good sort," said Zion.

"You can trust Jim Cooper. He's sound on the goose," Matthias said. "As for the wagon, you could check at Matheny's."

Zion recalled his first experience at the mercantile. The thought of doing business with Mrs. Matheny or her daughter Lark, a raptor in petticoats, did not appeal to him. Matthias detected Zion's hesitation and gave his question some more thought.

"Garth Eldridge just made a fine wagon he might be willing to sell."

Pansy Joy's eyes widened, her fork dripping with mashed potatoes and gravy stayed in mid-air. Pa was talking about her wagon, the wagon Garth made for them. She could not fathom why he would suggest selling it to Zion Coldwell. Fear loomed in her heart that Pa had changed his mind about the wedding and she would never be Mrs. Pansy Joy Eldridge.

"Don't get your dander up, Pansy Joy. Garth selling that wagon could be a blessing in disguise," said Matthias.

"A blessing?" Pansy Joy said. "How can that be?"

Matthias swigged a mouthful of cool cider before he gave his even-toned reply. "Garth has plenty of time before the wedding to make another wagon, and he could turn a nice profit on the one he already finished. You could use the money to buy some things you will need for housekeeping, like a cast-iron cook stove and some glass windows."

Relief flooded Pansy Joy. Pa had not changed his mind, and perhaps he was right. Having her own cook stove complete with the attached reservoir for heating water would make keeping house much more pleasant. Her normal cheerful countenance returned.

"You're right, Pa. That could be a blessing for both of us." The fork resumed its path from plate to mouth and delivered the mound of potatoes to their destination. Pansy Joy thought and chewed. "I could introduce you to Garth if you like, Mr. Coldwell. You'll pass the Eldridge farm on the way to the lodge."

"Thank you," said Zion. "I'll take you up on that, Miss Johnson. And thank you all for this fine meal. A fellow could get used to eating like this every day."

"Wait until you taste Pansy Joy's blackberry cobbler," said Marigold.

"Yeah," Lucas added. "With tipped cream."

"That's whipped cream, Lukey," Marigold said. "And I like it, too."

"Marigold, why don't you help me clear the table," said Rosalie. "I'll make some coffee and Pansy Joy can get the dessert."

After everyone was served, Zion took a bite of the cobbler, a delicious blend of buttery pastry and tangy fruit topped with rich, sweetened cream. "Perfection, Miss Johnson. I've never had better."

"She's a shoe-in for the blue ribbon at the fair," Marigold pronounced.

"We'll see," said Pansy Joy. "If the blackberries hold out, I'll give it a try."

Zion pushed back from the table. "As much as I've enjoyed being with you folks and the good food, I best head back to the lodge. If you don't mind, I'll just say goodbye to Penny, and then I'll be on my way."

Zion checked on his sister who still slept peacefully. Rosalie stood behind him as he peeked in the door. "I'll come back later this evening to check on her." He squelched the desire to hold her hand again or brush an auburn tendril off her cheek. "Thank you for everything, Rosalie."

CHAPTER 16

"So tell me about the fair," Zion said to Pansy Joy as they walked to the Eldridge farm. "I keep hearing folks talk about it. It must be big in these parts."

"Oh, it is. The competition's fierce." Pansy Joy grinned up at Zion. "Mrs. Matheny thinks her angel food cake tops every cook in Mason County."

Zion's experience with Mrs. Matheny concurred with Pansy Joy's appraisal. "Will Rosalie enter the baked goods contest, too?"

Pansy Joy smiled. She knew deep in her knower that Zion was interested in Rosalie, his interest made even more apparent by his question. "Rosalie said she won't enter the dessert competition, but she does make a fine rose-petal custard with caramel sauce."

"Why doesn't she enter it?"

"She said she doesn't want to compete with my cobbler. She's just considerate like that, not wanting to compete with family."

That seemed just like Rosalie to Zion. "The custard sounds delicious. Maybe I'll get to try it sometime."

"Maybe so." Zion and Pansy Joy continued down the road a ways in silence.

"What else?" Zion asked. Pansy Joy gave him a questioning gaze. "I mean what else do you and your sister enter in the fair?"

"Men folk mostly enter the livestock and agricultural events, and ladies the cooking, canning and sewing ones. Rosalie mentioned something about honeysuckle syrup. Her handiwork beats mine to pieces, but I'm not sure if she has anything to enter."

"Why not?"

Pansy Joy paused. She weighed sharing a confidence with Zion. Recalling the look on his face at the dinner table spurred her on. "Rosalie spends her time making things for others and things for sale to earn money for our needs. She has all the pieces collected and cut for a quilt, but she hasn't touched it since Mama died."

Zion wondered at Pansy Joy's revelation. Rosalie appeared to be well healed from the loss of her mother, but something restrained her from making the quilt. "What would keep her from quilting if she's got time for other handiwork?"

"Mama began collecting the pieces for this particular quilt when Rosalie was a baby. She picked all the colors and cut the pieces to make a Rose of Sharon counterpane for her firstborn's special day." Pansy Joy shrugged her shoulders and shook her blond head. "I guess Rosalie's not had the heart to work on it, especially after Clayton left."

Zion's ears pricked at the mention of another man's name. Had Rosalie been wounded, or was she still pining for this Clayton? A whirlwind of thoughts spun in his head as they turned down the lane to the Eldridge farm.

Katie was busy picking pole beans from the kitchen garden close by the farm house. She saw Zion and Pansy Joy coming down the lane and rose to meet them, basket in hand.

"Hi, Katie," said Pansy Joy. "It seems you're always carrying a basket of some sort or another."

Katie smiled. It seemed to her Pansy Joy was forever in good humor, cheering the folks she met along the way. "Hi, there. I was just picking beans."

"Bet they aren't as good as those doughnuts you brought by earlier today."

"I'd pick doughnuts over pole beans any day." Zion smiled at the girls and the thought of growing rows of donuts.

"It would be nice if doughnuts grew in the garden. I wouldn't mind picking them myself." Pansy Joy giggled and turned to her neighbor. "Katie, I'd like you to meet Mr. Zion Coldwell. This is Katie Eldridge."

"Pleased to meet you." Zion tipped his hat at Katie.

"You, too."

"We're here on business," said Pansy Joy. "Is Garth around?"

Confusion filled Katie's blue eyes, chased by humor. "Pansy Joy Johnson, since when have you wanted to see my brother on business?"

Pansy Joy thrust her hands on her hips and threw a good-natured glare at Katie. Her head waggled back and forth as she spoke. "Well, Miss Katie Sue Eldridge, since when did you get to know everything about everybody else's business?"

Zion watched the playful exchange, enjoying the mischievous banter between the girls. "Now Miss Eldridge, I assure you that Miss Johnson is correct and Simon pure in her intentions. She agreed to escort me on a matter of business with your brother."

"Is that right?"

"Right as a trivet." Zion grinned. Katie raised her eyebrows in doubt while Pansy Joy preened in victory.

"Garth's in the barn readying up the thrasher," said Katie.

"I can take Mr. Coldwell over," said Pansy Joy.

"More of that dutiful business you're on?" Katie asked.

"Yes, ma'am." Pansy Joy pranced past Katie and led Zion to the big outbuilding. On the backside of the Eldridge's traditional barn, a two-story addition housed a portable double-blast thresher. Garth moved about inside greasing the movable parts on the wooden machine.

"Hi, Garth." Pansy Joy greeted her fiancé with a winsome smile. Garth, delighted by the unexpected visit, set the oil can on a workbench and pulled a bandana out of his pocket. Wiping his hands, he crossed the floor to welcome his guests.

"This is a nice surprise."

"I'd like you to meet Mr. Zion Coldwell." Zion reached out his hand and gave Garth a firm shake. "This is Garth Eldridge."

"Fine piece of machinery you've got there." Zion looked over the threshing machine. "You'll be putting that to good use here in a few weeks. The crops look to be doing well."

"So far, it's been a good growing season." Garth rubbed a hand affectionately across the polished wood. "I'm counting on a good harvest so I can belt up to a steam engine come next year."

"I'd like to see one of those in action," said Zion. "There's no telling how many bushels an hour they can handle."

"Plenty more than my horses, that's for sure," said Garth. "What brings you out, Mr. Coldwell?"

"Matthias Johnson said you had a wagon you might be interested in selling."

Garth looked to Pansy Joy and then to Zion, confused and somewhat put out. "I have a wagon, but I hadn't thought on selling it. What's this all about, Pansy Joy?"

"When Pa first mentioned it, I had the same reaction, Garth." Pansy Joy placed a small hand on Garth's broadcloth sleeve and gave it a couple of reassuring pats. "But Pa had a good point. He said you have plenty of time before the wedding to make a new one, and we could use the profits to buy some things for our cabin."

Garth mulled the idea over. It had merit. He and his Pa had already cleared the parcel of land set aside for their cabin. A fall house-raising would see to the building of their new home, but they did need things to set up housekeeping.

"I would have been happy cooking over the fireplace for you, but the thought of our own cast-iron stove . . ."

"That would make life easier, wouldn't it?"

"Hot water ready for the dipping from the reservoir, coffee pot at the ready in a moment's notice . . ."

Garth looked from Pansy Joy's dreamy expression to Zion. "Looks like you've stirred up some interest in selling, Mr. Coldwell."

"I confess, I'd rather do business with you than the mercantile, especially if it would be a blessing to Miss Johnson. Her family's been more than generous to me and mine."

"I heard about your sister. Katie was by the Johnson place earlier today and said she was perking up."

"Gave me a scare, that's for sure."

"Scared us all," said Pansy Joy. "You've got to come by and meet her, Garth. She's just the sweetest thing. She reminds me of Marigold some, but her hair's a bit lighter, and she's more delicate."

"No offense now, Pansy Joy, but it doesn't take much effort to be more delicate than Marigold."

"You're right about that." Pansy Joy laughed. "But I wasn't talking about her actions—more her hands and cheekbones and eyes and such."

"Katie said she's a pretty little thing."

"She is."

"Back to the wagon," Zion said. "I'd like to see it, and then I'll need to speak with Mr. Coventry. He's the one making the purchase, but I'm sure we can come to terms."

"Why don't you go on up to the house, Pansy Joy, while Mr. Coldwell and I discuss the sale? Katie made some raspberry cordial, and I brought up some ice from the icehouse."

Pansy Joy nodded. "A cold drink sounds heavenly on a hot summer's day."

Zion and Pansy Joy parted ways at the road, Pansy Joy turning right, and Zion to the left toward the lodge. He covered the half mile quickly and stepped into the lane. The wagon was stored safely in the barn, Zion assumed, since the mules roamed freely about the corral. The stage and horses from the livery were nowhere in sight.

"The boy's shave tail." Zion heard Bug Perkins, presumably talking to J.T. Nester. He slowed his entry onto the property, waiting to hear the man's response. From his vantage point, Zion saw Nester sitting on a bench by the pond and Perkins leaning against the willow tree.

"That's to our advantage," Nester said. "Once we're out on the trail, we'll make sure the Coventrys and the rest of the folks see Coldwell's lack of experience. We'll earn their trust, and by the time we reach Virginia City, we'll plunder the lot of them."

"That beats playing the riverboat passengers."

"Folks heading west take everything they own with them." Bug rubbed his bony fingers together. "We'll get the whole kit and caboodle."

"We'll wind this up and disappear in the hills."

Anger roiled in Zion. He considered busting in on the conversation, telling the men he was wise to their plans and sending them on their way. Before he acted, Balim's words rang in his memory. "Remember what the good Book says, Massa Zion: 'He that is soon angry dealeth foolishly.'"

The weight on Zion's shoulders turned leaden. He couldn't afford to deal foolishly. If he confronted Nester, what would keep him and Perkins from following his party down the trail? Attacking by night? He had no evidence to go to the authorities, and if he approached him face to face, Nester could pull a gun on him right beneath the willow tree and claim it was an accident. What would happen to Penny and Balim then?

With the revelation of Nester's plans and the threat to his family and charges, something in Zion awoke–something he had tuned out in the months since his parents' deaths. He heard a familiar voice whisper in his spirit, *Return to me, my Son, and I will direct your path.*

Tears welled in Zion's eyes–not tears of sorrow or fear, but for the faithfulness and mercy of God. It seemed such a long time since he had heard the still small voice of God speaking to him or felt His presence ministering to His spirit. Zion had closed himself off and built strong walls around his heart, mind and spirit. And there God was right when he needed Him–with open arms, willing to take him back and give him guidance after he had rejected Him for so many months.

I need some time alone, Zion thought, *but that will have to wait. Lord, please give me the wisdom I need to respond to this situation correctly.*

Immediately, a song flooded Zion's thoughts. With worship in mind, he began to consider the situation in a new light. He recalled the time King Jehoshaphat's enemies were destroyed when the king appointed singers to praise the beauty of God's holiness.

I remember, Lord. I remember the time the Israelites sang and when they did, You stirred up the Moabites and Ammonites to fight each. When the Israelites worshipped You, their enemies destroyed each other.

Zion felt a boldness unfolding inside him, the bud of only moments ago flowering into full bloom. *I'll do it, Lord, I'll sing my way in.*

Zion placed his thumbs in his pockets and sang out in rich baritone.

Guide me o Thou great Jehovah
Pilgrim through this barren land
I am weak, but Thou are mighty
Hold me with Thy powerful hand.

Zion felt covered and protected as he walked up the lane to Comfort Lodge. He ignored the men under the tree and strode purposefully to the front porch steps. Balim poked his head out the barn door in disbelief. Master Zion was singing, and not just any song, singing to the Lord a prayer for guidance.

"Glory be." Balim felt the tears come and at the same time broke out in a teeth-baring grin. "Glory be to God."

CHAPTER 17

*Z*ion entered the spacious parlor full of renewed vim and vigor. His situation, though unchanged and unimproved, seemed somehow hopeful–and the heaviness on his chest removed. When he had happened on Nester and Perkins in the yard, a slew of "what ifs" and possible dangers surfaced, but now that he was listening to the Lord, Zion almost smiled at the challenge. *I think I know some of what King David felt when he picked up his sling and ran out to meet Goliath.*

Taking tea in the parlor, Thaddeus Coventry rose when Zion entered. The large room awash in afternoon sunshine, smelled of earl gray and cinnamon.

"Good afternoon, Mr. Coldwell." Thaddeus still wore the frock coat Zion had seen earlier in the day, but the missing top hat revealed a previously concealed bald spot amidst salt-and-pepper bristles. Wire-rimmed spectacles balanced on his nose overlooking a robust and thick handlebar moustache with an overhand twist.

"Good afternoon to you, too, sir." Zion took Sara Coventry's extended hand and leaned over it. "Mrs. Coventry."

Sara Coventry, an aristocratic lady from an upper class Philadelphia family, wore an air of grace and gentility. A middle-aged beauty, she sat in the parlor chair, her feet tucked carefully beneath her and her erect carriage not touching the back of the seat. Her tea dress of blue-green plaid overlaid a white chemisette with a high drawn lace neck tied with a thin black ribbon. Its full gathered sleeves puffed out like cottonballs beneath the gown's ruffled pagoda sleeves trimmed in black silk bows. The same plaid ruffle and black trim circled mid-sleeve and down the deep vee that plunged below her breasts, the edges meeting at a long black satin bow. The piped waistline came to a point at her narrow waist and then flared out in floor-length full skirts. A black snood encased her mass of blond hair.

"I trust your sister's condition is improved," Sara said, her pale blue eyes probing Zion's.

"Very much, thank you."

"Would you care to join us?" Thaddeus motioned to a chair, and Zion seated himself before the tea tray. Sara poured a cup for Zion.

"Cream or sugar?"

"Black's fine. Thanks." Zion accepted the delicate cup painted with pink blossoms and edged in fine gold. Placing a cucumber sandwich on a china plate, Sara passed the fragile dish into Zion's sizable hands.

"I didn't know the Erlangers had such fine china," Zion observed.

"I brought my grandmother's tea set," said Sara. "I know it might seem sentimental or even silly to you, Mr. Coldwell, but every time I use this set, I think of Grandmother Muriel and all the lovely teas we shared."

"Remembering loved ones is not something I consider silly at all, Mrs. Coventry, and you're right blessed indeed to have something special to remember your grandma by." Zion many times wished he had something of his parents to look at or touch. It would have been nice to have something tangible to bring them near to heart, especially for Penny's sake. Their memories would have to be enough.

A warm light filled Sara's eyes and she nodded her approval at the young man seated across from her husband.

"I hope your accommodations are satisfactory."

"Yes, indeed they are," Thaddeus replied. "And the children are enjoying the beautiful grounds. They are out now taking a walk along the edge of the woods."

Zion took a bite of the cucumber sandwich, the first ever to pass his lips. He surprised himself, enjoying the taste. "I'm glad to have a chance to talk with you privately, Mr. Coventry."

"Should I excuse myself?" Sara asked.

"That's between you and your husband. I have some information on the wagon you asked me to secure."

"That's fine," Thaddeus answered Zion, and then addressed his wife, "Please stay, Dear. This concerns our travel arrangements, and I want you to be involved in the decision making."

Zion finished his tea and set the cup on the service tray. "Today I met with a young man, a farmer in the area. He recently finished a new wagon made for his bride-to-be. It's never been used for hauling or fieldwork. His wedding is several months off, and he's willing to sell the wagon to us for a fair price."

"I'm sure he did his best with the construction, Mr. Coldwell, but not being a wagon maker by trade, do you think the conveyance will prove solid for our long journey?"

"I wouldn't have suggested it if I wasn't confident, sir. Garth Eldridge is a capable man, very mechanical. He runs and maintains the area threshing machine, and he did a fine job on the wagon."

Sara Coventry studied her husband. An accomplished businessman, Thaddeus Coventry, born into a wealthy family to begin with, increased his fortune speculating on railroad expansions and as a financial officer for the Pennsylvania Railroad. After the great fire of 1845, the age of rails arrived in Pittsburgh. During the rebuilding period, Thaddeus worked diligently with the Ohio and Pennsylvania Railroad until service was established between Cleveland and Allegheny City in 1851. Upon the completion of the line, he invested in the Pennsylvania Railroad, which established the line between Pittsburgh and Philadelphia. When that was finished in 1854, Thaddeus became restless, and the lure of the new frontier called him to adventure.

Leaving the metropolis to settle in a town still in the throws of the gold rush, Thaddeus's plans did not include mining in Virginia City. Already a prosperous man, he longed to see the country and discover what possibilities lay in it. The speculator in him thrived on challenge and industry, and he wanted the opportunity to be on the ground floor of the development of new communities and infrastructure in the west, perhaps even working on the transcontinental rail system. A nationwide transportation network would revolutionize the population and economy of the American West, and Thaddeus was privy to talks outlining the plans to link Omaha with Sacramento and the rails of the Eastern United States with California.

With all Thaddeus's business acumen, the purchase of a wagon proved to be an uncomfortable decision. Sara read his discomposure and offered her counsel. "With the others still making their way here, we have time to make the decision. Perhaps you would like to see the wagon before the purchase?"

Thaddeus looked at his wife with appreciation. "Yes. Thank you for the suggestion, Sara."

"Mr. Eldridge would surely welcome you to the check the wagon prior to purchase," Zion agreed.

"It may be unnecessary, but I would like to have something to make a fair comparison. Do you know where else in the area I might find a similar wagon?"

Zion held back a groan. He had hoped to avoid the mercantile, but he would not withhold the information. "I heard that out back of the mercantile the Mathenys have a woodworking shop where a body can get anything from whiskey barrels to wagons."

"I don't think we need any whiskey barrels, Mr. Coldwell," Thaddeus smiled. "But I would like to see a wagon."

"That'll be fine. We can ride into town tomorrow, and we'll check on the horses, too. Mr. Cooper's the blacksmith and comes highly recommended. He'll know who has a couple of good horses for sale."

"After breakfast, then."

Zion rose to leave as J.T. and Bug walked through the front door. "Mr. Nester, Mr. Perkins." Zion would have walked past the two, but J.T. put his hand on his arm to stop him.

"Mr. Coldwell," J.T. exaggerated the formal address, drawing out the word "mister" in disproportionate manner. "Might I have a word with you?"

"Certainly." Zion maneuvered J.T.'s hand off his arm and turned to face him. "What can I do for you?"

"As I mentioned, me and Bug are planning to head west with you. The Coventrys showed us the notice you placed in the *Pittsburg Post-Gazette*." He looked to Mr. Coventry for confirmation.

"Yes, I did," Thaddeus agreed.

"You wrote that folks with reliable transportation and the money for escort would be welcome to join the party." Bug nodded his head up and down several times looking like a scarecrow in the breeze. "Me and Bug plan to buy some horses and gear in town and ride out with you. Just need to settle up the fee."

Bug continued nodding behind J.T. Zion looked from one man to the other and silently thanked God for revealing their plans.

"I have guidelines, Mr. Nester. If you're willing to abide by them, you'll be welcome." Zion watched J.T.'s feathers ruffle under his leadership. He knew he was "shave tail," green and inexperienced as Bug called him earlier, but he also knew he had the upper hand this round.

"What guidelines?"

"I will write out a copy of the contract the others signed, but I can tell you the bare bones of it now." Zion paused for effect. "Besides the supplies and monetary fees, I have some rules of conduct.

"Number One: all input from travelers is welcome, but I have the last say on all decisions.

"Number Two: On the trail, everyone pulls his own weight, working together to set up and break camp, collect firewood and such.

"Number Three: Orderly conduct is required at all times. No sparking with the single women and no fighting.

"Number Four: No intoxicating drink. A small amount of liquor will be on-hand for medicinal purposes only.

"Number Five: Stay with the group unless asked to scout ahead or hunt."

J.T. made a show to be agreeable in front of Mr. Coventry. "Me and Bug will sign up. Just let us know the figures and supply list."

"I'll make you a copy of the list when I write out your contract."

"Whatcha gonna do if somebody breaks your rules?" Bug asked. J.T. glared at the scrawny man and forcibly restrained himself from bashing Bug up the side of his head.

"Between me and Balim, we'll see to any problems," said Zion. "And between here and Virginia City there is a lot of open space, but there are also settlements along the way with proper law enforcement."

"And if there ain't no law enforcements?"

"There are bullets." Zion patted the gun strapped to his right leg. "And there are always trees and rope."

"Surely you don't think there will be trouble," Mrs. Coventry said, her voice tinged with apprehension.

"You never know in the wilderness, ma'am, but we've got the good Lord looking out for us."

"Indeed." Thaddeus agreed.

"And Balim."

CHAPTER 18

"Lord, have mercy," Balim said. "I'll show them croakers who's a shave tail."

"Don't lose your Holy Ghost, Balim." Zion patted the big black man on the back.

Balim simmered down, a sparkle in his obsidian eyes, and beamed at Zion. "'Specially since you just found yourn agin." Zion chuckled. "Massa Zion, when I heard you walking down the lane singing that hymn at the top of yo voice, it done purged every bit of sorrow out of this ole soul of mine."

"Felt pretty good to me, too." Zion slapped his slouch hat on his knee and jumped down from the buckboard. The quiet of the barn provided a private meeting place for Zion and Balim to discuss the problem at hand.

"You have a plan for dealin' with the chiselers?" Balim asked.

"I haven't taken it to prayer yet, like I want to–haven't had the time."

"In all thy ways acknowledge Him and He shall direct thy path."

"That's what it says."

"That it do, Massa Zion." Zion looked up at his friend and gratitude filled his heart for the faithfulness of this man looking down on him from the wagon seat.

"You know, you don't have to call me Master Zion."

"You done told me that afore, and I knows it, but it's no never mind to me. The Bible says to obey yo massa, and black or white, slave or free, we's all got massas."

Zion smiled at Balim's wisdom. He was a man most of the southern world considered less than a person, unworthy of an education or the opportunity for one–a man who taught him so much through his words and example. "I'll call you Massa Zion fo now, and probly always will; but I only got one king, King Jesus."

"I'm sorry you have to take your meals in the kitchen."

"You's sorry I'm eating such fine vittles–don't have to cook 'em or even wash the pan when I'm afinished?"

"I guess it's better than we'll all have soon." Zion watched a field mouse scurry in front of the open barn door. "After supper I'm heading over to check on Penny. She'll be needing some clean clothes."

"That Miss Rozlee takin' good care of our girl?" Balim watched the expressions play out across Zion's strong features. His discernment, usually on target, zeroed in on a new development. Zion gave a slow nod.

"Yes, Balim. She is at that."

A slow smile spread out across Balim's face. "It might be fittin' to take her a gift a some sort . . . to show yo 'preciation."

"Do tell." Zion knew the jig was up. He locked eyes with Balim, threw his head back and let out a jolly laugh. "It's a good thing I don't have any secrets to keep from you."

Zion carried a bundle of Penny's clothes as he walked the path to Briar Hollow. He thought Balim had a good idea, bringing Rosalie a token, but what would be right for this special young lady? He passed clumps of vibrant orange tiger lilies, but decided against them–too flashy. Something about the Queen Anne's lace drew him to cut a few stems and tie them with a purple ribbon he pulled from his pocket. The flowers reminded Zion of Rosalie, long and lithe, and though she didn't wear fancy lace bonnets, Rosalie had a graceful elegance about her.

"That'll do." Zion continued, surprised his thoughts spent more time on Rosalie than on Penny and her condition. His sister had given him a scare, but he believed things would work out for the best.

Zion heard music inside the cabin before he rapped on the door. He waited just a moment before it swung open, Lucas behind it. Zion lowered himself, eye to eye with the stocky, brown-haired boy. "Hey, Lucas."

"Hi, Mr. Coldwell."

"All right if I come in?"

"Guess so." Lucas turned and yelled inside the room. "All right if Mr. Coldwell comes in?"

Flushing, Rosalie hurried to the door. "Lucas, don't yell like that. Of course Mr. Coldwell is welcome. He's come to see his sister." Rosalie, dulcimer in hand, ushered Lucas out of the doorway and motioned Zion in.

"Good evening, Rosalie." Zion's blue eyes scanned the face of the woman before him. He had noticed her auburn hair and celadon eyes the first time they met, but he took in more detail now—the way her chin, cheeks and forehead formed a heart shape, and delicate pink lips curved slightly upward in a pleasant expression. A smattering of freckles crossed the tops of her high cheekbones and the bridge of her nose.

She wore a simple dress of burgundy calico that complemented her auburn hair. A crochet collar, attached to a rounded fabric one, tied at the neck with a thin cream ribbon bow. Narrow sleeves accented her willowy limbs; and the dress's straight cut waist, her slender middle. Full skirts fell to the floor without ruffle or trim. Simple, sweet, just like Rosalie.

Zion extended the bouquet to her. "I brought these for you."

Delight and confusion coursed simultaneously through Rosalie. "Thank you." She set her instrument on the table and accepted the flowers, her small hand brushing Zion's in the transfer.

"I appreciate all you're doing for Penny."

Rosalie smile and dipped her head to hide the disappointment threatening to overtake her. *That explains the flowers,* Rosalie thought. *He's just thankful I've been nursing his sister. It has nothing to do with me as a woman he might care for.*

"They reminded me of you."

Rosalie's heart felt like a bucket going up and down the well rope, emptied one minute and brimming over the next.

"It's Queen Anne's lace," Pansy Joy said from across the room. For the first time since he saw Rosalie, Zion remembered the other people inside the cabin. "They say the red center is where Queen Anne pricked herself with a needle when she was making lace."

"That's just a tale," said Rosalie. "The Lord put that bit of red in the center to attract the bees and other insects."

"So they'll make honey," said Marigold.

"I like honey." Lucas rubbed his tummy and licked his lips.

"I know you do, Lukey. Want to go check the hives with me?"

Lucas turned to Rosalie for permission. She nodded, and the two were out the door before Rosalie could say, "Get your hats."

"Those two are always leaving without their hats." Pansy Joy grinned from ear to ear. "I'll take them out. I wouldn't want them to get a burn." Zion and Rosalie stood alone in the front room of the cabin. Rosalie, still holding the bouquet of flowers, broke the silence.

"Did you see Garth, then?" Rosalie walked to a shelf and pulled down a crockery pitcher. She dipped some water into it from a bucket, thinking it best to keep her hands moving and the conversation going. Loosening the ribbon, she freed the flowers and arranged them in the pitcher. Rosalie was certain that if she stood staring into Zion's blue eyes, just the blue of Mama's bachelor buttons in the wildflower garden, she might not be able to make intelligent conversation.

Zion watched her simple movements—so graceful and appealing. He looked at her hands and remembered their feel at the table when she had slipped one in his for prayer.

"Yes. I did."

"And did the wagon suit your needs?"

"I spoke to the Coventrys, and they were interested in making the purchase; however, they wanted to see what else was available first. They've never bought a wagon before. Living in the city they had no need."

"I see."

"I was hoping to avoid the mercantile, but it looks like we'll be heading out there in the morning."

Rosalie looked at Zion, curiosity brimming in her green eyes. "Why would you want to avoid the mercantile?"

Zion regretted setting himself up for the question. How could he explain that the Matheny women, one young woman in particular, made him very uncomfortable? "I guess it's like you said, I'm finding everything I need in Briar Hollow."

Rosalie felt the message behind the words, and crimson crept up her lithesome neck. Without a word of impropriety, Zion affected her senses in a way she had never experienced before. She turned back to the flowers and picked up the ribbon beside them. "Sometimes I have to go to the mercantile. I buy supplies there, like ribbons and such."

Zion chortled, and then confessed. "I think you bought that one. I pulled it from the lotion jar Penny was using at the lodge."

"Zion Coldwell," Rosalie joined his laughter, the feeling sweeping her senses with an unfamiliar giddiness. Zion loved hearing her laugh. What a day he was having. He had renewed his relationship with God, and now he was realizing he was coming to care for Rosalie. With everything in him he wanted to grab the young woman and swing her around the room. Sweet freedom abounded in a heart that seemed empty only days before.

"Zion." Penny called out to her brother from behind the bedroom door.

"May I?" Zion asked Rosalie. She smiled and nodded, and they went to the door together.

"Hi-ya, Penny."

"Hi, Zion." Penny looked at her brother's face, studying the light in his blue eyes. Something was different. "I heard you laughing."

"That you did. I was just confessing my iniquities to Miss Rosalie." He winked at the little girl who smiled up at him in return.

"That could take some time. Are you sure you finished already?"

Zion tousled Penny's golden hair. "You must be feeling better, Buttercup."

"I am, thanks be to God . . . and Rosalie." Penny looked fondly at the older girl.

"My pleasure, sweetheart," Rosalie smoothed Penny's covers, pleased at the progress her young patient was making. "Can I bring you something to drink?"

"That would be nice. I'm dry as cracker juice."

Zion laughed. "That's Balim's saying."

"I never heard of cracker juice," said Rosalie.

"Have you ever squeezed the juice out of a cracker?" Zion asked.

"Can't say as I have." Rosalie smirked, understanding the gist of the joke.

"It's dry, real dry." Penny guffawed and Zion slapped his knee at the look on Rosalie's face.

"What's going on in here?" Matthias asked, happy to hear and see the good humor filling the room.

"Penny was just telling me about cracker juice."

"Cracker juice? Seems that might leave a fella thirsty."

"I think you're right, Pa." Rosalie looked at Matthias leaning on his cane, a big man with a big heart. "Do you think you're getting the best of the worms?"

"I've been working on it, Daughter. Been out pulling the nests out of the trees."

"What kind of worms live in trees?" Penny asked.

"Did you ever walk by a tree and see a silky brown nest in it?"

"Yes, I have." Penny turned to Zion. "We used to get those on the trees back home, but I never paid them much attention."

"Those are filled with webworms. They build tough silky nests around a bunch of leaves and stay there feeding on them until all the leaves are gone. Then they move on and make another nest. They can kill a tree."

"Really?" Zion asked. "Our family raised horses, not trees. I never thought a few bugs could hurt a man's livelihood."

"They can at that. When I find a nest, I take a piece of wood with nails on it, snag it and turn the wood. The nest comes clean off the tree, and then I mash the worms on the ground."

"Ooh." Penny made a face at the thought of Matthias squishing worms under his boots.

"I don't enjoy mashing the worms myself; but if I let them go, they'll ruin my crop. A man's got to see to his family first."

"Yes, sir." Zion looked at Matthias and wondered about his injury. What caused this big man to depend on a carved stick to walk? He seemed a simple man, but Zion saw depth in Matthias Johnson. He recalled the strength of his hand when they prayed for Penny, and remembered the power of his faith.

"Speaking of squishy worms," Rosalie teased Penny, "It's time for your applesauce."

Fragile fingers flew to Penny's lips. "I don't think I'll be able to swallow it."

"We'll just have to think of something else for a minute," said Zion.

Matthias offered first. "How about the fireworks? They're coming up on the Fourth of July, just one week away."

Penny's eyes grew big with excitement. "Fireworks?"

"Yes," Rosalie confirmed. "First we have an ice cream social and some games, like sack races and horse shoes, and then a singing until dark. Once the sun goes down, folks set off all kinds of firecrackers and sparklers–even Roman candles."

"Lights and smoke and noise," Matthias added.

Penny looked longingly at Zion. "Do you think we'll be able to go?"

"I can't promise you, Penny. It depends on when the other folks get here and how soon they're ready to head out. We have several months of travel ahead of us, and winter will be here before you know it."

CHAPTER 19

"I hope our delay hasn't set things back." Louella Sweeney wiped soft tendrils of sandy hair off her forehead and tucked them beneath a calico bonnet.

"I don't think a couple of days will make that much difference," Clarence said. In gloved hands, Clarence held the reins of his pride and joy, a matched set of bays. He prided himself on his horses–enjoyed just sitting behind them on the wagon seat. He liked to watch the movement of their sleek reddish-brown bodies with black manes, tails, ear edges and lower legs. He admired their powerful muscles that moved together in unison as the animals plodded over the road into Washington.

"When you think we'll be traveling for about four months once we leave town, a day here and there'll be no nevermind." Clarence winked at his new bride and threw out an impish grin.

"Still, I'm sure everyone's anxious to get started out."

"Not as anxious as I was to marry you, darlin'." Clarence patted Louella's knee raising a blush on her cheeks.

Louella liked being married to her amorous husband, but was not yet comfortable with the intimacy and familiarity of being a wife. The daughter of a minister, Louella exhibited the utmost propriety, never having shown an elbow in public, or an ankle once she started wearing long skirts. She received her first kiss on her wedding day.

Clarence, on the other hand, didn't have a shy bone in his lanky, lusty body. He behaved himself during their courting time, a perfect gentleman, but once he stood before the preacher and said "I do," everything changed. He often reminded Louella that her own reverend father, right in the house of God, had given him permission to kiss his bride, and he took full advantage at every opportunity.

"How will we know how to get to the lodge once we get into town?" Louella asked.

"When we get to the macadamized road, we head north out of town one mile. There'll be a sign."

"I wish we could travel on pavement all the way to Virginia City. By the time we travel over two thousand miles, there's no telling how much dust we'll have eaten."

"You ain't kidding. Figure in the four hundred miles from North Carolina, and we'd probably have enough dirt to make a fine kitchen garden."

"I'm looking forward to getting settled and planting our own garden." Louella thought about the packets of seeds stored deep in the boxes on the wagon. She and her mother gathered them the previous year preparing for Louella to set up housekeeping, neither one expecting they would be carted off across the continent.

When Louella fell for Clarence, she knew he was a dreamer. Being conservative, she felt he was her perfect complement. God did say He took two and made one, and to Louella's way of thinking, Clarence's gumption would temper her reserve, and vice versa, making a beautiful Sweeney one. It seemed so, until a week after their marriage and Clarence came home from his work at Captain Slade's. He said curing Bright leaf tobacco for another man was not the way he intended to spend his life. He learned enough working in Piedmont County to start his own tobacco farm out west. If folks could grow Bright leaf tobacco in the infertile sandy soil of the Appalachian piedmont, Clarence felt confident it would do well in Virginia City. And with the new smoke-free, flue-curing techniques, he was certain he would be profitable.

The discovery of silver in the western Utah Territory caused Clarence considerable excitement. When news of Henry T.P. Comstock's claim hit North Carolina earlier in the year, he wanted to go then, though he hadn't told a soul. He had everything he needed now: a wife, a dream, and a back-up plan of growing tobacco, evidenced by the agricultural paraphernalia in the back of the wagon.

The Hobbs let out a long wail on the steam trumpet and shot puffy clouds out her gleaming diamond stack. The locomotive slowed, and then screeched to a stop, the inclined frame of the pointed cowcatcher nosing its way into the Louisville station on the corner of 10th and Maple. Known as an "American type," The 4-4-0 black locomotive had two driving axles coupled by a connecting rod, and a two-axle bogie, two small driving wheels on each side of the engine to help guide it into curves and keep it on the poor track frequently found on the developing American railroads. A black tender, edged in gold, with the words "Louisville & Nashville" also painted in gold, coupled to the steam engine, followed by two passenger cars, three freight cars and a red brake van.

Covering 180 miles in 5 hours, the trip from Nashville on the iron horse went without a hitch and proved quite interesting. Travis Ballard wondered what the next months would hold escorting two mail-order brides from vastly different backgrounds and one missionary lady across the continent. Of course, Zion Coldwell would be leading the group once they assembled in Washington, but until then, anticipation filled Travis. The situation also tickled his good humor.

Amidst the cacophony at the station, *The Hobbs's* bell rang out its signals to workers on the train and off. "This way, ladies." Travis held out his hand to assist the first woman descending from the train. Commotion met the passengers as people collected their belongings and exited while others waited to board. Porters assisted with luggage while crewmen filled the water and coal in the tender to fuel the train for its return trip to Nashville. The smell of sulfur from the burning coal mingled with the smells of the city.

First to disembark, Liza Waterson lit the platform in a purple and black satin dress. The fitted bodice accentuated her narrow waist and full figure with a scooped neckline trimmed in a wide black ribbon, a large purple flower and black satin bow perched on her right shoulder. Full sleeves were gathered at the wrist and trimmed in the same ribbon circling the neckline. Black and purple alternated in the gored circle skirt floating over multiple layers of petticoats. Atop her blazing red coiffure, Liza wore a pointed brim shirred bonnet in purple silk taffeta with scalloped, pinked and ruched trim on the outer brim, the underbrim decorated in black silk.

"At last." Shoulders back and full lips parted in a sensual smile, Liza scanned the station with hooded eyes and then turned to watch Penelope Ford accept Travis's assistance from the train. Brown-haired, brown-eyed Penelope's brown dress had a gathered fan front bodice with a fitted lining and gathered back, gathered sleeves and a dropped shoulder line. The full skirt, sewn to a separate waistband, closed in the center front at a miniscule waistline, and she wore a tan low-brim spoon bonnet with sepia trim.

"Thank you." Penelope gave Travis a diminutive nod, clutched her carpetbag with both thin hands and moved quickly out of the way.

"Thank you, Mr. Ballard." Beth Ann Sparks shot a friendly smile to her escort and slipped her hand in his as she descended to the platform. Her costume of crisp green polished cotton had two boned darts on the front bodice and a curved vee tucked back with piping at the neck, armscyes and waist. A large black embroidered bow tied beneath a white lace collar, and a band of black trim edged the coat sleeves. Knife pleats tucked the skirt's fullness in at a straight waistline, and topping her strawberry-blond hair, she wore a soft-crown bonnet of green silk trimmed in white flowers and pink paper roses. A white liner with a frilled edge garnished the inner brim, and black watered silk ties formed a perky bow under her chin.

"I wish we had time for a photograph," said Travis, "but I must see to our luggage and check the stage schedule." Excited about recording the emerging west and mining ventures in pictures, Travis also hoped to document each part of his trip. Initially trained in daguerreotype, Travis was eager to put the newer collodion process to work. Daguerreotype images were limited, for one because the finished product was very fragile, but also because they could not be reprinted. Using the collodion-based wet-glass plate negatives with prints made on albumen paper, Travis could make as many prints of an image as he wanted.

"Travis." Liza placed one hand on his arm and motioned to a building across the street with the other. "Look there, a tea house."

"Good eye, Miss Liza." Travis patted her hand. "I'll have a porter take our trunks to the stagecoach office, and then see that you ladies get some refreshments. Once you're settled I'll come back to make our travel arrangements into Washington."

In less than a quarter hour, Travis stood at the ticket counter of the Johnson, Weisiger, & Company stage line.

A beady-eyed, bewhiskered man stood behind the counter. "That's 10 cents a mile, 14 pounds of baggage allowed, and then

2 cents a mile for additional freight. One hundred pounds counts for one person," he said.

Travis wondered how the fellow ate. His moustache completely covered his mouth and would have made a great picture. Paired with a full beard, the abundance of whiskers made his mouth look like a hairy cavern when he spoke. "Payable in advance."

"And when does the next stage leave out for Washington?"

"In the morning at sunrise. It takes a full two days to get to Washington if conditions are good, and that's pressing the horses."

"That will suit just fine," Travis reached in his pocket to retrieve the money for the fares. "I'd like to book passage for five."

"I can sell you the passenger tickets, but you'll have to settle up any baggage fees with the driver."

"Actually," Travis grinned, "I'm purchasing a ticket for a spinning wheel. I'm assuming that can ride on top?"

"A spinning wheel? I never heard tell of the like."

"I know, but it's a sentimental item for a young lady relocating west."

The man behind the counter stroked his whiskers. "They say it takes all sorts of folks to make the world go around."

"That it does." Travis paid the man and took the tickets. He turned to leave the station and then remembered he needed sleeping accommodations. "Can you recommend a good hotel, friend?"

"The Galt House, northeast corner of Second and Main."

"And the telegraph office?"

"Western Union's the next building over."

CHAPTER 20

"Massa Zion," Balim called out to Zion as he closed the distance between the barn and the lodge. "I was thinking of paying a little visit to Missy Penny."

"I wanted to go myself, Balim, but I promised to take Mr. Coventry into town to check on the wagon and horses right after breakfast."

"Yes, suh." Balim knew Zion's schedule as well as he did. He also knew the planned trip to town provided an opportunity for him to check on his little missy and meet the young lady having such an effect on Zion. Since childhood, Balim had watched over Zion. In all their years together, he had never seen what he saw now–a young man enamored with a young lady. Behind the blue eyes, Balim recognized the flighty feeling of romantic excitement in a young man. It reminded him of sparking with Minnie, heart pounding, temperature rising and joy unfolding. Balim looked forward to meeting Miss Rosalie Johnson.

James hitched up his team and drove the Rockaway Coupe to the front of the lodge. "Thank you, Mr. Erlanger." Zion held the reins while James stepped down and Thaddeus, J.T. and Bug climbed in the covered carriage.

Balim watched the carriage roll down the lane and make the right turn towards town. Hands in his pockets, he rumbled a melody in deep bass and started down the path. Next to the pond, Balim spotted a snow white goose feather on the grass. He stopped to pick it up and twirled it by its tip in his sausage-like fingers. As he moseyed down the path, he began his song again, this time singing the words.

Who's that young girl dressed in white
Wade in the water
Must be the children of the Israelites
God's gonna trouble the water.

Wade in the water
Wade in the water, children
Wade in the water
God's gonna trouble the water.

Balim walked north on the main road and then turned in the lane to the Johnson place. After clearing the trees, he appraised the grounds in awe. "Glory be, if this don't look like a li'l patch a heav'n." The sun shone in the hollow. A slight breeze rippled the flowers in the wildflower and rose gardens, stirring an exotic cocktail of floral scents. Balim went to the back of the cabin, but found no door, so he cautiously took the front porch steps and knocked.

A black man, especially one traveling alone, never knew what type of reception to expect. Balim stepped back from the door and crumpled his worn slouch hat in his hands. The door opened and he lowered his head assuming a humble posture and avoiding eye contact.

Rosalie opened to the burly man. At 5 foot 9 inches, Balim was a bundle of taut, bulky muscles, yet something gentle about him touched her heart. "Can I help you?" Rosalie smiled at the man.

"Yes'm. Yes'm." Balim peeked at the willowy girl standing in the doorway. "I'm Balim. Belong to Massa Zion, and I's come to check on Missy Penny."

A mixture of shock and compassion assaulted Rosalie. Growing up in a slave state, Rosalie was well aware of the realities of slavery, but her family believed in freedom for all men. When Zion arrived in Washington exhibiting such love and tenderness to Penny, and wooing Rosalie's senses, she characterized him as a kindred spirit on the matter. Had she misjudged him?

Rosalie opened the door wide. "Mr. Balim." She paused until he lifted his dark eyes to hers. "Welcome. Please come in. Penny was just having some breakfast."

Peace swept over Balim. This Miss Rosalie was all he had hoped for. "Thank ya, ma'am." He nodded and stepped into the cabin.

"I'm Rosalie Johnson. It's a pleasure to meet you."

"You, too, ma'am."

"Balim?" Penny called out from the bedroom. "Is that you?"

Balim broke out in a wide smile, affection for the girl dripping from crinkled eyes. "Go ahead." Rosalie motioned Balim to the door.

Penny sat in the bed, her back resting on pillows propped against the headboard. Pallor clung to her small face, but her eyes sparkled when Balim entered the room. She clapped her hands and jostled the breakfast tray on her lap.

"Careful now, Missy Penny, you don' wanna spill milk on this fine feather bed."

"I sure don't." Penny calmed herself and stretched out a small hand that Balim engulfed in his. "Miss Johnson just changed the bedding and me."

"I hope she didn't change you too much. I liked you the way you was."

"You're silly, Balim." Penny released his hand and leaned back. "She just helped me wash up and put on the fresh nightgown Zion brought. She brushed and rebraided my hair, too."

"You's looking pert for a girl that nigh scared the liver out a ole Balim."

Rosalie watched the exchange. Penny treated Balim like family, and the look on Balim's face spoke volumes of tenderness. The warmth of their relationship eased some of the doubts she felt when Balim first arrived, but worry niggled in the back of her heart.

"She scared us all," Rosalie said.

"I was a prayin' for you, Missy."

"I knew you were." Penny sunk her head back deeply in a pillow, a small smile played on her thin lips. "As terrible as everything was, I knew I wasn't alone. I could almost see the angels hovering about, and I knew you were praying for me."

"Massa Zion, too."

Penny shot a glance at Balim. "He did?" Surprise crossed Penny's face. "Out loud? Did you hear him?"

"Sho 'nough, Missy Penny." Balim nodded and grinned.

"Thank you, Jesus." A delighted chuckle escaped Penny's lips. She closed her eyes and contentment bathed her features.

Rosalie wondered at the exchange.

"And thank Miss Johnson, too," Balim added.

"She has." Rosalie smiled. "I'll give you two a minute alone, but you should rest, Penny. You're still weak, and I can tell the washing and changing has taken a toll."

"I will."

Rosalie removed the tray from the bed and eased Penny back to a horizontal position. She fluffed the pillow around her golden braids and left the room.

"That girl lives up to her name, don' she?" Balim asked.

"Rosalie?"

"Yes, Missy Penny. Miss Rozlee–she's a gentle tonic, like a sweet-smellin' rose on a summer day–makes a body relax."

Penny liked Balim's analogy. Rosalie's name did seem to fit her. "Her ma had a real fancy for flowers. You could probably tell when you walked up."

"Nigh took my breath away," Balim agreed. "I brought you summpin."

"You did?"

"Yup." Balim pulled the goose feather out of his sleeve and tickled Penny's cheek. "Found this here downy feather by the pond on the way here."

"This isn't from one of the babies."

"No, Missy Penny. This here's a pointer, a big feather from the mama or daddy. I'm gonna clean it up and make a pen for you."

"Thank you, Balim." Penny took the feather from his hand and traced her own chin with the plume. "It's so soft."

"I'll cut a nib on the end, and you can use it to write and draw."

"I'll ask Zion to get some ink and paper before we leave."

"He's gone to town now looking at wagons and hosses for the trip," Balim said. "He wanted to see you this mornin', but I told him I'd come on by."

Balim looked at the girl, notably tiring before his eyes, and walked to the bedroom door. "I'll be going now, Missy Penny. You jist rest up and get better."

"Thanks for coming, Balim." Penny's breathing fell into a soft pattern and she drifted to sleep before Balim left the room.

From the kitchen Rosalie watched Balim shut the bedroom door and shuffle to the front room. "Before you go, do you think we could talk over a cup of coffee?" Rosalie smiled at the man and lifted a plate of molasses cookies to sweeten the invitation.

"You have a outside table, Miss Rozlee?"

"No need. You're welcome inside." Rosalie set the plate on the polished wood table and turned to get the coffee. Surprised and pleased, Balim walked to the table and waited for Rosalie's return before he sat.

"Please sit down." Rosalie poured Balim's coffee and sat in an adjacent chair. She offered him a cookie and took one for herself.

"I's always been partial to molasses cookies." Balim broke the treat in half, dunked it in his coffee and took a bite. "I believe that there's the softest molasses cookie I ever et."

"I'm glad you like it. They're a favorite around here, too."

Balim was curious, but decorum dictated he not initiate a conversation. He sat quietly, waiting for the girl to speak her mind.

Rosalie wasn't sure what she wanted to talk about, but curiosity compelled her to learn more about the man beside her, and ultimately his master.

"Have you been with the Coldwells long?"

"Since afore Massa Zion was born. Massa Coldwell brought me to the farm when I was eight years old."

"Eight? That's so young." The thought of a boy separated from his family at such a young age appalled Rosalie.

Balim sensed the girl's distress. "Massa Coldwell, he was a good man. I was born on a plantation near their horse farm, but the massa there fell on hard times. He needed money, so he sold my mammy and pappy. About six months later Massa Coldwell brought me to his house. He didn' say as much, but I knowed he did it so I wouldn' be alone." Balim smiled remembering Mr. Coldwell's kindness the morning he fetched him from the plantation and settled him into a room off the kitchen. "My Aunt Liddy was his cook."

The revelation pleased Rosalie. Still not happy with slavery as a way of life, at the very least, the Coldwells seemed good hearted people. "That big woman buried my face in her skirts and squeezed me like a lemon for juice," Balim said with a grin. "I miss ole Liddy. She was like a mammy to me."

"I know what you mean," Rosalie said, thinking of the last time her mother embraced her, certainly without the strength of ample Aunt Liddy, but full of love, just the same.

"Massa Coldwell let me help in the kitchen fo a couple of months filling the wood box and such, and then he took me out to the stables. Fine hosses, Miss Johnson, real thoroughbreds. Folks came from neighboring states to buy their stock from the Coldwells.

"At first I mucked the stables and fed and watered the hosses, but when I got older Massa Coldwell worked with me. Taught me everything he knew about breedin', raisin' and trainin' hosses—doctorin' em too." Balim quieted for a moment reflecting on the job and people he loved. "It's a shame it's all gone now."

"I'm so sorry."

"You and me both, Miss Rozlee. You and me both." Balim shook his big head in regret. "Every time I hear a crack of lightning I think about that day."

Rosalie reached across the table and touched Balim's arm. "I didn't mean to make you sad."

"It was a sad day, at that," said Balim. "But I don't mean to take on so. The massa and the missus already stepped into the arms a King Jesus, an' ole Balim'll see 'em again someday."

Rosalie smiled, joining Balim in the fellowship of sufferings and hope. "If we get to know each other in heaven, I'd be pleased for you to introduce me to them."

Balim's signature grin stretched from one side of his face to the other. "If that's the way of it, I'd be right proud to do it."

"I wonder if maybe Zion's parents know each other, or could have met my mom in heaven already?"

"We cain't know fo' sure, Miss Rozlee, but the good Book does tell about the ole rich man. After he died, he talked to Father Abr'm about Laz'rus, begging fo' a drop of water."

"And Moses and Elijah appeared together on the mountain with Jesus," Rosalie remembered. She brightened at the thought. "I'm not a scholar, but you just gave me a lot of hope, Balim. Thank you."

"We's called to encourage one another, Miss Rozlee, as brothers and sisters in Christ." Balim stood to leave. "I have to say thanks to you, for all you're doing for Missy Penny. I love that girl like she was my own."

"It seems she has a special fondness for you, too." Rosalie walked Balim to the door and watched him plod down the path and disappear in the woods. He left behind hope and faith so thick she thought she might scoop some up in a jar and save it for another day.

CHAPTER 21

"Mr. Coldwell, I'd like you to meet my husband, Donald Matheny." Martha Matheny bustled and preened like a rooster in the henhouse. Stuffed into a tight corset, her movements were stiff and breathing looked difficult in a dress more suited to afternoon tea than clerking in a mercantile.

"Pleased to meet you, sir."

Donald stood in high contrast to his wife, a trim bespectacled man with brown hair, he wore simple gray trousers held up with black suspenders and a white collarless shirt. He appraised the odd lot before him with unmasked curiosity. By his calculations he looked at a gentleman, a farmer, a swell, and a scarecrow with bug eyes and straw hair. "What can I do for you gentlemen?"

"These are my traveling companions," Zion said. He clasped Donald's gaunt hand in his. "Thaddeus Coventry, J.T. Nester and Bug Perkins." Hats and heads tipped in greeting. "We were told you have wagons for sale."

"I do," Donald answered. "I have a woodworking shop out back."

"Might we see your merchandise, Mr. Matheny?" Thaddeus asked.

"Why sure." Mr. Matheny led the troop out the front door of the mercantile and around to the workshop in back. Built like a large lean-to, the shop had only three wooden sides, the longest of which was the back wall of the mercantile. A canvas sheet rolled into a tight line was secured in place with ties that could be undone to provide cover in inclement weather. Tucked inside the shop, a young man not much older than Zion planed a panel of fragrant cherry. The smell of sawdust hung heavy in the air.

"Good morning, Mr. Matheny." The young man stopped working on the wood and brushed curled shavings to the ground beneath the saw horses.

"Good morning." Donald made quick introductions. "Gentlemen, this is Grant Taylor. Grant these men are interested in a wagon. How's it coming along?"

"Actually, Mr. Coventry is the one interested in making the purchase," Zion clarified.

"I'm finishing off the dining set for Sheriff Nash's anniversary, so the wagon got put on hold. It could be done in a week or so."

"I was hoping to be a couple hundred miles out of town by then," Zion said. He watched Thaddeus examine the wagon, a 3-board high buckboard with a spring seat and high wheels: the back set 52-inch, 14-spoke; and the front set 45-inch, 12-spoke. "The rest of our party hasn't arrived yet, so waiting a few days is a possibility."

"What do you lack to finish the job, Mr. Taylor?" Thaddeus asked.

"The horse tongue and the brakes," Grant said.

"Won't be going anywhere without those," Zion said.

"I was thinking to add a tail gate off the back, but you could travel without it."

"Could I have a word with you, Mr. Coventry?" J.T. raised his bushy eyebrows in appeal. Thaddeus nodded and walked a few paces with J.T.–beyond the hearing of the others.

Zion observed their quiet consultation. J.T., with experienced prowess, manipulated the man while Thaddeus nodded his head in naïve agreement. It ruffled Zion to watch Nester play Mr. Coventry like a square dancer's fiddle, but he was helpless to intervene.

The two returned to the shop and Mr. Coventry spoke first. "I'm very interested in your wagon, Mr. Matheny. It looks to be a quality piece of workmanship."

"Grant does good work."

"May I inquire as to the sale price?"

"The wagon will run you $30. Canvas is $1 per yard. If you want wagon bows to convert to a covered wagon, they're $3 for the set."

Mr. Coventry nodded. "I'll give you my decision by tomorrow noon, if that's acceptable."

Donald shook his hand in agreement. "You're the first to inquire after it. I don't anticipate a run on wagons before tomorrow afternoon."

"We're staying at the Comfort Lodge. I hope if someone does inquire, you'll give me first rights."

"Like I said, it shouldn't be a problem."

The men rounded the building and stepped on the walk at the front of the store. A jingle announced the opening of the mercantile door followed by Lark Matheny's sashay out into the morning sunshine. Flawless skin capped a meticulous up-do of golden ringlets. Lark, in a powder blue costume, shone against the drab wooden building at her back.

"Good morning, Daddy, gentlemen." She turned her attention to Zion, a demure smile played across her full lips. "Mr. Coldwell, what a pleasant surprise."

Zion gave a slight bow. "Good morning, Miss Lark." Self-disgust charged through Zion. Balim harped on the book of Proverbs often enough, and Zion knew Lark Matheny was just the kind of woman to avoid. Regardless, he could not help being attracted to her beauty and feminine wiles. He determined not to get too close, lest he become entangled in her snare.

"We were just on our way to the smithy." He took a step in the direction of Cooper's.

Lark stepped with him. "Did your sister like the bilbo catcher?" With all that happened in recent days, Zion had forgotten about the toy. "Why yes, she did."

"I'm glad." Lark gave a bright smile and a look of sweet concern. Zion wondered if he had judged the girl too hastily. It was nice enough of her to ask after Penny. "Maybe I'll get to meet your sister at church on Sunday, or at the Fourth of July picnic."

"She's been feeling poorly, so I'm not sure."

"Oh, I'm so sorry to hear that. The poor little darling." Lark drew near to Zion and placed a small hand on his arm. She looked up into his eyes, the picture of innocence. "Is there anything I can do?" Zion didn't miss the brush of Lark's bodice against his arm. The contact shot electric charges unbidden through his system. He shook them off, sure the connection must have been an accident, especially with her father standing right next to him.

"Miss Rosalie Johnson has been tending her. She has a way with herbs and things. Penny's doing much better, just weak."

"Thank the good Lord." Lark released Zion's arm and gave a little wave. "You have a nice day now."

"You, too."

The foursome headed down the walk in pairs; J.T. and Bug behind Zion and Thaddeus. Perkins turned to gawk at the pretty blond. "She'd go right nice with a dish of ice cream." Bug elbowed J.T. who gave him a hard look.

"Sweet girl." Nester said. He frowned at Bug and nodded at the backs of the two in front. Bug got the signal and closed his trap.

"Where's that beautiful horse of yours?" Cooper asked when the party arrived at the blacksmith's.

"West is taking it easy in the lodge corral. Mr. Erlanger loaned us his team and carriage this morning." Zion introduced his companions. "We've come to ask your opinion on the purchase of some horses. Mr. Johnson said you'd know best what is available in town."

"That I do–in the country, too, for that matter. Everyone brings their stock here for shoeing."

"We're traveling west and Mr. Coventry needs a team to pull a wagon."

"And me and Bug need mounts," J.T. added.

"Joe Smith's a hostler for the stagecoach. He's always got someone trading out or buying new animals. I shoed a team for him yesterday."

"Is he at the stage office then?" Mr. Coventry asked.

"He's usually at the livery across the street, but one of his mares is foaling, so he's out at his place today–about a mile east of town. Just follow the main road to the first Y and go left. It's the second place on the right. Tell him I sent you."

"I will. Thanks, Cooper."

Her unexpected meeting with Zion Coldwell stirred Lark. A kettle ready to boil over, his visit stoked her young fire. She had everything a girl could want, pampered by her mama, and with her daddy wrapped tightly around a dainty pinky finger– everything except a man. Being 14 and not having a beau riled Lark to no end. If she thought about it, she could work up a good headache. Of course, that hurt, but then her mama would send Evan or Ethan for ice, which she relished under the lace canopy of her white ironwork bed.

She watched the men walk from the mercantile to the smithy, repulsed by the jeering bug-eyed man who turned to ogle her beauty.

"You coming in?" Donald Matheny asked.

"Yes, Daddy." Lark lifted a coaxing gaze and paused for effect. "Daddy, I was thinking I might pay a visit out to Briar Hollow."

"Whatever for, Lark?"

"I was concerned when none of the Johnsons showed up for prayer Tuesday night. And now that I know Rosalie was nursing poor little Penny Coldwell," Lark clasped her hands, tucked them under her chin, and shook her head back and forth, "I just thought it would be the charitable thing to do."

Lark's uncharacteristic surge of compassion stupefied Donald Matheny. With a knitted brow, he stared in disbelief, but softened as he studied the innocent face of his daughter. "Why don't you take some candy with you?"

"You have the best ideas, Daddy."

A knock sounded at the door of the Johnson cabin just as they finished their midday meal. Marigold answered. "Hi, Lark." The family still seated at the table looked at one another in surprise. Lark Matheny was not a regular visitor to the Johnson home.

"Hello, Marigold."

"Won't you come in?"

"Yes, thank you." Lark entered the cabin and laid off her powder blue satin bonnet on the sideboard. "It's hot today." She dabbed her neck and forehead with an embroidered, lace-edged handkerchief.

"We have some cool cider," Pansy Joy offered. "Lucas carried some in from the springhouse before dinner."

"Something cold would be nice."

Rosalie stood and began clearing the table. "We'll have some plum pudding after I clear these dishes. Why don't you sit down and cool off."

"Are the plums ready?"

"Not really, but Pa brought a few early ones in yesterday. It's a tradition to make a pudding for the family with the first fruits."

"I got to lick the spoon." Lucas grinned up at Lark.

"So you like sweets?" she asked.

"I sure do. Doesn't everyone?"

Lark laughed. "I don't know anyone who doesn't. We sell lots of candy at the mercantile."

"Visiting the candy counter at your folks' store is Lukey's favorite part of going to town," said Marigold.

"Then you'll be happy to know I brought some candy with me."

"For me?" Lucas could hardly believe his ears.

"Yes, for you," said Lark. "There's enough for everyone." Lark made a show of pulling a paper bag from her reticule while looking around the cabin for signs of Zion's sister. Coming up short, she fixed her gaze on Rosalie.

"I heard you were nursing a sick little girl."

An alarm triggered in Rosalie. Lark looked innocent enough, but something didn't ring true. Rosalie could not remember a time Lark Matheny paid a social call to the Johnsons. "I have been. Penny Coldwell. She's in my room sleeping."

"I met her brother in town, and when he stopped by to see me again today, he filled me in."

Lark's comment raised hackles on the back of Rosalie's neck she didn't know were there. "I see."

"Could you wake her up? I've just been dying to meet her . . . ever since the first day I met Zion and helped him choose a gift for her."

The familiar use of Zion's first name and the revelation of their developing relationship did not bode well with Rosalie. Had Zion been playing Lark all the while he was bringing her flowers?

"She's still recovering," Matthias interjected. "It wouldn't do to wake a sick child for such a frothy reason."

Lark tried the pouty-lipped look that worked so well with her father, but Matthias wouldn't budge on the matter.

CHAPTER 22

Joe Smith proved to be a good source. With the arrangements for the purchase of a wagon team and two mounts complete, Smith agreed to stable and feed the horses until Zion's group set out on their journey. Mr. Coventry planned to see Garth's wagon after dinner, and Zion wanted to squeeze in a visit with Penny beforehand.

Pleased at their progress, Zion dropped the men at the lodge and handed the reins of the wagon to Balim. West answered his whistle, and without stopping to saddle the sleek stallion, Zion grabbed hold of his thick mane and heaved himself up on his bare back. In a matter of seconds he was out of the corral. Balim shut the door behind him with a sagacious smirk. "He's done got it bad, the boy do." Balim shook his head and watched Zion disappear down the lane heading toward the Johnson place.

Rosalie and Pansy Joy were working in the kitchen garden filling baskets with colorful produce. Rosalie picked meaty tomatoes from staked plants while Pansy Joy harvested yellow squash and cucumbers from their mounds. From where they worked, the girls heard the fast approach of horses' hooves. West pounded down the lane and barely slowed to a stop when Zion jumped off, unaware the ladies watched his arrival and dismount.

Pansy Joy cupped her hands around her mouth and yelled. "Is there a fire somewhere?"

Zion strolled to the garden, hat in hand, wearing a churlish grin. "Afternoon, ladies. I wanted to get out earlier, but I had to take some folks to town first."

"We know all about your day already," said Pansy Joy with an impish look on her face.

"How's that now?" Curiosity swelled in Zion. He studied the face of each girl. Pansy Joy was alight with her usual good humor, but Rosalie would not be read.

"Balim came by this morning to check on Penny, and then Lark Matheny paid us a call after dinner." Zion knew about Balim's visit, but Lark's came as a surprise. He didn't expect Lark and the Johnsons were bosom buddies, their personalities and lifestyles as far as the east is from the west.

"Do tell." Zion wondered if Lark's visit had anything to do with the stoic expression Rosalie wore. And although she appeared to be looking him in the eye, her focus rested somewhere higher than his pupils, on his forehead. "How are you today, Rosalie?"

"I'm fine, Mr. Coldwell. I'm sure you'd like to see Penny. Marigold's in with her." Rosalie pivoted, turning her side to Zion, and returned to the staked tomato plants heavy with orange-red fruit. Zion watched for a minute as she carefully examined the tomatoes for ripeness, peeking and poking around leafy stems. He gave Pansy Joy a questioning look, but she just rolled her eyes and shrugged her shoulders.

"I'll do that then." Zion adjusted his hat. He stuffed his hands in his pockets and walked to the front door.

"Rosalie, what's come over you?" Pansy Joy asked after Zion disappeared in the cabin.

Rosalie looked at her sister, the picture of apathy and innocence. "I don't know what you mean," she said. She returned to her task, carefully inspecting each tomato.

"Did something happen between you and Mr. Coldwell? The cold shoulder you gave him sent shivers down my back, and it's hot as blazes out here."

"No. Nothing's happened."

Nothing, my foot. Something was going on, and Pansy Joy was going to figure it out. Sweet, stable Rosalie was acting completely out of character. "I think I've got enough here. I'll go in and start supper. How about you?"

Rosalie kept her head down, concentrating on her work. "I have a couple more plants to check, and then I have some clipping to do in the rose garden."

Seated on the edge of the bed, a checkerboard between them, Penny laughed out loud at Marigold.

"What? You ain't never ate a mudbug?" Marigold asked.

"I've never even heard of them before." Penny studied Marigold's freckled face. "Are you joshing?"

"Well," Marigold drew out the word, a sparkle lighting her big brown eyes. "You might know them by another name."

"I knew it. You were teasing me."

"How can you say such a thing? I only tell the full gospel truth."

"You better, now that you brought the gospel into this."

"When you get stronger, I'll show you. We'll wade out in the creek, and catch some. They're all the time hiding out around the springhouse." Marigold lifted a black checker, took a double jump and landed her piece at the end of the board. "King me!"

"You were just trying to distract me, weren't you?" Penny glared at the vibrant girl seated across from her.

"How could you think such a thing? I was just filling you in on the local wildlife." Penny dropped a black checker on top of Marigold's and then studied the board to take her next move.

"I call them mudbugs, but some folks call them crawdaddies."

"I know what crawdaddies are," said Penny, "but to tell the truth, I've never eaten one."

"There's not a lot of meat on them, but if you get a bucket full, they'll fill your gullet."

"They kind of scare me with their pinchers. Did you ever get pinched?"

"Sometimes they pinch me, before I pinch them."

"You pinch them?"

"Suck their heads and pinch their tails." Marigold nodded her head matter-of-factly, honey braids jolting up and down. Penny's slight hand flew to her mouth in disbelief as a knock sounded at the door. Lucas rose from his favorite spot in front of the fireplace to answer it.

"Hi, Lucas." Zion filled the doorway. The sun beamed in the house behind his broad shoulders.

"Hi, Mr. Coldwell. Are you here to see Penny?"

"I sure am, but it's nice to see you, too." Zion stepped inside the cabin door. "Are you playing with those blocks?"

"Yup. Pa made them for me." Lucas lifted a smooth block for Zion to inspect.

"He did a very nice job. I used to love to play with blocks."

"You want to make a tower with me?" The sweetness of the boy touched Zion. He never had a brother to play with–just like Lucas.

"Let me check on Penny first, and then we'll see if there's time." Zion chucked him under the chin. "Thanks for asking."

Zion heard the giggling as he approached the bedroom. Penny sat up in the bed, a flush of pink on her cheeks. "You just proved it," he said.

"What's that, Zion?"

"A merry heart doeth good like a medicine." He smiled at the girls. "Look at you, Penny, sitting up there with the color coming back in your face."

"Wait 'til I get some mudbugs into her. That'll really help," Marigold teased.

"You don't really suck their heads, do you?" Penny asked, a look of refusal lingering in her blue eyes.

"Only after they're cooked."

Zion laughed at the pair and joined in the fun. "You've had them, too, Penny."

"No, I haven't!" Penny answered in disbelief.

"You don't remember Liddy's special boil?"

"Of course I do, but that was stew. It had potatoes and corn and sausage and onions."

"That was a recipe Liddy got from Emiline after she moved up from New Orleans."

Penny's disbelief turned to horror. "You mean there were crawdaddy heads in there?"

"Not the heads. She just used the tail meat." Zion watched relief cross Penny's face. "Balim sucked the heads."

"Oh, no!"

"Oh, yes he did. You can ask him."

Pansy Joy walked in on the ruckus. "What's going on in here?" she asked, hands on her curved hips.

"Just a little menu planning," Zion said.

"That's right," Marigold added. "You up to fixing some mudbugs if me and Penny bring some in?"

Pansy Joy caught the gist and the look on Penny's face. "With the tomatoes and peppers coming in, we could make up some spicy fritters."

"Do you use their heads for that?" Penny asked.

"No. Not enough meat to take the time to clean them," Pansy Joy said. Her expression softened and she patted Penny on the leg. "Are you feeling up to going crawdaddin'?"

"I am feeling better, but maybe not today."

"You're getting your strength back a bit at a time," said Pansy Joy. "You'll be out wading in the creek before you know it."

"I bet some plum pudding would perk her right up. She didn't get any earlier. She was sleeping," Marigold clarified for Zion.

"Would you like some, Penny?" Pansy Joy asked.

"That sounds wonderful. Do you think I could eat it at the table?"

"I think we better check with Rosalie since she's been nursing you. Mr. Coldwell, would you mind going outside and asking Rosalie if she thinks it's all right for Penny to sit up at the table for a spell?"

"I sure will." He tipped his head and left the bedroom.

"Come with me in the kitchen, Lucas." Pansy Joy said. "I'll let you lick the spoon again."

Zion stepped out in the sunshine. It took his eyes a minute to adjust to the bright light, and when they did, Rosalie was nowhere in sight. He could see she wasn't in the wildflower garden out front and considered she might be in one of the outbuildings, but decided to check the rose garden first. Circling around to the east side of the cabin, he spied her sitting on a bench beneath a grape arbor. Vines climbed the sides and top of the white wooden structure, and bunches of green grapes dangled beneath full, veined leaves.

Rosalie sat–scissors, gloves and hands resting on the skirt of her calico dress–staring at nothing, the same unreadable expression on her face Zion had seen earlier.

Not the bubbling beauty of Pansy Joy, or Lark Matheny for that matter, Rosalie's delicate features drew Zion. She sat on the bench, her tall carriage erect but relaxed beneath a wide-brimmed straw hat. Zion watched wisps of auburn hair play around her forehead and ears. The same auburn curved in fine brows over her startling celadon eyes, an unusual color that appeared yellow-green at times, more so as she sat beneath the grape vines in the summer sun.

She reminded him of a deer, graceful, yet skittish, and he wondered if she would run if she heard his approach. Zion wanted to cup her face in his hands and make her look him in the eyes. He didn't know Rosalie that well, but he had not pegged her as the moody type. She seemed distracted. With deliberate steps, Zion walked past the rose garden, his eyes focused on the girl in front of him.

Rosalie looked up. She saw Zion and her heart betrayed her reason. How could these waves of emotion flood her senses when Zion Coldwell was a slave-owning flirt? She watched him walk toward her, a shy smile on his face, unlike the gregarious grin he strode in with just a few minutes before. She glanced down at her lap, and then into Zion's face. The two locked eyes. Zion continued walking, until an exposed tree root brought him to his knees in a hard landing a few feet in front of Rosalie.

Startled, Rosalie jumped to her feet. The scissors fell, point down, from her lap onto the big toe of her right foot. "Oh!" she exclaimed. She reached down to grab her throbbing toe, lost her balance and fell on the ground inches from Zion.

Pride more injured than his aching knees, Zion reached out to help Rosalie into a sitting position. "Are you all right?"

The skirt of Rosalie's dress had received a slight tear when the scissors fell, but that was the least of her concern.

"I think so."

"I'm so sorry. It was all my fault." Zion's strong arm pressed against Rosalie's back. "Here, let me see."

"No . . . I can't . . . I mean, I'm all right." Rosalie had a secret. She loved the feel of warm soil between her toes and worked barefoot in the garden whenever the weather permitted.

Her flustered state befuddled Zion compounded by the wonderful feel of Rosalie tucked beneath his arm.

"Young man." Matthias stood on the path that led to the orchard and surveyed the scene on the grass. "Do we need to have a talk?"

CHAPTER 23

Heat flooded the faces of both Rosalie and Zion. "Sir." Zion scrambled to his feet. Reaching out, he aided Rosalie to hers. "I'm afraid in my clumsiness Rosalie's foot got hurt."

"You weren't a dancing out here?" Matthias watched the young man squirm. An observant man, and usually quiet, Matthias enjoyed the moment in good humor. He knew his girl–trusted her, too. Rosalie never gave him cause to worry. The way she mooned after Lark Matheny left–now that had concerned him. He had watched, too, the way she responded to Zion. A pa knows his girl.

The blush on Rosalie's cheeks deepened, and Zion stuttered in disbelief. Did Rosalie's father think he was sparking with her right on his property in the middle of the day?

"I assure you, Mr. Johnson, we were doing no such thing." Zion brushed the grass from his britches, still searching for the right words to say.

Rosalie balanced precariously on one good leg and the heel of her right foot. "Mr. Coldwell fell, Pa; and when I got up to check on him, I dropped my scissors on my toe."

"That's right. She lost her balance."

"I saw how you was helping her balance there, Son." Matthias fed the fire and waited to see how it would burn.

"Pa!" Rosalie could scarcely believe her ears.

"Well, if that's the way of it, let me see your foot, girl."

Rosalie tucked the injured foot behind her, upsetting her balance for a second time. She would have fallen again if Zion hadn't reached out and grabbed her. He gave a quick look to Matthias and released Rosalie as soon as she regained her footing.

"I'm sorry, Pa. I can't."

Rosalie never refused her father. Concern shot across Matthias's face.

"What's wrong, girl?"

"It's just, well, I don't have any shoes on."

Matthias understood the import of her statement. Sharon raised their daughters to be modest and upright. He moved to Rosalie, took her elbow and motioned for Zion to do the same. Together they assisted her as she hobbled to the bench.

"Go fetch Pansy Joy with some water and bandages," Matthias instructed Zion.

"Yes, sir." Zion, thankful to be out from under Matthias's scrutiny, hurried to the house. The door closed, and then flung open a moment later. Marigold and Lucas flew out.

Inside the cabin, Pansy Joy scurried for bandages. "Put some water in that basin," she instructed Zion. Supplies in hand, she joined her family under the grape arbor.

"What happened, Zion? I couldn't hear what was going on? Is everything all right?"

"I'm sure it will be, Buttercup," Zion soothed the girl. "Rosalie hurt her foot, but Pansy Joy's going to see to it."

"Is it hurt bad?"

"I don't know. She wouldn't let me see it."

"Why ever not?"

The corners of Zion's lips rose in a mirthful smirk. "It seems she didn't have any shoes or stockings on. It wouldn't have been proper."

"You see my feet all the time," Penny said, a confused look on her face.

"Things are different with brothers and sisters than with men and women."

"Can we pray for her?" Penny asked. Zion wondered what Balim had shared with his sister. Did she know he had taken to praying again?

"Sure."

Penny scooted over on the bed and patted the mattress. Zion sat beside her and held her small hands in his. "I'll start," said Penny.

"Lord, thank You for Miss Johnson and all the kindness she's shown to me. I pray that You will touch her foot and ease her pain. Please bring her a quick healing."

"And Lord," Zion began. Penny stared in reverent awe as she watched her brother pray for the first time since their parents died. "I pray there would be no infection or complications. Let Your abundant blessings rest over this household, in Jesus' name."

A peaceful smile spread over Penny's face and she squeezed Zion's hands. "Thank You, Jesus."

"How about a game of checkers?" Zion hoped to distract Penny from worrying over Rosalie.

"I don't think I could concentrate on it."

"That seemed to help Marigold's game."

"I think that was her intention all along," Penny said. "But I didn't mind. We had a grand time."

"I almost forgot." Zion reached in his vest and pulled out the bilbo catcher. "I brought this for you."

"I forgot all about it myself." Penny took the toy and flipped the ball, attempting to catch it in the wooden cup attached by a string. "Let's play best out of ten."

The two occupied themselves with their game until the door opened. Aided by Pansy Joy and Matthias, Rosalie limped into the cabin.

"To bed with you girl," Matthias ordered.

Zion stood and Penny scooted over to make room for her new bedmate. Zion gave them some privacy as Rosalie adjusted her skirts under the summer quilt.

"We need to get some ice on that foot." Matthias turned to Zion. "Would you mind running to town for some?"

"I'd be glad to. Where do I go?"

"The Matheny boys run the ice house on the south side of town. Just keep following the main road and you'll see it. It's a big building by the lake." Matthias looked around the cabin and saw the water bucket in the kitchen. "Pansy Joy, empty that bucket. He can fill it up and we can keep some extra ice in the springhouse for later."

As he mounted West, Zion regretted not taking the time to saddle him before leaving the lodge. Carrying a bucket of ice while riding bareback might prove a challenge, but it was a challenge he was willing to face. The sight of Rosalie standing, getting stabbed in the foot and falling to the ground replayed in Zion's memory.

He closed the miles to the ice house quickly and dismounted in front of the barn-like structure. A lanky red-headed young man sat in a rocking chair whittling on a piece of hickory. Zion did a double-take as his mirror image stepped out from around the building. Twins.

"Howdy." The seated man greeted Zion.

"Is this the ice house?"

"Yup." The standing man answered.

"Could I get a bucket of ice, please?"

"Just a bucket?" one man asked.

"Not a block?" said the other.

"Whatever will fit in here." Zion lifted the bucket.

The ice house, located near a freshwater lake, was filled each winter with large blocks of ice cut out of the lake and dragged by sledge into the building. A manmade underground chamber created a bed where ice blocks, insulated with sawdust and straw, were stacked high to be preserved for use during the summer months.

"I'll get it, Ethan." The ruddy man grabbed the bucket from Zion.

"No, I'll get it, Evan." Ethan fought his brother over the handle until it broke free of the bucket.

"See what you done, you ninny?"

"Hush your mouth or I'll clean your plow, blowhard."

Zion stepped between the two. "Pull in your horns fellows. I've got an injured girl that needs some ice before swelling sets in."

"Why didn't you say so?" Ethan looked at Zion.

"We can't have a girl suffering needlessly," said Evan.

"If you'll work on getting the ice, I think I can put this bucket back together."

"Sure thing, mister."

The twins disappeared in the building, followed by the sound of a chisel hammering into a block of hard ice. Zion sat on the rocker, placed the bucket between his knees and worked the handle back in place. His own receptacle in hand, Evan—or was it Ethan— carried the ice to Zion and filled the bucket.

"What do I owe you?"

"You just take that on out to the girl. Who'd you say it was got hurt?"

"Rosalie Johnson. She dropped scissors on her foot."

"That's my Katie's best friend and neighbor."

"She ain't your Katie, you deadbeat."

Zion intervened. "I thank you for the ice, but I have to run now. I'll tell Rosalie you sent this out for her. I'm sure she'll share your good deed with Katie."

"Tell her it was Evan."

"You tell her Ethan done it."

This town is loaded with Mathenys, Zion thought as he hurried back to the Johnson place. *It's a wonder it's not named Mathenyville.* Zion chortled at his own humor.

By the time he arrived at the house, Pansy Joy had Rosalie settled in the bed, her left foot tucked under the quilt and the right one resting on a slight incline covered with a towel. "It seems she twisted her ankle when she fell," Pansy Joy said. "She's going to have to stay off it for a couple of days. The ice should help, though."

Remorse filled Zion. He felt responsible for Rosalie's injury–a double injury at that. "I should take Penny back to the lodge. She's doing better now and you have a lot on your hands here."

"I wish you wouldn't, Mr. Coldwell." Pansy Joy lowered her voice to a whisper. "Rosalie's not a good patient. I won't be able to keep her in bed. Having Penny here might distract her and keep her off her feet."

Zion thought about it. The plan made sense. Penny's condition, improved for sure, was still weakened. "If you are certain, Miss Johnson, I don't want to be any more of an inconvenience than I already have been."

"Since we got through that first rough night, Penny's been no problem at all. I confess, I'll miss her sorely when you take her away."

"And I haven't seen Penny smile so much in a long while. She's thriving here with your family." Zion looked around the homey cabin wishing he could provide the same warm environment for his sister. Pansy Joy detected the longing in his gaze.

Capable and strong as he was, Zion didn't have a home; but he planned to. After this venture out to Virginia City, he thought he would know the best place for him and Penny to settle. And they could pick any place they chose, after he saw Balim on his way to Canada.

"I best be going then," Zion said. "Is it all right if I say goodbye?"

"Sure. I'll be in with the ice pack in just a minute." Pansy Joy scooped ice out of the bucket into a towel. "Marigold, I need you to run this bucket out to the springhouse as soon as I'm finished."

Zion poked his head in the bedroom door. The tender sight of Rosalie and Penny laid out on the same bed holding hands did something to his heart. They were beautiful, and they were beautiful together. He stepped into the room and leaned his back against the wall.

"Hey."

"Hey," Penny answered. Rosalie offered a weak smile.

"I just had the best plum pudding in the whole world," said Penny.

"You did?"

"Marigold said I was part of a Johnson family tradition this year."

Zion watched the content girl. "You were? How's that?"

Rosalie answered. "Every year Pa picks some of the first fruits from the plum trees and Pansy Joy makes plum pudding from Mama's recipe. Ever since the trees started bearing, we have had a little first fruits celebration."

"Mr. Johnson said it's his way of making a special acknowledgment of God's provision," said Penny, "like a festival in Bible times."

"First fruits are a promise of future harvest, and the Bible says Jesus is the fulfillment of the First Fruits Festival," said Rosalie. "Pa read the Scripture earlier, 1 Corinthians 5:20: 'But now is Christ risen from the dead, and become the firstfruits of them that slept.' Jesus was raised first, and there will be a harvest of resurrected souls to follow.'"

Zion recalled his Bible studies. "First fruits, then Pentecost, right?"

"Right." Rosalie smiled. The Spirit of God stirred in her bosom.

Reluctant to leave, Zion forced himself to bid farewell. "I guess I better head back to the lodge. Mr. Coventry wants to see Garth Eldridge's wagon before he decides which one to buy."

"When will I see you again?" Penny asked.

"I hope I haven't worn out my welcome." Zion looked at Rosalie, pretty as a picture with her hair fanning out on the pillow beneath her.

"We might need more ice," said Rosalie.

Zion grinned. Whatever was bothering Rosalie earlier in the day seemed to have passed. Talking about the Lord can do that, he supposed, his own heart warmed by God's sweet presence.

"I'll see you girls later, then." Zion winked and disappeared out the door.

CHAPTER 24

"**M**rs. Coventry would prefer to purchase the Eldridge wagon over the one at Matheny's, I'm certain." Thaddeus Coventry sat on the porch at Comfort Lodge in a padded ladder-back rocking chair situated next to the swing in which Zion sat.

Zion smiled at the thought. He doubted any woman would choose the brown unfinished wagon with a flat wooden buckboard over the shiny green wagon with yellow trim and padded seat. Beyond expert craftsmanship, Garth had detailed the wagon for Pansy Joy with tender loving care. "I can't say as I blame her. That bench seat looks a lot more comfortable, and we have a lot of miles to cover."

"Yes, it does; however, we could pad the one from the mercantile."

"That we could." Zion swayed back and forth in the swing in an easy, fluid motion.

"Mr. Nester mentioned we might consider purchasing both wagons."

"He did, did he?" Zion had wondered more than once what J.T. had discussed with Thaddeus that morning at the Matheny woodshop.

"Yes. He said with the length of the trip, one wagon could be filled entirely with supplies for the four-month journey. If weather got bad, we could use an extra wagon for the women to ride in and store the bedding and items we'll need on the trail."

"I see. Kind of like a rolling house." Zion worried his chin, fuzzy from the lack of a razor that morning. "I've got your furniture and house goods on the big wagon. I think we have adequate stowage and room for supplies, but with Nester and Perkins coming now . . ."

"I was thinking of my family's comfort," Thaddeus assured Zion.

Zion speculated at J.T. Nester's influence on Thad Coventry. He seemed willing to go to a lot of expense and trouble to have him along on the journey; but he had no clue what a rapscallion Nester really was, Perkins too, for that matter. If Zion told him what he knew, he doubted Mr. Coventry would believe him. *Lord, give me wisdom,* Zion prayed.

"That would mean purchasing another team of horses," Zion pondered aloud.

"Yes, but I've counted the cost and believe it would be a good investment. Settlers are certain to need fresh horses, a good wagon, too. I could sell the lot after we arrive."

"We would have to wait until next week to head out then," said Zion, "but truth be told, I'd be thankful for Penny to have more time to regain some strength. It's probably Providence at work, ordering our steps."

"I'm a believer myself, Mr. Coldwell."

"Would you like me to take you around to finalize your arrangements?"

"That won't be necessary, but thank you for the offer." Thaddeus stood and grasped the knob on the lodge's front door. "You have much to do to prepare for the trip, and Mr. Nester has offered to assist me. Good evening, Mr. Coldwell."

"Good evening to you, too, Mr. Coventry."

Thaddeus slipped in the door. Zion rose to his feet, and an uneasy feeling settled over him. He did have much to tend to before leaving Washington. He mentally scrolled down the list as he headed to the barn. Passing through the open barn door, he ambled onto a peculiar sight: beefy Balim sitting cross-legged in the hay scratching the chin of a mewing kitten.

"If you aren't a sight, Balim." Zion grinned at the man. "What are you doing with that kitten?"

"Well, Massa Zion, it's like this," Balim continued his ministrations, the cat arching her back under his big hand. "I finished with them mules and sat down in the hay to cool off fo a minute. This here tabby come alookin' for some lovin', and ole Balim gave it to her." Balim scratched the brindled feline behind her ears. "All a God's creatures could do with a kind stroke now an agin."

Zion watched in silence. A touch was a nice thing indeed. He recalled the feel of Rosalie leaning against his arm. Even with knees throbbing from the pain of a fall, the pleasure of a woman's touch compelled a man. "Cat got your tongue?" Balim teased. "I can send this little girl right on out the barn door."

"With one swift kick?"

"How cin you say such a thing, Massa Zion?"

"You know I'm just blowing smoke, Balim."

Balim studied Zion's face. "Somethin' bothering you? You ain't always ornery like this."

A sigh slipped out of Zion's parted lips, and his chest gave a weary heave. "I guess I have a lot on my mind." Zion fell back in the straw, plucked a piece and stuck it between his teeth.

"You want ole Balim to scratch you under yo scruffy chin?"

"Nah." Zion stretched and cupped his hands beneath his head. "You could tickle my ears with a little advice, though."

"You tell ole Balim all about it, Massa Zion, and we'll seek the Lawd fo His counsel. Yes, we will."

"That's good advice already." Zion turned to look in Balim's attentive eyes. Since childhood, he had found comfort with Balim. When he had fallen from the swing, he had run to the stables where Balim tended his scratches. When he was five and got a fishing hook stuck in his thumb, Balim pulled it out. Zion used to struggle to lift bales of hay into the feeder. Balim would reach an arm over Zion's straining back, grab the cord on the bale and help him heave it in.

"I don't know what I'm going to do without you, Balim." Zion grew melancholy.

"You don' have ta worry 'bout that just yet. We've got a lot of miles to cover 'fore we says goodbye. Who knows what the good Lawd has in store 'fore then."

"I was just talking to Mr. Coventry. It seems he's planning on buying two wagons." Zion paused before adding, "at the suggestion of Nester, of course."

"Don' really see no need fo that, but that's no nevermind. What the enemy means fo evil, God can turn to good."

A spark of hope lit in Zion's confused heart. "You're right, Balim, absolutely right."

"No bunko artist like Nester's gonna take down the children of the Lawd."

"Balim," Zion pushed himself to a sitting position and propped himself up with his arms locked behind him, "you make me feel like I could fetch some smooth stones and a slingshot and knock Goliath down for the slicing."

"Slice his fool head right off his contrary shoulders, messing with God's elect. Yes, suh."

"I know I've made things right with the Lord, but I'm still fighting for my faith. I think the accident pretty near knocked it clean out of me, and it's taking time to rebuild–like Penny after her bout with flux."

"She looked a might waterish this morning, but she had some color in her cheeks, some life in her eyes."

"I think she'll make a full recovery."

"Yes, suh, Massa Zion." Balim looked at the young man next to him with genuine affection. "And ole Balim thinks you will, too."

The sound of footsteps outside the barn quieted Balim and Zion. They were hidden from view behind the hay and listened in on the conversation taking place just outside the barn.

"He's taking the bait, then?" Perkins's heightened curiosity caused his bug eyes to protrude farther than usual. He rubbed his bony hands together, looking for all the world like a human praying mantis.

"Hook, line and sinker." J.T. stuck his thumbs under his suspenders, glad to be rid of the vest, tie and coat. "It's working like a charm. Coventry's eating right out of my hand."

"He's going for both of the wagons?"

"In the best interest of his family, of course." J.T. sneered and Bug snickered. "I think he's beginning to realize Coldwell can't live up to his advertisements, especially when we put a spoke or two in his wheels."

"Coldwell's wet behind the ears, anyway." Perkins pulled a flask from his pocket. "Did you get a lead on some whiskey?"

"I'm taking Coventry to town tomorrow. When he goes to the bank, I plan to stop by the Golden Goose. I'll see if we can't get some belly wash for the road."

"Nothing like a swig of oh-be-joyful to ease the trail dust down a feller's throat." Perkins took a long draw, and then offered his flask to Nester. "So this Coventry still has money in the bank? He ain't got it all with him?"

"No, but we'll have it before it's all said and done."

"What's your plan?"

"I'm still finalizing the details, but we'll wind this up and never have to shove the queer again."

"Folks on the riverboat was catching on, weren't they?"

"Making five or ten dollar bills would have been a better idea than drawing up singles. People see them too often and know what they're supposed to look like."

"We'll have a pocket full of the real thing soon, though, hey J.T.?" Bug swigged on his flask. Its contents warmed his innards and loosened his lips. "What about that big black boy? You think he'll give us any problems?"

"Nah. You know colored folks is dumb as doorknobs. He's got the brawn of a buffalo, but the brains of a banty chicken." J.T. hooted at his analogy.

"Yeah. Like a punkin'-headed jackylantern." Bug slapped a skeletal knee and almost lost his balance.

"You better lay off the spirits, Bug. You're gettin' all roostered up."

"I don't care a continental. I'll just take Sally up to our room and settle in for the night." Bug lifted his flask. "You ready, Sally? What's that? You want another kiss? Come to your Buggy-baby, sweetheart."

J.T. shook his head. "Bug, you're a lunatic. I'll be up after while. I'm gonna sit on the porch and smoke a cigar." He watched the tipsy man make his way up the path from the barn and then followed behind.

When the sound of footsteps fell off, Zion looked at Balim. Rage brewed behind his blue eyes. "That's about more than I can stomach."

"Why, Massa Zion, that's the blessin' of the good Lawd."

"How can you say that, Balim? They called you a pumpkin-headed jack-o-lantern with the brains of a doorknob. You call that the blessing of God?"

"White folks been calling black folks names a long time, but they words don' make things so. And they's some black folks that ain't got nothing good to say 'bout whites neither. It's the Word of the Lawd, Massa Zion, that's what we need to be a listenin' to.

"In the Book, Daniel was atalkin' to ole King Nebbykanezar, and he said they's a God in heaven that reveals secrets and makes 'em known to kings. See what Jesus done for you tonight?"

"Showed me I was being played for a fool?"

"Nah, suh. He's revealing the plans of the enemy so you can know how to fight and pray."

Zion took a deep breath and weighed Balim's words. They rang true in his spirit and eased his roiling thoughts. "Balim, those lowlifes don't know who they're messing with, do they?" Zion hoped that someday he would have the wisdom and maturity he found in his friend.

"The good Lawd takes care a His own."

"I know, but I was talking about you. I think you have more wisdom than anyone I know."

"The fear a the Lawd's the beginning a wisdom, Massa Zion."

"You know, you're not anything like the Balaam in the Bible."

"Lawdy, I hope not. He done beat his po' donkey who was a tryin' to save him."

"He did get to see an angel."

"And speak the Word of the Lawd to them Moabites."

"God filled his mouth with blessings and turned the plans of the wicked people."

"Well maybe King Jesus has summpin like that for this ole Balim . . . exceptin' for beatin' the donkey."

"Maybe."

CHAPTER 25

Penny and Zion sat at the table in the Johnson's cabin. "I'm sorry I didn't make it back out last night," said Zion.

"I know you're busy. I was fine. Rosalie is good company. We talked about all kinds of things."

"Like what?"

"Like how she uses Marigold's beeswax to make things. See how shiny this table is?"

Zion studied the smooth plane of the table, a fine patina with a silky finish. "It's shiny at that."

"Rosalie makes wood polish out of beeswax."

"You don't say?" Zion enjoyed listening to Penny's enthusiasm. Always a good student, he enjoyed learning as much as she did.

"Yes. She said she shaves beeswax into a canning jar and adds in some turpentine. And you know, Rosalie. She has to put something sweet smelling in there, usually lavender she said."

"She does seem to like sweet smelling things."

"Do you know how the polish gets its color?"

"Why don't you tell me." Zion smiled as he watched his sister's hands in motion as she described the process.

"She puts in a bit of lamp black for dark woods and yellow ochre for light ones. Then she seals it up tight and puts it out in the sun. She shakes it up every day, and when the wax is melted into the turpentine, it's ready."

"We'll have to try that when we get settled."

"Yeah. Maybe Awinita will give me some ochre."

"Who's Awinita?"

"She's an Indian lady–the Johnson's neighbor. She lives on the other side of the orchards and there's a clay deposit by the creek there."

"I didn't realize there were Indians around here."

"There aren't many. Awinita married a white man, and they have a baby named Sky."

"Did you get to meet them?"

"Not yet. But I hope to."

"It looks like we'll be in town until midweek," Zion said. "I heard there was going to be an ice cream social and fireworks on the Fourth of July."

Penny's eyes lit with excitement. "Really?" She grabbed her brother's arm. "Do you mean it, Zion?"

"It looks that way." Zion squeezed the hand on his arm. "And it looks like you are feeling much better. Are you ready to come back to the lodge?"

Penny let go of Zion's arm. An unusual reticence stole over her demeanor. Gliding the palm of her hand over the polished tabletop, she rubbed the surface in small circles with her fingertips. "I really like it here, Zion," she said in a hushed tone.

"I do, too, Penny. Washington's a nice little town."

"It's more than the town." Penny continued caressing the tabletop, eyes downcast. "I like the people–even the ones I haven't met yet."

"How can you like people you haven't met?"

"The Johnsons tell me about them." Penny turned her face to

Zion's. "I want to meet Awinita and Sky. I've never seen a real papoose before.

"And a girl named Lark came to visit while I was asleep. Isn't that a pretty name? She brought me candy, and I didn't get to thank her for it.

"Rosalie's best friend Katie lives next door, and she sounds so nice. Her brother Garth is Pansy Joy's beau, you know, and they're getting married at the stroke of midnight on January 1. Did you ever hear of such a thing?"

"No, I never did. But Pansy Joy has her own ideas, doesn't she?"

"She does." Penny stopped for a moment, searching her memory banks. "Oh, I forgot about the Matheny brothers. I guess they're both hog wild about Katie."

"I met them yesterday. They run the ice house." Zion chuckled. "They are quite a pair."

"That reminds me. There are two spinster ladies in town, Eleanor and Ollie May Goheen. They're always trying to outdo one another in charitable works, filling missionary barrels and such. And then there's Reverend and Mrs. Dryfus. They have a daughter about my age named Charity." Penny quieted, deep in thought.

"More than the people I want to meet, I really like the ones I know already–the Erlangers, the Johnsons, Rosalie. I don't understand how people can crawl right into a heart so fast, just like they always belonged there."

"Maybe God put an empty spot there because He knew they were coming along."

"Maybe."

Both elbows on the table, Zion cocked his head and rubbed his forehead with one hand. He studied Penny out of the corner of his eye, and realized how much he agreed with her, how much his own heart had been effected by the people of Washington–Briar Hollow in particular. He and Penny both had some empty spots in their hearts they needed God to fill–not the gaping wounds of several months ago, but still pockets of loneliness for their lost family and home.

"Penny?"

"Yes?"

"I have something to share with you." Zion weighed his words and decided to reveal part of his plans with his sister. "When we finish this trip out West, we're coming back here."

Penny could hardly believe her ears. "Oh, Zion! Really? It's all I've wanted these last few days. Can we get a place close by? I'll get to see Rosalie every day."

"Hold your horses. I didn't say we were moving here, just that we were coming back."

"What do you mean?" Confusion and disappointment mingled in Penny's blue eyes.

"I have some business to take care of, really important business I need to see to myself." Like a whirlybird twirling from the top of a maple tree, spiraling down into the dirt, Penny's soaring emotions crash landed on the wooden floor of the Johnson cabin. "Oh," she said dully.

"Hey, there." Zion lifted Penny's down-turned chin until she looked him in the eyes. "I didn't tell you that to make you sad, Buttercup. I thought you'd be happy."

"I . . . I will be." Penny said, offering a brave front. "I just got so excited and now I have to get used to the idea."

Zion watched Penny's emotions flying up and down like the handle on a butter churn, a handle he manipulated. "I tell you what."

"What?"

"Let's work on that supply list again. We'll get everything ready before the rest of the folks get in town. The quicker we roll out of Washington, the quicker we'll roll back in."

"All right," Penny agreed. "But you're sure we can stay for the Fourth of July?"

"I'll promise you that, Penny." Zion received a small smile for his promise. "Now let's look at that list." Zion pulled a sheet of paper and a nubby pencil from beneath his vest. He unfolded the paper and licked the lead pencil tip.

"Before we start, do you mind if I check on Rosalie? She's had an icepack on her ankle since after breakfast. I told Pansy Joy I'd take it away before it melted all over the bed."

Zion scooted back from the table. "I'll come with you." He rose and started walking to the bedroom door.

"Hold on a minute," Penny stopped Zion with an outstretched hand. "Let me make sure she's covered proper before you go in there."

Zion smiled at his sister, imagining Penny and Rosalie discussing the issue of modesty and bare ankles as they lay next to each other on the feather bed. "That's a good idea, young lady."

Penny opened the door and slipped inside, followed by the sound of rustling sheets. "All's clear."

Zion about lost his breath when he saw Rosalie laid out on the bed, waves of auburn hair billowing over a white pillowcase, a sleepy look on her cherubic face. He cleared his throat. "Good morning."

Rosalie stretched and yawned. "Good morning, Zion." Small pink lips turned up in a sweet smile, a fuzzy, contented look in her green eyes. Zion schooled his wild thoughts running like buffalo on a stampede. He saw the cliff ahead and averted his imaginings before they plunged into an abyss of no return.

"I'm sorry to wake you, but I promised Pansy Joy I'd take off that ice pack before you were swimming in your bed."

"Who's tending who now?" Rosalie patted Penny's arm. "Thank you, Penny."

Penny reached beneath the light quilt and pulled the towel out, which she handed to Zion. "Would you mind taking that out? I'm feeling a bit lightheaded."

Zion took the towel in one hand and grabbed Penny's elbow with the other. Easing her around the bed, he sat her on the edge and helped her lay down.

"I didn't realize how weak I still am. It felt so good to be sitting up visiting with you."

Rosalie swept a golden braid out of the way as Penny reclined onto the pillow in Zion's arm. He raised her feet and slipped them on the bed. Rosalie adjusted the quilt over the tired girl.

"Let me take care of this, and I'll be right back."

"Why don't you bring a chair and we can still work on the list. I'm not sleepy, just tuckered out."

Zion took the wet towel into the kitchen, grabbed a chair and carried it into the bedroom. The passage between the bed and the outside wall was too narrow for the chair, so he placed it next to Rosalie and pulled out his paper and pencil.

"We were just going over our supply list," Zion explained.

"This should be interesting." Rosalie placed her hands on the bed at her sides and pushed to sit up. Zion watched her struggle, but stayed seated.

"Why don't you help Rosalie, like you helped me?" Penny asked.

Zion rose slowly from his chair. He looked into Rosalie's face and she gave a small nod of permission. Clasping her hands, he pulled her to a seated position, adjusted the pillows against the headboard and eased her back on them. A flush deepened the smattering of freckles that dotted the tops of her high cheekbones and the bridge of her upturned nose. "Thank you."

"You're welcome." Zion sat in the chair. He heard the crumple and felt the poke through his britches. Eyes wide, Zion lifted his bottom out of the seat and reached underneath for his paper and pencil. Penny and Rosalie looked at each other and burst out laughing. Zion ignored them.

"Where were we now? Camp equipment: We need woolen blankets, they run $2.50 apiece. The Coventrys are converting a wagon, so they don't need a tent, and we already have one. Everyone else has their own except the folks coming from Nashville."

"How much do tents run?" Rosalie asked.

"Depending on the size, $5 to $15." Zion continued working down the list. We already have a camp stove, coffee mill and coffee pot, frying pan, stew kettle and bread pans. I packed a butcher knife and tin plates, but we'll need some more of those and some cups.

"We'll pick up some nails, they run about 7 cents a pound, and soap, about 15 cents a pound."

"I can send some soap for you," Rosalie offered.

"Would you?" Penny asked. "You make the best soaps ever."

"I'm glad you like them. I'll send some lotion, too. You're bound to get dried out in the desert."

"Candles," said Zion.

"I have candles, too."

"She makes them out of the beeswax, like the polish I was telling you about."

Zion smiled at the twosome on the bed. "That would be nice, and I appreciate it. We're going to need quite a few though."

"I'll send some, and you can buy some, too."

"All right, those run about 15 cents a pound. We've already got a washtub and buckets for water and axle grease. Still need an axe, shovel and hoe, those run about $1.25 each, and some hand tools and rope."

"You have so many things, and you didn't even mention food," said Rosalie.

"We'll get to that," Zion said. "Need some more powder and shot, a good hunting knife." Zion flipped the paper over and winked at Rosalie. "Now for the vittles.

"Let's see, for each person, we need 150 pounds of flour, 20 pounds of cornmeal, 50 pounds of bacon, 15 pounds of beans, 5 pounds of rice, 15 pounds of dried fruit, 40 pounds of sugar, 10 pounds of coffee, 2 pounds of tea, 5 pounds of salt, and half a pound of saleratus."

"We have some ciphering to do," said Penny, overwhelmed by all the numbers dancing in her brain.

"I can do that later. I just wanted to make sure we weren't forgetting anything. I need to get this order in."

"What about some potatoes and onions? Those will keep for a long time." Penny thought for a moment. "And meat?"

"We can't exactly crate chickens and haul them across the desert. We'll eat bacon and shoot game on the trail, maybe even catch some fish along the way."

"I'd be happy to send some dried apples and peaches," said Rosalie. "Some preserves and honey, too."

"That would be sweet, just like you." Penny smiled at Rosalie. "I'll think of you with every bite."

CHAPTER 26

A pink and purple sunset played across the western sky, marking the direction Zion's party would soon be headed. Zion sat in the swing contemplating the day, his visit with Penny, and all the arrangements being made for their trip.

Thaddeus Coventry, aided by Nester and Perkins, had traveled to the Eldridge Farm and into town to finalize the purchase of the two wagons, an additional team of horses and sundry other errands unknown. Zion rode out to the mercantile to drop off the supply list, and Mrs. Matheny gushed with delight at the handsome order. She assured Zion it would be ready by the first of the week. He left without seeing Lark, and that suited him just fine. The girl played havoc with his mind and body.

His talk with Penny replayed over and over, her joy at thinking they were to settle in Washington, and then her dashed hopes when she realized that wasn't what Zion was saying after all. A picture of Rosalie, pink-cheeked and droopy eyed from sleep smiling up at him from her bed surfaced repeatedly. A man could get used to waking up to such a sight. He had watched the way she touched Penny with her long, graceful fingers, and he wondered what those fingers would feel like on his own forehead, his own cheek.

The front door to the lodge opened. "Mind if I join you?" James Erlanger stepped out on the porch.

"Not at all." Zion scooted over to make room on the bench swing.

"This is my favorite time of day, and the best place to watch the sun set."

"I was just thinking how we're heading out that way soon. I remember when I was little I used to think if I ran fast enough, I could see the sun hit the earth at sunset."

"And I used to think the moon was chasing me," said James. "Little boys have their own ways of thinking, don't they?"

"Sure do." James crossed his arms and leaned back in the swing enjoying the cool of the day and the colorful skyline over the treetops. "I've been meaning to talk with you about something."

"Oh?" Zion looked to the man next to him. James's posture and countenance allayed his immediate concern of any serious problem. "What's that?"

"With Nester and Perkins staying over, we're going to run out of rooms when the rest of your party arrives."

Zion rubbed his tanned forehead. "I hadn't thought of that. Do you have any suggestions?"

"I've thought about it some." James stroked his trim beard between his thumb and bent forefinger. "Pansy Joy was by today; she helps Florence out now and again. She said your sister was more than welcome to stay out at their place."

"That doesn't surprise me. The Johnsons are good people."

"That they are. I've known Matthias since he and Sharon moved out to the hollow, right after he recovered from his injury."

"Sometimes I forget he has a limp. He's such a strong, competent man."

"That's how he got hurt, being strong and competent. He wasn't much more than a boy when he saved General Sam Houston's life in the Battle of San Jacincto."

James had Zion's full attention, and Matthias a new level of his respect. "How did it happen?"

"The Texas militia was incensed by the way the Mexicans flat out murdered their boys, and they whooped on Santa Anna like nobody's business. General Houston tried to stay the troops from running wild, executing Mexican soldiers as they fled; but someone started yelling, 'Remember the Alamo' and 'Remember the Goliad'–and they broke loose.

"Matthias was too young for the fighting, but he was there. When the soldiers marched, he was playing the fife next to a boy keeping time on a battered drum. He told me he was playing *Will You Come to the Bower I Have Shaded for You* when he saw an enemy soldier aiming his rifle for Houston. Matthias picked up a rock and threw it at the General's horse, and it struck the animal hard on the neck. The horse kicked up, and the Mexican soldier's bullet shattered Houston's ankle."

"Why didn't he throw the rock at the soldier?"

"He didn't have a clear shot, and you know how fast things can happen."

"So how did he get hurt?"

"The soldier that shot Houston saw what Matthias did. He was so mad he shot him, too. Hit him in the leg. The bullet is still in there, but that was the last trigger that soldier ever pulled. Houston plowed him down. Stayed in the battle to the end and then slid of his horse and fainted in the arms of Major Hockley, his chief of staff."

"That's an amazing story." Zion shook his head in disbelief.

"What's amazing is Matthias survived the infection. It raged on for days. If it weren't for Sharon's mother, he would have lost his leg, his life or both." James grinned. "Instead, he ended up finding a sweetheart."

"From what I gather at the Johnson place, they had a special relationship."

"That they did. The love of a good woman is something to treasure. When I found my Florence, I knew she was the one for me."

The directional change of the conversation piqued Zion's interest. "How did you know?"

James looked at the face of the young man seated next to him. Pansy Joy had hinted there might be some of Cupid's arrows shooting between Zion and Rosalie, and James could not help but notice the way Zion's features changed when he asked the question. "There are all kinds of women in this world, Coldwell. Some women can stir a man 'til he can hardly sit in his saddle, but there are other women that stir a man's heart. Instead of all riled up in the flesh, you get a mix of peaceful excitement. It's peaceful because you just like being with her; and it's exciting because there's a wonderful person to learn more about and experience life with."

Zion contemplated the older man's words, wondering how he so succinctly nailed his predicament. Not that he seriously considered a relationship with Lark Matheny, but she was pretty enough, and knew how to entice a man. Signal flares couldn't have been any bolder than her advances; she obviously had designs on Zion.

But Rosalie, she was of a different mold altogether; and Zion knew, he just knew deep inside she was the one. But did Rosalie feel the same way? She acted peculiar a few times, unreadable. What about that Clayton fellow Pansy Joy had told him about? Was she still pining for him? If she wasn't, and she was having feelings for him like he was having feelings for her, would she still be feeling the same by the time he returned in eight or nine months?

The ruffled edges of pink and purple ribbons nudged against

the horizon and then slipped away, marking the end of the day. "I appreciate your time, Mr. Erlanger." Zion stood to his feet. "I learned a lot sitting out here with you. Think I'll turn in now."

"About the sleeping arrangements?"

Zion smiled. "I'll sleep on it."

A peaceful slumber came to Zion, and he woke the next morning refreshed. "Thank you, Lord." Zion stretched and stepped out of bed in his long underwear. He slipped into his trousers and then his shirt and began fastening the buttons. "Thank You for another day and the promise that You're here with me." Zion sat on the bed and pulled on his socks and boots. "Thank You that today isn't just a day, but a part of eternity. Help me live it pleasing to You."

Accompanied by the sound of his boots clicking on the wood floor, Zion crossed the room and looked out the window. The willow tree rustled in the breeze, both above the water line and below in its reflection. "Life's like that, isn't it, Lord? Some things we can see and touch and some things we see but can't touch." Beneath the tree Balim sat on a bench watching the glory of the day dawning.

Zion left the room and went straight to Balim. He plunked down on the bench next to him and stuck his long legs out in front crossed at the ankles. "You's pert this mornin', Massa Zion."

"I am." Zion folded his arms across his chest and tipped his face up to the sky.

Balim watched. He knew he could out-silence Zion, but was not sure he wanted to. "You got plans for today?"

"Yup." Zion, eyes still closed, eked out a slight grin.

Balim shook his head and looked out over the pond glistening in the morning sunshine. They sat together in quiet for a few minutes, Balim's patience paying off.

"You know what I was thinking this morning, Balim?"

"No, suh, but if you's up to sayin', I'm up to listenin'."

"I was looking out the window at this pond, and it reminded me of the Pool of Bethesda."

Balim nodded his big head back and forth. "Yes, suh, I know of it well, a healing place."

"I was looking out my window looking at this pond . . ."

"Yes."

"I saw the reflection of the tree, and how it looks just like a tree, but it isn't. And sometimes that's the way life is. But maybe, it's really the opposite, some crazy mixed-up world where the things that seem real, like this tree we're sitting under, maybe it's less real than the one in the reflection."

"And how's that relatin' to the Bethesda Pool, Massa Zion?"

"I closed my eyes and sat here thinking."

"I done seed that."

"It was like I had a picture in my mind of the lame man at the pool. In the real world, there he was, lame, sitting by the pool, but in the reflection, I saw an angel lifting him up for his healing before he troubled the waters."

"Lawdy, you's given ole' Balim gooseflesh, Massa Zion."

"Don't you think that's the way of things sometimes? Things are happening in the spirit world before we see them in the natural?"

"I believe it. Yes, suh, I do."

"Take slavery, for instance."

"I done that all my life." Balim chuckled. Zion elbowed him playfully in the side.

"I'm serious. Don't you feel things are happening, like slavery is being fought over in the spirit world before we see a victory here? The 'tree' is standing, but something unseen is at work."

"I hope so, Massa Zion. Not everyone's got it as good as ole Balim."

"And then, there are women." Zion let out a long sigh.

"Now you're talking." Balim nodded, a wide smile replacing his previous thoughtful countenance. "You wanna talk 'bout my Minnie?"

"What?"

"You said you wanted to talk 'bout women folks, so I asks if you want to talk 'bout my Minnie. Or did you have someone else in mind?"

Zion knew Balim was teasing, but he went along with it. "All right. Let's talk about Minnie." Balim gave a strange look to Zion. The young man took him by surprise for a change. "How did you know you wanted to marry her?" Zion asked.

"I didn't plan on it, that's for sure. But when ole Liddy had Minnie over to help with the canning–her rheumatiz got so's she couldn' hardly get the lids on anymore, you know–I just couldn' help myself." Balim chuckled at the memory. "Minnie, she had a kerchief over her braids. She was a sweatin' over pots a boilin' water, gettin' those jars sealed tight. I looked at her servin' and smilin' and sweatin', and summpin jist crawled in my heart for that girl. It ain't left neither."

"I'm going to do everything I can to see you two together, Balim."

"I knows, Massa Zion. Ole Balim knows yo heart." He gave him a sideways glance. "You thinkin' 'bout Miss Rozlee like I thought 'bout my Minnie?"

Zion smiled. "I'm thinking I might be thinking like that, and I'm wondering what she'd think about that and how's she's thinking."

"That's a powerful lot of thinkin', Massa Zion. Maybe we should do some prayin' and trustin' along with it?"

"That's a good plan." Zion pulled one boot up to the bench and rested his chin on his knee. "It's like that Bethesda Pool I was talking about. You know, how things happen before we see them. I feel something happening in my heart for Rosalie, and sometimes it's like the waters being troubled, and sometimes it's as sweet as huckleberry pie."

CHAPTER 27

The breakfast dishes had been cleared away, and Zion sat in the dining hall finishing his coffee. The sound of plodding horse hooves and turning wheels announced the approach of a wagon. Zion threw back the dregs of his coffee, pushed back from the table and walked out the front door.

A beautiful set of matched bays pulled a covered farm wagon down the lane. Seated on the buckboard, a young couple beamed at Zion. The young lady had one arm wrapped around her husband's elbow and waved her free hand at Zion. The man pulled on the reins stopping his outfit in front of the lodge.

"I'm guessing you're the Sweeneys." Zion descended the porch steps and held out his hand.

"You guessed right. I'm Clarence, and this here's Louella." Clarence shook Zion's hand from his seated position and then jumped down to the ground. He reached up to help his bride down from the wagon.

"I'm Zion Coldwell. Pleased to meet you."

"We're sorry about the delay," Louella said. "I hope it wasn't an inconvenience."

"No ma'am. It looks like we won't be heading out for a few days anyway. The group from Nashville hasn't arrived and the Coventry's wagon isn't ready yet."

Louella gave Clarence a nervous glance. "That's all right. Do you think the lodge keeper will mind if we just camp out here?"

Zion understood their concern. The young couple's limited resources, already stretched to the maximum, couldn't sustain the unexpected cost of four or five nights at the lodge. "Mr. Coventry offered to pay for the additional lodging fees since we're waiting for his wagon to be completed."

The heaviness lifted off Louella's face, replaced by a bright smile. "That's right nice of him."

"It will be a pleasure to sleep in a bed for a few days." Clarence winked at Louella. Her face grew crimson, but she did not say a word.

"Why don't you come inside? I'll introduce you to the Erlangers and the Coventrys, and a couple other fellows who signed on. Have you had your breakfast?"

"Yes, sir. I married me one sweet little cook." Clarence pinched Louella's cheek. "She flipped out some fine flapjacks this morning. Don't know what I ever did without her."

Zion was taking notes: never talk about beds or pinch a girl's cheek in public. Louella looked mortified.

The three trooped into the dining room and Zion poked his head in Florence's tidy kitchen. "Mrs. Erlanger?"

Florence popped out from behind the pantry. "What can I do for you?"

"The Sweeneys just arrived. They already had their breakfast, but do you think we could get some coffee?"

"I'll be right out with it."

Zion directed the Sweeneys to a clean table and pulled out a chair for Louella. "I'll let the others know you're here. Be right back." He climbed the steps and knocked on the doors. "The Sweeneys are here," he announced from the hallway and then returned to the dining room.

Florence Erlanger came out shortly with a coffee pot and a tray of glazed sticky buns. "Those look wonderful." Louella lifted a pastry and drank in its sweet fragrance before taking a bite.

"Best get your fill now. You won't be eating like this much longer." Florence passed the tray to the men and then filled their mugs with steaming coffee.

"We have an oven, but I'm sure everything will be much different on the trail." Louella savored the sticky bun melting in her mouth.

"I put sugar on your supply list, so you can have a sweet now and again," Zion said.

"We thought we should spend the money on oats instead," Clarence said. "Louella's Ma gave us some maple syrup and sorghum for sweetener."

"I'll think about her with every bite," said Louella.

Zion flashed back to Rosalie and Penny. He wondered what they were doing and suddenly couldn't wait to ride out to the Johnson place.

"You sound like my sister." Zion wiped his hands and stood to his feet. "Which reminds me—I need to go check on her. Penny came down with flux. She gave us a real scare there, thought it might be cholera."

"Oh, my," Louella exclaimed. "That would have been awful."

"The flux was awful enough. She's gaining her strength back though. She got sick when we were visiting with a neighbor and they've been nursing her since."

"They must be dreadful kind folks to take in a sick stranger."

"Kind of like the prodigal's son?" Clarence asked.

Louella smiled at her husband. "I think you mean the Good Samaritan."

"I sure don't have all those Bible stories down like you do, Louella Sue."

"If your daddy was a preacher, then you would."

"Before we were certain it wasn't cholera," Zion said, "we thought we would have to quarantine. We couldn't take a chance on spreading it. Then Penny just kind of settled in over there, cozy as a flea in a thick winter coat."

"When are you bringing her back?" Clarence asked. "I know Louella would like to meet her. She taught Sunday school to the kids back home."

"Actually, the Johnsons offered to let Penny stay. Since we had more folks sign up for the trip, we filled up all the rooms here at the lodge." Zion headed to the door. "I'm going to head out now. Mrs. Erlanger will show you to your room when you're finished."

Zion left the lodge, chuckling at the Sweeneys. He wondered what brought two people so different together, and what it might be like to be married. When he arrived at the cabin, to his delight, Penny, Marigold and Lucas were out on the front porch. With chubby fingers, Lucas clung to the bilbo catcher. Penny's hand wrapped around his, showing him the motions to catch the ball in the cup. Marigold supervised while Daisy wagged her tail and loped down the steps to greet Zion.

"Hello, the house!"

"Hi, Zion." Penny smiled at her brother.

"You look great."

"Thanks. It's feels wonderful to be outside in the fresh air."

"Speaking of fresh air, that reminds me. I saw a quilt hanging on the Briar Hollow Orchard sign at the end of the lane. You think I should bring it in?"

"Why don't you ask Rosalie? She told Pansy Joy to hang it out there last night."

"That's odd."

"I thought so, too, but I didn't say anything. Mama and Liddy always aired the quilts out in the sunshine. Rosalie and Pansy Joy were whispering about the Paxton Inn visitors and Pansy Joy took the quilt out to the sign."

Zion shrugged off the question of the quilt and lowered his voice. "I've got news." Three sets of eyes and ears tuned in to Zion. Truly newsworthy news did not reach the hollow on a regular basis. "The Sweeneys drove in less than an hour ago."

"Who's the Spleeneys?" Lucas asked.

"He said Sweeneys, Lukey, not spleeneys," Marigold corrected her brother. "Spleens are part of your body, silly."

"What's spleeneys good for?"

"I'm not sure. Ask Rosalie," said Marigold.

"Seems like all the questions around here go to Rosalie," Zion observed. He turned to Lucas and grinned at the little tyke. "The Sweeneys are a newlywed couple going west with me and Penny."

"Can I go, too?"

"I'd love to have you along, Lucas, but your family would miss you. We'll be gone a long time, and you'll probably be a year older by the time I finish this trip. When's your birthday?"

Lucas looked to Marigold. "Do I get one this year?"

Zion and Penny laughed, but Marigold answered the question. "Yes, you get a birthday this year."

"Birthdays come every year, don't they?" Penny asked.

"Not if you're born on February 29," said Marigold.

"How old'll I be?"

"That depends on how you count it. In years, you'll be four, but it's really your first birthday."

"I never met anyone with a leap year birthday before." Penny looked at Lucas and wondered what it felt like to get a birthday once every four years. It seemed hers took forever to roll around, and she got one each year.

"I think 1860 is going to be a year of good things," said Zion, "and one of them being a birthday for a special boy."

"What else?" Marigold asked.

"We have a census starting, the eighth one since we became the United States of America, and an important presidential election."

"And my birthday." Lucas grinned up at Zion.

"And your birthday."

"Are Rosalie and Pansy Joy inside?" Zion asked.

"No," Marigold answered. "They went down to the barn."

"Why did they take food and clothes to the barn, do you think?" Penny turned questioning eyes on Marigold, and then Zion.

"Ask Rosalie," they answered in unison, followed by a round of laughter.

"I think I'll do that. Maybe they need a hand." Zion walked down to the barn and opened the door. Guilt and fear mixed on the faces of Pansy Joy and Rosalie, and a protective feeling welled in Zion. He looked from one girl to the next. Pansy Joy recovered quickly, her facial features and shoulders visibly relaxing. Rosalie appeared tense and apprehensive. "What's wrong?"

"Nothing's wrong," Pansy Joy answered in a light tone that seemed somewhat forced to Zion. "Why do you ask?"

"No reason." Zion stared at the girl feigning innocence and decided to play along. "I just came to see if I could help you out here."

"Everything's fine, but thank you." Pansy Joy answered again. Rosalie stood mute giving an occasional hard blink over enlarged eyes.

"I see you're putting hay in the stall. I can get a pitchfork and take care of that lickety click."

"No!" Rosalie stepped in front of Zion. In her haste she twisted on her good ankle and nearly fell to the ground. Zion scooped her up with ease, sat her on a bail of hay and grabbed the pitchfork hanging on the wall of the barn. Three long steps and he stood in front of the hay, pitchfork raised when he heard a scream.

"No, massa! No, massa!"

"Don't, Zion!" Pansy Joy ran in front of Zion and stepped between him and two sets of obsidian eyes peeking out from the pile of hay.

"What's this?" Adrenaline rushed through Zion. A flurry in the hay produced a petite black woman with saucer eyes and young girl clinging to her, her face buried in the older woman's ragged skirts.

"Please, suh. In the name o' the sweet Lawd Jesus, don' send us back to Massa Hayworth."

Zion appraised the situation, realizing the two must be runaway slaves who had just barely escaped being impaled by the prongs of the metal pitchfork. He dropped the tool to the ground and leaned back against the barn wall.

The woman crawled out of the hay and groveled at Zion's feet. "Massa Hayworth, he was a comin' fo my baby girl. I couldna let 'im take her. Have mercy." The woman wept, shoulders heaving, her daughter standing erect in the hay watching. A beauty, the girl's flawless skin glowed rosy even in the dim barn light. Full cherry lips blossomed beneath exotic almond-shaped eyes, and the beginnings of womanhood marked her lithe figure.

Stunned, Zion stood silent, absorbing the events that had unfolded so quickly. Without a word, he leaned down to the sobbing woman and gently drew her to her feet. Just as he did so often with Penny, he lifted her trembling chin until their eyes met. When she read the compassion on his face, the woman wept all the more.

"I don't know what's going on here." Zion swept the faces in the barn trying to glean more information. "But you have nothing to fear from me."

CHAPTER 28

Rosalie trembled as she sat on the hay bale. What she had witnessed made no sense–it befuddled her mind. Zion, himself a slave owner, discovering runaways in her barn and then treating them with such compassion–it just didn't seem real. But there he was, walking the woman over to her child and dropping to his knees before them on her barn floor.

"I'm so sorry." Zion addressed the girl. "I didn't mean to frighten you. I was just helping my friend with her hay. I didn't know you were in there." Slowly, the girl nodded and received a smile from Zion in return. "You scared me pretty good, you know. When I saw your eyes peeking out from the hay, I didn't know what I was seeing."

The corners of the girl's lips lifted in a quasi smile, wariness still lingered in her expressive eyes. Zion turned to Rosalie on the hay bale. "Have they eaten?" Rosalie nodded. "Good."

Zion sat down on the ground and motioned the woman and child to do the same. The twosome followed Zion's lead and tucked their feet beneath the hems of ragged skirts. "What's your name?" The woman looked at Rosalie, a silent question on her face. Rosalie nodded her approval.

"I'm Tawny. This be my girl, Jacinda."

"How did you come to be here?"

"It was too dangerous to go to the Paxton Inn last night. When I saw the log cabin quilt a hangin' out on the sign, I knowed this be a safe place to stop."

Zion realized the answer to the puzzle of the quilt airing in the dark of night stood before him. With incredulous eyes, he turned to the Johnson girls and stared at one and then the other. "Are you part of the Underground Railroad?"

Rosalie nodded again, still silent, still unbelieving.

Zion gave his knee a hearty slap and let out a hoot. "That's wonderful!"

Rosalie jumped on her hay bale and stared at him.

"I heard there was a major station in the area, but I thought it was Maysville. So there's a station at the Paxton Inn, huh?" The memory of the slave auctioneer in the lobby of the inn flashed in Zion's mind. "Isn't that ironic?"

"What do you mean?" Pansy Joy asked.

"Mr. Paxton is catering to slave sellers and buyers while all the time helping runaways escape to freedom."

"He probably gets a lot of helpful information that way," Pansy Joy observed.

"How does he do it, I wonder?"

"Runaways hole up in hidden staircases during the day, and then are taken to the next station after dark."

"Wait until I tell Balim." Zion, unable to contain his excitement, slapped his knee a second time and broke out in a do-si-do.

After the initial fright of being discovered, and the terrifying moment Zion held the pitchfork trained on the runaways, the realization that Zion not only approved, but was seemingly ecstatic slaves were being freed slowly seeped into Rosalie's shocked senses. What she thought she knew about Balim and Zion were two and two that did not add up to four. Curiosity mingled with the sweet surprise.

"But don't you own Balim?" Rosalie asked, questions still flittering in her brain.

"Legally, yes. Balim came to our home after his parents were sold away from a neighboring plantation. His aunt was our cook, and she worried so about him Daddy bought Balim. Daddy said the look on Liddy's face was something else when he brought her sister's boy to stay with her in the little room off the kitchen. It about broke her heart thinking of Balim alone on the plantation. Liddy never had any children and she treated Balim like her own."

"But he's your slave, isn't he?"

"Daddy brought Balim out to the farm when he was about eight years old. He was treated affectionately–as a servant, yes, but never less than a human being. To tell the truth, Balim has been my best friend as long as I can remember." Zion looked into Rosalie's green eyes and saw she still had reservations. "I'll let you in on a secret, since I've discovered yours. But you can't tell Penny."

"What's that?" Pansy Joy asked.

"Balim insisted on making this trip with me and Penny. When our folks died we lost everything but the horses. They were thoroughbreds, real beauties. I sold them all except West and invested the money in this expedition. I'm planning to earn enough to make a good start for me and Penny somewhere, and when it's all said and done, I'm seeing Balim off to Canada with half the proceeds and papers declaring his freedom in case he gets stopped on the way."

"That's wonderful." Pansy Joy walked to Rosalie and gave her shoulder a quick squeeze. "Isn't Mr. Coldwell something special?"

In her heart, Rosalie agreed, but she could not bring herself to say it aloud. "It is wonderful for Balim. But why don't you want Penny to know?"

"I'm afraid she'll spill the beans. I'm just playing things close to the chest for Balim's safety. When you're in slave states or dealing with strangers, there's always the chance you'll get it in the neck. Lots of blacks get kidnapped and drug back south, lost forever.

"Besides, Penny's such a romantic, she'd gush it out for sure once she found out Balim is going to find his wife Minnie in Canada."

"Balim's married?" This revelation astonished Rosalie yet again.

"Yup. He married a gal owned by a fellow that sold his place and planned to move out of state. She ran before they left, and word came back to Balim she was in Windsor. She said she rode the 'gospel train to the promised land' and she was waiting for Balim there."

"We's riding that train that don' run on no tracks," Tawny said. "Thanks to you folks and that quilt a hangin' out."

"I've heard stories about quilts used for signals, but I wasn't sure they were true," said Zion.

"We use whatever means we have," said Pansy Joy. "Most runaways can't read words, but they can recognize patterns. The log cabin with a black window means you're at a safe place."

"A black center isn't usual?"

"It's usually red," Rosalie offered, "to represent the hearth."

"This is incredible." Zion rubbed his forehead and tried to take in all the information. "What other quilts are used?"

"Flying Geese, Drunkard's Path, Jacob's Ladder . . ."

Zion laughed. "I wouldn't know them if I saw them, but I think it's a clever way to communicate."

"There are all sorts of secret words and signals people use. Levi Coffin started using the railway terms like conductor and station," said Rosalie. "Songs are important, too."

"That figures. Balim is all the time singing. Who would know if he was sending a signal or not?"

"Another slave would, and those involved in the Underground Railroad." Rosalie watched Zion's delight as he thought about the possibilities and then turned to look at her, another question in his eyes.

"How did you know to put out the quilt last night?"

"A runner came from the Paxton Inn. They put out their signal so Tawny wouldn't stop there, and we put out ours so she would come here."

Zion studied the tired faces of the runaways, once afraid for their lives, but now at peace. He reached in his pocket and pulled out some coins. "Take these."

Tawny shook her head. "No, suh. Jacinda and me ain't stopping at no stores along the way. You been good 'nough to us already."

Zion pressed the coins in her small hand. "I'm thankful people are providing for you along the way, but it might help when you get where you're going."

Tears welled in Tawny's bright eyes. "The good Lawd sho done take care a me an my girl today."

"Pansy Joy, show them what's in that basket." Rosalie motioned to the basket by the wall. Pansy Joy slipped off the blanket covering and lifted out Marigold's old calico dress. "Katie offered to lengthen this for Marigold, but I think it will fit Jacinda just right." Jacinda's eyes grew wide at the offering. The dress, well used by three Johnson girls, was the nicest thing by far she had ever owned. Pansy Joy put the dress in her arms and Jacinda clutched it to her breast and swished the full skirt in a half-turn.

"Look at all the material in this skirt, Mammy, and not a single patch on the whole thing." She turned to the Johnsons, a pearly white grin beaming in her beautiful brown face. "Thank you. Thank you so much."

"Here's one for you, Tawny." Pansy Joy pulled out her old dress. Both petite women, Tawny would not fill out the bodice quite the same as Pansy Joy, but that could be adjusted later.

Tawny's slender fingers covered her mouth in disbelief. She choked back a sob and shook her kerchiefed head. After she regained her composure, she spoke. "Massa weren't a good man. He used his women. Jacinda's his girl, and I just couldn' let him . . ."

Tawny paused for a moment to regain her composure and then continued, "He knowed what his overseer done to the women and the men folk, and he never put a stop to it. I heard tell of others had it worse than we did, but in my heart I always knowed they's mean white folks and they's good ones, same as they's mean black folks and good ones. Glory be to God."

"We're just glad we could help," Rosalie said. "Who can explain why one person is born white and another black, one free and one not? For some reason we were born free, and we're happy to do what we can for those who weren't."

"You done more than just give food and clothes and a place to stay to me and my girl. The three of you showed me my heart was right, and I've got peace like a river in my soul."

"That's a fine feeling, isn't it?" Zion rose to his feet. "But I better go, the young ones will be wondering what's going on. Let me pitch some of that hay so I can tell them I really did something while I was down here."

Zion grasped the pitchfork in experienced hands and moved a bit of hay quickly and efficiently into the stall. "Phew." Feigning a damp brow, he animatedly wiped his forehead with the back of his hand, a wide smile splitting his tanned face. "You Johnson girls could work a fellow to his death."

Zion walked to the door, stopped and turned back. "Can I pray with you before I go?" He looked in their faces for their approval and then brought the group together, Tawny and Jacinda in the middle surrounded by Zion, Pansy Joy and Rosalie still seated on the hay bale.

"Gracious God and Father, You are merciful and kind. I thank you for bringing Tawny and Jacinda out of the house of their bondage and believe You'll see them through this desert of hiding and fleeing into a promised land of freedom. I pray You'll keep Your angels all about them, keep them safe and provide their needs along the way, in Jesus' name."

Tawny whispered in prayer language undiscerned by Zion's mind but recognized by his spirit. A sweet presence filled the barn, a warm blanket of God's affirming love so thick Zion wished he could stay longer. He forced himself to the door and waved goodbye to his new friends.

CHAPTER 29

The rest of Friday passed in a blur of activity for Zion. Ballard's telegraph indicated the group would arrive Friday or Saturday, and preparations were made for their arrival. Since Travis would bunk with Zion, Florence Erlanger changed the bedding Penny used in his room and prepared the washbasin with fresh water and towels.

Once the purchase of Garth Eldridge's wagon was complete, Zion retrieved it from the farm and brought it to Comfort Lodge to prepare for the trip. Garth had fitted the colorful green wagon with a canvas cover, and the Coventrys puttered in and around it with much excitement making it ready with feather mattresses, pillows and such.

Out in the barn, Balim unloaded and reloaded the big wagon. He took off the things the Coventrys would use on their personal wagons and fastened down the large items and cases of books on their big one. He made room for the luggage yet to come and the supply order being prepared at the mercantile. In addition to the things needed for their trip to Virginia City, Zion stocked items for his return home and a large inventory of goods on high demand in the west. What sold for a quarter in Kentucky sold for a dollar in the west. Leather boots, aprons and vests used by miners wore out quickly. Rocks tore their shirts and pants. Zion carried some ready-made clothing and yard goods as well. He packed seeds, playing cards, ammunition and poetry books and ordered large quantities of white sugar and white flour from the mercantile. Zion looked forward to a lucrative profit, a new beginning for Balim, Penny and himself.

He wondered what Nester and Perkins had up their sleeves. They were up to no good, that was certain. He studied their movements, but learned nothing of their plans.

"Did you hear anything from J.T. or Bug today?" Zion asked Balim.

"Not a peep, Massa Zion. Nary a peep." Balim shifted their tent to the back of the wagon with the camping equipment.

"As much as I can't stand listening to the reprobates, I'd rather know what they were up to."

"They probly ain't figured it out theyselves."

"You're probably right." Zion chuckled and handed a box to Balim. "It's kind of funny. It reminds me of my birthday, anticipating a present, but not having a clue what it is."

"I don't think I'd open up a package from the likes a them, Massa Zion. You might find yoself facin' a rattler."

"I'm not expecting a gift from them, that's for sure. I was just comparing the situation with the anticipation of the surprise, wondering what they were cooking up." Zion leaned against the barn wall and chewed on a piece of golden hay. "Speaking of birthdays, I found out today Lucas Johnson was born on February 29. He's going to be four years old when he celebrates his first real birthday. Isn't that something?"

"Yes, suh. That's summpin. Po chile." Balim sucked in his lips drawing his mouth into a thin line and wrinkling his chin. "But if I know those Johnson girls, they took care a that boy."

"I'm sure they did, at that." Zion walked to the barn door and stepped outside. He looked around the property and then re-entered the barn and stood close to Balim. "They take care of more than little boys and girls, Balim," he said in a hushed tone. "Rosalie and Pansy Joy are part of the Underground Railroad."

"Lawd, have mercy!" Balim's eyes grew big as saucers. "I knew they was summpin special 'bout those girls. Yes, suh, I knew it fo sho and fo certain." He shook his head and bared a full set of white teeth. "How you done find this out, Massa Zion?"

"I saw two runaways today in their barn. They traveled during the night and stopped when Rosalie hung out a quilt on the Briar Hollow sign."

"The log cabin with the black center?"

Zion stared at Balim. "How did you know?"

"Ole Balim knows."

"I'm hoping you won't have to travel to Canada underground, but I suppose it's good to know the signals, especially until you're far away from the slave states."

The work on the big wagon complete for the time being, Zion and Balim headed to the kitchen hoping for some refreshments.

"Good evening, Mrs. Erlanger." Zion greeted the industrious woman setting beans to soak for the next day's meal. She wiped her hands on her apron and smoothed her hair back from her face.

"Good evening to you, too, Mr. Coldwell, Balim." Perspiration gleamed on the brows of the men. Florence's hospitality, as quick to surface as a trout on a mayfly, arose with a smile. "I see you two have worked up a sweat. Why don't you wash at the pump, and I'll get you some nice, cool cider."

"Thank you kindly," said Zion. The men retreated to the pump, splashed their necks, faces and hands with cool water, and then returned to the cozy kitchen where Florence had readied the table with tin cups of cider and a plate of apple fritters. The men made short order of the tasty treats and retired to the porch to watch the sun set.

"It's been a long time since I heard you a blowin' on yo' mouth organ, Massa Zion."

"I haven't felt much like playing, but I have it in my room." The two sat in silence for several minutes, the weight of Balim's unspoken request filling the space between the step he sat on and Zion's favorite perch, the bench swing.

"Oh, all right, Balim. I'll get it."

Zion stood so abruptly the swing lurched and continued its pendulum path, coming to a stop just before he returned with the instrument. "I'm sorry, Balim," he said. "I didn't mean to storm off like a spoiled kid."

Balim nodded and waited for the music. He knew the wind in the reeds would soothe Zion's spirit. Before the accident Zion used to play often, and was quite accomplished. He could bend in notes and shake in vibrato with his head or his hands in ways that set him apart from other players. Zion settled into the swing and lifted the worn instrument. The rich, plaintive tones of *Amazing Grace* ushered in a sweet peace on the porch.

Before Zion reached the chorus, the door swung open. Rachel and Henry Coventry joined Zion and Balim, followed a few steps behind by their parents. Silently the family filled in the four padded rockers on the lodge's expansive porch and steeped in the musical reverie of the hymn.

Zion played through the song and began the second verse. Sara Coventry's clear soprano united the sacred words with the song's timeless melody. When the last note sounded, no one spoke for a time. The peace on the porch was palpable and refreshing. The percussion of the katydids in the treetops continued the musical atmosphere, and Zion began Wesley's *O for a Thousand Tongues*. Sara sang again.

Rachel and Henry rocked back and forth listening to the music, but Henry quickly grew tired of the melancholy. As soon as Zion ended the last note of the hymn, he jumped out of his seat.

"Hey, Mr. Coldwell. Do you know *Cotton Eye Joe* or *Turkey in the Straw?*"

Thaddeus Coventry considered his son with a quizzical expression on his moustached face. "How do you know those songs, Henry?"

Henry sat down on his hands and rocked hard back and forth. "I heard them at Stephen's house. They have a darkie who works as a stable hand, and he fiddles like anything." The boy looked at Balim. "You play the fiddle?"

"Ole Balim plays some on the jaw harp and bones, but I'm not a fine musician like Massa Zion."

Sara and Thaddeus exchanged looks of concern. They had diligently provided their children classical educations in academics, music and literature. That their son knew floor stomping, frolicking barn dance tunes came as a surprise. Thaddeus mulled it over a moment and gave a slight shrug.

"Rachel and Henry will soon be exposed to a wide range of cultures and experiences, dear. We must do our best to make sure their education is well rounded."

"I suppose you're right. With the Chinese immigrants and settlers from all over the country, who knows what we will encounter in the west." Sara studied her son rocking back and forth, already knowing the answer before she asked the question. "So, Henry, have you practiced any of these new songs on your violin?"

"He has," Rachel volunteered. The picture of innocence, the delicate featured girl clasped her hands on her lap and shook her curls back and forth. "I've heard him while you were at the Anti Horse Thief Association meetings."

"Well, now," Zion interrupted. "I don't know those songs, but how about this one." Zion wet his whistle and began a rousing version of *O Susanna.* Contagious wiggles set Henry in motion to the music. He pulled Rachel to her feet, but she stood stoic as her excited brother danced an untrained jig. Before he finished the song, Thaddeus was tapping his toes and Sara kept time with a nodding head.

Wheezing and pale, Henry collapsed in his rocking chair.

"Are you all right, Son?" Thaddeus asked.

"I'll be fine, Father." Henry was familiar with the tightening in his chest. He sat up and exhaled as fully as possible and then inhaled as slowly and steadily as his constricting bronchioles allowed. The sound of his wheezing drowned out the katydids, and Sara moved to action.

"Rachel, get the Epsom salts. I'll have Mrs. Erlanger fill a tub with hot water."

Daily soaks helped Henry minimize his asthma spells, but he had missed several days in a row while traveling.

"I don't want to spend a half hour in the tub, Mother."

"I know, Henry, but you'll sleep much better tonight if you do. Listen to your wheezing."

"Miss Johnson knows a lot about healing herbs. Maybe I'll pay her a visit and see if she's got something to ease the boy's breathing."

"Thank you, Mr. Coldwell. I assure you we've been to the finest doctors, but if Miss Johnson knows of anything that might help, we'd be grateful." Thaddeus rose and walked with Zion down the steps. When they left earshot of the others, he confided his fears to Zion. "I pray Miss Johnson will find something to help as we make the trip. Epson salt baths will be hard to come by on the trail. But it's been my dearest hope that the dryer climate will help the boy's breathing." Thaddeus stopped at the end of the lane. Zion halted beside him.

"The air around this part of the Ohio is right thick. It could close up the best breathing passages." He offered a nod of encouragement and shook Mr. Coventry's hand. "I'll see what Rosalie has to say, and we can make this a matter of prayer."

"Thank you, Mr. Coldwell. That's most kind of you."

Zion covered the mile to the Johnson place in good time and knocked at the door of the cabin. Marigold answered. "This is a surprise, twice in one day."

"A good one, I hope."

"Oh, sure, come on in. We were just having a singing."

Rosalie sat in a chair, a fretted dulcimer on her lap. Penny sat next to Pansy Joy at the table with a limberjack. Lucas had a stick and a homemade drum, but the sight that surprised Zion most was Matthias with the handle of a singing saw tucked between his legs and a bow in his beefy hand. "Does a fellow need a ticket for this shindy?"

Matthias adjusted himself to stand, but Zion stopped him. "Don't get up on my account, Mr. Johnson."

"Hi, Zion." Penny greeted her brother. The light of health was returning to the girl's face and her eyes danced with merriment. "I was just telling them how much I enjoyed the music. It's been such a long time since you played your mouth organ."

Zion smiled at his sister. "Not so long, Buttercup. I played it tonight."

"Really?"

Zion pulled the instrument from his pocket. "See?"

Penny clapped her hands in excitement. Healing truly was underway in Zion's heart if he was playing music again. "What did you play? I bet Balim was happy as a fox in the henhouse."

"First, I played *Amazing Grace*. Wait until you hear Mrs. Coventry sing. It was like an angel dropped out of heaven on the front porch of the lodge."

"Marigold sings, too," said Penny.

"That's because I'm not coordinated enough for an instrument." Marigold laughed at herself.

"That's because God knew we needed a singer," said Pansy Joy. "And you have a fine contralto, Mari, rich and smooth as last year's maple syrup."

"Why don't you join us in a song?" Matthias invited.

"What's your favorite?" Zion asked.

"I'm right partial to *Rock of Ages*."

Zion found the beginning note and was soon joined by the other instruments in the room. The missed beat of Lucas's drum only sweetened the song as Marigold sang in a voice mature beyond her years. She swept the low notes, and the high ones resonated with clarity and perfect pitch. Only Lucas remained dry-eyed at the close of the song.

"That was beautiful." Pansy Joy dabbed a drop of moisture from her eye.

Penny blew her nose on a handkerchief. "Would you play *Fairest Lord Jesus?*"

"I will next time, Penny, but I can't stay long. I actually came to see Rosalie."

CHAPTER 30

Rosalie rose from her chair and placed the dulcimer on the table. "It's getting dark, but we could sit on the porch," she offered, wondering what brought Zion out to see her.

The Johnson porch chairs lacked the cozy floral cushions of the lodge rockers, but braided pads softened the wooden seats. Dim light radiated from the window and the bright stars and moon overhead kept the couple from total darkness.

"Did Tawny and Jacinda make it out all right?" Zion asked.

"I'm not sure. They slept during the day and planned to leave once it got dark."

"You should have seen Balim light up like a Fourth of July sparkler when I told him." Rosalie's pink lips turned up in a smile. The moon on her face illuminated her porcelain skin, and Zion paused, enjoying the feel of just sitting on the porch in the moonlight with this woman.

"Penny's looking well. Thanks again for taking such good care of her."

"You're welcome." Rosalie wasn't making things easy for Zion. She didn't have a clue why he was there or what he wanted, so she waited for him to speak his mind. Zion, confused by the quiet, wondered at her seeming aloofness.

"How's your ankle?"

"Much better."

"I was afraid you twisted it again in the barn today."

"I wondered why you scooped me up like a sack of potatoes and dumped me on the hay bale." Zion saw the humor in her eyes and relaxed.

"I'd say you're more like a sack of onions, not as heavy as potatoes, and you might make a fellow cry if he peeled away a layer or two."

Rosalie puzzled at his remark. "Who's layer? His or mine?"

Zion chuckled and gazed up at the stars. "I think most folks have some outer layers they show to the world." Zion's candid remark surprised Rosalie. Most men weren't open to admit vulnerabilities or sensitivities. She gave a small nod and found herself responding anew to the man beside her. Tipping his chair on its rear legs, Zion threw his arms over the back rest, looking completely relaxed on her front porch. Zion was big, like her father. Matthias was tall and broad like Zion, but much of his muscles had atrophied from lack of use. He had not regained full strength or mobility after his war injury.

"I'd like to stay and visit with you longer, but I have folks waiting back at the lodge for me."

Rosalie stood to her feet, a bundle of confusion. "Well, goodnight then."

Zion rose and grasped Rosalie gently at the elbows, his face inches from hers in the moonlight. The breath caught in his throat as the desire to kiss her overwhelmed his senses.

No denying it, this man confused Rosalie. She felt the same attraction, the same drawing Zion did, but stood blinking in the moonlight. Silent. Waiting.

"Rosalie," Zion whispered. He knew he had to do something, or he was a goner. He was sure to pull this innocent girl into a passionate embrace and make a fool of himself. Running his hands down her forearms, he took her slender hands in his for just a moment and then released them. The contact set both of their hands tingling. Zion stepped back and put his hands in his pockets. "Rosalie, I came to ask you something."

"Yes?" Rosalie's voice sounded quiet to her own ears.

"I mean, I . . ." Zion faltered. He didn't care if he made a fool of himself anymore. He pulled his hands out of his pockets and took Rosalie's again, further confusing the girl.

"I came to ask your help for a sick boy; but I have to tell you, I could stay out on this porch all night with you." Zion caressed her cheek with the back of his hand, silky and cool, just like he thought it would be.

Rosalie closed her eyes, reveling in the feel of Zion's touch and the tenderness of his voice. No words came, just sweet sensations, heightened when Zion brushed her lips with his fingertip. At that, her eyes flew open, probing the depths and passion in Zion's blue eyes boring into hers. A tremble in her lower lip worked its way down her arms. She removed her hands from Zion's and placed them palm out on his broad chest, rebelling against the desire to throw them around his neck.

Zion cupped the slender fingers on his chest with his big hands and gave Rosalie a warm smile. He lifted her hand to his own cheek, and cupped it again under his palm. "I wondered what your hands would feel like on my face, ever since I watched you nursing Penny with your gentle touch.

"I don't know what you've done to me, Miss Johnson, but I'm afraid I've come down with a chronic condition that's going to need some of your fine ministrations."

The mention of sickness seemed to break the spell long enough for Rosalie to gain control of her senses. Stepping back, she returned the conversation to the reason for Zion's visit. "You said there was a sick boy?"

"Henry Covington's got asthma in a bad way. He just had a spell. His ma's been treating him by soaking him in Epson salt baths, but his pa's concerned about the trip. Do you know of anything that might open up his pipes and help him breathe better?"

Rosalie sucked in a jagged breath. She could relate to the boy. Her response to Zion was closing off her own breathing passages. She nodded. "There are several things that can help–a tea of dried nettle leaves opens the pipes and passages of the lungs.

"I made a butterbur and mistletoe tincture. Half a dropperful every night will help with spasms. I can give you what I have and write out the receipt. That way Mrs. Coventry can make more when it runs out."

"I knew it."

"Knew what?"

"That you would know what to do and be willing to share it."

"I promised myself after Mama got sick to learn as much as I could and help others in need. Even if it's not life and death, easing someone's suffering is one of the most wonderful things I've ever experienced."

"I hope you'll have more."

"More what?"

"More wonderful experiences." Zion tipped Rosalie's chin with his forefinger and watched her expression in the dim light. "I happen to think you're wonderful."

A hot blush crawled up Rosalie's neck and spread across her face. "Is that what you told Lark Matheny when you went to visit her?" Rosalie regretted the harsh words, but she had to know the heart of this man who was rendering her own heart helpless.

"What are you talking about? I never went to visit Lark Matheny. I've avoided the mercantile as much as possible."

"She said she helped you pick out a toy for Penny, and then you came back to see her again."

Fury raged in Zion. The skunk had sprayed its foul scent, and Zion's nostrils flared. "That girl has made cow eyes at me ever since I walked into the mercantile the first day."

"You mean you didn't go to see her?"

"Never, Rosalie. I've had business in town, and she's happened to be there. I admit, she's a beautiful girl, but she's just a girl. I'm surprised her mother lets her wear long skirts. Any man with the sense the good Lord gave him could see she's scouting for a husband; but I for one, am not interested." Zion took a deep breath. As he calmed his stampeding emotions, his usual easygoing smile replaced itself on his tanned face. "I mean, I'm not interested in Lark. There's this other young lady . . ."

The front door opened. Matthias peeked outside. "Everything all right out here? You was getting kind of loud there, Son."

"I'm sorry, sir. I just heard a bit of a false report that upset me."

"It's getting late to be sitting our here in the dark. You two almost finished?"

"Yes, Pa. Mr. Coldwell was asking advice on medicine for a boy suffering with asthma. I'll just run in and get it, and I'll write the receipt down for you next time you come to see Penny." Rosalie ducked past her father and disappeared in the cabin door. Matthias stepped out on the porch.

"I'll keep you company 'til she gets back. Sit down."

Zion could not recall ever feeling quite so nervous. He wondered if Matthias suspected his feelings for Rosalie or if he considered his treatment of her inappropriate, especially after he found Rosalie in his arms the day she fell.

Matthias pulled a piece of wood from his shirt pocket and a knife from his pants before he seated himself next to Zion. He opened the folding blade and set to work on a shape he had begun carving in the raw piece of basswood. Curls of creamy wood drifted to the porch floor. Lightning bugs danced under the orchard trees. The smell of roses floated in the cool evening air. Between curls, Matthias studied the young man squirming in the chair next to him.

"Son?"

"Yes, sir."

"What are your plans?"

Zion wondered if this was a trick question. "My plans for what, sir?"

"You told us you were heading west, but what then?"

Drawing in a deep breath, Zion considered his answer. Rosalie had not confided to Zion the depth of her father's involvement, if any, in the Underground Railroad. Just how much information he should share, he weighed carefully. "Honestly, Mr. Johnson, I'm not planning to lead expeditions for my life's work. I've loaded up the wagon with items in high demand out west. They'll sell for a good profit, along with the mules and wagon I'm planning to deliver to a mining outfit in Virginia City. Between the merchandise, hauling for folks, and the escort fees, I should come out with a good profit, enough for me and Penny to find a place of our own. A girl needs a place to call home."

"That she does." Matthias scraped the knife across the wood once more than looked Zion in the eye. "Any idea where you might be looking to settle?"

"My plan was to travel west and make a decision after we saw more of the country."

"You said 'was.' Those still your plans?"

Zion looked at the man next to him. He knew better than to lie, but wasn't sure just what to say, unsure himself where things stood with Rosalie. "My plans are to follow the will of God, wherever that leads. I planned this expedition without consulting the Lord. After my parents died, I lost my faith and stopped praying; but I know that's no way to live. I've made my heart right with God now, and I'm trusting Him to show me the way."

"Can't give a better answer than that, Son. Not a one of us knows where our paths will really take us. I heard a proverb once, not in the Good Book, but right true. 'Man plans, God laughs'."

"I have to say, I didn't laugh much for awhile, but I feel kind of like Penny. She was so weak, but she's growing stronger every day."

"Jesus is faithful, Son. He'll show you the way."

"I plan to come back here some day." Zion's revelation caused the older man to stop whittling and study his face—to look for more meaning than what the words themselves offered.

"Do you now?"

"I have a business transaction in the area, so I'm quite certain."

"Just business?"

"There's all kinds of business, Mr. Johnson."

Rosalie opened the door, soft light from inside the cabin filtered around her slim silhouette. "Here you go, Mr. Coldwell. Make sure Henry takes half a dropperful around the same time each day and the tea as needed. A cup before bed would surely ease his sleep tonight." She placed a brown bag of dried nettle leaves and a bottle of tincture in Zion's hands. "A bit of honey or sugar in the tea will take the edge off the bitterness."

"Thank you, Miss Johnson. I'll see to it, and I'm sure the family would have me extend their gratitude."

"My pleasure."

Zion walked into the darkness thinking how a little Rosalie could take the bitter edge off any day.

CHAPTER 31

O vercast skies and drizzling rain greeted the stagecoach's arrival at the Washington station, an unusual looking coach topped with a spinning wheel battened down and covered with a white canvas flapping in the inclement weather. Seated on top, the driver hunched down in his jacket, his hat smashed down on his head. Travis studied the women inside, Liza to his left and Penelope and Beth Ann seated on the bench across from him. He wondered if such a high contrast of women were ever gathered for two-and-a-half days together in such cramped quarters.

Liza, usually asleep or at least inside in the afternoons, drooped in the heat of the day, constantly mopping her brow with a damp handkerchief. Penelope sat erect in her seat, her carpet bag firmly in place on her lap, speaking when spoken to from behind lowered lashes. Beth Ann wore a relaxed countenance, quick to smile and assist others. Travis appreciated her good humor and helping hands.

When the coach finally stopped at the station before noon, all on board happily gathered their belongings and prepared to disembark. Travis helped from within while the driver opened the door and assisted from the outside. Once everyone stood on the platform, Travis worked with the driver to unload the luggage. "Careful please, there's fragile camera equipment in that case."

"Right." Each man took a firm hold on a handle and eased the case on the platform. Penelope anxiously supervised the unloading of her precious spinning wheel and hurried to resecure the canvas protecting it from the drizzle once it was down.

"I'm going to the livery for fresh horses," the driver said.

"I'll go with you and see about a ride to the lodge. You ladies go inside the stationhouse. I'll be back as soon as I can."

Beth Ann led the women to the stationhouse and held the door open for their entrance. Flipping his watch open, Travis shielded it from the rain with his jacket, checked the time, and then closed the gold case. He slipped the watch in the pocket of his patterned Chinese silk vest.

Even when traveling, Travis cut a dapper line. He wore a single-breasted frock coat with a squared shape at the bottom front reaching just above his knees. As usual, with his morning dress, he wore contrasting fawn pants and a black silk stove pipe hat and black necktie.

The driver unhitched the team and the twosome made haste to the livery. Travis allowed the driver to conduct his business first and then inquired about transport to the Comfort Lodge.

"It's only a mile out of town," said Joe Smith. "Why don't you take a horse and have the keeper, James Erlanger, come out for you in his wagon."

"Most kind of you, sir." Travis took the horse and received the directions to the lodge. Enjoying the feel of the saddle after bumping on the wooden bench of the stagecoach, Travis let the horse pick the pace and quickly covered the mile to the lodge. A large black man came out of the barn as he entered the property.

"I believe this is Comfort Lodge?"

"Yes, suh. That it is," Balim answered.

"Is Mr. Coldwell in? I'm Travis Ballard. He's expecting me."

"Why yes, suh. Massa Zion's expectin' you. He was expectin' three women folk, too."

Travis thought it odd a slave would know so much of his master's business, but brushed it off.

"The women are waiting at the station for transportation. If you'll show me to Mr. Coldwell, I'll speak to him to see if a carriage or wagon is available."

"Mr. Erlanger owns the carriage, but I'm sho' he'd let you use it to fetch the ladies. Our wagon takes a six-mule team, so it would be much quicker to use the carriage."

Our wagon? The thought puzzled Travis. "Mr. Coldwell is inside?"

Balim heard the message loud and clear. Mr. Ballard would not deal with a slave. His patience had obviously been tried enough by the longer than necessary conversation. "Yes, suh. Massa Zion's inside." He bowed his head and retreated to the barn.

A few minutes passed and James Erlanger entered the barn through the big double doors. "Hey, Balim, will you help me with the horses?"

"Yes, suh." Balim and James made quick work of harnessing the horses and connecting one to the carriage and one to the flatbed wagon.

"You're good with the horses, Balim."

"I know hosses, Massa James. Massa Zion's daddy taught me all about 'em on his farm. A nicer spread an' finer animals you ain't never seen."

"If West is any indication of the animals he raised, I believe you. He's a beauty." James patted the flank of his horse. "Mr. Coldwell will need you to drive the wagon in for the luggage. We can't fit the ladies and all their belongings in the Rockaway."

"Yes, suh. Massa James." Zion backed the team out and climbed on the buckboard while James took the reins of the carriage horses. Stopping in front of the lodge, Mr. Erlanger hopped down and disappeared inside. He returned with Travis who sat next to him on the front seat of the carriage. James flicked the reins and headed down the lane, Balim close behind.

Memories of the slave auction flooded Balim's thoughts, but he pushed them back and focused on the task at hand. Once in town, Travis indicated the luggage and items belonging to his group. Balim and James worked together to load them on the wagon bed while Travis went in the stationhouse for the ladies.

"An open-air carriage sounds divine after that stuffy coach." Liza Waterson gave a dramatic wave of her handkerchief and allowed Travis to assist her into the back. "Just delicious, with padded seats, too." Liza adjusted her skirts as she lowered herself on the bench. "And thank God it stopped that terrible driveling."

Penelope made a quiet entrance and created the slightest bounce as she seated herself next to Liza. "Did you mean drizzling?" she asked.

"Whatever suits."

"I'll ride on the wagon," Beth Ann offered. "The carriage only holds four."

"If you're sure that's what you want." Travis walked Miss Sparks to the wagon and helped her onto the buckboard next to Balim. He returned to the carriage and the party rolled out of town.

Zion waited on the front porch and took the steps down to the lawn as the group approached. "Good to see you folks." Zion looked from one female face to another.

Travis made the introductions and Zion put the faces to the names. It wasn't hard to keep them straight. Each woman lived up to his expectations: Liza's colorful flamboyance and brassy personality, Penelope's nondescript appearance and demeanor, and Beth Ann's openness and helpfulness.

"Mrs. Erlanger has prepared some food for you. I'll show you to your rooms, and after you freshen up, come down to the dining hall. I know you won't be disappointed." Zion led the way up the stairs showing the three ladies their room on the left and Travis the room he would share with Zion on the right. Beth Ann oohed at the window seat in the gable while Liza made sure she got first dibs on the water basin. After a quick wash she fluffed her red hair and preened in the mirror. Penelope waited for her to finish before seeing to her own toilet, tucking strands of brown hair back in the tight bun she wore at the nape of her neck and scrubbing her hands and face. Beth Ann watched from the window seat where she released her braid and worked her fingers through her waist-length hair.

"Your hair reminds me of a Bible verse," said Penelope. "'Your hair is as a flock of goats, that appear on mount Gilead'."

"Why, Miss Ford," Beth Ann teased, "I do believe you're quoting from the Song of Solomon, a might steamy bit of Scripture."

Penelope blushed. "My pastor's wife recommended I read it before my wedding night."

Liza laughed, a lusty laugh from deep in the back of her throat. "Oh, Penelope, if you have any questions about your wedding night, you come to Miss Liza. I'll set you straight on anything you need to know." She lowered her voice and took on a confidential tone. "Keeping men happy has been my specialty since I was 17 years old. This marriage business is going to be a cakewalk. Just one man to tend should be a breeze."

Compassion swelled in Beth Ann's heart, a sorrow at a young girl's desperate choice to sell her body to make a living. "You have a big heart, Liza. I'm sure you and Ned will make a fine go of things. Are you up to the housekeeping? Because I'm an expert on cobwebs and rug beating, biscuits and bacon and such."

"My plan's simple." Liza placed her hands on her full hips and sashayed toward the door. "Keep him happy in the bedroom, and he won't care if his biscuits are as heavy as rocks." She opened the door and glided out, leaving Beth Ann and Penelope gaping at each other.

"That woman needs Jesus," Beth Ann said. "I hope we'll have a chance to reach her on the trip." She smiled at Penelope and motioned her to the door. "She's my first missionary assignment."

Penelope nodded and joined Beth Ann just as Travis left his room across the hall. "After you, ladies."

Travis Ballard had a regal comportment, a refinement that emanated from his polished appearance and meticulous manners. He followed the women down the staircase and into the dining hall.

"What a cheerful room," Beth Ann observed. "I love how the curtains and tablecloths match. And look, fresh flowers on every table."

"Quaint," said Liza.

Travis pulled out chairs for the ladies, starting with Liza. Beth Ann and Penelope couldn't help but notice Travis favored Liza with his attentions; but they weren't surprised. Miss Waterson was striking with her bright red hair and curvy figure wrapped tightly in a purple and black dress. The scoop of her neckline was well below normal daywear for most ladies, but quite modest for Liza's tastes. It hid some of her best assets, she thought. But even when she was more covered than was her preference, Liza knew how to play up everything she had, leaving men staring in her wake.

Sweeping into the room with a loaded tray, Florence Erlanger greeted her guests. "I wasn't sure when you would arrive, so I've made a simple meal and we'll have a bigger supper this evening." Baskets with thick slices of sourdough bread and little cups of honey butter and spicy apple butter were placed on the tables next to tall glasses of iced tea. "James made a special trip to the ice house this morning so you could have cold drinks, and we'll have Indian pudding with real whipped cream for dessert."

"I've never had Indian pudding before," said Travis, "but cold and sweet sounds good."

"Indian pudding is made with milk, cornmeal and molasses mostly, an egg and some spices. Quite flavorful." Florence dropped her empty tray and headed for the kitchen. "I'll be right back." She returned with a large kettle of beef vegetable stew which she placed on the sideboard and then ladled into stoneware bowls.

"That smells wonderful," Beth Ann said as Florence placed a steaming bowl of stew in front of her.

Penelope received her bowl with a nod and quiet thank you.

"Is that okra?" Liza asked. "Lands sakes. That stuff's too slimy in stew. Fried okra, now that's another story. I like it fried." She pushed the food around in her bowl. "Guess I can work around it."

"I hope so." Florence smiled at the woman.

"Where's Mr. Coldwell off to?" Liza dipped a piece of bread in the creamy brown broth.

"He's in the barn with Balim," Travis answered. "He said he already ate. This is delicious, Mrs. Erlanger." Travis enjoyed the homemade meal. Since leaving the plantation, he missed the fine meals set at his parents' elegant table. It was part of the price of freedom and adventure; and he was willing to pay it, especially since Daddy paid for everything else.

"All the other folks ate about an hour ago," said Florence. "The Coventrys went in to town with Mr. Nester and Mr. Perkins, and the Sweeneys went for a walk." Florence placed slices of Indian pudding on plates on the sideboard, ready for the cream when the meal finished. "Mr. Coldwell would like to have a meeting with everyone in the parlor at 3:00."

Travis pulled his watch from his vest pocket. "That's two hours. Plenty of time to enjoy this good food and a short respite."

CHAPTER 32

"We're all finally here." Zion scanned the parlor. Men, women and children from different backgrounds and cultures all looked to him for leadership, except J.T. and Bug, Zion was well aware. They were in the room, of course, needing to keep up appearances in front of everyone; but Zion wondered what they had up their sleeves. Regardless, he purposed to trust God for discernment and direction. Although he knew he had made the plans for this journey without consulting the Lord, he had repented and taken Proverbs to heart: "Trust in the Lord with all thine heart; and lean not unto thine own understanding. In all thy ways acknowledge Him, and He shall direct thy paths."

Of further comfort to Zion was the fact that Balim partnered with him in both the business and prayer.

"I'm sorry you haven't met my sister Penny yet," Zion addressed the gathering in the big room. "She took sick after we arrived. She's doing much better, but since the lodge filled to capacity with the addition of Mr. Nester and Mr. Perkins, she's staying on at the neighbors.

"Now that we've all introduced ourselves, I want to set the schedule for departure." Zion looked to Thaddeus. "Mr. Coventry's wagon should be finished by Tuesday or Wednesday at the latest. Since Wednesday's the Fourth of July, I thought we might as well start our trip off with a bang. Reverend Dryfus is hosting an ice cream social followed by a singing and fireworks. We'll have everything loaded and ready to head out Thursday morning."

"That gives us four days here," said Travis.

"I think when we look back on this trip, we'll be thankful for the time we had here to rest and prepare. We'll make the most of our time—we'll take inventory and check our supplies. If you're all set, that's great, but as we talk amongst ourselves, we may find we've neglected to bring a few things of importance."

"I've got everything I need in my valise," Liza said. "Ned's got the house ready. All I need to do is show up and make it a happy home."

"I'm glad you don't have to worry about any details, Miss Liza, but others are going to start from scratch, so it's good to review supplies. There is a well stocked mercantile in town, and any tack you may need you can find at the livery. Check your horses' shoes. Cooper did a fine job on my stallion. You may want to pick up some extra shoes and nails. The horses and mules will be putting over 2,000 miles on before we arrive in Virginia City.

"I've got our supplies and food coming out on Monday. We'll stow what we need in workable containers and configure it on the wagons beginning Monday afternoon, with the exception of the items Mr. Coventry plans to take on his wagon. I'll be sitting in the dining hall with my list after our meeting, if anyone wants to compare what they've brought with mine. I'd appreciate looking over yours. You might have thought of something I didn't."

"Being this is your first trip west, that's highly likely, ain't it, Coldwell?" J.T.'s lip curled as he spit out Zion's name.

"Is that true, Mr. Coldwell?" Sara Coventry asked, concern for the safety of her family playing across her delicate features.

Zion nodded. "Yes it is, Mrs. Coventry. I suppose everyone has to have a first, don't you?"

"Like my first railroad investment." Thaddeus encouraged his wife who looked up with wary eyes. Mr. Coventry knew of Zion's inexperience, but neglected to share it with his wife for fear she would not agree to entrust herself and their children to his care.

"The most important first, I believe, is trusting God. He's given us knowledge and wisdom, but He also still speaks to His people today, giving us what we need to face the challenges and obstacles life brings. I trust He'll lead us and protect us on this journey. That's why we don't start one day of travel without prayer. After breakfast, we'll gather for devotion and ask the Lord's blessing on our day." Zion broke out in a big grin. "Just look at what He did for the Israelites in the desert. Their clothes and shoes never wore out."

"And they wondered around dying like flies for 40 years." Bug snickered at his humor, proud he remembered a Bible story from so long ago.

"It might seem like 40 years, but if we make good time, we can be in Virginia City in just over four months. You'll be spending Thanksgiving in your new homes." Zion made eye contact with everyone in the room before he spoke again.

"If you're not willing to abide by my terms, or the terms on our signed contracts, then I'll refund any money you've fronted and we'll part as friends. Otherwise, I'm happy to see you to your futures in America's new frontier."

"I wish you could have been there, Penny." Zion held his recovering sister's elbow to keep her steady as they walked a circuit in the Johnson yard. "Wait until you meet everyone."

"I'm looking forward to it. Do you think they'll come to church tomorrow?"

"I don't know. I told them about the service." Zion watched as Penny maneuvered around a hole in the yard, ready to help if she should stumble. "I'm looking forward to meeting Reverend Dryfus. Rosalie told me he stopped by to see you this morning."

"He did." Penny grew animated. "He brought Charity with him. She's the sweetest thing. You'll never guess what she did."

"What?"

"She brought a basket."

"Well that's just exciting as can be, Buttercup. You never saw a basket before, did you?"

"Oh, Zion. You're silly. This basket was special because it had five puppies in it. They were soft as down and the cutest little shepherds you ever saw."

"How old were they?"

"Seven or eight weeks, Charity said."

"That must have been a heavy basket."

"Her Pa carried it for her, but when she got here we put it on the ground and had the most fun playing with the pups—Marigold and Lucas, too."

"You sure they were shepherds?"

"Of course. They looked just like Gypsy—black bodies with fluffy white bellies and brown markings. Same pointy noses, too."

"Gypsy sure helped out on the farm, didn't he?"

"I used to love to watch him work," Penny said. "What was it Pa used to say about shepherds?"

"They're a farmer's helper, a loyal companion, and a child's shadow. And old Gypsy was all that, wasn't he?"

"He was." Penny reached for Zion's hand and the two walked a bit in silence gently swinging their arms in time with their steps. "It's getting easier now."

Zion looked down at Penny's thoughtful expression. "What's that, Buttercup?"

"I mean, it's easier to remember the good things about home, like Gypsy, and not feel that terrible hot burning in my chest."

Zion recalled the pain and agreed with his sister. "I know what you mean."

"Why do you think terrible things like Mama and Daddy dying happen, Zion?"

"I wish I had the answer for that. I'd be lying if I said I did, but I'll tell you one thing I learned. It's plumb fool-headed to run from God when He's what you really need most."

"I know you're right. And I don't believe God sent the storm, but sometimes it's hard to accept that He could have stopped it– but He didn't. I think that's the hardest part about faith."

Zion wondered at his sister, still so young and dependant, even weak from her recent sickness, but mature and strong in her faith and understanding of deep spiritual matters. For the first time in months, the voice of Zion's mother rang in his memory, and with it an answer for her little girl.

Zion felt his chest tighten. He stopped Penny and dropped to one knee in front of her. Still holding her hand he looked deeply in her blue eyes, so similar to his own. "Penny, what was Ma's favorite verse of Scripture?"

Penny knew the answer without having to think about it, but as the revelation dawned, tears welled in her eyes. "Romans 8:28."

"Let's say it together, like a prayer."

"All right," Penny whispered, reverence filling her spirit.

Zion stood, took Penny's other hand and turned his face to the sky. "And we know that all things work together for good to them that love God, to them who are the called according to His purpose." Something broke free in Zion. A river of healing washed away his doubts leaving behind a peace and a joy Zion had never felt before. He had known this Word, heard it almost every day from his own mother, but today it lived in His heart.

"Do it again." Tears spilled out the corners of Penny's eyes and ran down her cheeks–not tears of sorrow, but sweet release. Zion lifted his hands to the sky and Penny clutched hers to her chest. "And we know that all things work together for good to them that love God, to them who are the called according to His purpose."

"If I was at one of them brush arbor meetings, I think I'd have me a shout right now," Zion said, beaming from ear to ear.

"Oh, Zion, God is so good."

"Yes He is–faithful, too. Do you remember Pa's favorite verse?"

"Of course." Penny smiled. "He just about beat us over the head with it every time we got in trouble."

"Those weren't the only times he said it, but you sure felt the impact more under a scolding." Zion laughed. "It was 3 John 4. 'I have not greater joy than to hear that my children walk in truth.'"

"I guess that's what we have to do now."

"That's what I plan to do now, Penny. As God gives us the strength, we can walk in His truth knowing all things work together for good."

Rosalie watched from the window of the cabin. Not knowing the subject matter in no way diminished what she felt as she watched brother and sister stroll through the yard and break out in spontaneous prayer. Zion's uplifted arms drew Rosalie to him this morning as much as his outstretched hands had in the darkness the evening before. She knew she was falling for him, and she felt helpless to do anything about it. Her life, so routine and stable, had turned upside down by a man she met only a week before, a man who was leaving soon.

Pansy Joy watched the expressions playing across her sister's face. She wondered what she saw out there, but was unwilling to interrupt. "Marigold, help me with these sheets."

Marigold began to protest. It wasn't her room after all, but the look Pansy Joy threw at her silenced her reply. "All right." Marigold followed Pansy Joy into the room she shared with Rosalie.

"Let's pull these off and get the clean ones on."

"It's not wash day yet. Why the hurry?"

"When folks have been sick and spent a lot of time in bed, it's good to put clean bedding on. Just be thankful you weren't the one who got flux or twisted your ankle."

The girls worked together to strip the sheets and pillow cases. "What's going on with Rosalie?" Marigold asked.

Pansy Joy studied her sister, wondering if she should share her thoughts. Marigold's interests were more on bees and fishing than boys. Still, Rosalie was her sister, and since Marigold was astute enough to pick up on her feelings, Pansy Joy felt they could talk about it. "I'm thinking Rosalie might be having feelings for Zion Coldwell."

Marigold absorbed her words, reflecting on the way Rosalie had been acting ever since Zion arrived. She cocked her head to one side and looked at Pansy Joy. "I think you're right."

Pansy Joy tucked a pillow under her chin and slipped a case over the end. "In a way, I'm happy for her, but I'm concerned, too." She shook the pillow into its case and placed it on the bed. Marigold smoothed the air bumps from beneath the quilt.

"Why's that, PJ?"

"The Coldwells are pulling out for Virginia City next week. Even if the two have feelings for each other, it might just end up breaking Rosalie's heart again."

Marigold nodded. "Like Clayton?"

"Like Clayton."

CHAPTER 33

A buzz filled the lawn around the church building–so many visitors on one day, and such a variety of them. Reverend Dryfus had delivered a sermon he hoped ministered to all, encouraging the saints and sharing the love of God with the sinners. Before the dismissal he extended an invitation to everyone for the ice cream social and fireworks on Wednesday, an invitation enthusiastically received by the congregation.

Lark Matheny eyed Liza Waterson with interest. Of course, being a principled young lady, she would never think of wearing such a garish outfit to a Sunday morning service, but the sensuality the woman exuded was a power Lark desired to wield for herself. Men flocked around the red-headed beauty. She seemed to accept it as nonchalant—insignificant, but Lark knew how it felt. She knew Liza was relishing every minute she was the center of so much male attention.

Liza's moves looked so natural that Lark decided to practice some for herself. Pulling the fan from her reticule, she flipped it open and turned her wrist, just so, like Liza did, and then fluttered her eyelashes behind it.

Marigold watched Lark from across the lawn and bit her bottom lip to keep from bursting out in raucous laughter. Lark, only two years older than Marigold, seemed like an actor to the younger girl—like a member of one of those traveling theatrical productions. She was all dressed up in a stage outfit, playing the part of someone she was not in real life, but someone she wanted very much to emulate.

Marigold observed Lark methodically place one hand on her hip—like Liza—while batting her eyes behind the fan she held in the other. As she began her choreographed approach to Zion and Penny, her hips pendulated like the regulation in the Matheny's grandfather clock. Once she reached Zion, she offered him a coy smile and a stiff arm, expecting Zion to bend over and kiss her hand the way any gracious gentleman would in the presence of such a fine lady.

Zion offered an impish grin and grabbed Lark's hand with a beefy paw. "Howdy, Miss Lark." Zion rotated the girl's hand with animation and pumped it up and down like a man priming a dry well pump.

Taken aback, Lark regrouped and tried another tactic. She waved the fan a couple of times and batted her eyes in what she was sure gave a come-hither look while still appearing sweetly innocent. "Hello, Mr. Coldwell. It's so nice to see you in the house of the Lord this morning."

"It's good to be here." Zion tucked his thumbs in his Sunday best suspenders and rolled from heel to toe, backward then forward, then back again, in a way that reminded Lark, in a less-than-compelling way, of her gangly twin brothers. Something seemed amiss.

Maybe I interrupted some bizarre conversation. Surely something's going on between Zion and his sister for him to act so strange this morning. Lark turned her attention from the oscillating Zion to an equally befuddled Penny. "And you must be Penny. Aren't you a pretty thing?" Lark stroked Penny's silky hair at the crown and gave the girl a smile that broadened her mouth but failed to reach her probing eyes. "And look, you have the same gorgeous blue eyes as your brother. I just love that color." Lark turned to Zion. "A young lady could find herself lost in pools so blue."

Penny did not know what to think about Lark, unsure just what kind of woman she was talking to. "Yes, I'm Penny. Pleased to meet you."

"Did you enjoy the candy I brought for you? I wanted to meet you last week when I walked all the way out from town in the heat of the day, but Rosalie refused to let me see you." Lark puffed out her lower lip in her most charmingly pathetic way.

Refusing anything to anyone didn't seem like the Rosalie Penny knew and loved, but she did recall eating the candy, and she hadn't met Lark when she stopped by. "Thank you, Miss Lark. I love rock candy best of all, and I'm sorry I didn't get to thank you for it before."

"That's quite all right." Lark patted Penny's fair cheek. "If you can talk your brother into bringing you out to the mercantile, I'll get you some more."

"Your pa's delivering my big order tomorrow, so I don't think I'll have a need to go back into town for anything."

"I see." Lark shifted her weight from one foot to another with a dramatic sweep of her full skirt and petticoats. "Then perhaps I'll see you at the Fourth of July celebration. I love watching the fireworks shoot off in the moonlight. It's so romantic. At least, it would be terribly romantic if the right fellow was standing close by." Lark blinked her eyes and waved her fan again.

Zion felt sorry for the girl, at the same time he wondered what had gotten into her. If her behavior before had been aggressive, today's was downright tawdry.

"Miss Matheny," Zion addressed Lark in a slow, deliberate voice. "I'm sure one day some lucky fellow will be standing by your side at the fireworks, and it will be everything you're hoping for."

Lark could not miss Zion's dismissal. Delivered in a way that offered to keep her dignity in tact, Lark still felt its stinging blow to her ego and fledgling girlish passions. Drawing her shoulders back, she lifted her chin and threw a venomous look at Zion. "I must be on my way now." Lark tossed her golden ringlets. "Mother and Father are having the Dryfus family for dinner, and it would be rude to keep the minister waiting."

Zion and Penny watched Lark promenade across the grass. "I never met anyone like her before," said Penny.

"She's just trying to grow up too fast." Zion squeezed Penny's shoulder. "Trying to rush things before their time just sets a body up for frustration."

"Life's frustrating enough sometimes without adding extra to it."

"That's for sure." Zion spied the Johnson family talking with the Eldridges and the Erlangers. "Why don't you go see Mrs. Erlanger? She's been asking about you. I'd like to speak to Reverend Dryfus, and I'll meet you there in a minute."

He watched Penny walk into Florence's embrace and then turned to meet the pastor.

"Fine message today, Reverend." Zion extended his hand.

"Thank you. Good to have you with us, young man. What brings you to Washington?"

"I'm Zion Coldwell. You met my sister Penny out at the Johnson place."

"Oh, yes. She and Charity had a wonderful visit."

"I heard they had some kind of picnic." Zion chortled.

"Picnic?" Warren Dryfus furrowed his brow in thought, and then let out a chuckle. "Would you be talking about a puppy picnic?"

"That's the one."

"My Charity believes the coats of puppies are a pure conductor for God's healing virtue."

"It seemed to work for Penny."

"She is much improved since I was out to see her."

"I wondered if you had plans for all those pups."

"Actually, Mr. Coldwell, I'm looking for homes for them. Are you interested?"

Zion lifted his index finger to his lips. "If you could just keep that on the quiet, I'd appreciate it."

Reverend Dryfus nodded. "Fine. Fine. I won't say a thing."

"Penny said the pups were seven or eight weeks old. Do you think they're ready to wean by Thursday morning?"

"Oh, yes. Charity has already been supplementing their milk with solid food. They're doing well."

"Great." Zion put his hat on and smiled at the minister. "Thank you, Reverend. I look forward to the ice cream social Wednesday."

"Me, too. God bless you."

"You, too."

Louella wiped her eyes with her fingertips.

"What's wrong, Apple Blossom? I thought you'd be pleased as punch to be in the gospel mill this morning." Clarence handed his bride a rumpled bandana. She blew her nose and turned a sorrowful face to her husband's.

"It just made me miss Ma and Pa, and reminded me . . ." Louella sniffled. "It just made me think I'll probably never see them again." A sob choked out behind the red bandana.

"Aw, Sugar." Clarence put his arm around Louella's shoulder and she buried her face in his forearm.

Across the church, Liza turned to Penelope. "See what I mean?" she declared. "This doxology works is no good for a girl's complexion. Just look at Louella. She's as splotchy as a griddle cake ready to be flipped."

"Miss Liza!" Penelope exclaimed. "I can't believe you'd say such a thing!"

"Hardly needs saying, the evidence speaks for itself." Liza looked Penelope over. "But at least it brought a little life out of you. I never heard so much excitement in your voice. I was getting worried for your intended, wondering if he knew he was paying for a mouse instead of a purring feline who knows how to scratch a man's itch."

"Claws down, Miss Waterson." Travis spoke firmly and locked eyes with Liza. "What's gotten into you this morning?"

She shook her head and set her jaw in a firm line. "I haven't been to church since I left home, not even for a wedding or a funeral. I don't know what made me decide to subject myself to a gospel sharp today."

"I know," said Beth Ann.

"What would you know about it?"

"I know that I've been praying for you, asking the Lord to soften your heart so you could feel His love."

Liza harrumphed and gave Beth Ann a haughty look over her shoulder. "I've had more love than one woman could ever need."

Beth Ann looked in Liza's eyes, behind the mask. "Do you know there's a story in the Bible about a woman who went to a well? She had to draw water every day, and it was a big job. Jesus told her He had water to drink and the woman would never be thirsty again."

"Listen, Miss Missionary Society, I know that story, and I know what kind of woman she was. I don't need you looking down your holier-than-thou snoot at me."

Beth Ann offered a smile that further aggravated Liza's foul mood. "I can see you're not ready to hear the rest of the story, but I'll be glad to share it with you when you are." She turned to Penelope and thrust her hand in the narrow bend of her arm. "I feel like walking back to the lodge. Would you like to join me?"

"Looks like you and Sally had a rough night." Nester pushed back the curtain. Dust particles frolicked in the bright shafts of light that charged across the darkened room.

"Hey, cut that out, J.T."

"I'm cutting nothing out, Bug. If you're gonna dance with Sally on Saturday night, you better be ready to roll out Sunday morning." Nester crossed the floor and ripped the blankets off the bed. "I'm only letting you in on this deal because of your dear departed sister, God rest her soul. We missed church this morning because of your shenanigans."

Bug hooted. "Since when did missing a preaching get you this riled up?"

"Since it was an opportunity to build trust with these dupes—I mean our distinguished traveling companions." J.T. grabbed the flask nestled in Bug's scrawny arms. "Instead of making headway, I was making excuses for your sorry carcass."

"My head is pounding." Bug smiled, revealing a dilapidated set of teeth. "And that is the gospel truth, J.T."

"What do you know about the gospel truth anyway?" J.T. checked his reflection in the small mirror hanging next to the washbasin and adjusted his cravat. "It's a good thing Marcy gave me that copy of *The Neckclothitania*, or else I'd never be able to manage these fancy harnesses."

"You saying you didn't wear your best bib and tucker in Auburn State Prison?"

"Shut your mouth, Bug."

J.T. had spent five of his prime years working in a black-and-white striped uniform. The Quakers ran the prison, and set a rigid schedule of prayer and contemplation, requiring the prisoners to work to help support the prison's upkeep. J.T. ran his fingers through his hair recalling the years he was forced to wear it close cropped, feeling like an old bald man, and walk in locked step, head bowed from place to place. He could almost feel the hand of the prisoner behind him and his hand on the shoulder of the person in front as the men maintained a rigid separation traveling from their private cells to the communal dining room to work and back again in complete silence.

J.T. shook off the memories and focused on his plans for the future–a flush one full of anything he wanted, most of all his freedom. "We need to finalize plans before we set out, in case we need to bring anything from town."

"Speaking of things from town, did you get the whiskey?"

"I knew when I saw that Taylor character he was an abolitionist. I heard he has his own squaw and papoose, too." J.T. cackled. "I told him I was a conductor on the Underground Railroad, so he's making a false bottom on the wagon with a nice big opening. We'll load it up with jugs of Kentucky bourbon."

Despite his splitting headache, Bug let out a roar. "You beat all, J.T.!" He grabbed his temples and squinted his eyes. "Ooh, my head."

CHAPTER 34

M onday dawned clear and full of promise. Donald Matheny and his boys arrived immediately following breakfast with two wagons full of supplies. Balim and Zion spent hours repackaging and organizing everything they needed for the trip. They stopped for a quick lunch of cold ham sandwiches and applesauce and then went straight back to it.

"Did you forget you had a sister?" Zion looked up from his work to find Penny smiling at him, Rosalie at her side.

"If you two don' make a fine picture standin' there looking fresh as a mornin' breeze," said Balim.

Balim and Zion stood to greet the girls, Rosalie in a pretty pink calico and wide-brimmed straw hat and Penny in a new indigo bonnet that accentuated the blue in her eyes.

"I think I'm going to have to rename you, Penny," said Zion.

"What do you mean?"

"You look more like a blue bonnet than a buttercup today."

Zion took Penny's chin in hand and turned her head left and then right, up and then down examining the calico poke bonnet. "Where'd you get such a fine chapeau?"

"I made it."

"You did not." Zion was certain Rosalie or Pansy Joy had made the bonnet, not his little sister who had minimal sewing skills. Just last month he helped her sew a button on her dress. "She did." Rosalie affirmed Penny's prowess with needle and thread. "Pansy Joy cut out a new dress for Marigold and she had enough calico for bonnets for both of the girls."

Zion grabbed Penny by the shoulders and turned the beaming girl in a full circle. "I'll be." Penny glowed under Zion's praise.

"Hey, Zion," Penny tugged on her brother's belt loop. "Where's your whip? I was telling Marigold about your fancy tricks. She thought I was talking about a yo-yo." Penny rolled her eyes, full of spunk and sarcastic drama.

Zion tugged on a blond braid. "You don't want your big brother to show off now, do you?"

"It feels good to do something well. You liked my hat, and I came to show it off."

Zion rubbed his fuzzy chin. "You got me there. I tell you what . . . I'll come by after dinner for a bit, if that's all right with Miss Rosalie."

"That's fine, Mr. Coldwell." Rosalie tipped her head and smiled. "I'm making some gingerbread. We'll wait for you to have our dessert." She turned to Balim. "You're most welcome, too, Balim."

"Why thank ye, Miss Rozlee. Gingerbread sounds mighty fine. Yes it does."

"We better get back." Rosalie reached for Penny's hand. "I thought a walk would help build Penny's strength up, but we have things to do at home."

"Home is a right nice place to be, isn't it?" said Zion.

Balim watched the interchange, fascinated at the turnaround in Zion and his response to the willowy Miss Rosalie. Yes, the good Lord was at work, for sure and for certain. "A walk with Miss Rozlee seems to do a body good, yes, suh."

"If you hurry, maybe you can catch up with them," Zion said. Balim let out a hearty laugh and the two returned to their work.

"I'm going to wash up Balim, and put on a fresh shirt."

"I didn't know a feller needed a fresh shirt to crack some whip tricks for little girls." Balim feigned concern. "Do you think I should put on my Sunday-go-to-meetin' clothes?"

Zion shook his head at his friend. "You can go smelling like a mule if you want. I'll be down in five minutes."

The two traveled the road to the Johnsons, excitement building in Zion. Months had passed since he had handled his whip, and he wondered if he would be rusty. Planning to do a few simple moves first, he considered which of the fancier ones Marigold might enjoy–and Rosalie, if she happened to be around.

"Did you see the dragonflies hovering over yon by the pond, Massa Zion?"

"I didn't pay too much attention today."

"Maybe not to the dragonflies, but ole Balim thinks you was payin' some special attention to another of God's fine creatures."

"Maybe." Balim's grin was contagious and Zion soon wore one of his own. "So what about the dragonflies?"

"They's summpin else, yes, suh. I never noticed they had spikey legs. They was a chasin' after the mosquitoes and they didn' have a chance, no suh. The dragonflies attacked from underneath, wrapped those spikey legs around 'em, and they couldn't get away."

"And I'm sure there's a spiritual lesson in that, if I know you."

"Sho there is." Balim grinned. "I ain't figured it out yet, but I know there is."

Zion slapped Balim on a broad shoulder. "You're something else, Balim."

Running down the lane from the cabin, Penny, Marigold, Lucas and Daisy met Balim and Zion before they cleared the trees. "We heard you coming." Penny, breathless, grabbed her side.

"Slow down there, Penny," Zion said. "You aren't full strength yet."

"I know. It just felt so good to run, and I've been looking forward to seeing you all day."

"You saw me already today." Zion tousled the panting girl's hair.

"I know." Penny sent a bashful look to her brother, and Zion chuckled at the girl so anxious to share a little excitement with her new friends.

"We had dinner a few minutes ago. Rosalie and Pansy Joy are just finishing up the dishes." Marigold studied Zion's waistline and the coil of braided leather fastened to his belt. "You really do have a whip."

Zion laughed. "Penny and I were raised on a horse farm. Everyone knows how to use a whip on a horse farm."

"I don't," said Penny.

"Most everyone, then."

"Did you beat the horses?" Lucas looked up at Zion with horror in his big brown eyes.

"No, we used whips to train horses to do things like lunges and to give them signals." The tense expression on Lucas's baby face relaxed, replaced by his usual infectious grin. "Would you like to see some different ways to use a whip?"

The children egged him on. "All right. First is the forward crack. It flows vertically in front, then I swing up. It's kind of like hitting a nail with a hammer." Zion ran through the motions, ending with a sharp crack in front at face level.

"Wow. What else can you do?" Marigold asked.

"There's the snake killer." Zion followed the same moves, this time drawing the whip tightly overhead. "And one of my favorites is the side crack." Holding the whip at his side with the end trailing behind, he lifted his arm, and the end of the whip came out from the side, cracking in front.

The quick movements and intense cracking sounds awed Marigold. "How do you do that?"

"It takes some practice, but once you get the hang of it, it's like throwing a ball. You aim with your thumb and let it go." Rotating his wrist, Zion began a full figure eight with double cracks, further impressing his audience.

"He didn't even show you any of his tricks yet. Wait until you see what he can do." Penny bragged on her brother.

"I bet Pa would like to see this–the girls, too." Marigold headed for the cabin. "I'll be right back." Before she reached the door, it opened.

"What's going on out here?" Matthias, leaning against his cane, filled the doorframe, a large smile on his face.

"Good evening, Mr. Johnson." Zion wondered what Matthias was thinking of him as he played with his whip for the children.

"Mr. Coldwell was showing us some whip cracks," Marigold said, her brown eyes sparkling with excitement.

"Well, now, I used to play with a whip some myself, back in the day."

"Really, Pa?" Lucas said, disbelief on his young face.

Matthias called Rosalie and Pansy Joy outside for the show. When everyone was gathered he turned to Zion. "Set your whip down on the ground, the tip facing me." Zion followed Matthias's directions. Leaning on his cane with his left hand, Matthias bent and grabbed the whip by its popper with his right hand. With a flip of his wrist, the whip curled, and the handle raced into Matthias's firm grip.

"That's amazing, Pa," said Rosalie. "I never knew you held a whip a day in your life."

"Don't need such things to tend plants, child, nor fetch Clover into the barn for milking." Before Matthias's injury, his plans had included herds of cattle and a bonanza ranch out west. Accepting his disability took time–a long process and the loving support of a Christian woman who helped him dream new dreams. Sharon's love of nature spawned the idea of tending their own orchard, the reason they moved from arid Texas to Kentucky's humid clime.

Lucas giggled. The thought of his pa chasing Clover into the barn with a whip tickled his funny bone. "What else can you do, Pa?"

"I don't know tricks really, but I'll show you the cattleman's crack." Matthias released a forward snap that cracked in front of him. His son clapped. Matthias looked at Zion and asked, "This is an eight-footer, isn't it?"

"Yes. I have a longer one, but I don't do tricks with that." The single-tailed whip was made of four leather strands braided together. The thong connected to a thin replaceable fall. A horsehair popper tied to the fall with a larkshead knot; while at the opposite end, an intricately braided leather cover encased the 12-inch wooden handle. Zion looked at Penny. "You ready?"

"I'll be right back." Penny walked to the wildflower garden and retrieved a black-eyed susan. Holding the long stem between her teeth, she turned to her side and nodded.

Horror registered on Rosalie's face. "Don't!"

With a flick of his wrist, a crack sounded and the flower fell to the ground, its decapitated stem still in Penny's teeth.

"That could take a fellow's breath away," said Matthias.

"I think my heart stopped for a second." Pansy Joy clutched her hands to her breast. Rosalie stood stock still, eyes enlarged, while Marigold and Lucas jumped up and down. "Do it again! Do it again!"

"I think I scared the ladies. How about I show you something else?" Zion looked at Lucas. "Can you bring me a small rock?"

The boy scurried to the side of the cabin and returned with a rock in his pudgy hand. Taking the stone, Zion placed it on top of his head. "Stand back." He drew the whip to his side. The thong circled around him raising the popper over Zion's head and knocking the stone to the ground.

"Whooey," Matthias hooted. "You didn't move a hair on your head, Son."

"I wish you could be here for the fair," said Marigold. "You would be sure to win some of the competitions."

"I'm not sure they have a whip cracking competition," said Matthias, "but it's a sure thing folks would like to see this kind of skill."

"Jump rope." Penny smiled at Zion, reminding him of her favorite stunt.

With a whoosh the whip cut through the air. Zion jumped and the popper cracked under his feet. He kept the whip moving and repeated the trick several times before the final crack. Zion gave an exaggerated bow. "Thank you, ladies and gentlemen. You've been a wonderful audience."

"How about we close out that fine performance with some of Rosalie's gingerbread?" Matthias said. "Did you whip up some of your sweet cream, Pansy Joy?"

"I sure did, Pa. You want to have it outside or in?"

"It's right nice out this evening."

"Come on girls," Pansy Joy called to her sisters. "Let's feed these men folk." Penny followed the procession into the cabin.

CHAPTER 35

A mixture of gloom and excitement played back and forth in Penny. The thought of leaving broke her heart. Even with Zion's promise they would come back and the company of the darling new puppy, the thought of being separated from the Johnson family weighed heavily. And Zion hadn't said how long they would stay when they did return. Not long enough for Penny, she was certain.

Fighting for equal time in Penny's emotions, the anticipation of the ice cream social and fireworks scheduled for the next evening was building higher and higher. It was like shoveling more and more coal into a steam engine until the steam just had to let off or explode.

Rosalie sensed the girl's unrest. "Penny, would you mind helping me with these?" Penny lifted her head from drawing lazy circles on Marigold's slate. The wash complete and hanging on the line, Rosalie looked forward to sitting for her next task. "I need to snap these beans for supper."

Penny took the crockery bowl from Rosalie and began snapping the ends off the pole beans, her melancholy displayed in the lethargic movements of her hands as she dropped the beans in a pan of water and let out an occasional sigh.

Rosalie watched the girl in silence and tried to think of

something to take her mind off things. "When we're finished, I was hoping you would help me pick some roses for Pansy Joy's wedding. We're drying them out so they'll still look pretty come the first of January."

Penny sniffed and snapped another bean. She held it a long while in an upturned hand, and then Rosalie watched a tear slide down the girl's cheek, just about breaking her own heart.

"Oh, honey." Rosalie scooted her ladder back chair next to Penny and wrapped the slight girl in her arms.

"I'm sorry," Penny said. "I don't know what's gotten into me."

"I think I do." Rosalie wiped a straying tendril out of Penny's face. "It's hard to leave friends, isn't it?"

Penny clamped her eyes shut, trying to quench the threatening storm of tears. She took a minute to compose herself and turned to look Rosalie in the eye. "I love you, Rosalie." Penny bit her quivering lip and took a deep breath.

Rosalie rubbed the girl's back in soothing circles. "I love you, too, Penny." Rosalie prayed for words to comfort the disquieted girl. "I'm so thankful our paths crossed this side of heaven. I'm never going to forget you, Penny."

Rosalie smiled. "I just thought of something."

"What?" Penny sniffed and Rosalie handed her a handkerchief.

"Our getting to know each other is going to give God praise."

A confused look crossed Penny's face. "I don't understand. How can God get praise when people who love each other are separated?"

"There's a verse in Philippians that says 'I thank my God every time I remember you,' and I'm planning to remember you every day, probably lots of times every day."

"I know what you're saying." Penny turned her face from the table and blew her nose. "It's just hard to say goodbye again so soon."

"Are you thinking about your ma and pa?"

"I think about them all the time, but it's gotten easier being here with you." Penny dropped her hands to her lap. "I hope once we get on the trail things won't go back to the way they were."

"What do you mean?"

"I mean after the accident, Zion lost his faith. He was quiet and hardly talked to me. He wouldn't pray, and I could tell he was angry when I read my Bible. He listened to my nighttime prayers, but I'm sure he just felt obliged to do that. Since we've come to Briar Hollow, it's like having my brother back again."

Rosalie remembered the Zion she had met the first day they made acquaintance at the Erlanger's place. He did seem different than the man who just last night stood outside cracking whip tricks with her family.

"I remember after my mother died," Rosalie began, then paused. She had Penny's full attention. "Healing takes times, and everybody grieves different. The way one person handles pain, isn't the same as someone else, right in the same family."

Penny thought about Zion and Balim, even herself and agreed. "That's true."

"When Mama passed on, it hurt the most right at the start; but over time, the pain eased. I would think I was all healed up, and then another wave of remembering would fill me with the loss again. Those waves come, but they are like the ocean tides. Did you ever study them before?"

Penny nodded and Rosalie continued. "That first crashing wave can just about drown a person, but the next one doesn't come as far, as high. It's like that with grief. When we're hurting, we get up and stand to our feet, and then another wave comes. But you know what? Each wave is a little more removed, the pain a little less, and then one day we can look onto the sandy shore and find all kinds of lovely things we never noticed when the water was high."

Burrowing her head under Rosalie's arm, Penny drank in the sweetness of her embrace, the reassurance of her words. "I'll be praying with you, Penny, that if another wave crashes, it won't knock your brother down. He's a good man."

Penny looked up at Rosalie. "Do you think so?"

"I do."

Florence and James Erlanger had their hands full boarding and feeding their many guests. In addition to the regular daily needs, these folks were preparing for the adventure of a lifetime, and they needed extra help with washing and packing. Every free moment Florence spent in the kitchen whipping up recipes for their journey. She made hard tack, fried doughnuts, stewed dried fruit and planned to cook a ham and several chickens Wednesday.

The Coventrys employed Pansy Joy to assist in readying the wagon they had purchased from Garth. To compliment Garth's paint job and make the interior comfortable, she lined the inside with a green cloth with several large pockets on each side to hold looking glasses, combs and brushes and such. After the men loaded boxes and trunks on the floor, she arranged bedding on the flat surface. Mr. Coventry had purchased an India rubber mattress for his wife which Pansy Joy filled with 50 gallons of water. The mattress served double duty as a water carrier and a nice bed.

Zion and Balim completed packing their wagon. In the removable box under the seat they stored food items, bacon, salt and other staples. Balim whittled four sturdy sticks to points that inserted into holes in the corners of the box converting it into a table to use along the way. Packing their newest items in the bottom of the clothing crate, they planned to discard used items along the way as necessary.

Louella and Clarence's wagon looked like a cabin on wheels. With just the two of them starting out, they didn't have as many things to pack, and beneath the treated canvas cover they created a cozy nest. Clarence installed some cleats on the floor of the wagon to keep things from slipping around as they drove. The clothing chest was packed in behind the food storage box and there was enough room on the floor for Louella's rocking chair. When she tired of sitting on the buckboard on the trip from North Carolina to Kentucky, she rode in the back rocking away the miles under her canvas shade. Another trunk contained household goods and wedding gifts, her grandmother's china, curtains and things to set up housekeeping in Virginia City. One corner housed a butter churn, washtub and basket of tin dishes for the trip and in the other, sacks of flour, cornmeal and other food items. To the side of the rocking chair, she rolled up a feather mattress, pillows and blankets that she spread out at night over the boxes to make a reasonably comfortable bed. Her ironware and cooking utensils were stashed in a box hanging on the outside of the wagon.

Grant Taylor had promised the Coventrys their wagon would be ready by the close of the day. J.T. and Bug planned to pick it up after dinner and load it up in the morning with their gear and the additional items the Coventrys had ordered from the mercantile. Their large furniture pieces and many boxes of books were already loaded on Zion's big wagon, along with Penelope's spinning wheel, Travis Ballard's photography equipment and the personal belongings of Eliza, Penelope and Beth Ann. Not having a wagon of their own, the ladies planned to take turns riding inside on the crates, on Penny's or Balim's horses, or on the buckboard with Balim. Travis purchased a saddle horse, and at the pace of 15-20 miles per day, everyone would walk from time to time, as well. Zion provided tents for their sleeping arrangements.

The long day of preparations finally came to a close, and Zion headed out to the Johnson place to check in with Penny.

"Step back, Son," Matthias called out to Zion from his position in the front yard. "I feel a ringer coming on." He pitched the horseshoe at the stake, but instead of circling the target, it leaned against it.

"That's only two points, Pa, and both of mine are closer," Marigold said. "I win!"

"Sorry I didn't make it out earlier," said Zion. "We got most everything ready though. The truth is we could pull out in the morning." Zion winked at Matthias. A tragic look registered on Penny's face and Zion burst out laughing. He pulled a blond braid and tipped Penny's nose with his finger. "Don't worry, Penny, we'll stay for the fireworks."

"I think you almost set some off right now," said Matthias.

"Why don't you go check with Rosalie. She's out in her drying shed over yonder." Zion crossed the yard. Through the open door he spied Rosalie moving about between ropes suspended like clotheslines dripping with different flowers–some drying in bunches and some individually. A little workbench with a hutch and several small drawers lined one of the walls. Rosalie had not heard his approach, and Zion stood silently watching her work.

No windows graced the shed walls. The only light entered through the door of the small building. Amidst the shadows, Rosalie inverted a flower and shook it against the inside of a metal pail. The pinging of seeds against the metal rang out a pleasant sound.

Light played on Rosalie's face as she moved, highlighting first one feature and then another–fine, curved auburn brows arched over incredible celadon eyes; freckles dotted defined cheeks, just enough to make them interesting; pink lips turned slightly upward revealed the young woman's satisfaction in her work. Rosalie reached in the pail, withdrew some of the seeds and allowed them to slip through her long fingers. A second chorus filled the air as the seeds hit the bottom of the pail. She stepped to the workbench, retrieved a pencil from a drawer and wrote something on a paper before pouring the seeds out and folding them inside the paper.

Zion watched Rosalie begin to turn in his direction and cleared his throat unwilling to be discovered spying on her. The look of undisguised pleasure on her face sent hope charging, and he gave Rosalie a smile and a slow nod before removing his hat. Blue eyes locked with green, and Zion held his hat in both hands in front of his wildly thumping heart. "Good evening, Rosalie."

"Hello, Zion." Thick auburn hair in a loose arrangement lost a whispy tendril that found itself spinning in Rosalie's fingers. "I almost thought we wouldn't see you today."

"You look nice." Zion hadn't meant to say it, but it slipped out. "I mean, you look like you're enjoying yourself in there. This is quite a place you have."

"Mm." Rosalie, intoxicated by the warmth of the shed and the fragrance of drying flowers, smiled a sultry smile, oblivious to the affect she was having on Zion. "Next to the rose garden, this is my favorite place."

"What are you working on?"

"A surprise." Zion watched her gentle sway, the same movement Lark used to entice him at the mercantile, but so different in Rosalie's innocent delight.

"Oh?" Zion grinned. "For me?"

"Actually," Rosalie drew the word out in elongated syllables. "Yes. It is for you."

Zion was undone by her unexpected reply and stuck a finger under the band of his collarless broadcloth shirt to loosen it and make a passage for the lump in his throat.

Rosalie lifted her chin and grinned. "But you can't have it until tomorrow night."

CHAPTER 36

Sleep evaded Zion. He tossed on his bed and tried to keep from disturbing Travis, all the while thoughts of Rosalie and his future played out in a variety of repeating scenarios. Crazy ideas, like Reverend Dryfus marrying them at the ice cream social tomorrow night and taking her with him out west. Like staying in Washington and letting J.T. run the outfit to Virginia City, he wanted it so bad, after all. The possibilities that warmed Zion's heart most weren't viable or fair to Rosalie or the men and women he contracted with on this business venture. And, of course, there was Balim. Zion would not forget his commitment to seeing him free and with a full purse for his faithful years of service to his family.

Zion rose with the sun and walked barefoot to the window. Shadows of Perkins and Nester in the dim morning light slowly registered in Zion's sleep-deprived brain. Standing next to the tailgate, they tinkered at the back of the wagon they had picked up in town the night before, but from his vantage point, Zion was unable to determine what they were doing.

Slipping into his clothes, Zion stepped quietly down the stairs and out the kitchen door on the side of the house. Slowly, quietly, he approached the men, keeping covered as much as possible by the trees and landscaping in the front of the lodge. He realized sneaking up on them was impossible, so when he got close he walked quickly to the back of the wagon attempting to catch Perkins and Nester in the act of whatever no good thing they were undoubtedly knee deep involved in. With a bold "Good morning" Zion strode to the back of the wagon. A quick scan revealed nothing out of the ordinary.

"Good morning to you, Mister Big Bug," Perkins greeted Zion, sarcasm dripping, and tipped his slouch hat. Zion smiled, but no humor lit his stony eyes.

"What brings you out so early in the morning, Coldwell?" J.T. asked, a smirk on his smug face.

"I was wondering the same thing about you two."

"Nothing much," J.T. said. "It was dark when we picked the wagon up, so we wanted to check out the workmanship."

"Right," Perkins added. "You can't trust a fellow that would marry up with a squaw."

Zion realized he stood on a cold trail and left the two without a word.

Excitement reigned in Washington, but no place more than Comfort Lodge. The travelers, after completing their final preparations for their journey, made their way to the church lawn for the ice cream social.

"I'm so glad it didn't rain," said Mrs. Coventry. "The children would have been disappointed."

Thaddeus held his wife's elbow and the couple watched their daughter and son walking before them on the road to town. The nettle tea and butterbur had alleviated Henry's asthma considerably, and the whole family breathed easier as a result. Rachel walked, every bit the young lady, with her porcelain doll in hand. Henry rolled a hoop on the smooth tar surface.

"I wish the trail to Virginia City was paved like this," said Henry. "I'd roll my hoop all the way there."

"As old Fred the bartender always said," Liza began, "Wish in one hand and . . ."

"Now Liza," Travis interjected. Familiar with the saying, he stopped Liza from embarrassing herself in front of the Coventrys, not that she would notice. Penelope's eyes got big, but she clamped her lips together in a tight line. Beth Ann was clueless.

Florence and James were finishing up the dinner dishes and closing up the lodge. J.T. and Bug claimed to need some time readying up their wagon. Mounted on West and Star, with Absolom saddled and ready, Balim and Zion waited at the lane for the Johnsons to come by in their wagon. They heard the sound before they saw their approach and Zion rode out to meet them.

"Howdy!" he called as West turned and sidled up to the wagon. "I brought you a surprise, Penny."

Looking past Zion, Penny saw her horse waiting for her in the lane. "It's Absolom!"

Matthias chuckled. "Be careful riding that one in the woods. I don't want to hear about your hair getting hung up in the trees."

Penny smiled. She knew the story about King David's proud son. "I'm careful, Mr. Johnson. I don't go too fast riding side saddle."

"What a beautiful horse, Penny," said Rosalie.

"Thank you." Penny longed to mount Absolom, but thought about all Rosalie had done for her. "I'll be riding him all the way to Virginia City. Would you like to ride him into the churchyard?"

Trained to ride sidesaddle by her mother, Rosalie warmed at the idea. She couldn't remember the last time she had ridden a horse. Matthias sold Sharon's saddle years ago to raise money to buy goats, not realizing at the time it would be difficult to replace. "I'd love to."

Matthias reigned in his horse, and Zion jumped off West to assist Rosalie out of the wagon. "Oh, there's no mounting block," said Rosalie.

"I'll give you a leg up." Zion knelt in the road to help Rosalie mount the horse.

"Look, Pa," Marigold said. "Look's like Mr. Coldwell's proposing to Rosalie." Pansy Joy tried to get Marigold's attention, but she was trained on the scene ahead. "Hey, Mr. Coldwell, don't you want to talk to Pa first before you offer your hand to Rosalie?"

Stiff as the wash on the line on a winter day, Rosalie's leg refused to lift her booted foot into Zion's hand. Crimson shot through her face, and Zion watched her reaction wondering what it meant. Was she embarrassed by Marigold's insensitive joking, or did the thought of him proposing mortify her? In his heart, Zion knew the answer. Rosalie would have shaken off Marigold's comments with a laugh if her words had not meant anything to her.

"That's enough, Marigold." Matthias spoke sternly to his daughter. "I'm gonna take these gawkers on ahead." He clicked the reins and set his wagon in motion. Balim met him, and the group continued down the road.

Zion stood. He brushed off the knee of his trousers and settled his hat straight on his head before finally looking into Rosalie's face. "Little sisters."

Rosalie eked out a weak smile. "Little sisters."

"What do you think he would say?" Zion asked.

"Who? What?" Confusion swirled in Rosalie's green eyes.

"Your Pa." Zion's words settled heavy on Rosalie. "If I was to ask for your hand?"

"I . . . I don't know what to say." Rosalie clamped her trembling hands together, willing them and her wobbly legs to be still. Zion's expression told her he wasn't playing games, even if Marigold started all this with her nonsense.

"If your Pa was agreeable, would you be?"

Her practical side knew the realities. Zion was leaving tomorrow morning. But her heart knew, was blatantly aware, that it was heading off on the journey with him. She peered into Zion's cornflower blue eyes and gave a slow nod.

By the time the couple reached the church, women were laying out food on cloth-covered tables and men were cranking on the ice cream machines. Young children gathered in a game of drop the handkerchief, while teens carried on with a round of blind man's bluff. Zion couldn't remember the last time he had seen so many people in one place. Mr. and Mrs. Matheny stood next to Reverend and Mrs. Dryfus, Martha making it clear her fine boys had donated the ice for the shindig.

Among the crowd were the Eldridges, Sheriff Eudell Nash, his wife Jane, Cooper, Jenkins from the post office, Joe Smith from the livery, the Goheen sisters, and so many other folks he had met in town and at church on Sunday. Of course, the Coventrys and the rest of Zion's traveling party were there, except Nester and Perkins.

Off to one side, Pansy Joy, Katie, Garth and some of the older youth gathered around Evan and Ethan Matheny like petals on a flower with tall red stamens popping out of the center. "Shall we see what those Matheny boys are up to?" Zion asked.

"You never know with those two," Rosalie said as she and Zion headed their way. Rosalie stopped short when she heard Katie let out a frightful shriek.

"Don't you do it, Ethan Matheny!" The crowd backed away creating an opening that allowed Rosalie and Zion a peek at the twins. Evan cupped a miserable bullfrog in his hands while Ethan held a match ready to ignite the firecracker stuffed down the helpless amphibian's throat.

"Let the poor thing go," Katie begged.

"If you insist, Katie darlin'." Evan dropped the dazed frog. But Ethan moved quickly, struck the match and lit the firecracker before anyone had a chance to think twice. Young people scattered in horror as a muffled explosion rang out.

"Dear Lord in heaven, what are those boys up to now?" Almira Dryfus wondered aloud, not really wanting to know the answer.

"Boys will be boys." Martha Matheny gave a syrupy smile to the reverend's wife.

Monsters will be monsters, Almira thought.

After things calmed down from the explosion and its resulting fall-out, Sheriff Nash shot off the signal for the sack races won by Garth for the third consecutive year. The three-legged races followed, also begun by a shot from Sheriff Nash's gun.

"Look at them go, Marigold!" Lucas scanned the field in amazement watching the couples race from the start to the finish line.

"I see, Lukey." Marigold chortled when the Matheny twins passed.

"What's so funny?" Pansy Joy asked her sister, obviously amused by her own thoughts.

"Those two look like a spider with the spasms crossing the grass with their spindly legs all tied together." Marigold looked from Pansy Joy to Garth and the threesome burst out in laughter. Lucas ignored their comment until the twins neared the finish line.

"Well those spider boys are gonna win the race!" Lucas shouted a moment before the Mathenys broke through the ribbon held between Lark and Charity Dryfus.

"Yup. They won all right." Garth chuckled and ruffled Lucas's hair. "Let's go get some of that ice cream."

After the ice cream, folks gathered for a singing. With all the instruments in Washington, nothing sounded as sweet as songs sung a capella in the open air. Hymns and patriotic tunes ushered in the darkness and Sheriff Nash began the fireworks. "You boys stay back," he ordered the Matheny twins. "Cooper's got this under control."

Fireworks lit the sky, followed by the smell of gunpowder. Bursts of stars and streams of cascading color floated from heaven punctuated with bangs and whistles. Zion stood with Penny leaning against his chest. With Rosalie at his side, he celebrated the nation's 83rd Independence Day relishing the freedom he felt in his heart and spirit. Tired and happy, the children made no complaints when Matthias and Pansy Joy led them to the wagon for the return trip home.

Rosalie, Zion and Balim mounted the saddle horses and rode out of the churchyard. When they approached the lodge, Balim said goodnight and Zion continued with Rosalie, escorting her to the safety of her home. Under the tree-canopied entrance to the hollow, Zion reigned in his horse and Rosalie followed suit.

"Can we talk before we go up to the house?" Zion asked.

Rosalie nodded. "Would you like to dismount?"

"Better not." Zion grinned. "It's safer this way." Iridescent moonlight slivered to the earth between the trees. Twinkling lights and a bright moon sparkled in the heavens.

"Penny and I stopped here the first day we came to visit you. She found a fairy ring and she wanted to make a wish."

"It does seem a magical place at times. Pansy Joy has a wishing jar right in the middle of the ring," said Rosalie. "It's silly, I know."

"I'm not so sure." Zion guided West next to Absolom, the two stallions stood neck and neck bringing Zion and Rosalie close. "You could be the fair Lady Gwinevere sitting on horseback in the forests of Camelot." Zion smiled at Rosalie. "I believe she wore her hair down, though."

Zion stroked Absolom's mane, and Rosalie blushed at the thought of unpinning her hair in front of a man. Goosebumps rose on the back of her neck. "Medieval tales of knights and ladies may seem romantic, but life isn't always like story books."

"I think we both know that firsthand, Rosalie."

"I know. I'm sorry." Rosalie studied the lines of Zion's handsome face. "I just don't know what to think or say." Rosalie twisted the loose ends of the reins in her hands. "I don't want to play games, Zion. We both know we have feelings for each other, but you're leaving in the morning, and I have to wonder where that leaves us."

Zion reached over and placed his hand over Rosalie's. "You don't know how much I want to stuff you in the back of my wagon and take you with me. I even thought of forgetting the whole excursion and asking your Pa if he needs help collecting plums and apples." Releasing her hand, Zion straightened in the saddle. "I know I have to do what's right, even if it's the hardest thing to do. I have to put any possible future we might have in God's hands . . . and yours.

"I have to fulfill my obligation, Rosalie, but I'm coming back. I can't ask you to wait for me, but if all goes well, I'll be knocking on your door sometime in March of next year to see if you did."

"You and Penny will be in my prayers every day."

"Now, Miss Johnson, I believe you told me yesterday you had a surprise for me tonight."

"I've changed my mind." The corners of Rosalie's lips turned up in a slight grin. "You'll have to come back in the spring for it."

"Now that is not nice, young lady, not nice at all." Zion laughed. "You are full of surprises, Rosalie–and I like them all."

CHAPTER 37

They had been gone less than 24 hours, but thoughts of Zion and Penny crowded Rosalie's mind. The routine of caring for family and home, once so rewarding, now left her feeling empty. Watching the hummingbirds, a delight on previous summer days, was just another part of her work clipping roses for Pansy Joy's wedding. She wondered how Pansy Joy was holding up waiting so long for Garth to be her husband. At least their pledge was true and the date set.

Rosalie did not hold to the old wives' tale that the eldest daughter must wed first; but a wedding sometime sure sounded nice, especially since Zion rode into her life and awakened the desire with his affection.

The plums came in, providing plenty of work for the Johnsons, followed by the pecans and a bumper crop of Granny Smith and Red Delicious apples. Matthias kept with the tradition established by his wife, and with the first apple plucked from the orchard showed Lucas the star hiding inside.

Take an apple, round and red
Don't slice down
Slice through instead
Right inside it you will see
A star as pretty as can be.

With the cutting and the poem, Matthias reminded his children to think beyond routines and habits, to be willing to try new methods and ideas, and perhaps they might find a surprise, like the star in the apple. By the time all the apples were sold, canned, dried, stored, smushed into cider or otherwise processed, the pumpkins were ready to harvest.

The apiary yielded a good supply of honey. Marigold smoked the hives to lull the bees to sleep and then pulled out the honeycombs. She left enough for the bees to eat, sending them back to work to produce more. Leaving some of the honeycomb intact to be eaten whole, she removed the wax caps from the remaining cells with a knife and gave the excess wax to her sisters: to Rosalie, for making candles, furniture polish and moustache wax, and to Pansy Joy for wrapping the creamy cheeses she made from Clover's rich milk.

A full week of activities surrounded the Mason County Fair. Rosalie entered her honeysuckle syrup, which took second place, and Pansy Joy's blackberry cobbler beat out Martha Matheny's angel food cake. The house of mirrors received several visits from Lucas and Marigold, and Charity Dryfus won the longest ponytail competition. The results of the horse races and plowing matches were published in the paper along with a picture of a hot air balloon giving folks rides. Katie's quilt received honorable mention, and God smiled on Lark Matheny when the judges voted her "fairest of the fair" and placed a crown on her golden curls.

After Garth finished his rounds with the threshing machine, his father organized a cabin raising. The first day saw the walls erected, and the second the roof shingled. With the structure in place, the families took their time getting things ready on the inside, including the cast iron stove purchased with the proceeds from the wagon Garth sold the Coventrys.

When the cones appeared on the junipers, neighbors gathered for the fall hog killing, a messy and laborious task, but one that created a social occasion for friends to gather for work and fellowship. Pansy Joy served up the annual treat, fried skin cracklings, while Rosalie and Katie stuffed cleaned intestines, creating spicy sausages. Matthias blew up a bladder for Lucas and Marigold who used it to play a game of ball while the hams and bacons were set to cure.

After the hog killing, Garth and Lowell Eldridge put in their winter wheat followed by a joyful Thanksgiving. With the onset of the holidays, final preparations for Pansy Joy's wedding hit full steam ahead.

Rosalie worked on the potpourri. Saving out the whole roses that had maintained their lovely shapes as they dried, she mixed the rest of the roses, buds and loose petals in airtight containers with fragrant juniper wood shavings, pine cones, rose hips, cinnamon bark, and orris root. To scent the mixture, she added precious rose oil skimmed from the top of her homemade rosewater. Hundreds of petals and much time were spent to make a small amount of the essential oil, but the smell, especially in the middle of winter, was worth the effort.

Over the weeks before the wedding, Rosalie intermittently shook the potpourri containers, stirring the contents. The second week of December Marigold opened the lid of one and gagged at the rotten smell. "You aren't really putting this out at Pansy Joy's wedding are you?" she asked.

"Give it some time. It will smell sweet by then." And it did. New Year's Eve Day Rosalie and Pansy Joy took the wagon to Comfort Lodge and filled bowls with the fragrant mixture. Setting them on wooden trays, she dressed the tops of the bowls and the trays with the whole pinkish-yellow cabbage roses and golden beeswax candles wreathed in dried wildflowers. They dressed the mantle in like manner.

Maggie Eldridge helped her future daughter-in-law make up a beautiful wedding costume of forest green cotton batiste and rich apricot trim. The deep lower floor-length flounce of green was topped with peachy petals that fell gracefully over the skirt around the knee. A short, snuggly fitting green zouave jacket trimmed in gold soutache braid around the edges and wide sleeves, was worn open over a creamy blouse with a high neckline and full, cuffed sleeves. Fit to perfection, a cream veil trimmed in apricot ribbons and velvety green leaves capped the ensemble.

Lucas and Marigold squawked about taking a nap, but Matthias enforced his decision, insisting his children would be thankful come midnight and Pansy Joy's wedding began. While the younger ones rested and Matthias worked on a secret project out in the barn, Rosalie and Pansy Joy sat at the kitchen table drinking chamomile tea with honey.

"Are you nervous?" Rosalie studied her sister. Pansy Joy fit the picture of a glowing bride, a mix of excitement and peace that her wedding day had finally arrived.

"Not really."

"It seems like just yesterday we were cutting the flowers and making plans, and now here it is."

"I know. Back when Pa told Garth we had to wait until I turned sixteen, it felt like an eternity, but here we are. Everything's ready."

"Is your dress over at the lodge?"

"Mom Eldridge took it over and gave it a final pressing yesterday. It's hanging in one of the guest rooms."

"She did a beautiful job. You do look like a pansy in it with that petal skirt." Rosalie sipped her tea. "I have something for you."

"Rosalie, you've done enough already. I don't know how I would have managed without you."

"That's what sisters do." Rosalie stood and walked to her father's bedroom. "Pa let me hide my gift in here." Rosalie moved to the wooden chest at the foot of her father's bed, the hope chest that once belonged to her mother. Reaching inside, she pulled out a package wrapped in an embroidered basket liner. "Here you go." She placed the package on the table in front of her sister.

"Rosalie, this is beautiful, and it's just like you to be so resourceful with your wrapping." Pansy Joy smiled. She untied the string and flipped open the fabric revealing a set of linen curtains scalloped along the edge with bits of fabric that matched the prize winning Double Wedding Ring quilt Katie pieced for her and Garth. "Oh. They're perfect. I can't imagine when you found the time to make these." Pansy Joy lifted one of the curtains and heard a clank. "There's more?"

"Just a little something to let the sunlight in."

Pansy Joy pulled out the second panel and uncovered a set of gilt brass curtain bands.

"You've always done that for me, you know?" Rosalie smiled. "You bring sunlight wherever you go, Pansy Joy."

Tears welled in Pansy Joy's eyes and she clasped her sister's hands in her own. "I hate to leave you, Rosalie."

Rosalie pulled a handkerchief from her sleeve and wiped the tip of her nose. "A half a mile isn't so far, I guess."

"I could come on Tuesdays and we could do the wash together." Pansy Joy offered.

Rosalie laughed. "You hate the wash."

"Exactly."

Matthias buffed the polish one last time, thoughts circling with his hands as he rubbed the cloth against the gleaming maple.

With deft fingers, he traced the scrollwork edging and then the engraved Scripture.

He debated on when to give the gift to Pansy Joy. With the peculiar timing of the ceremony, the reception would be simple, just coffee and raspberry cordial served with the cakes Almira Dryfus and Florence Erlanger had made for the special day.

Picking up his cane from the workbench, he rose to his feet and walked to the cabin where he found, not to his surprise, his two oldest wiping tears and laughing at the same time. "You got an extra cup there, Rosalie?"

"Sure, Pa. I'll get one for you." Rosalie stepped to the cupboard for the cup and Matthias crossed the floor, the plaque tucked behind his back.

Pansy Joy watched her Pa and knew he was up to something. "What you got there, Pa?"

"Just a little something I've been working on."

"Have you been keeping warm out there?" Pansy Joy asked.

"I put some wood in the little burner. It seems the more I stayed out there the more wood shavings I kept coming up with." Matthias placed the plaque in his daughter's hands. "I hope you like it."

Pansy Joy choked and fresh tears moistened her eyes. "Oh, Pa. It's just beautiful. I love it." Pansy Joy rose to her feet and threw her arms around her father, almost knocking him over in the process.

"Whoa, there, little girl. If you want your pa to walk you down the aisle you best not injure me anymore than that old Mexican soldier already done."

"What does it say?" Rosalie asked returning from the stove with a steaming cup of tea.

"It's a dedication plaque," said Matthias. "Read it, Pansy Joy."

Hear, O Israel:
The LORD our God is one LORD:
And thou shalt love the LORD thy God
With all thine heart,
And with all thy soul,
And with all thy might.
House of Eldridge est. Jan. 1, 1860

"The Good Book says to keep these words in our hearts, and teach them to our children–when we're sitting in our houses or walking by the way–when we're lying down or rising up." Matthias felt a fatherly speech welling up, but he kept it short knowing Reverend Dryfus would take care of the wedding message. "You know in Bible days God's people used to write Scriptures in boxes and tie them to their hands and on their foreheads. They wrote them on the posts of their houses and gates.

"This verse here, Pansy Joy, this is the most foundational Scripture in the Bible. If you and Garth will always keep this first, remembering that there's only one God and loving and serving Him with all your hearts, souls and might, well, there's just no better way to live."

Pansy Joy sniffled while Rosalie swept tears from her cheeks. "I'll hang it right next to the door, Pa, so we'll never forget."

"I can't help but think about your ma on a day like today." Matthias paused and took a sip of tea. "She'd be right pleased for you, girl."

"We best not go there, Pa, or Garth will have a blotch-faced bride with blood-shot eyes." Pansy Joy smiled, and then softened. "You know I've been thinking of her myself."

"I wish she was here to give you the mother-of-the-bride talk, but I trust Maggie filled you in on everything you need to know."

Pansy Joy's eyes grew big as silver dollars and her creamy complexion turned crimson. "Oh, Pa!"

CHAPTER 38

"Can we go watch Ethan and Evan?" Marigold asked Rosalie.

"They're starting today?"

"I heard them talking about it at church Sunday. They already cleared the snow and Cooper put the special ice walking shoes on Mandy."

Rosalie considered the request. School would be starting back up next week, but for now the young ones had cabin fever. An outing might help them work some wiggles out, and quiet in the cabin appealed to Rosalie. "Go ahead," she said, "but I want you to bundle up good."

The Matheny boys planned to begin their annual ice harvest. Fascinated with the process and their beautiful Clydesdale Mandy, Marigold looked forward to watching the horse and plow make the first passes on the clear ice. Farming a lake intrigued Lucas as much as his sister. Making the grid first, farmer and horse marked off two feet by six feet blocks with the plow, and then made the first cuts. They made several passes with the plow, and once deep enough and too dangerous to take the weight of the horse and equipment, the Mathenys finished the cutting with a one-handled crosscut saw. Blocks broken apart with a giant wedge and hammer were floated though a channel to the lake's edge where a horse-powered block and pulley system was used to lift the ice out of the water on to a wagon and transport it to the icehouse.

"Do you have your caps?"

Marigold laughed. "It's not summer Rosalie. We don't go anywhere without a hat in this weather."

"It never hurts to check with you two." Rosalie tucked the ends of Lucas's muffler inside his coat and pulled up the collar. "I want you back before lunch. It's too cold to be out for long."

"Can we visit Pansy Joy?" Lucas turned woeful eyes on his big sister. "I haven't seen her since the wedding."

Rosalie missed her sister, too. "Why don't you see if she'll feed you some lunch . . . at least warm you up with some hot chocolate." She smiled and kissed Lucas's pudgy cheek. "Tell her I love her."

With Matthias gone to the Taylors, Rosalie had the cabin all to herself. She stoked the fire and sat in the rocking chair. Lucas, growing like a weed, needed new socks and was always loosing a mitten, keeping Rosalie's knitting needles busy. Reaching in the basket beside her, she pulled out a half-finished sock. With the toe and heel turn complete, finishing was an automated process, leaving Rosalie's thoughts to roam.

She wondered how Penny's and Zion's socks held up on their trip west, and if they were having a cold winter, too. Traveling in the desert they wouldn't see snow she imagined, but nights could be chilly. Surely they were on their way back by now. Zion said he should arrive in Virginia City no later than Thanksgiving and had promised Rosalie he would see her in March. Her heart wanted to trust him, but thoughts of Clayton taunted her. He had said he was returning for her, too, but not even one letter made it back to Washington.

How she wished the telegraph ran through to Virginia City, but messages traveled no faster than the people on foot, wagons or horseback, taking months to transmit. The cabin door opened and Matthias came in stomping the snow from his boots.

"It's mighty quiet in here. Where's Lucas and Marigold?"

"They went to the Matheny's to watch the ice cutting." Rosalie slipped a strand of yarn over her needle and looked up. "They asked to visit Pansy Joy, so I told them they could stop by on their way home for hot chocolate."

"They're missing the girl, too."

Rosalie nodded and set her needle in motion. "How are the Taylors? I hope Sky is feeling better."

"Awinita said the bloodroot you sent helped his cough. The poor little fellow sounded like a dog barking a few days ago."

"That's good."

Matthias debated discussing business matters with Rosalie. Over the last years she filled the role of her mother in more ways than just cooking and caring for the young ones. Rosalie had intuition and insight into the ways and runnings of a profitable orchard, and he valued her opinion. He did the books himself, but having someone to sound things out with helped a man sort through his thoughts.

"Grant's thinking of selling."

"Really?" Rosalie's knitting needles stood still. "I know they've been feeling hemmed in with all the people moving out this way."

"That's it." Matthias hung his hat and coat on a peg and pulled the coffee forward. Opening the door of the cast iron stove, he inserted some wood and stirred up the fire. "They wanted to give me first rights on their place."

Grant Taylor had settled on the property opposite the orchard five years previous, a pastoral homestead bordering the same creek that flowed through Matthias's land. Matthias had hoped to purchase the land himself, but never raised the finances. He squirreled away a good sum, but not enough, and shied away from borrowing money at the bank. When Grant bought the place to build a home for himself and his new bride, Matthias let the idea go, until his visit with the Taylors opened the possibility again.

Rosalie set her knitting aside and joined her father in the kitchen. She served up two slices of pumpkin pie and placed them on the table. Matthias retrieved the coffee pot and another mug.

"Are you considering buying, Pa?" Rosalie worried about her father. He functioned well with his disability, but additional responsibility might be more than he could handle.

"What do you think about it?"

"I think it's a big decision." The fork slid easily through the creamy pie, and Rosalie took a bite.

"That it is."

"The Taylors have been good neighbors," Rosalie mused aloud. "We never had to worry about our crops with them living on the other side of the orchard."

"That's true."

"If we don't buy now, we may never have another chance." Rosalie sipped her coffee and rolled her thoughts around. She hesitated to question her father's ability, but decided to broach the subject frankly. "Is this something you really want to take on, Pa? Expanding the business would mean a lot more work."

Matthias looked at his practical daughter, unconsciously kneading his bad knee. "I know I'm not getting any younger, and I'm not looking to expand the business right now, but a man likes to leave a little something for his family."

"Don't talk like that, Pa." Rosalie shook her head. "Pansy Joy has been gone less than a week, and I'm not ready to think about any more changes."

"Is that right?" Matthias studied Rosalie over the rim of his coffee cup, doubting she would mind the change a tall young horse farmer from Virginia might bring, but he held his tongue.

Rosalie gave a firm nod. "Yes, sir."

"Well, it's just something to consider. They won't be leaving out until spring anyhow."

"That's a ways off yet." Thoughts of spring always brought Zion to mind and his promise. *I'll be knocking on your door sometime around March.*

Marigold and Lucas returned to the Washington schoolhouse the second week of January, leaving Rosalie time to work on her soaps and lotions and make candles. She attended weekly quilting or sewing bees organized by the Goheen sisters who hoped to fill several missionary barrels before folks started heading west when the weather broke. In the meantime, in the cold of winter, Rosalie busied herself caring for her family, heating foot warmers on the stove every night and then tucking them in their quilts before bedtime.

A February blizzard dropped a large amount of snow on the region, and until it melted, Marigold made a variety of ice creams. Each night she tried different flavorings: first vanilla, then honeysuckle syrup, and then canned peaches. Horse drawn sleighs jingled to the pond where Reverend Dryfus organized a sledding and ice skating outing before the spring thaw. A winter warm-up followed at the lodge. The Erlangers invited everyone for hot chocolate and a potluck dessert where Mrs. Pansy Joy Eldridge unveiled a new pumpkin cream roll to rave reviews. The month closed out with a festive celebration of Lucas's first-fourth birthday.

When the calendar turned to March, Rosalie worked at keeping her thoughts under control. March had thirty-one days, and she did not want to spend each one of them tormenting herself with thoughts of Zion's return. The first of the month, the Johnsons and Eldridges all pitched in to tap the maple trees. Pansy Joy and Katie worked with Rosalie to boil the sap and make the syrup. With one last winter storm, the children insisted on a sugar-on-snow party, making a chewy candy by drizzling hot maple syrup in the snow. The candy was "just like downtown," Marigold pronounced.

Pansies pushed through the cold earth to brighten March days. In the wooded lane, dogwoods burst with pink and white blooms on a mossy carpet sprinkled with crested dwarf irises and patches of purple valerian. Seemingly overnight the orchard's apple and plum trees were in full bloom. Lowell Eldridge and James Erlanger organized a spring turkey shoot leaving a clutch of hunting widows and single ladies to gather at the lodge for a quilting bee. Marigold, out for a walk in the woods with Lucas, stumbled across a fawn, and with no mother in sight, she folded the spotted babe in her arms and carried her to the lodge.

"But Rosalie, she doesn't have a mama, I looked all around."

"You need to take her right back where you found her, or you just might love the poor thing to death."

"Rosalie's right," Florence said. "Deer don't have fangs or claws. To defend themselves they either run or try to blend in with their surroundings, especially the young ones. That's why God gave them spots. This little one's mama is probably nearby feeding."

"Wild things were never meant to be brought home and tamed," said Rosalie.

Reluctantly, Marigold turned, shoulders slumped, and began a slow trek back into the woods, Lucas in tow. Rosalie considered her own words, thinking about Zion and wondering if perhaps he was like the little fawn, born to a different destiny. Would he come out of his world to live in hers? If he did come, would she be willing to leave her world for his?

As new life sprung all around, Rosalie's hopes began to fade. March turned into April with no word from Zion. Easter Sunday, April 8, Pansy Joy invited her family to her home to serve up her first holiday dinner with all the trimmings. Lacking adequate seating, Garth set up a sawhorse and plank table and brought in thick logs for seats. The smell of ham, sweet potatoes and yeast rolls filled the cabin crammed full of Johnsons and Eldridges.

"That was a fine meal, Daughter." Matthias leaned back on his seat and rubbed his full belly.

"I'm glad you liked it. I hope you saved room for sweets," said Pansy Joy.

"After all this settles down first."

"I have a sweet that won't bust your trouser buttons, Pa." Pansy Joy laughed and locked eyes with Garth, a radiant smile on her face.

"It might bust your skirt, Pansy Joy—in a few months, anyhow." Garth grinned.

"For our first dessert, we have sweet news." Pansy Joy looked around the cabin into the dear faces of her family. "What better time to tell you there's a new life coming than on Resurrection morning."

The news of Pansy Joy's pregnancy sent the room into a spin. A baby, a grandchild, a niece or nephew—the Johnson and Eldridge families celebrated together in the cozy cabin. Mingling with the excitement, Rosalie experienced some concern for Pansy Joy's and the baby's health. She determined to take the matter to prayer every day and learn as much as she could about possible complications before, during and after delivery. Silently, she thanked God for the baby and the new doctor in Washington.

CHAPTER 39

Throughout the first two months of the trip west, J.T. and Bug challenged Zion's authority and judgment at every turn. Too many mornings Zion woke to find things around the camp in disarray, or minutes into their journey something would break and set them back for hours. Frustration mounted among the travelers while J.T. and Bug looked on clucking their disapproval at Zion's incompetence.

Certain he smelled alcohol on their breath more than once, Zion searched but never discovered a source to prove his suspicions that they were drinking strong liquor. He worried over the men's influence on Thaddeus Coventry, especially when they convinced him to join a friendly game of poker one evening after dinner.

"I know you holy rollers ain't interested in the devil's pastime," J.T. snickered and shuffled Thaddeus to a makeshift table where they played cards until the wee hours of the morning. Zion watched as Bug filled mug after mug from his canteen for Thaddeus and they played on. He whispered a prayer and turned in for the night.

The next morning Thaddeus came down with a mysterious sickness. His head pounded and he couldn't hold a thing down. Their start delayed, the group prepared to roll out with Thaddeus moaning on a bed in the back of the green wagon. The sickness delayed morning devotion, but everyone gathered after a quick breakfast and prayers were offered for their safe travel and health. Thankfully, no one else was sick.

During prayer, Zion felt a strong impression to check his wagon. Later, as everyone worked to break camp, he circled around the conveyance, compelled to a stop beside the wooden storage box lashed on the outside of the wagon base. An image of his whip raced through his mind, and he reached inside the box and pulled it out. Pressed by an urgency he didn't understand, Zion exchanged the 8-foot whip for the 25-foot whip.

Zion questioned himself. He wondered if he was loosing his mind in the desert heat, but he reminded himself how he had been praying diligently to hear the voice of God. He remembered Balim's encouragement, telling Zion that God spoke to lots of folks in their deserts. *Fool or no, I'm going to listen and obey.*

With the exception of the occasional breakdowns and problems, Zion was pleased that everyone was safe and sound, even if they were behind schedule. The river crossings had run smoothly, and after the first week, everything became routine. People learned to set up and break camp with minimal effort, and once their bodies became accustomed to the long hours of walking and riding, each person slipped into their roles. Liza most often rode in back of Zion's big wagon out of the dust and sunlight, while Penelope, Beth Ann and Penny took turns riding Absolom, on the buckboard next to Balim or walking.

When Penny walked, Rachel often walked beside her, and the girls developed a close bond as they covered the miles with Penny's pup scampering at their heels. Mr. Coventry's wagon followed directly after Zion, hoping the lead position would limit Henry's exposure to trail dust. He rode in the back or beside his father who delighted the boy by giving him the reins when the terrain allowed. Henry drank Rosalie's nettle tea whenever asthma symptoms rose, but generally fared well.

Behind the Coventrys, J.T. and Bug drove Thaddeus's second wagon, followed by the Sweeneys, and lastly by Balim in the big wagon.

"You have a canopy bed?" Penny asked Rachel as they walked beside the Coventry's green wagon. Penny's puppy trotted along at her side.

"With a blue comforter and curtains. I can't wait to sleep in it again."

"My bed got burned up in the fire, but Zion said I could pick whatever kind I want once we get settled."

"That will be fun. Do you think you'll get a canopy bed, too?"

In a move that took the girls off guard, the monotony of walking beside the line of wagons broke when Nester whipped up his horses and pulled his wagon away from the convoy. He reigned the animals in and Bug jumped down with a weapon in his hand. He walked briskly to the girls.

"Howdy." Perkins bared a decrepit smile and tipped his dusty slouch hat. The girls exchanged puzzled looks. Bug customarily avoided contact with everyone except J.T. and Thaddeus Coventry, unless he was taunting Zion. Something was off-kilter.

A shot rang out in the desert. The walkers stopped in their tracks while those riding and driving worked to bring their animals under control. Zion, at the head of the convoy, pulled West around in a hard turn. He rode onto the scene, jumped off his horse and reached for his gun.

"Drop your gun, Coldwell." Seated on the buckboard, J.T. trained his Colt revolver on Zion's chest. Bug aimed his carbine at Penny and Rachel ran to her family.

"Nobody move," J.T. yelled. "I'm calling the shots now."

The surprise attack caught Zion off guard. He stood motionless, weighing what he should do, until he saw the gun aimed at his sister. "All right, Nester."

Zion slowly pulled his revolver out of its holster by the handle and threw it on the ground. With the hunting rifles stored in the wagons, Zion had the only gun readily available besides the ones Nester and Perkins carried.

"Good choice. Kick it out, Bug."

Perkins sidled up to the gun and kicked it several yards away— too far for Zion to lunge and retrieve. Nester smirked, and with a sinister laugh set his revolver in his lap. "I think it's time you learned a lesson on respecting your elders." J.T. pulled a cigarillo from his pocket, struck a match and lit his smoke. He picked up the gun and casually aimed it once more at Zion's chest.

"What are you planning to do, Nester? Kill us all? You won't get the Coventry's money unless they withdraw it from the bank in Virginia City."

"It's time you saw the elephant, Coldwell." J.T. blew smoke rings above his head. "Me and Bug are tired of this gig, and we're ready to pull out. Coventry signed everything over all legal like just last night. Tweren't nothing to pass a last will and testament off as a promissory note on a man once he's good and soaked."

Zion seethed inwardly, but he knew he had to keep his cool. *Help me, Lord Jesus.*

Nester took a long draw on his cigarillo, blew a puff of smoke and continued in a cocky monotone. "I don't need to shoot you . . . unless you force the situation. I wouldn't want to have blood on my hands."

J.T. snickered and scowled at Zion. "Me and Bug will just let the horses go. I'll take your stallion there, Coldwell, and the desert will take care of you soon enough."

Zion prayed under his breath, knowing Balim was calling on Jesus, too. An idea came to him, and he turned to face his sister.

"Penny, I want you to come to me," Zion said. "Just walk slowly."

"Don't do it, girl." J.T. stiffened and commanded from his perch. "If she moves, shoot her, Bug."

Bug's eyes grew large and his lower lip seemed to unhinge. "I wasn't necessarily planning on shooting a kid, J.T."

"If you let her go, her brother's gonna try something," said Nester. "Just look at him."

"Penny, trust me," Zion said. Penny looked to Nester, and then to Bug, and then to Zion. Slowly she moved one foot in her brother's direction.

"Bug, pull the trigger," Nester ordered.

"She's just a kid."

J.T.'s anger burned. His eyes flashed pure venom as he swung his arm around and pointed his revolver at Bug. "And you're just a washed up drunk that makes love to a metal flask of whiskey every night. I don't need you if you won't follow directions–not even for Marcy's sake, God rest her soul."

In one smooth motion, Zion took advantage of J.T.'s momentary distraction. He pulled his whip from its holster. With a quick lift of his arm, he released a side crack that wrapped around Bug's wrist. Bug's hand jerked, and the barrel of the gun he had been pointing at Penny discharged a bullet that screamed toward Nester on the wagon.

"Hit the dirt!" Zion yelled and threw himself over Penny a moment before a massive explosion shook the earth. Bug shrieked, set ablaze in the blast of the wagon loaded with bourbon. J.T. was nowhere to be found.

Balim jumped down from the wagon and ran to Bug. He rolled him in the dirt and quenched the flames. Mercifully, he passed out from the pain of the extensive burns.

Following a traditionally rainy April, May flowers bloomed in Rosalie's gardens. America was blossoming, too, it seemed, with the Pony Express now running correspondence from St. Joseph, Missouri, to Sacramento, California. Messages raced across the developing country in only ten day's time.

Exciting things were happening all over. The Washington newspaper ran a story of a meteorite shower less than 200 miles away. A shooting star fell from the sky on May 1, killing the horse it landed on in New Concord, Ohio.

In addition to fiery stars falling from the heavens, things were heating up politically. Word of Abraham Lincoln's speech at the Cooper Institute reached Briar Hollow. The Kentucky-born politician attacked slavery and declared the federal government should restrain the institution. On May 9, the Constitutional Union Party nominated John Bell for president, followed by the Republicans who chose Abraham Lincoln on May 18. The presidential election, a matter of great debate, became the most popular topic of conversation any time men folk gathered.

Things were changing all over the land, except for Rosalie. She was busy enough. With Pansy Joy gone and a baby coming, she put in long days in the gardens and the kitchen. At night, after she tended the needs of her own household, she knit soakers and sewed diapers. She made gowns for the new baby, adding delicate tucks and embroidery to the simple garments.

She rocked and worked, wondering what it would be like to make the precious things for a child of her own, and then tried not to think about it at all. She forced herself to remember the long, exhausting nights with colicky Lucas. She decided she should just be thankful she would be sleeping peaceful when Pansy Joy was bound to be walking the floor with a little one. Rosalie could visit the baby and be free from all the extra responsibilities. She even chuckled thinking about how much extra washing Pansy Joy was going to have once the baby came.

Something happened inside Rosalie. When Zion failed to return, she started questioning herself. Had he really said the things she remembered? Was her mind playing tricks on her? Had his intentions been less than what Rosalie imagined? Perhaps with Pansy Joy's wedding preparations she had wanted someone to love her so much she built things up to be more than they were. What could have been accidental touches may have triggered her emotions to play tricks on her. Had she mistaken Zion's good manners as interest beyond friendship?

Dinner finished, and the dishes cleared and washed, Rosalie rocked and knitted, all the while her emotions perked like a coffee pot on a hot stove top. Matthias watched. He saw the thoughts whirling behind those eyes so like his dear Sharon's pale jade ones. He read her turmoil, easy enough as she knitted faster and rocked harder until she finally shook her head and stood up.

"I'm going out for some fresh air." Rosalie put her hands on her hips and looked around the room. "When I come back in here, I want to see all those blocks put away, Lucas; and we need more wood." She turned to Marigold. "I spent a half an hour cleaning up sticky honey off the table and floor today. The next time you want to experiment with your bee business, I'd appreciate it if you would clean up after yourself."

Matthias locked eyes with his daughter, amazed at her rampage. Rosalie's lower lip trembled, but she bit it down and reached for the door handle, escaping into the darkness before she said anything else she knew she would later come to regret.

CHAPTER 40

M atthias allowed his daughter to leave without comment, but moments later he followed Rosalie outside and down the porch steps into the moonlight. The song of the katydids accompanied their amble along the familiar path to the orchard. Matthias leaned on his cane and followed his daughter's soft steps in silence.

Rosalie stopped in front of the grape arbor. Beneath the vines, Matthias spotted the bench–the one he had hewn from a fallen hickory tree what seemed just a few short months ago.

He remembered dragging the trunk up from the woods to surprise his new bride, and how Sharon's eyes had danced when he unveiled the gift on their one-year anniversary. She had thanked him with a thorough squeeze, sat right down on the bench and then presented him with her anniversary gift.

"Matthias. We're having a child." The words echoed in the halls of his memory, the wonder and awe of a first-born baby growing inside his beloved wife.

Rosalie stood before him now with the weight of so much more than she should carry upon her slender shoulders. Matthias looked at her bowed head. Compassion swelled in his heart for this gentle daughter God had blessed him with.

"Rosalie, honey." Rosalie turned, but kept her sad eyes downcast. Matthias tipped his daughter's chin upward with a big warm hand. Their eyes met, and he hoped she would see the depth of his feelings in his expression.

"Yes, Pa."

"I used to sit here with your mama, and we'd have the nicest talks. Do you think we could do that?"

Rosalie was taken back. Matthias rarely talked about his private relationship with his wife.

"Sure, Pa. That would be nice." Rosalie swept a fallen leaf from the bench and sat down. Matthias joined her and together they looked out over the trees alight with the soft glow of a feathery moon. The damp spring air was fragrant with scents drifting in from the orchard.

"Your Ma was a special woman, Rosalie," Mathias began. "I'm thankful the Lord gave us every day we had together."

Rosalie looked at the man beside her, and for the first time thought of him as more than a father, more than a husbandman, more than a caring neighbor and deacon in the church. Her father had once been a young man in love. Perhaps he understood more of her situation than she imagined.

"Did I ever tell you how I met your mama?"

"No, Pa." A flicker of an old memory skittered across her mind—a long ago conversation with her mother. They had been working together hanging gold and garnet mums out to dry. Each year they planned ahead, collecting flowers, seed pods and such to fill winter days with projects like decorating grapevine wreaths to sell in town. "I remember Mama saying something about a corn maze, but I'm fuzzy on the details. I'd like to know more if you're up to the telling."

A lazy grin worked its way up from Matthias's curved lips and crinkled his eyes. "It was a harvest moon that night, girl.

The crops were all in and the canning done. It was time for some fun.

"I guess Preacher Smythe thought the young folks could use some recreating after all the hard work, so he ordered up a picnic. Everyone was flustered with excitement, buzzing about like those bees your sister keeps when they get riled up. One of the local farmers offered his spent corn field for a maze, and all the young bucks headed out with their scythes. It was like one of those labyrinths your mama read to me about in a book on English gardens with openings here and dead ends there.

"By the time Friday supper rolled around, we'd all nearly burst our buttons with anticipation. Baskets of fried chicken, cold bean salads, biscuits with honey and jams and great hunks of watermelon were set out on sawhorse tables. Preacher Smythe offered up a thanksgiving prayer, and we all dug in.

"The gals and the fellows, they pretty much stuck to their own during the picnic, but I know more than one or two were looking forward to coupling off in the corn maze." Matthias paused, and pointed a work-worn finger at Rosalie. "Now don't get the wrong idea. Tweren't no shenanigans going on. Nothing inappropriate a-tall. Just a time to let intentions be known, if you know what I mean."

Rosalie nodded her understanding, and Matthias continued.

"We lined up to go in the maze, and I confess, I got right close to your mama a-purpose. She was such a pretty thing. Didn't think she'd give the likes of me a second look, but it didn't stop me from wanting to be with her.

"Now being one of the fellows that cut the maze, I had a bit of an advantage when Preacher Smythe pulled a fast one on us."

Rosalie looked puzzled at that. "What do you mean, 'a fast one'?"

"Well, leave it to a minister to bring the good Book into every activity." Matthias chuckled.

"What did he do?"

"The reverend opened a basket full up with red bandanas. He said, 'Young men, young women. I want you to know the truth of the Scripture today. There's a verse in Proverbs that says *The path of the just is as the shining light, that shineth more and more unto the perfect day, but the way of the wicked is as darkness: they know not at what they stumble.*

"Gertie near turned tail and ran when the reverend took Sally Ann and Douglas and tied bandanas around their eyes. They stumbled into the maze and started working their way through, feeling their way as they went. Since Douglas helped with the cutting, he thought he knew where they were going, but he soon discovered Preacher Smythe had spent the morning adding some obstacles and cutting some additional connections in the maze.

"Preacher gave them a couple of minutes, then he took hold of Beatrice and Johnny. He tied a bandana on Johnny, but not Bea, then he sent them into the maze. We could hear Sally Ann and Douglas stumbling around, and we could hear Bea trying to guide Johnny past the obstacles and through the passageways.

"Another couple of minutes passed and then the preacher grabbed your mama and me. He put narry a thing on our eyes, but sent us through with full sight. You can imagine we hurried right on past the other two couples and beat them out of the maze nothing flat. Beatrice and Johnny came next, and the first couple came out last."

"The last shall be first, huh, Pa?" Rosalie's facial features had relaxed during the story, and Matthias was pleased to see a genuine smile fill her heart-shaped face. Rosalie twisted a strand of auburn hair around her finger and nodded at her pa.

"That's a truth, Daughter. But the preacher man was trying to get a different lesson across. He explained it this way. He said, 'These three couples had very different experiences in the maze.

With the first couple, both were blinded. They couldn't see where they were going. Just like the Scripture said about the way of the wicked. When we don't have the light of God showing us the obstacles in our paths or the clear paths we should follow, it will be difficult to navigate the passages of our lives.

"'Now Bea and Johnny, they gave us a good example of what the Bible calls being unequally yoked. When one can see and the other can't, it's frustrating for both. One's trying to explain what the other one can't see. God's ways are best, for sure and for certain.

"'And did you notice how Sharon and Matthias cleared the obstacles and made it through the path without a scratch? Why, they went in last, but they came out first. That's what it's like to have the blessing of God on your life–like the path of the just I was telling you about that gets brighter and brighter each day. Walking with Jesus is like that. Each step, each day brings us closer to Him.'

"He kept on with his preaching, saying, 'Young men. Young women. I want you to remember this maze when you start thinking about your futures and who you'd like to spend them with. Life is like this maze with obstacles and dead ends, opportunities and different paths to take. We all walk on our own paths, but it's up to us to make the wise decisions that will help us as we travel and make it through to the other side.'"

"I can just picture you and Mama bursting through the maze all laughs and smiles."

"You're right, girl." Matthias looked up at the Milky Way lighting the night sky. A grin split his face from ear to ear. "That was it for me. When we walked through the maze, I held your mama's hand. It was the softest thing I ever touched and she smelled like lavender. I'd steal a glance at her, and she'd be looking at me kind of shy like. Then we'd laugh as we passed the other folks. You know, we weren't always sure which path led to the end, especially since Preacher Smythe threw in those surprises. A couple of times we had to turn around. We jumped an overturned butter churn, and at the end of the maze I lifted your Mama over the plow that blocked the way out. The end came too quick for me. I surely didn't want to let go of her sweet hand."

"What happened next?"

"Well, following Preacher Smyth's surprise Bible lesson, he let us all go through without the bandanas. I walked through with your mama again, but I didn't dare touch her with everyone else around. After everyone came out of the maze, we loaded up on a hay-filled wagon and jostled along a bumpy path. We rode for awhile, took a turn through the fields, and then circled back. Around the bonfire we filled tin cups with warm mulled cider and finished off the evening with a gospel singing."

Rosalie sighed. "I always loved to hear Mama sing. When I was little, all tucked up in my bed at night, I felt such a peace listening to the creak of her rocking chair keeping time with her sewing and singing, song after song. I remember *Fairest Lord Jesus* the most. Was that her favorite?"

"Near as I remember, it was."

In a clear, sweet soprano, Rosalie began the first verse:

Fairest Lord Jesus, ruler of all nature,
O thou of God and man the Son,
Thee will I cherish, Thee will I honor,
thou, my soul's glory, joy, and crown.

Fair are the meadows, fairer still the woodlands,
robed in the blooming garb of spring:
Jesus is fairer, Jesus is purer
who makes the woeful heart to sing.

Fair is the sunshine, fairer still the moonlight,
and all the twinkling starry host:
Jesus shines brighter, Jesus shines purer
than all the angels heaven can boast.

Matthias was swept into the glory of the song that seemed so appropriate on this beautiful starry night. He joined his rich baritone with his daughter's sweet melody.

Beautiful Savior! Lord of all the nations!
Son of God and Son of Man!
Glory and honor, praise, adoration,
now and forevermore be thine.

A hush filled the hollow—an engulfing silence that wrapped Matthias and Rosalie in its tender beauty. Even the bullfrogs and katydids seemed captured by the magic of the moment and quieted.

Matthias spoke, his voice just above a whisper. "I think that was your mama's favorite because it told about so many things she loved—the flowers, the woodlands, the heavens. They're all the work of God's beautiful creation, but nothing is as fair as the One who created it all."

Matthias felt a shift in his spirit. It was time to come to the point. He felt rather like Preacher Smythe with his corn maze, searching for a way to reach into a young girl's life with wisdom and guidance. *Help me, Lord,* his heart cried.

"I heard a poem once. It said something about a fellow who overlooked an orchard in search of a rose." Matthias rubbed his chin and gave a shake of his head. "I've been thinking, and you know what? I think I've been doing just the opposite of that. I've been so busy with my orchard, the work of tending plants and raising a family, I've been missing a rose. You, Rosalie."

"Pa." That was all Rosalie could choke out. This big bear of a man propped up by a gnarly cane had a heart of gold. Tears that had been contained by sheer force of will over the last few days glided down Rosalie's porcelain cheeks and dripped on the slender hands clasped tightly in her lap.

Matthias reached over and covered Rosalie's hands with one of his own. "Remember, Rosalie, what I told you about the corn maze. Sometimes the last comes out first, and just because two people coupled up and went in first doesn't mean their time inside was more rewarding."

Rosalie gave a soft smile and nod to her father.

Matthias returned her expression. "I believe the Lord has something special for you, Rosalie."

CHAPTER 41

O ver the next few days, Rosalie thought often of the conversation she had with her father. She wondered at all the lessons a person could learn when they looked at God's creation.

She pondered on seeds. How in every apple seed was the potential for an apple tree, and in every apple tree, the possibility of an orchard. She prayed the Lord would help her bury her seed, let it die and then grow it into a beautiful tree.

In Galatians she read about the fruit of the Spirit, and she realized that fruit wasn't for the tree, but for others. She prayed the Lord would grow the fruit in her life she needed to bless the world she lived in with love, joy, kindness, gentleness, and so on.

As she worked in her mother's rose garden, she remembered the oil she made for Pansy Joy's wedding. She had used a cooking process that pulled the oil from the petals and then caused it to float on top of the water. Rosalie prayed the Lord would use the difficulties in her life to create a fragrant, healing oil.

Thinking further on oil, she meditated on how nice it would be to pick oil from a tree, but how God designed pressure to release the valuable commodity. When her "fruit" got pressed–when she felt impatient or got out of sorts–she prayed she would release oil, too, for lubricating the squeaks and rubbing into the wounds of life. Rosalie discovered that when she submitted to the pressings and released her oil into the lives of others, it brought healing into her own hands.

The third week in May drew to a close, and Rosalie determined to begin the fourth with a cheerful disposition. First thing in the morning, she pulled her dress from the peg and purposed to put on some thanks with her calico.

Thank You, Jesus, for this day and the hope I have in You. Thank you for my loving family and home and all Your bountiful provisions.

She left her room and began to prepare breakfast. As she poured batter on the griddle, she realized her spirit felt lighter than it had in months. Humming *Fairest Lord Jesus* felt wonderful as she flipped the griddlecakes and watched them rise.

Matthias sensed the change as soon as he walked in from milking Clover. Marigold and Lucas responded with fresh smiles and happy hearts. After the meal, Marigold fetched Matthias's Bible.

"I was reading from the Prophet Isaiah last night." Matthias paused and looked at Rosalie. "Read here, Daughter."

Rosalie took the worn book from her father's hands and read the verse.

"Isaiah 61:3. 'To appoint unto them that mourn in Zion, to give unto them beauty for ashes, the oil of joy for mourning, the garment of praise for the spirit of heaviness; that they might be called trees of righteousness, the planting of the LORD, that he might be glorified.'"

Rosalie lifted her eyes to her father's. "What a perfect passage for today. Thank you for sharing it, Pa."

With Marigold's help, the dishes were quickly washed and returned to the shelves. Afterwards, Lucas enticed his golden-haired sister to take him on a trip to the fishing hole.

Rosalie thought about the woods lining their lane and how they were brimming with lily of the valley. A longing to fill her lungs with their clean, sweet scent persuaded her to set aside her household chores for a few minutes and go for a walk.

As she left the cabin, she noticed the wildflower garden coming to life with pink and yellow lady slipper, columbine, primrose and buttercups. On an impulse she stopped, plucked a yellow buttercup, and twined its stem around her fingers before entering the wooded lane. She ambled a bit, drinking in the scent and scenery of the spring woodland, and soon found herself off the path.

Rosalie stood beside the fairy ring. The blue Mason wishing jar, although tipped over, still held its secrets in the center of the ring. Rosalie leaned over to right the jar, but curiosity overwhelmed her usual pragmatic sensibilities and she unscrewed the lid.

With nimble fingers, she pulled out the first note and recognized Pansy Joy's script. "I want to marry Garth Eldridge, the handsomest fellow in Mason County."

Rosalie grinned and reached in for another wish, this one from Marigold. "I wish we could get a new school teacher that wasn't a Matheny."

The third and final paper she recognized immediately–a sheet of the stationery she had given Katie for her last birthday. She unfolded the paper and read the message.

"Dear Lord, You said to ask and it shall be given. You said to call those things that are not as if they already are. So I ask You to bless my dear friend Rosalie with the desires of her heart, and I thank You for bringing a godly man to cherish her and partner with her for Your glory. In Jesus' name. Amen."

Dumfounded, Rosalie stood in the middle of the fairy ring with the jar tucked under her elbow. In one hand she held Katie's note and the buttercup, with the other she wiped the tears coursing down her cheeks.

The sound of a horse turning into the lane pulled her thoughts back to reality. Rosalie stood stock still, hoping the rider would pass by without seeing her, but the steps slowed. She turned to see who it was.

Something about the large black horse caused a jolt in Rosalie, and when she saw a large man dismount and walk toward her, she could hardly believe it. Zion.

Zion Coldwell saw the calico in the trees and prayed it was Rosalie. When he saw her turn her watery green eyes on him, he thanked the Lord. How many months he longed to see her, and there she stood, hatless, her beautiful auburn hair shining as shafts of morning sunlight pierced the leaf canopy.

Zion joined Rosalie in the fairy ring. The two stood in silence. Rosalie was mute, shocked and confused. Zion was apprehensive and curious.

"Hi," said Zion.

"Hi."

"I wrote a song while I was gone." Zion grinned at Rosalie with a mix of merriment and concern in his cornflower blue eyes.

Rosalie gave a light chuckle of disbelief. "Is that right?" Of all the times she had mentally played out Zion's return, she had never envisioned the scenario unfolding now.

"Yep." Zion stuck his hands in his pockets. "You want to hear it?"

"Sure." Rosalie gave a slight shake of her head and her pink lips curved slightly in an amused smile.

Zion cleared his throat and threw back his head, releasing a booming baritone.

I headed west to travel cross the country
Passed fruited plains and amber waves of grain
I saw the mountains and I saw the sea
But one thing always haunted me
A green-eyed girl from Kentucky named Rosalie.

Rosalie wanted to laugh and cry at the same time. *Where is he going with all this*, she wondered. *And what kept him so long if I was haunting his thoughts all the way from Kentucky to Nevada.*

"You're too much, Zion Coldwell."

"I'm hoping I'm just enough," said Zion with a sheepish look on his rugged, tanned face, "at least just enough for a green-eyed girl from Kentucky named Rosalie." Zion took Rosalie's free hand in his. "I'm sorry it took so long for me to get here. I missed you every day."

"What happened, Zion? And where is Penny?"

"It's a long story." Zion looked deeply in Rosalie's eyes. "Have you got a few decades?"

Rosalie laughed. She put the lid back on the wishing jar and set it down, and then tucked Katie's stationery in her apron pocket. "Aren't you being rather presumptuous, Mr. Coldwell? You've been gone a long time."

"Right," said Zion. "About that." Zion noted the teasing in Rosalie's voice, but knew she deserved an honest answer.

"I came as soon as I could. Bug and J.T. were up to no good. Balim and I knew it all along, but we didn't have any evidence. They played their hand out in the middle of the desert, planning to take all the horses and leave us there to die. But the Lord had a different plan."

"Is everyone all right? Did anyone get hurt?"

"I'm sorry to say J.T. was lost in an explosion of his own making, and Bug Perkins was so severely burned we couldn't move at all for a couple of weeks. When we did start traveling again, we had to take things slow. With the delays J.T. and Bug caused earlier in the trip, we were a month behind schedule before we finally pulled in to Virginia City.

"Getting all the travelers settled in and selling all the goods we brought, along with the wagon and mules–it all took longer than I expected, and then we had to re-outfit for the trip back."

"What happened to Bug?"

"It seems he had an explosive conversion experience." Zion grinned from ear to ear. "He knew he wasn't living right. Bug's pa was a sanctified Methodist minister. By the bye, his name is Beauregard. When his little sister Marcy tried to say Beauregard, it came out Bug, and the name just stuck over the years."

"It's hard to imagine him as a little boy."

"He was crying like a baby when he came to after the explosion. It wasn't from the pain, either, although that was something fierce, I can only imagine. He was repenting and calling on the name of Jesus."

"Praise God for that."

"He said as bad as he was hurting from the burns, there weren't no way he planned to spend his afterlife in eternal flames." Zion looked at Rosalie, a penetrating study from eyeball to eyeball. "I've got my afterlife plans all settled Rosalie. I booked a ticket on the gospel train, Acts 2:38, but I have some options to work out in the here and now."

"Maybe discussing them with a seasoned deacon in the Washington church might help," Rosalie offered. "Pa's out in the orchard."

Zion beamed. He grabbed Rosalie at the waist and swung her around the fairy circle. Setting her back on the ground, he took her hand and walked her out to the lane. "Penny's waiting by the sign. I bet she'd like that buttercup you're holding onto."

Rosalie looked in her hand, surprised to see the stem threaded through her fingers, the yellow bloom still intact. "I'll get her and bring her up to the house."

When Penny saw Rosalie coming toward her she ran to meet her in the lane followed by a shepherd that was no longer a pup. They embraced and walked hand in hand back to the cabin. The dog yapped and wagged his tail as the girls gushed the highlights they had missed over the last months: the trip west and Pansy Joy's wedding and baby news.

Rosalie enjoyed Penny's company, but her thoughts kept racing to the orchard where Zion was talking with her father. An hour passed before the men entered the cabin. Relief swept over Rosalie as they crossed the threshold wearing big smiles.

"Did you know your Pa bought the Taylor place?"

The news surprised Rosalie. "I knew they offered it to him." Rosalie gave a questioning look to her father.

"Grant gave me a fair price, and I took it. He and Awinita are clearing out the first of June, and I plan to move in and work the orchards from the other side for awhile."

Understanding dawned on Rosalie. She ran to her father and squeezed him hard. "Oh, Pa. What a wonderful idea."

"I've been considering taking on a business partner. I'm not getting any younger, you know, and Mr. Coldwell is looking for a place to settle."

Penny and Marigold shrieked for joy. They grabbed Lucas's hands and made a merry circle dancing around the kitchen floor. "I can't believe it," said Penny. "When Zion told me he wanted to marry you, Rosalie, I was as happy as I thought I could ever be, but to live here is almost more than my heart can take."

"Looks like you'll be getting your old room back," said Marigold.

"You feel like riding in to see if Reverend Dryfus is available the first Saturday in June?" Zion asked.

"Let's walk."

Zion and Rosalie walked the two miles to the parsonage, some in comfortable silence, just enjoying being together after such a long time, and then filling the steps with chatter and news, plans and dreams.

"So Balim is on his way to Canada?"

"We stopped at Maysville before we came here. I drew up his papers and sent him across the Ohio River. I never felt more free in my life."

"That's funny," said Rosalie. "You gave Balim his freedom, but it liberated you, too."

"It was a good feeling." Zion walked with Rosalie beside him, one arm tucked under his elbow and the other clasped on top. "After our folks died, I didn't think I could ever feel this happy or settled again."

"I'm glad you're healing." Rosalie smiled up at Zion, thankful for the clarity in his blue eyes that revealed a peaceful spirit. "You never talked much about the accident. Does it hurt still?"

"Not like at first."

"What happened, Zion?"

"Lightning struck the big bebb oak growing between the house and the stable. The tree split in half and lit up like a match, one half igniting the barn and the other half the house."

"That's terrible."

"It was. A huge limb hit the roof above Ma and Pa's bedroom. They didn't have a chance to get out.

"I ran to Penny's room and we climbed out the window, but we lost everything in the house. The horses escaped into the corral. The barn was beyond repair."

"I'm so sorry."

"Life comes with sorrow, Rosalie, but it also comes with beauty."

"That's a lesson I learned in Mama's rose garden. Life comes with thorns, but with the thorns come roses."

*E*PILOGUE

*Z*ion lifted the corner of the quilt and pulled it over the pillow. Rosalie did the same on her side of the bed and then ran her hand across the top to smooth out the air bubbles.

"Every time I make this bed, I still can't believe it."

"I can only imagine." Zion winked at Rosalie. "With so many of the Washington ladies hoping to have me for their own, it is amazing you landed such a fine catch."

"Oh, you. If I didn't have the bed made already, I'd hit you with my pillow."

"*You* have the bed all made? I thought *we* made it."

"You know what I mean, Zion Coldwell, and you know I was talking about the quilt, too. I never received a gift that surprised me more in my life."

Zion grinned at his wife. He loved mornings with Rosalie. Every night she braided her waist-length auburn hair, and every morning Zion unfastened it and fanned it out over her pillow. He ran his fingers through the thick mass and then watched it float around her shoulders before she pinned it up for the day. "Did I tell you Pansy Joy told me about that quilt when I first came to town?"

"No," said Rosalie with a look of surprise in her sparkling eyes. "What did she tell you?

"We were walking over to the Eldridge place to see if Garth wanted to sell his wagon to the Coventrys. She told me how your had ma collected the pieces for the quilt ever since you were a baby, but you hadn't had the heart to work on it, even though it was your own special Rose of Sharon quilt."

"She was right about that." Rosalie paused for a moment and then laughed. "You know what's so funny?"

"When I tickle you right here?" Zion tickled Rosalie under her chin, and she slapped his hand.

"No, you silly. Behave yourself." Zion lifted his offended fingers to his lips, and Rosalie shook her head. "What's funny is I was spending my nights knitting soakers and sewing baby gowns, and Pansy Joy was spending hers piecing Mama's quilt together."

"For little Maggie Rose's sake, I'm glad you got those soakers finished."

Rosalie stepped into Zion's arms. Nestling her head against his broad chest, she thrilled at the feeling–the feeling of loving and being loved, and knowing the Lord blessed their union. She lifted her head and gazed into his cornflower blue eyes, thinking again how the color matched the bachelor buttons that grew in her wildflower garden. She sighed and gave a contented smile. "Are you going over to Pa's later?"

"Yes. We're moving Clover and the goats over to his new barn this afternoon." Zion glowed with excitement. "I'm itching to finish the expansion on our barn and corral. Cooper arranged for the mare to be transported from Lexington in two weeks."

Matthias and Zion had been working together in the orchards. Zion enjoyed the occupation, but he had horses in his blood. He looked forward to breeding the three-year-old thoroughbred with West, the beginning of a new season in the Coldwell horse business. After breakfast, Zion rode into town. Fifteen minutes passed, and the sound of West's shoes pounding down the lane brought Rosalie and Penny quickly out the door.

"Is something wrong?" Penny asked.

"It's Balim!" Zion, out of breath, reached inside his vest and pulled out a paper. "I got a telegram!"

"What does it say?" Rosalie and Penny rushed down the steps to stand beside Zion as he dismounted.

"He found her." Zion ripped his hat off and threw it up in the air. He shook his brown hair and let out a yell. "He found Minnie."

Penny clapped her hands and jumped into Zion's arms. "Thank you, Jesus!"

"Did he say anything else?" Rosalie asked.

"She was staying with Reverend Josiah Henson's family in Dresden, but they're planning to buy their own place in the Dawn Settlement. Balim's going to work at a manual labor school set up to train former slaves for jobs as mechanics, blacksmiths and such."

"That's wonderful," said Rosalie, beaming from ear to ear. "And it's just amazing we're able to get this information so quickly. Think how long it took for him to travel there."

"I know what you mean." Zion shoved his hat back on his head. "And now that the Pony Express is running, we can get a letter back and forth from the West Coast in nearly three weeks."

"Can I send a letter to Rachel?" Penny asked.

"You sure can." Zion tipped the end of Penny's nose with his finger.

"It's a changing world we're living in," said Rosalie.

"That it is." Zion wrapped one arm around Rosalie and one around Penny and steered his girls to the house. "The census is going to tell a lot about how our country is shaping up. And with the election, who knows what the future holds."

"Do you think Mr. Lincoln might win?" Penny asked. "He seems like a good man, and he wants to free the slaves."

"I read in the paper an 11-year-old girl named Grace suggested if he grew his beard out, he might have a better chance of winning," said Zion.

"What does a beard have to do with politics?" Rosalie asked.

"About as much as monkeys have to do with birthing humans, I imagine. Ever since that Darwin fellow's book came out, people are questioning the Bible and creation like never before."

"Did Pa share the notes on Mr. Spurgeon's New Year's Day sermon with you?" Rosalie asked. "He was so excited when he got that copy from Reverend Dryfus."

"He did. And did you notice Mr. Spurgeon gave that message on the same day Pansy Joy and Garth got married?"

"Isn't that a coincidence? I loved the message. What was the text? Do you remember?"

"But the God of all grace, who hath called us unto his eternal glory by Christ Jesus, after that ye have suffered a while, make you perfect, establish, strengthen, settle you."

"That's right. He said the verse had four jewels in it: perfection, establishment, strengthening and settling, and those jewels are laid out on a jet-black setting of *after that ye have suffered awhile.*"

"We get the 'jewels' after we have suffered a while. That's the point, isn't it?" Penny asked.

"That's right. He said it's a fact that men must suffer, and that sorrow assists in working out our blessings. We can't discard sufferings, but take them from the same hand from which we receive mercy."

"That sounds like something Balim would say," said Penny.

Zion laughed. "I always told Balim he was the wisest man I ever knew, but I don't think he would compare himself with Charles Spurgeon."

"I don't think so either." Penny reached the door first and stepped aside so Zion could open it. Rosalie entered the cozy cabin and walked to the stove to warm the coffee. "I'd like to ask him a question."

"Mr. Spurgeon or Balim?" Zion asked.

Rosalie laughed. "Charles Darwin, actually."

"Really?" Penny stared at Rosalie.

"What would you ask him?" Zion asked.

"I'd ask him, according to his theory, if he thought rose bushes developed thorns or thorn bushes developed roses."

Zion rubbed his forehead. "I guess that's a good question, but what makes you think of it?"

"The Spurgeon message. If we can't discard sufferings, but take them from the same hand from which we receive mercy, then wouldn't it be the same with thorns and roses? Don't you think God made them both at the same time, and for a purpose?"

"I suppose," said Zion. "I'm just glad my sweet 'Rose of Sharon' doesn't have any thorns. Otherwise, you might prick me in the bed at night."

Rosalie smiled. "You might not know this, husband, but your 'Rose' doesn't have any thorns at all."

"That's not likely, is it?" Zion asked. "Don't all roses have thorns?"

"Mama named me after the Rose of Sharon, and those aren't really roses. They are flowering bushes."

"Well I'll be." Zion rubbed his chin in thought. "I never knew that."

"What about Jesus?" Penny asked. "Doesn't the Bible call Jesus the Rose of Sharon?"

"It doesn't actually say Jesus is the Rose of Sharon. Sharon is a valley next to Gilead known for its fertility and beauty. The Rose of Sharon represents the flowers in the field, the same field King David fed his flocks."

"So Jesus is like the flowers in the valley."

"Those flowers do have healing and beauty, like Jesus."

Zion grinned at his wife. "You know, I did an in-depth study of the Song of Solomon before our wedding." Rosalie blushed, but kept her thoughts to herself. "The person who said 'I am the rose of Sharon' was actually Solomon's bride, and she represents the church, not God."

"That's a good point, too," said Rosalie. "So if we read it literally, that means we, the church, are the flowers in the field that bring beauty to the valley and food for Israel's flocks."

"And these kinds of roses don't have thorns?" Penny wondered aloud.

"I guess they shouldn't." Rosalie nodded. "Or I suppose I should say, I guess *we* shouldn't."

Penny smiled at her sister-in-law. "I think we all need Jesus to help us with that."

Zion, full of the joyous news of the day, grabbed his girls in a group embrace. "As Balim would say, 'That's the way it is. Yes suh, that's the way it is.'"